CEREUS & LIMNIC

Keith Hayden

Social Arts

2021

Acknowledgements

Many thanks to my eternally supportive wife, Dr. Joanna Ho, for providing love, space, and encouragement to make this work possible.

Thank you to my brother, Dr. Ajani Abdul-Khaliq, for believing in, polishing, and fueling my writing.

Thank you to all readers who believe in change and building a better world and society.

CHAPTER 1:
BARTO AND THE MACHINE

Human society is a great machine. When parts of it break down, the resulting defect disturbs all who make use of the vital component, and may cause the entire apparatus to shudder and smoke. The loyal employee, the naive and trusting citizen, its defenders and detractors, the leaders; none are spared the hindrance of the malfunction. The bigger the part, the greater the upheaval and cost of repair.

This is how Barto Khuni thought of things. He knew, based on the decision he made today, that the damage to the ever-turning gears of civilization would be extensive and lasting. *When the bill comes due for the repair, we may have to invent a new unit of measure to quantify it. Then harness all of our human ingenuity to correct it,* Barto thought to himself, feeling the slickness of sweat begin to build on his hands.

He sat alone at his desk in a suit tailored to match his large round frame. He felt the cool breeze of the air conditioner tickling his scalp. It easily wafted through his thin grey hair, caressing his partially exposed brown scalp beneath. The skin on his face was remarkably smooth, the jolly eyes fit for laughter. Lines around his mouth and eyes told half the tale of a lifetime of telling and reacting to bad jokes, mostly at his own expense. His lips were thin, and arched slightly upward, telling the other half of his story. But today, his normally jovial features were veiled in apprehension, reversing the direction of the normally upward lines of his face.

Small glowing lines of light filtered into his office via thin openings between the industrial-sized shades covering the windows. The morning sun and the bustle of downtown San Francisco hundreds of feet below were blocked out, minimizing his distraction. Barto's eyes tracked a single beam of light from the window behind him. It bounced off of a metallic umbrella holder near his sealed office door, forming a small shadow behind it. The dark diversion held his attention for several seconds. Then a light from a small screen on his desk caught his attention.

The device was black with a thin rectangular shape, able to fit completely in the palm of his hand. It had been manufactured by Samsung, and like the smartphones of his youth, housed a universe within a galaxy of potential. Barto was old enough to remember the days of single purpose cellphones. Now, he was old enough not to care about anything other than the basic functions of the gadget everyone referred to as a 'device.'

There was a message from Lili on the screen. It read:

Don't hesitate. You're making the right call and I support you. We will deal with the fallout together. The other two will have to get over it.

He grinned in response, grateful for her friendship and support even after all of these years.

Really, there wasn't much that he had to do. A simple voice command and it would be done. Yet he hesitated. Waiting for a phone call, a beep from his device, or some other source to act as an excuse to delay the inevitable.

Barto slackened his tie to allow cool recycled air to reach his chest, then cursed under his breath. *Why do I always tie the damn thing so tight? Even after all these years, I still make the same mistake almost every day.*

He interlaced his fingers together and rested his chin upon them as he leaned forward, thinking, stalling. As one of the Founders of the organization others viewed him as an intellectual, a leader. George Washington of the modern age. Yet, he had never been a decisive person. For many decisions in his life big and small, he often relied on decision trees to weigh and consider his options. Under each canopy, time froze, providing him with ample time to contemplate potential actions and futures. He must have planted thousands of trees in his life. *I am a planter, just like Washington.* He smiled to himself. The amusing observation made him less aware of his thundering heart and the dots of sweat on his forehead.

The tree for this decision had already been planted, and he had selected the superior option hours ago. The only thing left to do was execute. He had run the numbers, consulted with Lili, done his customary toilet time thinking, and after each activity, had come to the same conclusion. *The others may not be ready, but this was what we agreed on. How it has to go down. I never thought it would have to be me, but it must be done.*

He sat up straight in his chair with new confidence and sureness surging through him, then picked up the device from the surface of the desk. After punching in a series of long codes, and bypassing the authentication gates, he came to the executive approval screen. *Are you sure you want to proceed?* It asked, in a small gray text box. Barto stared at the box then gave the voice command "Yes." Then the final screen appeared on the device. He had to say the name of the order precisely or it would not work.

Enter executive order number. It prompted.

The authoritative tone resonated from somewhere deep inside of him. The sound from his lips seemed to mix with light waves sneaking into the great room, providing weight and sonority to his words.

"Execute order DD-5428."

There was a pause as the device fulfilled his request. As the machine worked, Barto's mind began to create a list of the possible events that could follow from his decision. Each one more catastrophic than the last. Overwhelmed by the abundance of probable scenarios, he abandoned the effort. *There's no way to tell what will happen now.*

Device still in hand, he dictated a voice message to Lili and the other Founders then sent it off. In under a minute, they would know what he had done, and nothing would ever be the same.

Then he reached for his desk phone and called the number for air transportation, casting aside his acrimonious thoughts about flying, to focus on his desire to leave San Francisco as soon as possible.

A sweet sounding, yet untrained artificial intelligence (A.I.) assistant answered the call. Their exchange was brief, but littered with awkward starts and stops, another minor irritant for Barto. After three minutes, the voice asked, "When would you like to be in the air Mr. Khuni?"

Barto scratched his head, "By this afternoon."

"Got it, sir. It will be standing by at 1300 hours."

CHAPTER 2:
FATHER AND DAUGHTER

A distant buzzing drifted through the air, floating into her consciousness. Initially, she thought it was a component of the bizarre dream that her sleeping mind had conjured to entertain her, so she listened. Seconds faded into minutes as she strained the limits of her hearing. Frustration gave way to fatigue as she stood silent, unable to find the origin of the tone.

The noise was accompanied by recurring visual elements of the dream: fields of grass tinted with the color of ocean water, her father, herself, and an ancient computer monitor with a flashing blue screen awaiting an input command. With hopeful trepidation, she approached the glowing terminal, extending a trembling hand to a yellowed brownish keyboard. Without hesitation, her young fingers began gliding across sticking keys, attempting to manipulate the machine. Yet each keystroke failed to bring the machine to life. It remained dormant, unyielding, with only a blinking cursor winking mockingly at her entries, void of caring or empathy.

It's broken. The thought flashed in her mind, repeating itself with the rhythm of the blinking command line cursor. Then the beeping sound began. First faintly, barely above an audible frequency, but eventually the volume increased to an almost deafening tone after a few seconds, only to fade away until it became a quiet whisper again.

Where is it? Why can't I find it? Her inability to find the source of sound, made her feel lost in the blue void. A prisoner of the expanse, subjected to an unexplained wavering tone. Her vexation rising along with the awareness of her thumping heart drew her back into her conscious mind. She lay there with her eyes closed for a few moments more, grasping in vain at wispy dream fragments. It was an exercise in futility, but she forced herself into a momentary calm seeking to extend her limited physical senses. After several seconds, she still heard the beeping. It was close, closer than she had ever been.

What!? Wait! It worked!?

Her eyes shot open. In a flurry of motion, she threw her thin sheet off of her and rushed to the window of her room flinging open the curtains, squinting through her sleep-clouded vision to see past the wide lawn, and the imposing black gate at the end of a long driveway. The source of the sound had been a garbage bot performing his collection duties. The machine's shape in the form of an old-timey silver trash can was an ironic reality, not lost on her. It made her picture the old world of her father. A mixture of mismatched fashion styles, green lawns, and for some reason mustached men, converged in a sepia tone in her mind's eye. A caricature of a past she never knew or fully understood.

The bot used alloyed arms to lift the black bag of refuse into a gaping dark hole in its center, letting the door glide shut after the waste was deposited deep within its interior. From her vantage point, she could not see evidence of the tiny explosion inside of the machine, turning the garbage into ashes and energy. But she was always curious about it. Wanting to understand how they packed such a powerful explosion into such a tiny space. *Ignition method? Fuel source? How?* The unanswered questions left her with an uncomfortable 'in the dark' feeling. She wasn't afraid of the dark, but she preferred the bright illumination of knowledge to guide her steps.

The garbage bot continued its movement down the street, taking her tension with it. She let her shoulders relax, and took a deep breath to fill her lungs. *False alarm. How silly of me to think that I would be able to hold on to it*, she thought, pondering the dream again.

Her disappointment was quickly displaced by a strong desire to get her day going. Moving away from the window and around her bed, she picked up her device from its appointed position by her bedside. Her device was gold, adorned with a sticker of a rocket spitting a flame from its exhaust, another of a black infinity sign, and a third of a single white gear on the back. The decals were scratched and faded from countless transfers in and out of her pockets. A vocal command from her lips brought the limitless device to life.

"Calendar."

Setting the device in an old yet functional robotic circular swivel, she angled it toward a barren wall behind her nightstand, waiting to view her calendar, but nothing appeared.

Oh dammit. I forgot to set it to project mode. She was still getting used to the new model with improved projection features. "Project mode." Her voice produced a tiny echo in the room, a clear sign of sleep fog lifting from her mind's surface.

The calendar flashed onto the wall in a complicated matrix of social and academic suspense dates. A hidden code only she and possibly her best friend and rival, Harpreet, could decipher. They had competed in all things academic ever since their fateful meeting during the Basics of Language committee some twelve years prior. Both having been tutored at home by the finest artificial intelligence teaching programs optimized to their unique learning preferences, they became fast friends, leaving the other five-year-olds behind. With perfect grades, both agreed to race to see who could test out of the committee the fastest. Her competitive nature manifested early on, and she won the contest by one day. That had been the beginning of a rivalry that continued to this day, with each girl taking the lead in every other contest year after year. Both enjoyed the shared rivalry and friendship. It drove them to greater heights, and kept life interesting.

She found her mind wandering, but managed to focus it back to her projected calendar. Her vision focused on the date: June 14th, 2062. Two events, one with a green rhombus, the other with a red pentagon in front of it, populated the line. A calculus lesson at 1000 and dinner with Dad at 1900. A light day.

Feihao. Plenty of time to chill.

Sunlight, warm and bright, made its way through the window, heating her skin. *I should get going.*

She made her way to the body length mirror fastened to the back of her door and admired herself for longer than she wanted to. A single gold colored shirt and an old yet reliable pair of purple panties were all she wore. Her long black hair was a mess, falling in every direction except down. Gangly long arms appeared to sway in the breeze of the air conditioner. Her eyes, umber brown, shining and thin, reflected brilliance, hinting at unrealized greatness. She allowed a small smile onto her lips at the thought of her eyes. They projected her presence and intellect, and made her more memorable. *Unforgettable.* Some told her that her gaze was as intense as it was beautiful; she tended to agree with that observation. Her face was slim and flat, with a small nose set in the center. Her eyes scanned downward, toward her (in her opinion) unremarkable breasts, when she noted a tiny red swell on her cheek. It was sensitive to the slightest prod from her finger, and stung whenever the muscles of her face moved. She twitched her face several times to confirm its presence

A pimple. Great. She reached for nearby facial cream in her nightstand and began to methodically apply it to the red menace. As she made tiny swirls with her finger, a knock on the other side of the door startled her.

"Jinhua? Are you up?" The voice of her father resonated clearly from the opposite side of the door.

"Yeah I am. I'll be out in a minute." Jinhua finished applying the cream, then hurried to her closet and to dress herself. The night before she had set aside a simple green t-shirt and shorts. The clothes swayed on plastic white hangers, undisturbed, until Jinhua hastened to rip them down and throw them on her body, after changing out of her sleepwear. She hadn't realized how behind her usual schedule she was. *Damn dream. Stupid trash bot.*

When she opened her door, her father stood before her, a neutral expression on his face.

"You have to get ready for committee." He paused, noting his daughter's uncharacteristically disheveled appearance. "Did you sleep alright?" There was concern in his tone. He knew that she was usually ready to go by this time in the morning.

"I slept great. Are you heading to the office?"

He was dressed in a sharp looking steel-colored suit accompanied with a sky-blue dress shirt. The tie was neatly pressed, accented with cerulean and white stripes. It looked new even though she had seen him wear it off and on ever since she was little. His face shared Jinhua's features, but was wider and rounder, making his brown eyes less pronounced to a casual observer. A full head of grey hair sat above the chiseled wrinkles carved at specific points on his face. Her father's face reminded her of a weather-beaten statue. After decades exposed to the elements, it had history, and related a different story when viewed from distinct angles. Every Wednesday he made the two-hour journey down to Sacramento to meet with the city government down there. Though he never really discussed the details of the meetings, he always came home with a mantle of sadness about his slim shoulders.

"I'm about to leave right now. You know how slow the bus can be," he said.

"Slower than the orbit of Mars." Jinhua covered her mouth to conceal a giggle. Her father chuckled as well.

Li Ma looked at his daughter, the little girl turned young woman, now 17-years-old. In a flash of nostalgia, he recalled the first time that he took her to the Powerhouse Science Center in Sacramento. She was only a girl then, but she already had a sparkle in her eyes whenever she viewed something she liked. The sparkle appeared as soon as they entered the planetarium. The infinite collection of projected stars seemed to stretch beyond the walls of the physical space, swallowing him and his inquisitive daughter by his side whole. Though the room was packed with a sprinkling of other parents and a class of elementary school children with chaperones, it felt like they were the only two in the room. At that moment, it was Li and Jinhua's planetarium.

Li had watched her eyes glowing with wonder, captivated by the endlessness and untold frontiers of space. Swirls of overwhelming emotion, threatening to break the surface of his stoic veneer, manifested as a hint of satisfaction and silent joy on his face. Jinhua was oblivious to his gaze. Her entire being was focused on the astronomical projection. To her child mind, the blanket of stars beamed back at her, calling her to wonder, imagine, and explore. *My future is up there,* she had thought.

Ever since that day, Li had tapped all of his connections within and even outside of the organization to find her the finest resources and mentors to fuel her interest in space, science, and mathematics. First, he started her out on books for children, but she quickly devoured them and subsequently surpassed all of her peers in her honors basic Space Science Committee. He found his old Arduino robot kit, thinking that it would serve as a suitable challenge for a nine-year-old. But by her tenth birthday, she had designed three of her own projects with no assistance from him or any of her committee scholars. It was unheard of within the organization for someone so young to study directly under a scholar, but with a few back-door connections, he had made it happen for her. She was truly gifted.

"Dad…are you ok?"

Jinhua nudged Li back from his thoughts.

"Fine, fine." He smiled warmly. "Don't forget dinner at seven tonight."

"I'll be there." Jinhua looked back at her device in the swivel, feeling slightly embarrassed. "You know, we don't have to go out… we can just eat something here."

"No, we should. It's not every day they let teenagers into the Junior Space Cadets. It's a big deal."

She didn't protest. Despite all of her academic success throughout her life, it still felt awkward when others talked about it directly, even if it was her dad.

"Don't be late." He leaned forward and gently kissed her forehead, then walked down the long corridor toward the staircase to go downstairs. His small, yet powerful footsteps left faint impressions on the thick carpet as he walked away.

There was a time many years ago when she would walk behind him to try and fill those footprints with her own tiny feet. Jinhua felt the urge to follow him now, but stopped herself when she remembered that her feet were slightly larger than his now. Instead, she stood and watched the impressions for a few seconds until they were completely swallowed by the carpet material. *Have a good day dad. I love you.*

CHAPTER 3:
FRIVALS

As soon as Jinhua stepped outside of her house a blast of heat slammed into her face, causing her to gasp. It took her body a few seconds to adjust to the drastic difference in temperature.

Before she left the house she had picked up an object that appeared to be an ocean blue colored bar leaning in a dusty corner of the expansive entry way of the house. The pole was two and a half long, smooth, and was her preferred method of transportation around town. *Perfect day for rippin'.*

Jinhua smiled at herself as she gripped the bar. It reminded her of how far she had come since she had purchased it for her birthday three years prior. In those days, all she had wanted to do was finish her homework so she could ride her ripboard with Harpreet. She spent days learning how to deploy the board's retractable wings from the bar. At first, treating the device as a delicate object, then trying to add flair to her board deployments. After about a week, she moved on to the analysis phase. She had meticulously documented the make-up of the various composite materials of the personal transport: aluminum alloy, painted fiberglass wings, and some kickass grip tape. After another few days she was ready to ride.

The first race against Harpreet had ended in crushing defeat. Jinhua hadn't quite worked out the optimal positioning for her levcer, the vital balancing component without which there was no levitation. No levitation, meant no rippin'. A misplaced levcer meant an uncentered magnetic field, which bungled the ripboard's fickle glide profile when the wings were deployed. These were facts unknown to Jinhua the first time she stepped on the board. Real world gems of experience that her scrutinizing analysis could not account for. During that first race, her slipshod foot placement and graceless handling of the levcer had left her off balance and slow. A sharp turn at a high speed was all it took to send her flying onto the street, leaving a deep gash on her knee. It was a mistake she never made again.

The bitterness of that loss fresh in her mind, she grasped the pole and hastened out of the front door, locking it behind her. By the time she reached the imposing black security fence at the entrance of the driveway, she was already beginning to feel beads of sweat forming on her exposed forehead. Wiping the perspiration away with the back of her hand, she continued to move as if she had no place to go.

She pulled out her identification card from her pocket and held it toward the gate's scanner. The card was tomato red in color and housed her picture, social security number, driver's license number, links to her major bank accounts, medical records, as well as money. All of the information had somehow been smashed within its microscopic computer components. *I can't believe my entire life is on this card.* She always had the same thought whenever she used the thin slice of technology. The all-in-one card was convenient, yet it made her feel vulnerable to have the entirety of her person housed within one easily pilfered or misplaced item.

The security panel made a series of beeps, signaling that her card had been accepted. The old black gate emitted the sound of aged metal on slightly oxidized tracks as it slid open. Jinhua sidled through the opening to hasten her trip. The heat of the morning was already beginning to make its ever-warm presence known to her face and skin.

Upon reaching the street, her device chimed in her tiny shorts pocket. With practiced skill, Jinhua pulled it out and examined the screen. The message from Harpreet was brief, yet provoked an excited smile onto her face.

Barter race? Meet at the Old Veterans' Park in 10?

Jinhua dictated a voice message reply: *I'll be there in 5.* A small sticker of a checkered flag accompanied her words on the display screen. Within a second the device was back in her pocket.

In a fluid motion, she used an underhanded swing to fling the blue pole in front of her, while simultaneously activating the wing deployment. Sky blue wings extended from the pole ready to accept her feet. Before it hit the concrete with a dissonant clang (a noise she had named the sound of shame), Jinhua expertly positioned and activated her levcer at the precise moment, then leapt toward the hovering board with style. The sun gleamed and the ripboard took flight just as her feet landed on the safety of reinforced grip pads. She was suspended only by the harmonious equilibrium between the balancing forces of the levcer, her stance, and the board.

I won't lose this time.

With a determined look on her face, she kicked at the ground, propelling the board forward.

Five minutes later, Jinhua arrived at the park to find Harpreet waiting under the shade of a large tree. In her jean shorts and burgundy tank top, she stood tall with her arms at her side, hands open, eyes closed as if she were an offering to the sun. Just as they had competed in all things related to school, so too did the two young women often compare their physical characteristics, as if they were professional athletes preparing for a championship. As Jinhua approached the unaware Harpeet, she mentally compiled a list of random attributes, assigning herself or her best frival (*friend-rival* her own created word) as the victor. *Height: Her, only by two inches. Weight: definitely her, by several pounds. Chest size: Harpreet. Hair length: draw. Intelligence: don't make me laugh, ME. Smile: I guess her. Ripboard skill: Me by a mile.* The mental exercise made Jinhua grin to herself as she floated toward her friend, whose cinnamon toned skin glistened with a film of sweat in the morning heat. When she was close enough, Jinhua jumped off to the side of the ripboard at the optimal position, retracting the sky-blue wings, and kicking the pole back into her right hand in a smooth fashion. It had taken her months to master the movement, and she was proud of it.

"Practicing your mountain pose?" Jinhua said in a soft voice.

Harpreet's eyes fluttered open. A big grin formed on her lips. "Gotta do something in this heat. It's so hot! And it's only 9:30!"

"Yeah it is. I think it's supposed to get up to 116 degrees today."

"Hot enough to cook a whole meal on the sidewalk!" Harpreet said. Both girls laughed.

Harpreet put her hands on her waist, sticking her chest out. "You ready to lose?" Her tone was challenging, defiant. She reached for an orange pole leaning against the tree, then twirled it in her hands, thrusting it down near her feet in dramatic fashion. Waiting for Jinhua's usual reaction. A reaction that never came. *Something's on her mind. I wonder what?* "You alright?"

"I had *the* dream again…"

"Which one? The one about Derak?"

"No!" Jinhua slapped her arm with enough force to sting, but not to bruise. "And, ew!"

"Ok, ok! Just had to be sure!" Harpreet said laughing. "You mean the one about the broken computer, right?"

"What could it mean?"

Harpreet stood silent for a moment. Striking a pensive pose with arms crossed, chin on fist, she looked at Jinhua, wanting badly to find answers or explanations where both knew there were none. *She looks so vulnerable sometimes.* After a minute of the ambient noises of nature, people walking by in low conversation, and the occasional vehicle passing by, Harpreet spoke.

"You know what would help you right now?"

"What?"

"A little bit of rippin'! You always feel better after that!" Harpreet placed a warm, slightly sweaty hand on her shoulder. Jinhua smiled. The unexpected contact was helpful.

The details of dream fragments still lingered in her mind, but she was ready to let them go. To allow them to drift away in the wind behind her board.

"You're on."

"That's my girl!" Harpreet said, jumping with excitement.

With flair, she waved her orange pole around her head and tossed it at the ground, while in the same instant activating her levcer with the opposite hand. Jinhua flinched when she heard the sound of metal clashing against the sidewalk. Harpreet fell backwards onto her backside, letting out a string of exaggerating expletives in English and Punjabi.

"Goddammit! One day I swear I'm gonna get that thing that you do down!"

Jinhua giggled. "One day. Good thing you fell on your oversized 'safety cushion'."

Harpreet stood up, as a group of crows vacated a nearby tree at the sound of her laughter. "No kidding. If it were you, you would've probably shattered a hip."

"Hey! Mine's just taking longer to inflate!" Both girls laughed, extending the moment of levity.

Harpreet redeployed her ripboard, activating it with more caution this time. As she stepped her right foot onto the wings, a look of surprise made her eyebrows arch and her eyes grow wide. Her hand dug her device out of her shorts to check out the notification. "Shit!"

"What is it?" Jinhua asked with concern.

"Committee time got moved up. Apparently old Master Scholar (MS) Rhodes is bringing in a new student from Sac, and wants us all there early."

"How long do we have?"

Harpreet brought the device closer to her face as if she were an old woman with a vision impairment "Uh…five minutes."

Lines of determination drew themselves onto Jinhua's face. "Then we'd better rip it." Her frival mirrored her expression, returning a challenge-accepting smirk. She lowered her center of gravity, ready to begin the contest. "Ready?"

Harpreet nodded, hovering her right leg at a 45-degree angle above the widened sidewalk for a stronger first kick.

"GO!!"

CHAPTER 4:
A NEW SOCIETY

The feeling was electric. Jinhua felt the fresh rush of adrenaline propelling her long legs to thrust her through the open air in front of her. Each kick was precise, optimized to give her maximum force, while keeping the amount of time off of the ripboard to a minimum. Half an inch in front of her, Harpreet's attention was just as focused on winning the race. Her balance was questionable. But what she lacked in grace, the power and length of her legs more than made up for, making her an even match.

After passing under the old highway ninety-nine, Jinhua nearly lost her balance as she weaved through a throng of elderly walkers casually enjoying a morning chat. A man with a sun-spotted, warm beige complexion mumbled obscenities as she and Harpreet cut through.

"Going left!" Harpeet shouted from up ahead.

Jinhua, quickly adjusted her trajectory, wondering why she had not taken a right on Gray Avenue toward the old mall and their committee meeting, which was scheduled to begin in three minutes by the time on her device. *Where is she going?*

Let's see if you can keep up. Harpreet's thoughts rushed by like the wind under the wings of the board, as she gave a hard kick, widening her lead.

Jinhua's board edged only six inches behind, gliding over large cracks and great circles of discolored gray in the sidewalk. The filled holes were grim reminders of a flood disaster that had killed millions and left the entire city underwater for months, years before her birth. When was the flood? Was it in the twenties? Or maybe thirties? She never could get historical numbers right. Unless the figure was attached to science, her memory, like an efficient computer operating system, flagged it for disposal, then tossed it into the digital dustbin.

They had reached the intersection of Washington and Gray Avenue. Distracted by her thoughts, she gasped as Harpreet made a sudden U-turn, cutting across the width of the street, without pausing to look for oncoming people or cars. Safely on the opposite side, she resumed her kicking and gliding, throwing up tiny rocks every time her foot touched the concrete.

"Got you loser!" Harpreet yelled over her shoulder.

Damn you Harpreet! I'm not gonna lose!

Jinhua made a swift U-turn across the street to follow her. She looked right, becoming fixated on a large white pickup truck that was headed right for her. Panicked, she sped up, narrowly reaching the other side of the street before being struck by the honking vehicle. What she hadn't seen was the hapless middle-aged cyclist who had turned onto the street between her and Harpreet's rapidly shrinking frame at this point some fifteen feet down the sidewalk. By a narrow margin, Jinhua avoided the man, who had stopped in the middle of the sidewalk with a dumbfounded look on his face.

She attempted to shift her balance, but acted too late and plummeted onto the sidewalk, her roll dampened by dry grass under a small tree. As she staggered to her feet, the sting of a cut registered in her brain, warm blood trickled down to her shin. Harpreet rushed back down the street. A look of triumph was quickly replaced by concern.

"Wow, crazy wipeout. You ok?" Harpreet reached out her arms to clasp Jinhua's slim shoulders. She looked her up and down, performing a motherly scan. "Nothing looks broken."

"Thanks Doc," Jinhua said.

Harpreet dusted clay-colored dirt from Jinhua's shoulders and arms, as a devilish grin crept onto her face. "…Looks like I won…"

Jinhua gave her a playful slap on the arm. "Looks like it." Her eyes fell to her bleeding knee. The gash looked like a jagged red mark, oozing a steady stream of dark blood. She applied pressure using a single tissue from a small plastic pack she carried in her back pocket.

A habit she had picked up from her father at a very young age. *Always good to have them on you,* he had told her on some random day in the distant past. Now, she was thankful for the advice.

Harpreet clenched her teeth and tensed her jaw at the sight of it. "Looks pretty deep. Might have to hit the market to get it wrapped up."

"Ugh. I'll probably have to give his daughter ripboard lessons in exchange. So boring! She just runs around with the pole the entire time and can't even open the wings!" Jinhua complained.

Harpreet shrugged, "Maybe you can trade the babysitting time for something else?" The mocking tone bled skepticism.

"Doubtful." Jinhua exhaled frustration, glancing down at her device with her free hand. She remembered that the committee meeting had begun five minutes ago. "Shit. We're late."

Harpreet's expression remained unchanged. She was undaunted by the threat of being tardy. "Is that right? Ok then, let's get going space cadet."

It didn't take long to make the short walk to the old Yuba-Sutter Mall and make the exchange. Jinhua recalled through rose-tinted nostalgia endless hours roaming the rows of stalls of the barter market with her father as a young girl. The experience left a lasting impression on her psyche and stoked a sense of home within her. A comforting feeling.

The open-air market of the old world clashed in broad daylight with mid-twenty-first century technology. The result was a uniquely distinct ambiance characteristic of all comvil barter markets nationwide. It was possible to trade money, credit, or any type of service, for almost anything here. Biohacked humans hawked t-shirts, beside heavy-set clear-skinned middle-aged artisans, craftsmen, and specialists of all disciplines. A group of farmers traded baskets of almonds for the latest digital entertainment, a source of infinite pleasure and intrigue. Music from various sources mixed in the air around the girls as they walked the main path through the market, greeting friends and neighbors along the way. Harpreet raised her nose, large nostrils flaring, in response to the smell of fresh baked bread, honey cinnamon rolls, mangos, and chocolate drifting in the air around them. Her eyes followed her stomach's calling. Though hungry too, Jinhua urged her forward through the increasingly dense packs of early morning shoppers and traders. Her bent over position, holding bloody tissues over her knee, was beginning to attract unwelcome attention.

The trip to the doctor's stall hadn't lasted long. He was an old man with a stubborn looking face, but was caring at heart. His bushy white mustache contrasted with dark brown skin, but also made his teeth appear brighter than they were. Dr. Ross had been a longtime friend of Jinhua's father, Li, and always made time for his daughter's cuts and bruises.

Harpreet stood by with the vigilance of a well-paid mercenary, as the doctor sanitized and wrapped the afflicted knee. After the services were rendered, he scanned her all-in-one life card. Though his daughter was at home sick, the scan digitally obligated Jinhua to provide ripboard lessons at some unknown date in the near future. She was thrilled to escape the lessons for the moment, but dreaded the day when she would have to make good on the debt. There was no getting out of it. The consequences for *trade-jumping* (as it was colloquially known) worked on a tiered progression system. The first offense was a suspension of services from the aggrieved person's specialty (in this case medical services) for one week. The second, was a thirty-day suspension from *all* similarly categorized services throughout the entire comvil, which in her case would be no access to local medical care at all. The third, and final offense, was potential expulsion from the comvil. Though Jinhua had never heard of anyone actually being removed, she imagined that getting back in and reestablishing trust within the community was a monumental task that few were willing to undertake. So it was better to keep your promises, and pay your debts as quickly as you were able.

Her knee wrapped, Jinhua walked with a slight limp behind Harpreet, weaving through the growing crowd with quick steps on their way to the community center. Once inside, it took them another minute to reach the back of the building. The committee room was located in an old furniture store. The large open space, where once upon a time, eager retail workers showcased overpriced sofas, beds, dining room tables, and cushions, had been partitioned off by tall white room dividers that did not quite reach to the ceiling. The dividers could be rolled by a very strong person or a machine to rearrange the layout of the committee rooms at any time. This allowed them to be adaptable for almost any academic purpose. Jinhua had heard that it had even served as a physical fitness committee room at one point in time. The rumor crossed her mind as she and Harpreet arrived outside of the door to their committee room. A simple door housed within one of the wall dividers. Jinhua felt as if she had completed a brisk warm up in a gym committee, heart thudding and breathing uneasy from the exertion of the race and her power walk.

Made it. Only 15 minutes late. Jinhua thought.

She opened the door and walked casually to her seat in the center of the space, ignoring the pairs of eyes of her ten committee mates. Most gawked at her wrapped knee and overall disheveled appearance with curious glances, each forming a personal narrative concerning the cause of her rough image.

"Mind your own business!" Harpreet snapped, in an echoing whisper.

Jinhua flashed her a grateful glance as they both sat and adjusted themselves into their seats, and began to remove their needed supplies from a locked compartment under the desk top. Jinhua held her all-in-one card to the desk then heard the click of the lock, concentrating on organizing her supplies to take her mind off of the events of her morning so far. When she was ready, she straightened her back, and her face switched into academic mode. Her pupils widened like a camera aperture, facial muscles relaxed, her lips formed a perfectly straight line. It was the position of a model student, one any teacher would be delighted to see on the first day of school. Eyes staring straight ahead, she realized for the first time that their instructor was not there. Jinhua swiveled her head as if it were a security camera around the front of the room, but saw no sign of him. "Hey, where's Master Scholar (MS) Rhodes?"

"Hasn't showed yet." A dark-haired man with a brown complexion and a serious face spoke. "No idea where he's at."

"Thanks Derak," Harpreet cast a flirtatious wink in his direction. He seemed not to notice the gesture and returned his attention to a video playing silently on his desk screen.

"He'll come around eventually. He knows he wants all this," Harpreet said, bringing a flask of water from under her desk to her lips, viewing him out of the corner of her eye..

Jinhua shook her head. Her mind was still on MS Rhodes. Creeping concern replaced the look of academic readiness on her face bit by bit. "He's *never* late. I wonder if something happened?"

In the next moment, they both heard the heavy footsteps of MS Rhodes approaching just beyond the thin wall. The door opened slowly and MS Rhodes entered the room, squeezing his fat body through the door frame. A few steps behind him, a young man with a quiet countenance walked in.

Instantly, Jinhua felt a large quantity of blood gather in her face at the sight of the youth.

Who is that!?

CHAPTER 5:
THE NEW KID

The boy was gorgeous. He towered over MS Rhodes at about six something feet tall with well-groomed brown hair. He wore plain white jeans and a royal blue t-shirt that revealed the slight curves of a developing muscular chest connected to his two noticeably thinner arms. His two hazel eyes gleamed under the humming fluorescent lights while they scanned the room.

Don't stare! Jinhua said to herself. But the warning came too late. She felt the keenness of his gaze lock on to her, running over the skin of her face as if etching every detail of it into memory in order to reproduce it with flawless accuracy at a later date. The intensity of his glare made her face grow warm under the buzzing lights of the room. Her eyes darted to the empty space on her desk in front of her, providing a grounding moment of calm. Next to her, Harpreet noticed her discomfort, mouthing the words *'he's hot'* with hushed lips. She was entertained by the mystery boy's effect on her best friend.

The boy was a paragon of youth and strength, which made their instructor, MS Rhodes, appear older, fatter, and more drained than usual. In Harpreet's mind, she made an attempt to picture her committee scholar as a young man. Perhaps he had looked like the new boy at some point, and was a young scientist with hopeful dreams of being a changemaker in physics? Maybe he had lofty dreams of ending water scarcity and destroying the millions of tons of plastics in bathtub warm water oceans? She envisioned the root of his descent into academic corporate stupor. What went wrong? Too many compromises? Too many empty promises? Too many false victories? She tried to see his former greatness, yet, could only see a man curved and bitter from a lifetime serving as a key component in a sputtering machine. A wave of sadness washed over Harpreet at the thought. She returned her eyes to the boy, to make it go away, intrigued by Jinhua's visible response to his entrance.

MS Rhodes began to speak in a droning tone.

"Students, this is Daniel. He's been approved to join our committee by the citizens' council." A sudden coughing fit interrupted his speech. He pulled a small miserable cloth out of his pocket to spare his audience from the expectorants shooting from the depths of his lungs. *Damn smoking. I knew I should have given it up years ago.* After several seconds, he caught his breath, using a high amount of restraint to suppress more coughs. "He's just moved here from Sacramento, so please welcome him to our committee with open arms." He gestured unceremoniously toward the youth. The boy gave a small smile accompanied with a slight waving of his hand to acknowledge his new classmates.

Jinhua pretended to busy herself on her screen to avoid his eyes. Out of the corner of her eye Harpreet observed her, entertained by her rattled state. The other students gave a curt acknowledgement of Daniel's presence, but quickly returned to their respective personal worlds of physics notes and videos. They didn't seem excited for another person to join the committee, no matter how good looking he was.

As she did her best to avoid Daniel's eyes, Jinhua thought of a cartoon she used to watch when she was very young. It depicted old world school life with farm animals representing all of the characters in the school. The show focused on Wendell (a talking pig) and his friends as they teamed up to foil their antagonist teacher, a cyborg human named Mr. Jones. Most of the episodes ended in Mr. Jones' humiliating defeat in comedic fashion at the hands of Wendell and his friends, which always brought a sense of joy and justice to her then young mind. One day, her dad watched an episode of the show with her. The only thing she remembered was his comment after the credits were rolling. "Things are different now here in the comvils. But many things about human nature remain the same. People will always be people and fight for dominance over others," he had said. The words stuck in her head for weeks afterward. It would be another decade before she clearly understood the weight of his words. *Nobody wants another competitor*, Jinhua thought. The reaction of the committee reflected this sentiment.

The rest of the morning's events were an afterthought for Jinhua. It was rare for MS Rhodes to lecture for an entire session. He simply did not have the stamina for it. However, he seemed to be especially passionate about their unit on thermal physics and talked in short bursts in between violent coughing fits for the entire time.

Daniel had taken an empty desk closest to the windows of the committee space and arranged his digital notebook and two digital ink pens with geometric precision in front of him. He occasionally looked to the bustling barter market outside, but was primarily focused on listening to MS Rhodes. Jinhua did her best to focus during the lecture, but the pleasant seed of attraction flowering inside of her distracted her usually laser-focused academic brainpower. She caught herself daydreaming about Daniel, in desperate need of more information about the mysterious boy from the city.

As soon as MS Rhodes dismissed the committee for the afternoon, Jinhua collected her belongings and walked outside into the main concourse of the old mall. Harpreet followed close behind, flashing a wry smile, looking at her in a way that mocked and demanded to know what she was thinking. Out of earshot of the other students, and Daniel, she pulled Jinhua aside and said in an ear-splitting whisper, "Damn, you were practically drooling when you looked at him during the entire session! You like him don't you?"

Jinhua's gaze fell to a cracked tile on the floor beside her right foot. The crack exposed a layer of brownish old concrete in what would have otherwise been uniform patterns of teal triangles. "Maybe I do...I don't know. I guess I don't know anything about him yet." A small smile crept onto her face.

"What do you mean you don't know anything!? You know he's super cute and looks like Captain America from the old Marvel movies. What more do you need than that?"

Jinhua laughed louder than she expected to. "Good point," she admitted, her gaze rising to meet Harpreet's eyes once again. "What should I do? Physics and ripboarding I can handle. But boys aren't really my thing."

"That is true. You *are* hopeless when it comes to the male species. Remember that boy Davian at Space Camp back in the day?" Harpreet shook her head, "That was poor form."

"Hey! I was like ten back then. Who knew he would turn out to be a booger eater!" Jinhua protested.

"You're welcome that I saved you from that one." Harpreet said triumphantly.

Jinhua looked back toward the committee room. Daniel seemed to be discussing something privately with MS Rhodes. He looked like he was shifting his weight to leave the room.

"Be serious for once! What should I do?" Jinhua said, her tone pleading.

"Well…you should start by inviting him to come to Star of India with us for lunch."

"What if he doesn't like Indian food?"

"Everybody likes Indian food!"

"I don't know. What if he's one of the few people in the world that doesn't like it? Maybe we should just go to the river or maybe to the movies." Jinhua's face distorted with confusion. A rare emotion for her.

Harpreet gave an impatient sigh. Jinhua's tolerance for risk was high in almost every area of her life except when it came to people. Her friend was cautious, almost overly so. Afraid of the potential messiness that was often paired with close relationships (especially potential romantic ones). Sometimes she wondered how they had become close friends at all. She pushed those thoughts aside, and adopted her gentle big sister tone.

"Hey, why don't we just invite him to the river with us."

"Us?" Jinhua's bewilderment gave way to levity. "What is this *us* all of a sudden? Why do you need to be there?"

"You know…so I can make sure he's not an asshole or something. He's the product and I'm quality control. I have to make sure he's not defective, y'know. If he *is*, then we'll return him." She swung both of her arms as if tossing a dripping bag of garbage into a waste chute with little care for where or how it landed.

Jinhua's lips formed a lighthearted smile, "You mean so you can be *nosey* and see if anything happens between us."

Harpreet feigned astonishment, "Me! Nosy? Never! Buuut, somebody has to look after you—"

Suddenly Harpreet fell silent, then made a small pointing gesture toward the door to the committee room. Peeking out of the side of her eyes, Jinhua followed her finger to see Daniel emerge from the room. He adjusted the straps on his small backpack and began to rotate his head from side to side, most likely searching for the exit of the community center. Despite her effort to avoid them, his hazel eyes locked with hers for a second. A fleeting grin ran across his face.

Dammit! He's seen me! She felt the urge to leave the community center, but her thought process was interrupted by Harpreet's boisterous voice. "Hey Daniel! You need some help finding the way out?" She waved at him with excitement. *Oh no he's coming over here! Damn you Harpreet!* Jinhua felt the muscles in her back and abdomen tense, bracing herself for the now inevitable first encounter with the boy.

Daniel's smile beamed as he cadenced steps toward them. His almond hair swayed to an inaudible rhythm as he appeared to glide across the floor. Harpreet reached out an eager hand to shake his. "Hi, I'm Harpreet and this is Jinhua, welcome to the only physics committee in Yuba City." Her hand remained suspended in the air for some time as Daniel studied it. He seemed unsure how to respond to the gesture. Harpreet held her hand out. Jinhua held her breath. Seconds later, he returned the handshake. The firmness of his clasp projected strength and confidence. *So far so good.* Harpreet thought.

"Hello, nice to meet you." The tone of his voice was resonant and clear, with a touch of bass. *He would have been a successful podcaster back in the day*, Jinhua mused. Standing to the left and slightly behind Harpreet, she could see him in stunning detail. Up close his erect posture was evident, transmitting poise and dignity. A detail Jinhua had not noticed before from the seated vantage point of her desk. The skin on his face glowed with a touch of tan, perfectly unblemished. A well sized nose and a flawlessly cut jawline contributed to his attractiveness. His good looks and serious demeanor made him more than a little intimidating.

"So Daniel…" Harpreet began, with a playful tone. "Would you like to come with us to Star of India?"

"What is that?" Daniel gave a perplexed look.

"It's only the best Indian restaurant this side of the Feather River! Y'know, we figured you might be hungry after listening to all that boring lecturing back there."

Another long pause punctuated the silence between them. The only things Jinhua could hear clearly were the sound of a loud echoing conversation towards the intersection of the concourse of the mall and her own fluttering heartbeat. She feared it might be visible to Daniel and any onlooker.

"I'm sorry but I can't. I have soccer practice this afternoon." He shifted his weight to turn and go. Harpreet opened her mouth, most likely to protest, but the sound of Jinhua's voice cut through the silence and the ambient sounds of the old mall.

"Hey, maybe we could meet at the river after your practice…uh what time does it end?" She managed an inquisitive tone, despite the overwhelming desire she had to shut up and let Harpreet speak for her. Daniel stopped and turned to face her. He seemed to be unsure if he should answer the question or not. "At 3PM."

A look of alarm appeared on Harpreet's face. *What is she doing!?*

"Ok…do you mind if…," Jinhua had to consciously prevent her words from spilling out of her mouth, "…*I* meet you near the river bank at River Front Park at four?"

Daniel smiled brightly, "Sure, let's do it." He extended his hand in a smooth gesture of acceptance. This time it was Jinhua who delayed five seconds before returning the handshake. To her it was a long time, but Daniel didn't seem to register the odd gap. "It was nice to meet you Jinhua. I'll see you later at the river around four." With that he turned and walked toward the center of the concourse. Jinhua watched him depart, eyes glued to his athletic buttocks. The tightness of his jeans made her breath catch in her throat, freezing her temporarily in place. It wasn't until he turned right toward the exit and disappeared from view, that her breathing returned to normal, reanimating her entire body.

Harpreet stared at her friend, mouth open in disbelief. Then she began to clap her hands, in a congratulatory manner. "Wow, I must say, I'm impressed! Didn't expect for you to go for it straight out like that." Jinhua returned a confident toothy grin. "You know I have to go to temple at 4 right? So I won't be there to back you up."

Jinhua let out a low giggle, and slapped her arm. "That's why I chose the time."

Harpreet shook her head while her laugh reflected off of the walls. *So magra.*

CHAPTER 6:
PROTEST - PART 1

Li walked with purpose toward the bus stop. It was only a ten-minute walk, but he was already running late for an early meeting in the old city. He needed to make up for lost time. He carried a small black briefcase with him. What it lacked in volume it more than made up for in utility and portability. *Besides, it's more than enough for everything that I need,* he thought to himself as the bus approached.

The bus coughed and sputtered as it lumbered to a stop, emitting thick black smoke and a vaporous sigh when the autobrake engaged. The once white sides of the vehicle had an old-style ad for a local dentist who promised whiter teeth with just one bleach treatment. The phone number was so faded that Li couldn't make it out. Under the windows, the ad strips appeared to have been attached by hand and clung to the side as if they might fall into the street at any moment. A video image flickered onto the strip closest to Li, advertising the latest summer action movie. It was the remake of a popular movie released ten years ago that the film studios down south were hoping to make another big pay day on. *Some things never change.*

An elderly woman with a grim expression on her face and a cane hobbled toward Li and stood beside him. There both waited, under the sparse shelter of the otherwise abandoned bus stop. He couldn't tell if her vision was impaired in some form or if she just didn't want to acknowledge his presence. Upon seeing the bus, she removed a worn pair of red glasses with cloudy thick lenses and produced a small silver case from her purse. With shaking hands, she clicked open the case and pulled out an unblemished pair of silver glasses. Not long after she put the glasses on, the stern expression on her face molded itself into a crooked smile, showing yellowed teeth. Li wasn't sure what advertisement she was viewing, but whatever it was had instantly changed her mood.

He silently stepped around the woman and entered the bus. A blast of cool air from the overworked air conditioner helped to relax his turbid thoughts. The frigid air made him reminisce about how he had gotten started in his current line of work.

*   *   *

Born in Fuyang, Zhejiang Province in Eastern China, Li Ma had come a long way from the small mountain town of his youth. At the age of 9, Li's father uprooted his entire family from China and moved them all to San Francisco. A reticent boy with a brilliant mind for pattern recognition and mathematics, Li excelled in the American public school system with ease. He found the curriculum mildly challenging, yet tedious when compared to the rigid academic and cultural standards of the Chinese educational model, but still put maximum effort into his school work. Upon his high school graduation in 2018, he was accepted to the California Institute of Technology (Caltech) as an engineering major. Like any other college student from an immigrant family, Li endeavored to study hard in order to earn his degree then get a good job. However, for Li his transition from the son of a poor Chinese immigrant, to the son of a wealthy self-made business magnate, would come to be a footnote in the biography of his life.

Two years after enrolling at Caltech, on a balmy September afternoon, Li was walking back to his dorm room after a lecture, when a woman approached him. She had pale-ivory skin with dark auburn hair and intelligent jade green eyes. Her full lips were angled ever so slightly upward into a friendly grin. Even at his young age Li could tell this was no ordinary woman. She walked as if she were accustomed to carrying heavy things long distances, yet her posture was straight as a board. Her clothes: snug pink jeans, a white t-shirt, revealing her navel deep-seated in taut abdominal muscles, were too new and clean for her to be an average college girl. She carried a black backpack with no logo that flopped on her back as she moved toward him, indicating she carried little or no books at all. By the time she flashed a quick smile and introduced herself as Sarah, Li knew she was not a college student.

During that first encounter, they only exchanged pleasantries and some small talk, before Sarah continued on her way. The entire meeting lasted less than five minutes, and left Li wondering who she *really* was and what she wanted from him.

Over the next six-week period, Li ran into and noticed Sarah in the oddest of places. During his early morning runs, he would see her auburn hair bouncing on an adjacent route, slowing only to greet him with a smile and a sharp wave, as she sweat and took lengthy strides to maintain her pace. While walking on campus, she appeared on benches and in common areas. Sometimes she was reading on her phone, or listening to music; other times she just seemed to be hanging around. Anytime he saw her, Li gave a small wave, then went about his business.

On the few occasions that he had time to stop and speak with her, strangely, he found himself doing most of the talking. Sarah was a good listener. Smiling and nodding at the proper intervals, contributing her own perspective and jokes at ideal moments, and occasionally even flirting a little with him. But despite the fact that she was an excellent conversation partner, Li didn't know much about her, for she rarely talked about her past. Without explicit revelations about herself, Li was forced to assemble her identity based on contextual clues he had gathered. After weeks of observation, he knew the following information: age: late twenties early thirties, marital status: definitely single, interests: running, Billy Eilish music, playing chess, weightlifting (he had seen her doing all of the above at least twice), personality: astute, introverted, hard-working. He also knew she had probably grown up in nearby Orange County and most likely had close family members in the area (he had watched *her* talking on the phone animatedly one day without her being aware).

One afternoon, under a steely gray sky in November, they met for tea off campus. Outside in the nippy open air, Li wore a light jacket over an orange Caltech shirt, and jeans. Across the table, Sarah sat in black winter leggings with dark red rectangles on the sides, wearing a coal gray Caltech hoodie. Beside their cloth face masks, steaming cups of tea had been placed before both of them. Li ordered red tea, while Sarah had black herbal tea. At the proper moment during their chat, Li disclosed all of the personal facts he had gleaned about Sarah's personality, background, and hobbies. When he finished, Sarah's face flushed with uncharacteristic embarrassment, providing a momentary glimpse at her genuine self. The *real* girl behind the mask. Seconds later, she recovered her usual cool facial features, lowered her voice, and made him an offer.

She said she represented *important* people in the United States government. Her people were looking for scholars and young college students like Li, to help them get a better understanding of Chinese culture in America. She also explained how the coronavirus pandemic of that year had already claimed nearly a quarter million American lives, and that Li's support could *possibly* prevent another quarter million more from being lost. After the pitch was complete, Sarah blinked her pretty eyes casually, crossed her legs, sipped her herbal tea, then leaned back in her chair, hands folded in her lap, eyeing him with anticipation. Her refined jade eyes reflected anxious impatience beneath their composed luster.

Li had been only mildly surprised by her proposition. He had watched enough American movies and read enough articles online to know somewhat how these things worked, without having experienced them first hand. There was no doubt about it, Sarah was some type of U.S. government agent, most likely working for the infamous Central Intelligence Agency (CIA). She (They) wanted to recruit him because he was born and raised in China, spoke Mandarin fluently, and was an engineering major. He was also a young 20-year-old male at the time, which was probably why they had specifically chosen her, an attractive, White female, with jade colored eyes for his potential recruitment. They had thought of every detail. His school schedule, daily routine, even down to the cultural nuance of the jade eyes to remind him of his birth country. Had they really gone through so much trouble for him? Possibly.

Li sat at the table as Sarah's eyes bored into him. The way her foot bounced in the air, and her neck muscles tensed, Li could tell she was very uncomfortable when she had no control over things. He did not want to trouble her, but this was now about him. It was his decision. With her true purpose unmasked, Li wondered what he should do?

It took him a week to mull the decision over. Sarah offered to pay a hefty sum in exchange for Li's junior intelligence gathering efforts. She told him his talent as a brilliant engineering student, and native Mandarin speaker, would be helpful in keeping America safe. Li thought long and hard. Though he had no need of extra money thanks to his father's wealth, he found his engineering path dull and monotonous. When he was honest with himself, he enjoyed the *study* of engineering, more than he did the *application* of it in a sterile laboratory or corporate office. Although it had been strange being followed by Sarah for almost two months, he had been able to figure *her* out with only his powerful instinct as a guide. Sarah herself had reluctantly admitted that to him. How good could he get if he actually had her training? He decided to find out. A week after they had met for tea, he contacted Sarah and formally accepted her offer. He had no idea that decision back then would lay the foundation for a long career in the intelligence world. A career that would take him around the world, allow him access to society's labyrinthine under chambers, back alleys, and sewers, and culminate in his current position as Chief of Intelligence of Cereus.

*   *   *

Comfortable in his bus seat, Li's mind focused on the message he had received only an hour prior.

Could it really be happening? Order 5428?

After all these years, he never thought it would occur so unexpectedly. No training scenario or exercise had prepared him or any of his colleagues for this situation; now, essentially, they were all flying blind.

He rubbed his temples with his fingers in a circular motion to help clear his head. He needed to focus on who he should meet with first when he arrived at the capitol building. Should he speak with the governor? Or maybe the mayor might be the better choice? He allowed himself to lean back in his seat and relax his shoulders as he developed a concrete plan of action.

First, he needed to call a meeting with the state leadership to calm and reassure them that he and the organization had everything under control. Next, he would need to get on a conference call with the other remaining Founders, to determine how they could conduct an organized transfer of power and leadership to all of the comvils.

That will be the hard part and it might not go as smoothly as we surmised.

Outside of the window, the bus sped past patches of open farmland south of Yuba City and was quickly approaching the newer suburbs on the west side of Lincoln. Most were single family houses that repeated themselves in a uniform pattern after a block or two, with a few wealthier properties sprinkled in for those fortunate enough to be able to afford them. The entire area north of Sacramento had seen explosive population growth in the early twenty-first century. This necessitated a large number of homes to be thrown up fast with little regard for how to sell them. As a result, Li knew that over fifty percent of them were vacant, with few to no pending inquiries. The thought and the sight of the homes made him feel like a failure. *If only we had intervened sooner.*

His moment of regret was interrupted by the distant chime of a bell from deep within his inner ear. The chime echoed softly, slightly beyond the edge of his awareness at first, but loud enough to make itself known. He had personally chosen the tone because it was calming and neutral, which made it easier for him to focus when he needed to use it.

Identify caller. His thought triggered a prompt response from the device resting in the jacket pocket of his suit.

"Call from Rodan." A distant male voice spoke into his ear. Li's neutral expression now gave a hint of uncertainty. With the events of the morning, he was unsure about the conversation he was about to have with his closest colleague and long-time friend.

Whenever he thought of Rodan Mitchell, the ox came to mind. Loyal. Steadfast. Diligent. Indomitable. These were the classic positive traits of one born in the year of the ox. Born in 2021, Li knew that the element associated with Rodan was metal. The elemental pairing brought the image of a detailed pewter figure to Li's mind. Crafted with precision, but heavy and hard to move, especially if it was very large, like Rodan. According to dominant belief, oxen were also introverted, indecisive, and skeptical people. So focused on their gradual and unbroken march toward their objectives, they were prone to self-centeredness and sometimes had difficulty understanding and expressing their true thoughts. Li knew all Chinese zodiac traits were anecdotal. They were based on thousands of years of Chinese folklore, superstition, and countless generations of parents' attempts to frighten unknowing children into becoming good people. Even with that knowledge and decades of lived experience, he still found kernels of truth in the old-fashioned beliefs. He had seen Rodan's personality and, at times, the trajectory of his life and career, manifest just as the animal wheel of fate had ordained. Rodan, as an ox, was oblivious to these things. It was only natural.

Call from Rodan. The voice repeated itself three times, providing Li with a moment to collect his thoughts.

Answer call.

Rodan's voice boomed in his mind, inciting a brief feeling of nausea. *Must be the new implant*, Li thought.

"What's your ETA?" Rodan asked.

"I'm on the bus right now. Should arrive at the capitol by 1030."

"Gotcha. Just wanted to give you a heads up that there's an active protest scheduled for today."

"Is that right? What time?"

"Our sources are sayin' around 1100. But you know how reliable they can be."

"Right. Peaceful or armed?"

"Right now, word says it's one of the peaceful groups. Some treehuggers from Napa. I don't think they should be much of a problem. But we'll keep an eye out."

Break. He put a mental stop in the conversation to consider Rodan's words. *A protest? Today?* Most peaceful protests were scheduled weeks in advance, and he hadn't read any reports or received any notifications from any of his sources about one this morning. Something was off.

Continue.

"You still there?" Rodan's voice pierced his thoughts and coincided with an abrupt lane change that the bus had to make. Li felt bile surge up his esophagus, he swallowed hard to force it back down.

"Yeah still here. Have they said anything about next steps?"

"Naw not yet. Still waiting on word from one of the big bosses. We still don't know which one pulled the trigger yet."

"Got it. We'll find out more soon enough. Ok, I'm signing off."

"Li, one more thing…watch your back out there. We don't know what's gonna happen from here."

"I will."

End call. Li's eyes moved to the slim black briefcase stowed on the floor of the bus between his legs. It had been nearly ten years since he used his service weapon while on the job. He stared at the case and hoped that he could add another day onto that number, although he had his doubts. In nearly thirty years of service with the organization and prior to that in the military, he had received countless hours of various kinds of training. During all that time he knew that his greatest asset in any foreign situation was his instinct. It was a skill that rarely failed him and had even saved his life on more than a few occasions.

Once again, his internal alarm was active and warning him that today was going to be a very long day.

CHAPTER 7:
PROTEST - PART 2

Thirty minutes later, Li peeled his attention away from his device and gazed out of the window as the buildings of Sacramento's city center came into view. To him, the downtown corridor seemed to open its jaws and devour the bus as it rumbled off of Interstate Five and on to J Street. The morning sun reflected off of the shining glass window panes of the US Bank Tower. Once a centerpiece of human economic progress, the nearly half-century old building now stood as a fractured beacon among crumbling skyscrapers. Many of the other high-rise buildings that made up the city's skyline looked no better than weathered old apartment complexes and were replete with shattered windows, failing power, and dilapidated interiors. Li had taken tours of a few of the towers over the years and it wasn't pretty. The entire downtown area reflected old world values. Obsolete. Broken. Ineffective.

As the bus pulled toward its stop at the Golden One Center, the sky appeared to darken. A small patch of clouds blocked the blazing sun in an effort to stifle the heat of the morning. Li spied discarded trash and food wrappers blown by hot gusts of wind tumbling down fissured sidewalks. The people outside of the bus seemed not to notice or care. Desensitized to the filth at their feet, they scurried by in haste toward some unknown destination, hands concealed or holding large signs, wearing improvised face coverings for obscure purposes. Some walked, others jogged. The scene produced a tightness in Li's throat. He knew the feeling well. It was his body's physical signal of readiness. The equivalent of a warning sign in red letters before a hazardous road, prone to rock and mudslides. While his bus decelerated, the roar of its engine drowned out the sound of voices out on the street. But when it began to idle, and passengers began to trickle out, the unmistakable commotion of many vocal cords gathered in one place arrived at Li's ears. They didn't sound happy.

The protest.

With a series of well-practiced silent movements, he keyed in his suitcase combination, unlatched the briefcase, and slid a silver three dimensionally (3D) printed M1911 into a shoulder holster sewn into his suit jacket. He took extra precaution not to alert the drowsy younger man staring into his device across the aisle from him. His weapon equipped, he stood up and made his way off the bus.

Li walked with a brisk pace down a side street, eyes forward, yet scanning, avoiding small bands of people with agitated faces on J Street. After rounding the corner, he could see the backs of dozens of people holding signs, shouting, and shaking their fists in the air with vehemence. The throng of protesters was so thick there was no way he would be able to take his usual direct route up to the capitol. He needed an alternate approach. His eyes shifted down L Street. He could continue that way, but it appeared that more and more of the angry mob was spilling over onto the side street. Although his face wasn't very recognizable to the average person, he had been in the media a time or two in the past. Every time it had been in relation to the organization, with each occurrence giving him more exposure to its enemies and detractors.

I need to get off of the street. The tension seemed to be escalating rapidly on the other side of the block near the capitol. *I thought this protest was supposed to be peaceful.*

"Hey, hey! I think that's one of em'! One of the weird commune freaks from the news!" The voice blasted from a large man with a protruding gut and full head of greying brown hair who separated himself from the group of protesters half a block from Li. "Let's go beat his ass!" The man and two of his friends, both tall and lanky, advanced in Li's direction, fists clenched, eyes of fury. Two held protest signs. The other appeared unarmed. Though he saw no weapons, all three looked like the type to fight dirty, and probably would not hesitate to use the wooden rods of the sign to beat him down if given the chance.

Li thought about engaging the three men and subduing them, but in quick fashion abandoned the idea. He couldn't risk more bad press falling onto the organization's shoulders because of his actions. Due to his textbook knowledge of the downtown area, the perfect hiding place stood out clearly in his mind. With long strides he turned back in the direction toward the highway and sheltered himself in a battered old parking garage. Secure in his hiding spot in the shadows of the structure, he peered from around the corner just in time to see the three men standing where he had been only seconds before. One faced in each direction. As a result of the exertion, all three panted with open mouths, like a pack of wolves on the hunt. They were drenched in sweat and had consumed most of their stamina running down the short block. They darted their heads from left to right searching for him. From his place of concealment, Li could read the protest signs. On the simple white board in handwritten red lettering read the words: "Down with Cereus! Down with Limnic!" The other sign read: "Give me liberty and land, or I give YOU death!" From the signs, Li's vision floated to the man with the gut. Then he saw the gun. The large man gripped a glock so hard that the veins in his bloated forearm were visible.

So much for the peaceful protest.

Li's left hand slowly moved to the sidearm concealed within his suit jacket. His instinct caused his body to tense and sharpened his senses. It was a familiar feeling that overcame him anytime he drew his weapon, even if it was only on the practice range. It reminded him to exercise extra prudence while holding the power to end a life. Li waited for several seconds. One minute, then another thirty seconds passed before he dared to peer around the corner again. When he did, his pursuers were nowhere in sight. He scanned both sides of the street twice before returning his firearm to the holster in his suit jacket.

Too close.

A sound in his inner ear caused his muscles to go rigid. It was a call from his telepathic communicator, or TP comm for short. He dropped his shoulders, in a bid to relax himself and his mind. The technique took some of the edge off, but his body was still in alert mode.

Answer call.

Rodan's voice echoed in his head. *"Where are you?"*

"I got chased by some protesters. But I evaded them. Who told you this protest was going to be peaceful?"

There was an awkward silence before Rodan gave his response. *Damn, I'm not sure who provided the intel! I just read the first report that I received. Ah fuck, how embarrassing! I should have fuckin' verified that shit. Now other people might be in trouble too!! Gotta think of a way to unfuck this…why did I drink so much coffee this morning, I really need to take a leak.*

Rodan's unfiltered thoughts filled Li's mind. It was giving him a headache.

"Rodan…your 'mic' is on…" A soft musical tone played, then the connection went silent. Li sighed heavily. As amusing as it was to hear Rodan's inner dialogue, he had no time for it right now. The mass of voices, screams, and yells from the protesters seemed to be inching closer with every passing minute.

The melodic tone sounded again, signaling Rodan's return to the call. *"My bad Li."* The volume of Rodan's voice was lower than before.

"It's ok. We need to verify that intel source. I saw an armed protester."

"Is that right? You think someone slipped us bad info?"

"Yeah. And I want to find out who it was." Li put a mental break in the conversation. Had it been Rodan's careless oversight that gave them the incorrect information? Or had one of his sources gone rogue? He had made plans to meet with one of them that afternoon. Perhaps he needed to contact him now and request an emergency meet? The questions gave way to more questions, each one making him feel increasingly uneasy about the bizarre events of the morning. The only thing that he was sure of was that he needed to get off of the street. Now. *Continue. "Can you send me a data map with the locations of the protesters? That will help me avoid them."*

"Sorry Li. Network has been shaky since the order went out this morning, so no can do." The bass had returned to Rodan's voice just in time. It was accompanied by a mocking tone. *"You a super soldier though, so you should be able to get around a bunch of lightly armed protesters right? Compared to the shit you did in the war, this oughta be a walk in the park."*

Li rolled his eyes and forcefully exhaled air from his nose, forgetting to mentally block out the laugh that resonated in his and Rodan's minds.

"You're right. I'm getting too old for this."

"Aren't we all. Might be time to get some of those happy augmentations and retire in a digital haze. You know how a lot of people do nowadays."

"I'm not quite ready for that. Not my style."

"Oh yeah that's right. You Mr. Integrity after all."

Li became silent. The unmistakable sound of footsteps scuffing the pavement made tension return to his body. His hand went for his gun. After thirty seconds, the sound faded. He dared not peek around the corner.

"You still alive over there?" Rodan asked. More impatient than concerned.

"Yeah. I need to move. I'll see you, in say…twenty-five minutes?"

"Look if you can't make it in under fifteen, you're gonna buy me lunch."

Li allowed himself to laugh. *"You're on."* The tone went dead, signaling the end of the call.

He pulled out his device and gave it the vocal command to open the map. A 3D holographic map of downtown Sacramento appeared to hover above the surface of his device. He rotated it with his finger in midair and mentally mapped his planned route to the capitol service entrance. When he was sure he had memorized the turns, he closed the map and took a deep breath before he stepped out of his place in the shadows. *Now or never.*

No one seemed to notice him emerge from the old parking garage. His eyes scanned left, then right with practiced discernment. Years of training converged, allowing him to detect potential threats while maintaining constant steady steps. The sirens of several patrol cars rushed past him. No doubt they were rapidly mobilizing to establish a perimeter around the block surrounding the Capitol Mall. Taking advantage of the increased police presence, Li took long strides down 8th street, then took a sharp right turn on K Street. Upon turning the corner, he witnessed a group of protesters throwing bottles, cans, and whatever else they could get their hands on at a group of uniformed officers manning a checkpoint. One of the officers, a blonde woman with an ample chest and a thin waist, resorted to secondary force in defense of herself and clubbed an angry demonstrator on the side of his head. He fell to the ground in a heap of sweaty flesh, no doubt unconscious from the unexpectedly heavy blow. At the sight of their fallen comrade, five of his friends became enraged and looked prepared to tear the woman and her squad mates to shreds.

Li's heart bled at the sight of the overwhelmed and (most likely) outgunned cops, but he had no time to go to their aid. His destination was less than two blocks away.

He hurried down the street and turned the corner onto 11th Street. With the capitol building in sight, he slowed his pace to a brisk walk. He was so focused on reaching his objective that he narrowly avoided being hit by an old Tesla that was speeding away from the direction of the protest. *Too many close calls this morning.*

The final push to the capitol's service entrance went without incident. One sentry blocked his path when he reached the side of the building. He was well armed, much more so than standard street cops. Li wondered who he was working for.

"You have some business here?" he asked. He was tall with thick black eyebrows and a matching mustache on a dry sand toned face. It was the face of one who had spent long hours standing in the sun for no good reason. Probably ex-military or local cop turned mercenary. Both were bad news if they fought for the wrong reasons.

Mustache seemed as if he had been waiting for an excuse to draw and use his weapon all morning. But Li did not provide him with one. With diplomatic decorum, he produced his Cereus organizational badge, signaling that he was a high-level member. The guard scowled in response, but allowed him to pass.

The chaos of the protest continued to unfold outside as he walked into the building. The black service door slammed behind him, leaving an echo in his ears. Inside the poorly lit service corridor he could no longer hear the screams, shouting, and the unmistakable pops and bangs of small arms fire on the other side of the door. As he moved toward the service stairwell, he questioned the details of the morning, wondering why the protest had become violent and who fed them the bad intel. He had a feeling that he wouldn't like the answers to either of those questions.

CHAPTER 8:
STRATEGY MEETING

Rodan knew he should close the browser, but his scattered thoughts wouldn't allow it. *Research, I'm doing research.* Words he repeated to convince himself of his work ethic and commitment to detail. The sustained half-truth made him feel better about how he had spent the last fifteen minutes.

Seated at his desk, in his battered dark blue suit pants, with white dress shirt and midnight blue necktie, he recalled his younger days as an eager and idealistic beat cop in the Sacramento Police Department. Serving as a police officer in the city that raised him was a great honor, and prepared him for his current role as Director of Operations in his small liaison office for the organization. In those days, he was fresh off of his first and final enlistment in the U.S. Army, and was keen to commence with the next chapter of his life. After four years of drudgery and *'embracing the suck'*, he returned to his beloved hometown, and filled out a job application to become a cop the day after his plane landed. Nine months later, he was standing on the corner of Grant Avenue and Marysville Boulevard. Lean and trim, clothed in a crisp uniform, a shining seven-pointed gold star badge over his heart, gun on his hip, he stood on that corner, eyes gleaming, as he observed the traffic flow by. He had been fortunate to be assigned to North Command, District 2, Beat A. The location of his alma mater Grant Union High School (Go Pacers!). He beamed with pride on that day and everyday he was on the job.

Back then, he embodied service for others over himself, often volunteering to take on extra duties or shifts to cover for his peers or to just become a better cop. His fellow squadmates called him *'Brain'* because he always seemed to know random details about certain parts of the city, and would recite them to others even if unsolicited. His knack for taking in knowledge was only rivaled by his steadfast commitment to serving and protecting his community, a neighborhood notorious for crime and drugs.

In 2045, after a two-week period of non-stop rain, the neighborhood had been flooded. Schools were closed. Elderly people, confined to their homes due to limited mobility, died. Hundreds lost their jobs or businesses overnight. Officer Mitchell viewed the scene with sorrowful eyes and a heavy heart. So moved was he by the scale of the tragedy, and his unfailing obligation to *all* things greater than himself; he immediately leapt into action.

He volunteered to lead a recovery effort that spring, mobilizing hundreds of hands within the local area, and coordinating outside agencies to assist with flood relief, even going as far to establish and head a food bank for needy families from within his dear Grant High. He had no idea how many lives he impacted or saved as a result of his effort during that and other similar emergency situations throughout his first three years of active service.

Little did he know, someone was watching. Li Ma had heard about his herculean endeavor to lift his beleaguered community up following a series of disasters, and as a result, had scouted him from afar, for an unknown amount of time (Li still would not tell him for how long specifically). Eventually, when he approached young Rodan, he told him he was destined for bigger things. Things that would not only help his community, but potentially help move the whole of *humanity* and *society* to a better place. Always called to serve at the highest level possible, with great hesitation, Rodan turned in his badge, and joined the ranks of Cereus shortly afterward.

Sitting there at his desk, his thoughts in a jumble concerning the roaring protest outside, and his closest colleague caught up in it, sometimes he wondered what happened to that slender youth. What happened over the years that had weakened his once fantastic brain's ability to absorb, store, and arrange data? Was it early onset dementia? Had he burned himself out too early in life? On some days he worried he had been so focused on stacking disparate factoids and tidbits of information in the open space of his brain, that he had neglected any organization of the vast storage closet that was his mind, leaving a disordered collection of unusable litter. He was the equivalent of a large obese man, confined to his home. Trapped, among piles and piles of once useful things. A prisoner of memory, who had no idea where to begin how to dig himself out from among the clutter. Staring at his computer, these were the thoughts that entered his mind. *Maybe this was my fate all along.*

Like many of his work tangents, his search began with purpose. He had been researching possible weaknesses in the perimeter of the California capitol building. He worried about the security of the old building, hoping to find valuable information about how to protect it and its occupants should the protest outside penetrate into the building. *How did I fuck up the intel report?*

After fifteen minutes he had learned various details about the ancient government building. Among them, novel tidbits he had never known, and would probably never remember. *Began construction 1861,…granite archways…something, something, something…Corinthian columns…ooh! Something about the American Civil War…lead architect was accused of being a Southern sympathizer…Reuben Clark…oh shit!…died in an insane asylum in Stockton, California in 1868.* Only the last detail planted roots in the hard earth of his mind. The others were washed away by the rising tide of tasks he needed to complete, flooding his overwhelmed brain like spring rains inundating a wheat field.

Rodan contemplated Clark's tragic end as he stared at the sea of papers and electronic document readers on his desk. *I might go insane if I can't unfuck this.* Unable to focus on his original objective, he abandoned it for a more attainable one. Find the previous year's report and hope he included details about building security in it.

After another ten minutes of rummaging, he still couldn't locate the intelligence report. *Dammit, I thought sure it was here.* He slid open a file cabinet to his right only to find documents for the previous year that he had yet to organize, file, and digitize. He knew he should clean and arrange, but it always felt like there were more pressing matters at hand. This time was no exception.

A ring from his desk phone interrupted his search and his thoughts. It caused him to jerk himself in the direction towards his desk and to hit his forearm on the side of the metal shelf. *Son of a—!* He shut his eyes and let the throbbing pain dissipate, then reached for the receiver, arm still stinging with pain.

"Yeah."

"It's me. I'm at the conference table. Can you come over?" It was Li. He didn't sound like he had just navigated his way through a violent protest. *Damn him. Why does he have to make everything look so easy?* Rodan stood, adjusted his tie around his bulging neck, and his pants around his curved belly. For some reason he felt the need to up his game whenever Li was around, even though he knew his glory days of youthful physical prowess and presentation were long behind him.

The meeting room was so small that an old oak conference table consumed the majority of the floor space, leaving only small aisles between the wall and the chairs at the table. It always took Rodan considerable effort to navigate his tall, dark-skinned, 230-pound frame through the tiny room during meetings, while the svelte Li was able to spend hours reviewing files and even conducting liaison meetings in the space. Despite his physical discomfort, their small liaison office in the state capitol had become a home away from home after all of the time they had spent there together.

When he entered the room, Li stood behind the chair closest to the left of the head of the table, his eyes rapidly scanning electronic documents on his device. Rodan cleared his throat in an obnoxious fashion to get his attention.

"You made it." Rodan made no attempt to conceal a playful tone.

Li diverted his attention from his electronic documents and grinned. "I did. What was my time?"

"Looks like that lunch will have to wait for another day." Rodan laughed.

The small smile that wrinkled Li's face was quickly replaced by a straight line of seriousness. "I'm looking for any messages that I received concerning today's protest. You find anything in the old intel reports?"

Rodan placed his giant hands on the back of a chair for support, feigning casualness. "Nothing yet. Still working on it." Li flashed him a disapproving eye. Rodan pivoted to change the subject. "I just got word that the local cops are breaking it up already…with the help of local mercs of course."

"That's good to know." Li straightened his posture and rotated himself toward Rodan, displaying a hint of puzzlement that made him look even older. "Which mercs?"

"They were mostly the Hornets from South Sac, mixed in with a few of the Fighters from Folsom." Rodan chuckled. "The Fighters aren't the strongest, but they've got some of the most advanced warrior bots in town to do the dying for them."

Li mouthed a laugh, but no sound came out. He knew Rodan was right, but it still did little to calm the voice of his instinct that blared with sustained intensity as it had the entire morning. "The Terminator and his crew didn't show up?"

Rodan's eyes sank toward the floor. "Not that I know of. I wonder what's up with him…he's usually one of the biggest supporters of the local cops."

A pensive expression dominated Li's face. In all the years Rodan had known him, that face usually meant that some revelation was dawning in his mind that would be beneficial for both of them. Though technically they were both equal in position and pay, Li's experience and strategic brain made him the de facto boss. The producer and approver of most ideas their small detachment came up with, and ultimately followed through on.

"What are you thinkin'? Is it possible that The Terminator, his boys and bots had something to do with this?" Rodan asked.

"Exactly. Otherwise, why wouldn't he show? He never misses an opportunity to flex his muscles or his machines."

"There's only one way to find out." Rodan reached in his pocket, produced an old smartphone with a visibly cracked screen, then extended it toward Li. Smartphones were outdated tech, but they were much safer to use when communicating with potentially untrustworthy sources.

Li gazed at the phone suspended in Rodan's hand. Hesitating, as if an invisible force had frozen him in place. "…We said we wouldn't use that unless it was an emergency…" Despite the rising impatience that he noted in his long-time colleague's mannerisms, his doubt about whether to use the phone or not lingered in the air between them.

"Just make the damn call."

Reluctantly, he sighed deeply, took the phone, and said, "If we're wrong about this, it could endanger and possibly burn one of our best sources."

"C'mon Li, with silence from HQ after giving the order and a violent protest right on our doorstep, I'd say this qualifies as an emergency." Rodan reasoned.

Li knew he was right, yet his instinct continued to silently tap him on the shoulder from the shadows of his mind. The Terminator had only been on the books for six months and in that brief period of time had been one of his most productive sources of information in the city. His network and clout extended all the way down to San Francisco, the surrounding Bay area, then up to as far north as the comvil in Chico. He and others like him were a big reason why the deconstructionist philosophy of Cereus had been able to survive against the daunting pressure of the old world after all these decades. It had garnered them major land and property acquisitions, that were then repurposed for practical needs like housing, community work centers, or places for social gathering. In addition to land conversion, it also prevented old world companies from demolishing dilapidated structures and building anew on the same land. Many of the people protesting outside held this as their principal grievance.

The term 'deconstructionist' was something of a misnomer. It did not mean tearing things down, so much as it meant preventing the need to erect more structures for the sake of incessant old-world economic expansion. Information from sources like The Terminator had helped move deconstructionism from the philosophical realm to the real world. But he wasn't always the easiest or cheapest person to work with.

I wonder what we'll have to pay this time? Li thought as he keyed in numbers on the smudged screen of the smartphone.

The familiar tone of a ringing phone tingled in his ear. It rang once…twice…three times. *No response.* On the fourth ring, a deep voice that sounded as if it was being passed through a metal filter answered the phone. "Hello?"

"I could go for some Thai food today. How about you?" Li's voice came out clearer than he expected, fighting mounting nervousness.

"Sorry…you must have the wrong number. I'm not hungry today." The canned voice dragged his words, then abruptly ended the call.

Rodan watched Li, unaware that he was holding his breath. He noticed that his old friend looked physically sick after he removed the phone from his ear. "Well? What'd he say?"

Li looked up from the phone with sagging shoulders. A betrayal of his usual erect posture. "I think our source has been compromised."

CHAPTER 9:
NOE

The sound of her feet scratching the pavement and her heavy breathing were the only noises apparent to her. Light clothing and a pair of worn sneakers were all she wore as she made long strides down the pavement. The heat of the morning on her exposed legs and muscled abdomen made no impression on her. Just the road and the thought of completing her daily three-miler were the only things on her mind. She passed restaurants, bars, shops, and houses, without glancing at their names or the patrons emerging from them. Didn't need to. She could almost run the route with her eyes closed. Her pace was so swift onlookers expected to see some wild animal, jaws gnashing, teeth bared, on her heels. To her, the pace was irrelevant. She only wanted to move. Whether she was prey or predator did not enter into her clearheaded state of mind.

As she rounded a corner to turn south on 5th Street, a passing cyclist, face deep into his device, emerged from behind an obstructively placed evergreen tree. She sidestepped to avoid the man, feeling rising irritation from his lack of awareness and her broken runner's trance.

"Imbécil! Watch where you're goin'!" she said, raising her voice with a slight Spanish accent.

The man on the bike swerved, then skidded to a halt at the edge of the sidewalk just in time. He narrowly avoided entering the already busy street, replete with rushing vehicles on their morning commute. Relieved, he breathed a sigh of relief, before noticing the woman standing before him. "Oh disculpáme Noe! I didn't see you running there!" His eyes roamed up and down her body before falling unapologetically on her sweat glistened breasts.

Noe rolled her eyes, then reached out a hand to raise his chin with her index finger. "Gabriel...um hello. I'm up here." She shook her head, smiling inwardly to herself. He had maintained a lifelong crush on her, an unrequited one-way relationship. One where she only reciprocated in private fantasies in the depths of his mind. She was sure of it. *Aye Gabriel…what am I gonna do with you?* Despite his constant ogling, she knew he was harmless. A loyal *amigo de infancia* who provided her with updates about her mother and her large extended family through complex familial networks she never had time nor patience to keep track of. Even though he was six years her senior, Gabriel had never quite gotten a handle on his vices and looked as if he were well into middle age. He was not a very big man, but he was tall. A beer gut swelled under his black shirt, like a bosu ball placed on a flat surface. It did not fit well with his long arms, and when paired with his bad posture, made him appear to be constantly sticking his stomach out. His lips were dry, and his face lacked plasticity, hinting at constant dehydration. His only redeeming quality was his full head of black hair sprinkled with flecks of grey. Combined with the matching bushy black mustache below his nose, it would have almost made him look regal, if Noe hadn't known that he dyed it regularly.

Gabriel's eyes fluttered, then finally focused on hers. It helped to break the spell she had on him, and to return much needed blood flow to his brain. "I'm sorry Noe. You know I couldn't help it. Es que eres tan chula." His eyes showed boyish innocence, providing sincerity to his words.

"Ya sé. That's what you always say," she said, hoping to strike a sarcastic, yet playful tone. Judging by the sad response in his eyes, it was a failed effort.

Gabriel smiled at her as if he had not heard the comment. *She didn't mean it that way. Don't be so sensitive*, he told himself. With great effort, he kept his eyes on her face, allowing himself glances toward her soft lips between blinks. In his eyes, she was an angel, perfect in every way. Blackish-brown hair, feminine orange-brown eyes, a slender neck, crazy hot athletic body with a year-round tan; she could have easily been a successful model if she wanted to. But he knew that wasn't her style.

Ever since high school he had been entranced by her beauty. It was the odd name that first piqued his boyhood curiosity. "Noelani Acosta? What type of weird name is that?" he had thought. A few weeks later, seated next to her in their Integrated Math class, he had asked her this very question and had received a very direct answer. "My mom is Hawaiian, my dad is Mexican. I'm mixed," came her blunt answer. From that day (it took several months), they eventually became friends, staying in touch even throughout her time in the military. When she got out years later and returned to Sacramento, Gabriel looked her up again. She was just as beautiful, but different. Though they still hung out from time to time, he could tell she had seen some shit while she was in. Whatever it was, she hadn't gotten over it.

"So what's up?" Noe asked him, hands on hips, "besides getting in the way of my running route."

"Just heading into the market early. Got a few things to sort and organize before the lunch rush."

"Cool." Noe moved to resume her run, expecting the chivalrous flourish of his arm he usually offered as a joke whenever she passed by him. This time though, he remained locked in place on his bike seat. "What is it? Something wrong?" Concern crept into her voice unknowingly.

"It's your mother. I…uh spoke with her today. She says she really needs to talk to you…says it's urgent." Gabriel's words were delicate. Like a doctor giving a patient bad news. "Have you spoken with her yet?"

Noe folded her arms across her chest. "No." Her eyebrows slanted, lips pursed, her breathing became heavy again, despite standing in place for the last minute. She wanted to punch something, anything, and Gabriel stood within arm's reach.

"Hey, don't shoot the messenger!" He raised his hands in defense, "She told me you haven't been returning her calls."

"And? ¿Entonces qué?"

"C'mon, mija, I've known your mother a long time and I know when she's worried about you…" He hesitated before continuing. "She said she wants you to go and visit her." Noe's nostrils began to flare. *She needs to hear this.* "She said it was important that she talk to you in person." A visible vein near the side of her left temple began to throb. It looked as if her head might explode any second, yet her eyes arched in surprise. *She didn't expect to hear that.* Gabriel shut up, out of consideration for her and his own well-being.

Noe let out a deep sigh to relax herself as she had been instructed to do so many times in the past whenever she felt overcome by rage. After several seconds, the wave of anger subsided, but threatened to return again at any moment. She managed a flat tone, hoping to sound indifferent. "Ok thanks for letting me know Gabriel. I'll give her a call today and see what she wants." The attempt failed. *Nope, I'm still angry, really angry. Gotta calm down.* She began her breathing exercises again. They were somewhat effective.

Gabriel smiled at her effort. "I know you haven't had a good relationship with her but, Noe, y'know we only get two parents in this life, if we're lucky. You gotta try and appreciate them while they're around."

Although she knew that he was right, she couldn't bring herself to express it on her face. Staunch neutrality was her only response. He opened his mouth to say more, but before sound could come out, she forced her way past him, almost causing him to tumble from his bike. From over her shoulder, Noe said, "Buen día, Gabriel." Her eyes scanned from side to side before she stepped off to resume her run.

Gabriel eyeballed her glutes until she turned another corner and vanished from sight. It was difficult watching her struggle, worse knowing she was going through it alone. He and her mother had always tried, but she never accepted the help. Gabriel shook his head, pitying her. Noe's mother sounded scared on the phone. Of what, she hadn't said. But whatever it was, it was something she wanted to share with her estranged daughter. *I hope you call her this time Noe. There might not be much time left.*

Around the corner, Noe had been aware of the presence of Gabriel's eyes lingering on her ass while she moved down the block, but didn't dwell on it. Reasons for why her mother desperately wanted to talk to her crowded in her brain, making her forget his wandering eyes. This wouldn't be the first time she *urgently* needed to speak with her. *What the hell could it be this time? Trying to set me up with someone? Or get me to join the family business again? Or could it be something more dire?* She felt her chest tighten. The anger was returning again. It always did when it came to her mother.

Noe was on the final straightaway of her run. A clear sidewalk. She increased her speed. The boost provided a much-needed catharsis from the cloud of fury hanging over her mind. As she felt her legs beginning to burn from additional exertion, a small smile drew itself on her face. Her "angry runs" always gave her the best workouts.

*   *   *

The fire from the creaking gas stove burned with a brilliant arrangement of blue, orange, and red. It danced in a controlled frenzy below the iron skillet Noe held with a loose grip over it, heating her lunch. A modest helping of synthetic bacon and eggs from a carton, or as she liked to call them, "fake" eggs, sizzled, cracked and popped emitting a delicious aroma. Cooking them both at the same time wasn't the best way to take advantage of their flavor, but it was much faster and efficient.

Standing at the stove, the undulating circle of fire before her sparked wildfires of involuntary memories on the surface of her mind. *What the hell does she want?* Noe's thoughts of her mother always came in brief flashes. An image of a little girl with arms outstretched, desperate for the kind of love only a mother could give. A teenager turning her back on a pseudo-repentant face. The hours-long arguments during her precious moments of leave. The final physical and emotional barrier erected in her mother's honor. Yet despite the scorched earth campaign she had waged against her mother's sins, withered clusters of charred patches survived, igniting curiosity, bitterness, and sometimes, on rare occasions, hope.

Mesmerized by the flames, it wasn't until the familiar smell of blackened food reached her nose that she realized her breakfast was burning. *Shit.* With a jerk she removed the skillet from the fire, whirled toward the nearest open window, waving her free hand violently over the grotesquely burned concoction. *They'll need DNA records to identify this.*

Smoke from the pan choked the kitchen air, filling the tiny apartment within seconds. Noe reached for the knob on the stove and switched it off. It gave her time to set the skillet on the cool side of the stove top. She exhaled air from her nose, exasperated and hungry. Her ever present inner critic raised its voice, berating her for sub-par cooking skills. *How will you ever be able to survive without the military or your family!?* It mocked. She clamped her eyes shut to force it quiet. It complied.

A loud buzz from her device drew her attention to a small glass coffee table in the living room. With quick steps, Noe reached it in time to see "Mom Calling" on the front screen. She stared at it, willing it to shut up with her cold gaze. It obeyed.

The living room had one window, and light from the late morning filtered in on to Noe's skin. She stood there for several minutes, hands on the window sill, letting the heat warm her overworked muscles. The usual view of the gleaming golden Tower Bridge sitting over the toxic Sacramento River greeted her. It was a distraction from the seed of worry taking root somewhere deep on the scarred frontier of her psyche. The instinct to destroy any attempt at new life there was strong, but she resisted. *What if something is really wrong this time?* She pondered, more curious than concerned. Fifteen call attempts in one morning was excessive, even for her uncaring mother.

With a decisive motion, she faced the device and commanded it to redial. Her body became rigid, accelerating into a higher gear of anticipation. It was an automatic action forged from years of military training, readiness, and general awareness of all of the dangers in the world. Although she wasn't in the mood to fight, she would be prepared if the need arose.

CHAPTER 10:
THE UBER SHEPHERD

In the back of a cramped car, Noe condensed herself as much as possible in a failed attempt not to make contact with the older man sitting next to her. He smelled of an odd mixture of strawberry vape smoke with hints of shitty schwag weed. She knew the odor well from her early days in the military.

The old man's wrinkled tree bark-textured ivory complexion twisted into grotesque shapes as he spoke directly into a camera held by his female companion. The woman, a probably once beautiful Filipina looked to be about the same age, though Noe could never tell an older person's exact age thanks to all the widely available anti-aging treatments. She held a camera in one hand, while encouraging tree bark face to keep talking with the other. In their makeshift mobile studio, she was the camerawoman and executive producer; he, the on-air talent. His role was to say things that were supposed to be witty, edgy, and provocative all at once. He wasn't doing a very good job at it. Noe did her best to make herself small, avoiding potential contact with the man or becoming an unwitting guest on their live broadcast.

I hate Uber pools, Noe lamented. The car was self-driving, navigating lines of traffic on the crumbling U.S. Highway Fifty in short, sometimes jarring, thrusts of movement. *Must be an old model.* The vehicles had come a long way from the early designs at the beginning of the century. But after several unfortunate accidents, and general public dislike at the weirdness of seeing a car moving with no driver, the rideshare company agreed to post bodies in the driver seats to "increase the public confidence in the service that we provide," their message online had stated decades prior. They called them drivers, but everyone knew no actual driving was involved, so they became colloquially known as Uber shepherds.

The current shepherd was reading an actual physical book. From her disadvantaged position, Noe couldn't make out the title. She leaned to the side of the seat to get a better view. All she could see was a thick book with lines and lines of words. *A real book! How rare.* He was an Asian guy who looked like he could be fifteen, but was more than likely around her age. *I swear Asians never age, how lucky*, she thought. He was even a little more handsome than she originally noticed. With his black-rimmed reading glasses, stylish loose-fitting button-down shirt, he looked like he would have been more at home down south in the Bay Area than up there in sleepy Sacramento. His appeal was only diminished by his dimwitted decision to use the front passenger seat as his personal office. All manner of document readers, papers, books, writing instruments, and snack containers competed for space in the improvised setup. Somehow, he had even managed to hang two neatly pressed half-folded spare shirts on wire hangers from the door of the glove compartment. *Very resourceful, but sloppy.*

"You never know when you'll need a spare."

The young driver's voice startled her. A set of playful eyes met Noe's gaze in the reflection of the vehicle's rear-view mirror. The mouth wasn't visible but his eyes looked happy.

Noe let out a single breathy guffaw. "I'm impressed that you were able to fit all of that up there."

"It's either this or my dad's place. I actually feel like I have more room here." He laughed, but it was tinted with sadness. "You headed to Folsom?"

"Yeah…" Noe's voice became soft and low, "…gonna visit my mom over there."

He set his book aside in his 'office' in order to give her his full attention. The old influencers lost in their own personal illusion continued their show in the corner of his eye. They whispered to one another about how to edit the video, unaware of him or their stunning ride companion seated right next to them. The shepherd felt a generous helping of pity for the two. *It's probably been decades since they influenced anyone other than themselves.* Ignoring them, he focused his energy on her. She was by far the prettiest fare he had ride within weeks. He made a conscious decision to violate the unwritten policy of "don't engage in long unwanted and awkward conversations with passengers" he had learned in his early days on the job.

"I heard Folsom is one of the last decent neighborhoods in town…I mean one of the ones that wasn't that messed up after all the flooding and earthquakes in the thirties," he rambled, unsure if he should keep talking; he did. "…That's at least what my parents told me. They're Bay Area transplants. We left during the height of the exodus ten years ago, only to move here, which of course wasn't much better off because the same shit was happening. People just got fed up with dealing with all the inequality and lack of public services. It really sucked."

Noe's mind drifted. He wasn't saying anything profound or interesting she didn't already know. Her lack of interest manifested into an expression of absentminded consenting, though she was not completely aware of it. A series of short vocal acknowledgements were all she offered him.

Sensing disinterest, tiny beads of sweat formed below his hairline. *Be more interesting!* "Uh…I'm sorry. I'm running my mouth again. I know I can talk too much."

"No, it's alright. I was listening." A pang of guilt hit Noe square in the chest. Her mind had wandered again. It was a habit she had been trying to rid herself of for years. She sat up as straight as she could in her seat without making contact with tree bark face next to her, who was busy using crooked fingers to manipulate the old smartphone camera. The woman had fallen asleep. "You're right. Up here isn't much better. But even though it's a little run down, I liked growing up here."

The shepherd's eyes bounced in the rear-view mirror. *She still wants to talk to me! Ok keep it cool.* He told himself to be less wordy. *Gotta listen more! This is a real woman!* "You grew up here? Nice! Which part of town?"

"Del Paso Heights," she made no attempt to conceal the pride in her voice.

"Cool, I've never been up there, but I've heard it's nice," his answer was breathless.

Doubtful, Noe thought. The area typically had a reputation for being one of the poorest and most dangerous parts of the city going back at least to the beginning of the century. Things only got worse as the years went by. The coronavirus of the early twenties and resulting economic downturn blighted the area right before her birth. Throughout the thirties and forties, the valley had been hit by a series of biblical natural disasters, always arriving whenever overall conditions seemed to be improving. They could never catch a break before the next fire, flood, or rare earthquake rattled, scorched, or inundated the area. In February 2045, when she was only 15-years-old, she recalled torrential rains falling for nearly two weeks straight. It was so bad, she had needed to go to her school, Grant Union High School, to get whatever food and supplies she could grab.

The media dubbed these calamities the 'great disasters.' To them, it was a sensationalist tagline. A pithy two-word summary of a string of tragedies for eager viewers to digest as they downed their coffee in the morning or prepared for bed at night. But for select residents of the ghetto, each one was a world-shattering event that forever altered the course of their lives. Thanks to her father's blue-collar work ethic, and her mother's 'extracurricular activities,' Noe had been one of the lucky ones to survive through it all, but she had not gone completely unscathed. Like a second degree burn with fractured but healthy skin, the collective trauma from decades of pain had been seared onto her memory. The wound was a grim reminder of ever-present grief. As a result of these catastrophes, her childhood had been marked by longtime residents fleeing the area in droves. First the Parkers in third grade, followed by the Acevedos in middle school, then the Carbajals when she was fourteen; that one hurt a lot. Those were just the people she knew personally. The area felt less like home after that, which eventually prompted Noe herself to leave via the military. Guilt from the hard decision still lingered over her shoulder like a low hovering steel cloud threatening cold rain. She felt it upon seeing the faces of people like Gabriel and others she knew in the community. The feeling left a dull ache in her heart. It was an affliction she had learned to live with, though she never truly stopped looking for a remedy. In the back of the auto car, the memory of her anguished personal history forced her eyes closed. It was her attempt at prayer.

"Are you alright?" the shepherd asked.

Her eyes flew open. "Fine." The feeling of tear ducts opening reached her awareness. She willed them to close. They complied. "How much further to Folsom?" her unexpectedly hard voice surprised her, and made the shepherd's eyes grow wide with surprise or fright. Noe couldn't tell the difference.

He consulted his old smartphone, "Uhm…let's see…my phone says about twenty minutes. They really need to get this middle console fixed so the passengers can see the trip progress." The place in the vehicle where a stylish touch screen should have been was covered with a black makeshift plastic cover. The handy work looked shoddy. Clearly a rush job for someone in need of a quick getaway or someone trying to get out of work. It shuddered as if it might come loose at any second as the vehicle traversed under-maintained streets.

"That your handy work?" Noe asked, motioning toward the center console.

The shepherd laughed, "Naw, I'm horrible when it comes to fixing stuff. Must've been the owner. Guess he's about as good as I am when it comes to vehicle repairs."

Noe exhaled a single laugh. "You're probably right about that."

"I reported it a few weeks ago. I guess someone jacked the computer."

"This isn't your car?" Noe asked with genuine curiosity.

The shepherd laughed showing all of his teeth. The Filipina woman stirred in her seat at the sound. The old man continued to struggle with the camera. "No way. I could never afford one. Now that I think about it, I don't know anyone who actually *owns* a car. Way too expensive to buy the fancy fuel. And the old school gas is hard to find at a reasonable price. I guess we can thank our parents' generation for that."

Our parents? "How old are you?" Noe challenged.

"I'm twenty-nine," he continued laughing. "I know, I know, I look like I'm fifteen. I get that all the time."

A smile found its way onto her face. "Wow, you had me fooled."

"It's cool. You can make it up to me by giving me a good rating and…maybe requesting to ride with me again?"

Her eyes darted to his front passenger seat, then down to the device in her lap, she could see the shepherd's name was Van. *Van Tran.* "Only if I can ride in the front seat next time." She giggled openly, and felt her mood lighten for the first time since entering the car.

To Van, her laugh was like music. A symphony of pleasant tones from sonata to allegro. "Sure! I've got a place I can stash my stuff. I don't do this for everyone, but for you—" he consulted his phone, "—Miss Noelani Acosta, I'll make an exception." *I made her laugh!*

Noe had been so caught up in their conversation, she hadn't noticed the change in scenery outside. The drab gray of the city had been replaced by houses with large lots with imposing security gates providing exclusivity and privacy to wealthy residents. Large patches of green, trees, grass, and brush populated the spaces in between each house, adding to the character and look of the neighborhood. The place stank of money from unknown shadowy sources. Noe felt her foul mood returning as the car followed winding streets toward her mother's house.

Van noted the change in her mood. He allowed a minute of silence to pass between them, unsure of what to say. A minute later, he sighed with relief as the car slowed near Noe's destination. He considered making a comment about the upscale neighborhood. But the look of bitterness on Noe's face as she stared out the window made him keep his comments to himself. "Looks like we're here," Van said, less buoyant than before. "Even great rides must come to an end."

"So true." She made a quick series of swipes and low vocal commands on her device, then looked up at the fuzzy mirror. "Ok, I left you five stars and a comment too. Have a good day." Noe smiled warmly as she opened the door and stepped out. Van was nice and had done a great job getting her out of her head, but she hated dragging out goodbyes, even if it was with someone she had just met. And her mind was already focusing on the next task at hand: facing her mother.

Back in the car Van watched Noe walk away from the vehicle. She was so stunning in her lemon tank top and fitted white capris that he almost felt a feeling of shame looking at her naturally tanned skin and curvy figure. He gave the command to open his Uber app and scanned the screen to find her comment: "Nice guy and driver for someone who lives in his car. Clean your fuckin' front seat! :P". Van laughed out loud.

CHAPTER 11:
MOTHER AND DAUGHTER

Noe never liked talking on the phone. It wasn't something she had grown up doing and it felt awkward every time. The entire process of it—needing to have the voice encoded and decoded by electric currents only to have some phantom on the other end transmit a message that sounded like her, but was not—made her feel impersonated. It was as if it was not truly her, but some doppelganger, a spotted crocotta, that stole her voice to speak to the entity at the other end of the connection. The distressing process felt inauthentic and fake. Not at all like the real her.

Noe felt the absurd personality feature surface in the form of a tightness in the back of her neck during the conversation with her mother prior to her surprisingly engaging Uber ride. It had been a brief exchange, with her mother doing the majority of the talking. Her phantom phone-self mostly listened, while the flesh and blood Noe did her best to suppress the desire to let loose expletives and audible expressions of surprise.

Her mother insisted on seeing her in person right away to discuss the details of a will that she was drafting. Details too sensitive for the highly monitored phone lines (according to her). She had always been an anxious and neurotic woman, her mother, but this new attempt at communication was a new low. *If* it wasn't true. *She sounded terrified.* Noe went through every possible source of the cause of the genuine fear she heard in her mom's voice over and over again, but she couldn't come up with anything. Her efforts to block anything related to that woman out of her thinking brain had been too efficient over the years. But some instinct deep inside would not allow her to stay away this time. Her mind wouldn't be at peace unless she knew what it was.

Noe agreed to see her through a combination of single words and vocal acknowledgements. It had been difficult not to let the old wounds open. To cover the cauldron of rage, anger, and sadness that had churned into an ungodly mutation over the years. But she managed it. Noe inhaled a deep breath while standing at the base of the hill in front of an imposing black iron gate that led to the smooth extended driveway up to her mom's house. As she exhaled, her mind continued to roll with possible explanations for her mother's pressing urgency to see her besides the will. She found none.

The sound of several clicks accompanied by metallic grinding refocused her attention as the large gate began to slide open. Her mother must have noticed her on the security cameras and opened the gate remotely. The path was wide enough for a vehicle as large as a tank to pass through and, if given clearance, to reach the front door of the house. A scenario Noe had fantasized about more than a time or two. Presently, the thought brought a devilish grin to her lips as she marched toward the house. She felt as if she were climbing the stairs to Dracula's castle like in the old Castlevania games. The thought, along with her burning legs and climbing heart rate spurred her body into a state of physical preparedness. Her vision and spatial awareness were heightened, her muscles primed, as if she were about to begin a live combat military exercise. *Always good to be ready when dealing with Mom.* She quickened her pace to intensify the feeling.

After a minute more of climbing, she reached the large circular driveway in front of the house. Landscaped and well-manicured bushes symmetrically placed around the perimeter stood like vigilant sentries around her. They provided a sharp contrast to the shaggy coyote bushes and Oregon ash trees that surrounded the property. A set of thick decorative oak doors were neatly framed by majestic marble pillars and gave the property a hint of royalty in what would have been otherwise a standard mansion. At least that's how Noe saw it. *Ever the queen.* She rolled her eyes at the pretentious facade, then extended her finger to press the doorbell.

The hulking door to her right opened slowly, and a small woman peered out. Her bead-like brown eyes scrutinized the space around her house guest, shifted from right to left, examining the environment. Sensing no sign of immediate danger, they settled on Noe.

"Mom it's just me. Will you open the door? It's hot out here," Noe said, with irritation in her voice. Her mother's excessive security procedure always took too long and was completely ineffective. *Check BEFORE you open the door Mom!* When she finally opened the door completely Noe performed a perfunctory scan of her person, searching for any obvious signs of distress. Upon inspection, nothing seemed troubling about her mother's appearance. She looked, more or less, like she always did. She wore a dark blue dress with pink plumeria scattered around the design. Noe noticed (though she did not want to) her ample bosom resting on her slightly bulging belly, her cleavage on display for all to see, as usual. Her hair was black and thick, with a strategically undyed ring of gray forming an arch just above her forehead. From a distance, it might have appeared as a silver tiara, but up close it just looked like a half-assed dye job. For all of her frustration with her mother, Noe had to admit that she had aged well. The skin of her face had, for the most part, resisted gravity, and appeared soft to the touch. Outside of expected creases at the lips and forehead, she had few wrinkles, though Noe was not sure if this was genetic, proficient use of cosmetics, or because her mother rarely smiled or laughed. Her expression was eternally stuck between a resting bitch face and the scowl of a disapproving and, or, angry mother. Noe never knew her to be fun or jovial in any way. A genetic trait she herself had surely inherited.

From the doorway Lili regarded Noe, performing a similar evaluation. She was thin. *Not eating enough.* Her skin was dry even with a film of sweat on her face. *Not drinking enough water and or too much booze.* She looked tired and overworked. *Not enough sleep or sex.* She was alone. *No ring on her finger.* She had no social life. (Probably.) *A mother just knows these things.* But her hair and boobs looked great. *Both gifts from me.* She kept her comments to herself, of course. She and Noe had never had the type of bond that would allow them to discuss such things. Lili knew this was her fault, but would never admit it openly. Her gaze moved to Noe's face. Her upturned lip and her stiff posture hinted at deep resentment ready to burst out at the slightest provocation. Lili questioned herself for making the decision to contact her. *The child still doesn't understand, I can tell. How can I ever bring her to understand? Will I ever? This is the best course of action. This time she will understand.* Noe's eyes burned with old and misguided anger toward her. Her temper and skeptical nature were hereditary, Lili knew that. She allowed a brief moment of pity to descend over her. Then watched it vanish as quickly as it had come.

"Yes, yes come in and get out of the heat." Lili waved a hand, signaling her to enter.

The circular foyer of the lavish house was decorated with rare and expensive flowers placed methodically on the sides of the entrances to the great room, dining room, and hallways. Juliet roses, Moloka'i white hibiscus, and other varieties made the space smell like a garden. The mix of fragrances made Noe's head spin. She curled her toes in her sandals to keep her balance and prevent herself from puking.

"You look good Noe. Can I get you anything? Water, juice?"

Noe detected apprehension in her mother's voice. *What is going on with her?* "No Mom, I'm fine."

"Are you eating? You look like a stick."

"I'm ok. I just workout a lot."

Lili's eyes scanned up and down again. She wanted to ask more questions, but knew she would not receive honest responses. The thought would have saddened her years ago. Now, she simply nodded her head, then extended her arm toward the right. "We should go sit down."

Her mother's voice was softer than usual. It lacked the fierceness and attack that Noe was accustomed to. She followed her into the adjacent great room where they both sat on a surprisingly simple wicker couch with cushions. Its presence felt odd in the large space. As odd as the large gap both women instinctively placed between them when they sat. From a distance they appeared as strangers, despite their shared facial features.

"Mom, what is this about? You asked me to come and now I'm here. What do you want?"

Lili hesitated. "Noe, I'll get to the point. I want you to be the beneficiary for my estate. I know I've mentioned it before, but today I have notarized papers ready for your signature."

Noe shook her head fiercely. "No Mom. We've been through this before. I don't want all of this." She gestured toward the room and its surroundings. "You know how I feel about this shit. I don't want your dirty money." The anger began bubbling toward the surface. "After what happened with dad…I just can't."

"Your father was a good man. He worked hard trying to be the image of what this country made all of us believe was the key to a life that was happy and good. And like millions of others, he was fooled and robbed of his life in pursuit of capitalist wealth. Ultimately, he died because of it."

"Don't you talk about him like that! He did all of that for you! For us!" Noe's words came out with explosive force.

Lili closed her eyes and waited. She was well practiced in dealing with her daughter's volatile temper. "I know my life has been far from perfect, but I can assure you that the things I have done over the years, I did with you and Victor in mind. So we could have a better life, free from the oppression of old world thinking," she said, her tone reasonable and soft.

Noe crossed her arms across her chest and scowled. "Yeah Mom. You can tell yourself that all day if it makes you feel better."

"It's the truth. I'm sorry I didn't do a better job when I was younger of explaining that to you. I tried to make your father understand, but he was too well conditioned in the ways of the old world to get it. Through no fault of his own, of course. The economy and society of this country has always been a well-oiled machine with people as its energy source. That, combined with the efficient indoctrination of false ideals like '*The American Dream*' are one of the best ways to keep the entire thing functioning to destroy lives and the planet." She paused. "I couldn't just stand by and do nothing knowing that."

Noe glared at her mother with narrowed eyes. She had heard all of this before and it was boring. "Don't pull that Chomsky bullshit on me now. If your goal in joining and helping those fanatics all this time was to save the planet, equality, and all that other utopian shit; why'd you have to build a fuckin' mansion on a lake? Why do you collect super rare flowers while most live in poverty and squalor?" Silence. Lili looked away. "Uh huh that's what I thought. You're such a fuckin' hypocrite."

The fire burning in Noe's eyes and her incendiary tongue had little effect on Lili. *Poor child. Will she ever understand? Can she?* Her lack of ability to influence her daughter's mood, debilitated her, made her old bones feel weak and heavy. "Baby, who among us are not hypocrites in this world? Just by existing in the design of the old world causes even *you* to consume content, resources, and everything else without end. I'm just honest about the things that I like and how I get them."

Noe sunk her shoulders, exhausted from arguing. *I knew this would be a waste of time.* She stood to leave. "Look Mom, I won't sign the docs. Ever since you joined that cult all those years ago you've wasted your life in the service of Cereus. I don't want that for myself."

Lili looked disappointed, shaking her head at the floor. "Noe, think about it, you were in the military and ever since you left, what have they done for you? You risked your physical and digital life for what? For freedom that you already had before?"

Noe turned to face her, stung by the truth of her words.

Lili continued. "Cereus offered a solution to the widespread economic inequality, waste, and environmental destruction that was the norm in the old world. Trust me, I know it has its flaws and is an imperfect solution for an imperfect world, but it's better than where we were headed as a species before it was created." She could see the conflict and doubt on her daughter's face. *How to make her understand?* "Noe, I want you to take this." She produced a faded business card from a small pocket stitched into her dress and handed it to her.

Noe received then read the card with suspicious eyes. It was jet black in color, with gold embossed lettering. She ran her finger over the name "Rodan Mitchell". *Who is this?* Printed a space above the name in bree serif font was "**Cereus**" and a phone number. The card contained a gold crescent moon with a single arrow piercing through its center on the upper left-hand side. The figure was rotated at a forty-five-degree angle appearing star-like, floating on the black surface of the small business card. Noe shuddered upon recognizing Cereus' logo. She had grown up seeing the symbol on her mother's mail, and had associated it with bad news for as long as she could remember. "What's this for?"

"He's an associate of mine that you need to contact as soon as possible."

"And why should I contact him?" Noe asked testily.

Lili sighed. "Because I've just been informed that some of our enemies might be coming for me. And he may be the best way to protect you should anything happen."

CHAPTER 12:
DATE BY THE RIVER

Daniel stood motionless by the river, staring into the stillness of the water's surface. There was a lightness to his being, that made him appear to sway in the gentle summer afternoon breeze. He looked thoughtful, almost princely. The wind ruffled his brown hair, providing charm to his otherwise noble stance.

I wonder what he's really about? Jinhua thought. She observed him from behind a public restroom building near the river's edge. *He's only a boy. I can do this.* The desire to seek counsel with Harpreet was strong, but she repelled the instinct to pull out her device and contact her. No doubt, she had left her numerous messages already with hopes to experience her 'date' first hand. If her device was full of unread correspondence, Jinhua didn't know it. *I want to do this on my own anyway.* She felt tension-fueled excitement rush through her body. It made everything around her appear in higher contrast with crisper sound. The hyper awareness nearly caused overload to her senses. It took her several seconds to calm herself through conscious muscle relaxation. Another skill she attributed to her father. Feeling more relaxed and ready, she straightened her posture then emerged from her concealed position behind the small brick bathroom. *Now or never.*

Upon hearing the crunching of sandals on dry grass and tiny pebbles being scattered, he turned to face her. A wide grin formed on his face. "Hello, I was beginning to think that you weren't going to come."

Jinhua returned the smile while she brushed a strand of hair behind her ear, "I had to take care of some errands for my dad during lunch," she lied. She had really been stuffing her face at Star of India with Harpreet, and receiving pre-date advice of course. "How long have you been waiting?"

Daniel's head swiveled toward the river, where tiny ripples caused by small aquatic creatures disturbed the previously placid water. "Not long, maybe ten or fifteen minutes."

"Oh I see."

A long pause formed between them. Daniel turned toward Jinhua, looking at her, almost through her, as if he were studying her in order to produce a detailed report later on. She felt the urge to cover herself up, but resisted. Instead, she stared back mimicking his unflinching eye contact. *This is getting weird. Maybe I should go.*

"You're really good at this conversation thing," Daniel said, allowing himself to blink for the first time in what seemed like minutes.

She put her hands behind her back, twisting from side to side, head bowed, "Well, I'm not sure what to say. I'm just…glad you showed up y'know. I know you just got to town." He nodded his head up and down in response. The motion looked odd.

Daniel took several steps forward, then stopped about three feet away from where she stood. His rare earth metal-colored eyes began to glow as he fixed his gaze once again. "I'm sorry. I didn't mean to embarrass you. I was just trying to make a joke. You know, be sarcastic."

'Make a joke', …interesting choice of words. "No, it's feihao," Jinhua replied.

Daniel's face twisted with confusion. "Fei…hao? What does that mean?"

Jinhua's hand raised to her mouth to conceal an involuntary giggle. "It just means it's 'all good' or 'alright'. It's Chinese. I guess it used to be two words and then people started saying it as one or something like that. I'm not really sure. I learned about it from a video I saw online."

"Ah, I see. I don't know any Chinese. Are you from there?"

"No, I grew up here. I've lived in Yuba City my entire life. What about you? You moved from Sac, right?" Daniel's eyes appeared to blink at irregular intervals. His ratio of eye contact was completely off.

One moment it was a stare, the next his gaze diverted far far away. It made Jinhua more nervous.

"Yeah, that's right. The city isn't what it used to be, at least that's what my parents told me."

"Yeah my dad told me the same. He says with all the so-called 'freedom groups' fighting each other that a lot of the city isn't safe anymore. We used to go down there more when I was younger, but now it's pretty rare."

On the opposite side of the river, two black crows swooped down near the shore. They addled around the rocky grey earth, pecked a few times, then flew off disappointed. Jinhua and Daniel viewed the scene in silence, seeking distraction from the stale conversation.

This is getting awkward again! Maybe I should have invited Harpreet, she's the talkative one. Daniel appeared unruffled, an indistinguishable expression on his face. The sights of the river captivated his attention from time to time, when he wasn't staring at her.

"So, I heard you're in a cult," he said.

Jinhua recoiled from shock. "Wh-who said that!?"

"My parents. They told me that your dad works for the cult and that this whole town had been taken over by it. Said it was like a hostile takeover back in the day, or something. That this whole thing wouldn't last. They used the words 'pipe dream.' Is it true?"

She planted her feet firmly on the ground to suppress the urge to hit him. "No way! Cereus isn't a cult! How could you say that?"

He maintained firm eye contact. It made his response seem colder. "I just wanted to know if it was true. That's all. And I figured since your dad works for them, you could set it straight for me."

"How do you know where my dad works?"

"Saw it on your social media posts," he replied, blinking for the first time in minutes.

Oh right. Pictures of her standing with her father, his associates, and other big shots in the area in front of their large house came to her mind. *I completely forgot, how careless of me.*

"I see," her tone lowered, but her body remained rigid from his insult. "But still, it's not a cult. My dad and his friends help people. They just want to allow *all* people to have the dignity and respect that they deserve, no matter how much money or perceived value they have to society. The old ways turned everything and everyone into a commodity, into competition. Cereus at least tries to give people a chance to have the life they want without worrying about money." She realized her voice had risen to an unrecognizable higher pitch. *All looks, no brain, this guy. Just my luck.*

He fidgeted in front of her, blinking rapidly. Confusion seemed out of place on his face. It made him appear more human. "What you say is valid, however, the conditions in the cities have shown the inability of Cereus' model to work with a large portion of the population. And it's not just down in Sacramento. San Francisco, Austin, Atlanta, New York City, have all had similar issues. My parents say that they rely too much on technology. That the common person can't get in on the deal. That's why the 'freedom group' vigilantes have been able to recruit so well in the past few years."

"You're talking about that 'Back to Humanity Movement'?"

"Yep."

"Oh." Jinhua's eyes fell to the ground. She saw a trail of ants marching toward her open sandals, then shifted her foot away in a fighting motion. "Well I don't know much about that," she muttered, "Just that a bunch of people don't want machines ruling their lives." Her eyes rose to lock with his. "But anyway, that's not true that Cereus relies on tech too much. I see people getting together to walk, chat, trade, and live every day! People here and in comvils around the world care less about making money than just trying to be good and happy. Sure they use a lot of tech. Who doesn't these days? But they care more about building relationships, than building wealth. I've seen it. I've lived it." Daniel's hand raised to his chin in a thinking motion. One of his eyebrows arched with inquisitiveness.

I've got him now, Jinhua thought. She continued her rebuttal. "And besides that, the whole barter market and committee models are grounded in people being able to use whatever talents that they have to be better connected with each other, the environment, and themselves! How is that relying too much on tech!?"

Daniel was silent. His face was passive but the shoulders were slouched in a sign of defeat. Satisfied her defense had been effective, Jinhua turned to go. After two steps, she heard his footsteps moving in her direction. *He wants another verbal beating I see. I'll give it to him.*

"Wait…Jinhua…I…I'm sorry. Don't leave…please," he pleaded.

His lips had turned slightly upside down. The marble-like eyes reflected the most sincere remorse. He was sulking. Although her annoyance at his clumsy offensive speech gave her cause for a swift exit, she felt the magnetic force of empathy preventing her early departure. Hands on hips, Jinhua examined his face and body language for signs of insincerity. There were none. "What you said was pretty stupid, especially with someone you barely know. You understand that right?"

He nodded, hanging head low with guilt. "I get it. Those are just opinions that my parents have. I don't believe all that stuff. That's why I was asking about it." An out-of-place pause filled the air between them. Only the cawing of crows and insects buzzing filled the void. When he spoke again, some levity returned to his voice. "I have an uncle, who encourages me to try and understand the perspectives of others. He's older, so he grew up in the 2000s and 2010s. During that time, he said there were a lot of nationalist movements all over the world and the internet at the time became a very polarized place."

Jinhua shifted her weight to her right foot. Her feet were becoming sore standing on rocks of varying size and shape. The afternoon heat caused the back of her neck to tingle, an early indicator of a sunburn. Both factors contributed to her peevishness. *There'd better be a point to this history lesson.* She feigned interest. "Mhm, and?" The impatience in her voice was intentional.

Daniel, sensing her irritability, hurried to finish. "Ok, I'll get to the point. Long story short, he told me that the polarization led to conflict, economic then eventually military, in the form of the 5G Wars and the First Cyber Space War. Said that all of it could have been prevented if more people were actually willing to *really* listen to the viewpoints of others, instead of living in the bubbles of information that their preferred news sources provided. Don't you agree with that?"

Jinhua softened her stance. He had made a valid point. "Yes, I do." She swallowed hard. It helped remove some of the bitterness caused by his inconsiderate statement. "You know, you really could work on your approach a little more. Unless being rude is your go-to method for hearing the opinions of others," she quipped. The tiniest of smiles flashed on her face. Although she remained aware of her pre-date jitters, she felt herself begin to relax in his presence. *Harpreet said that's a good sign.*

Daniel returned a hint of a smile, then took two small steps forward to close the distance between them. "Maybe I need your help to do it better."

"You really do!" Jinhua smirked. "Because you're *feicha* at it right now!"

"*Feicha?* What does it mean?" He said through small fits of laughter.

"It means, you really bad at it!" She said in a country twang. They both laughed openly. Jinhua unconsciously lifted her hand then jabbed his shoulder in a playful motion. The light physical contact caused his eyes to dilate. Their moment of joy ceased, they stood in a soundless stare. Each one's eyes searching the other for something. Daniel looked confused, but ready for action. Jinhua felt warm, her senses tingling, as she began to lean in closer to his face. She was close enough to sense the heat of his body, and feel the toes of his shoes scraping the borders of her sandals. Jinhua's heart fluttered with sharp beats, unaware of her overall diminished perception of time's flow, as she closed her eyes and inclined her neck upward to meet his enticing lips. *Should I…?*

The vibration of the device in her pocket broke the spell. Daniel backed away abruptly, nearly falling backward to the rocky shore. Jinhua's hand reached instinctively in her pocket. Red-faced and still worked up, she stared at the sky to reawaken her logical brain, before she looked at the device. *It's probably Harpreet being nosy and checking up on me anyway.* A minute later, feeling more like her usual self, she viewed the message. What she saw on the screen caused icy fear to crawl up her spine. A tsunami of emotion and despair crashed down on her, drowning, choking. It was hard to breathe.

Daniel saw her turn away from him, heard the low sobs coming from her. Saw the long straight jet-black hair droop over the sides of her face forming a cocoon of darkness. "Jinhua…what's wrong? Did something happen?"

On Jinhua's screen, below Harpreet's multiple messages were two lines of text from an unknown source. The capital letters conveyed the urgency of the statement: SOMETHING HAS HAPPENED. YOUR DAD IS MISSING. PLEASE CONTACT ME ON THE EMERGENCY LINE ASAP.

CHAPTER 13:
URBAN COMBAT

A stray dog padded its way down a street in Midtown. He was a golden-brown German shepherd with muscular haunches accompanied by a face that invoked compassion and intimidation in all who saw him. His canine intuition was attuned to street rhythms, allowing him to determine friend or foe with ease. It helped him decide which face to show in public. The only way he knew how to survive.

The morning had been eventful for the mutt. He had made good use of his sad face to earn a good helping of synthetic meat from a family of three posted in a battered tent on the corner of Q and 21st Street, just steps in front of the old Sacramento Bee building. He salivated at the thought of having his fill right there in the presence of the needy family, but thought better of it. The meal would taste better in the privacy of his home.

Initially, he thought to take the most direct route down 21st Street. However, his acute senses warned him of potential danger, so he opted to loop around the block, take a sharp right on 23rd, then another on S to arrive without incident.

Once on S Street, he passed an old Victorian-style house. It stood like an ancient relic from a bygone era. It was in stark contrast against the surrounding mix of slums, incomplete 3D-printed homes, and modern offices. All of this detail was lost on the dog as he trotted then stopped in front of the house. He titled his head to the side, ears raised. The property owners always offered him good chow when he used the really sad face on them. Thoughts of a second helping of grub tempted him, but with his breakfast quickly turning to mush between his jaws, he continued his march toward the only home he knew.

The alley had everything. A sturdy old box to provide shelter from the rain. Old concrete slabs arranged like a small obstacle course provided ready-made exercise equipment. And an old dog bed, ripped at the sides for impromptu napping. Free water was available from the runoff of a nearby air conditioning unit. It was his little corner and it was perfect.

Just around the corner from the entrance of the alley, the dog halted his gleeful trot. The saliva soaked meat fell from his mouth to the cracked street. Without a second glance at the food, the dog raised his snout at an angle for confirmation, contracting the nostrils of his damp nose repeatedly at the air. Something was off. An unfamiliar mixture of dog sweat, wet fur, and a hint of blood floated around him. A low growl escaped from his mouth. On alert, he snatched the meat off of the ground, then retreated to a small patch of open earth in the small front yard of the Victorian. Paws, abled and calloused, dug a strategic hiding spot for his meal. He would return for it soon enough.

He went back to the alley. Upon inspection, everything was in its usual place, with the exception of the fly infested carcass of a smaller black Border collie. The mouth was forever open, its tongue hanging out of it in a pool of its own blood. A mangled brown collar with a nametag had been ripped from its appointed position around the neck. Remnants of the once identifying mark were glued to blood soaked fur.

The German shepherd approached the animal remains. Sniffing, sniffing. Upon closer investigation, an unmistakable scent informed him of the dog's identity. He had belonged to a group of people a short ways down the block. He had known him well. Memories of shared meals and physical pleasures of female street dogs flashed into his mind in quick succession. It was his friend and he was dead.

From the shadow of his box, two dogs emerged into the grey afternoon sunlight. The taller of the two only by its pointy black ears was a doberman. The second was a chunky rottweiler with slobber running down its mouth. Upon noticing the German shepherd standing there fangs bared, profile lowered, and emitting angry growls; they swiftly entered an attack formation around him.

The German shepherd lunged first. With animal velocity he closed the distance between him and the flabby rottweiler. It let out a loud bark, tried to swipe with the right paw, but the nails had been trimmed and the attack was ineffective. Soon after, the former police dog's fangs entered the rottweiler's tender jugular. Its body flailed from the force of the vice grip-like jaw clamped on its neck, shaking him belligerently from side to side.

While the rottweiler yelped and kicked at the air, blood oozing from its neck wound, the doberman attacked from behind. Its first bite found its target on the German shepherd's back leg, making the dog wail. In a reflex movement, his leg kicked backward, scratching the doberman in the right eye. It staggered to the side, giving the golden-colored dog valuable time to drop the now lifeless corpse of the rottweiler, then whirl around and face his enemy. The barking was loud and vigorous as it faced the wounded doberman with its body slanted in a pre-attack position. The dogs barked and postured themselves, each one paying no heed to their respective wounds, hoping to win the contest through intimidation alone. The doberman had trespassed on his property and killed his friend. In the eyes of the German shepherd, these atrocities were unforgivable. There was no mercy or redemption for him. At least none he would find in that alley.

The sound of a single gunshot from close range caused both of their ears to perk. In the next instant, the German shepherd witnessed the formidable doberman fall on its side. A pool of warm blood flowed from the abdomen. A sign of another dead dog.

The surviving dog's attention turned to the source of the deadly blow. A single man, tall, wearing a ball cap held the gun. A sadistic smile formed on his old lips under the shadow of the visor. He held the gun with an experienced grip. His aim adjusted from the lifeless doberman, to the German shepherd.

Facing the barrel of the weapon, the capability of his hind leg reduced due to the dog bite, the dog knew that there was no escape. He let out a low growl and straightened himself in a dignified posture, eyes fixed on the man. It held his gaze for several seconds, unfazed by the possibility of death. Instinct told him to wait for the blast.

Slowly the man lowered the gun, tucking it away in silence.

"You're a bold one," he said with amusement. He dropped to one knee, and beckoned the dog to come to him.

Instinct forged by years on the streets told the animal to obey or die. There were rarely few other options in his world. It limped over with great effort, letting out low whines and whimpers.

The man inspected its injuries. *He's banged up, but salvageable.*

"Let's go." The man bent over, lifted the dog, then carried him into the adjacent building. He left the bodies of the other two to rot in the sun.

CHAPTER 14:
THE ENCAMPMENT

The building was old. It appeared abandoned to undiscerning passersby. A patchwork of mismatched colors of metal, wood, and plastic covered what once had been the display windows of a hardware store, displaying crude graffiti art of local vandals. An overgrowth of healthy vines clawed their way from the sidewalk through the face of the building. Like jagged veins, they split the wood where a sign had boasted the name of the store decades prior, further diminishing its curb appeal. A single door camouflaged itself among the odd mixture of natural and manmade blemishes. It blended in among the sun-bleached grey bricks, and was only visible to those who had a need to pass through it.

Like me. The man checked his surroundings multiple times in a paranoid fashion before entering the building with the injured dog. He waved his hand over the center of the door. The action initiated an unlocking mechanism, emitting a series of clicks from the door's interior. The man pushed the door open with his leg, then entered into darkness. Once inside, the door closed with a slam, and relocked itself. It took his eyes a moment to adjust to the dark entryway, but he could see dim light further back in the facility. The sound of disparate conversations and vibrations from the bass of a hip-hop song made his feet tingle in his boots. The man moved deeper into the structure, the light gradually increasing along with the volume of the music, with every step he took. *The crew must be all here…good.*

As he moved through the space, he realized his right leg had become fatigued from carrying the surprisingly heavy dog. A prickling sensation gave way to small shooting pains, causing him to nearly drop the animal. *Dammit! Augment right leg 50%.* Within seconds, he felt a numbing sensation, followed by coolness, then strength deep within the leg. He could almost see the microscopic repairs occurring in his thigh at the cellular level. The sinews of his muscles sewing themselves back together felt like getting a good pump during a heavy lift. It was an intoxicating feeling. It made him feel powerful. *Godlike.* A grin curled itself onto his cracked lips.

"I see you found yo'self a pet! Ah ain't he cute!" A dark-skinned man with a bulging belly chided. He wore dark green cargo pants along with an untucked wrinkled tan shirt and held a partially disassembled M-4 rifle in his hand. His name was Lloyd Owens, and the man had known him for years. A lifetime ago, they had served together in the Army when he was a butter bar, quick to melt in the sun or under the heat of a hot desk lamp. Lloyd was a young enlisted troop then. They rose through the ranks of their respective tiers together, until both retired from service. Despite their differences in their former pay grades, they had always considered themselves to be kin and remained close, linked by the unbreakable bond of military brotherhood. Considering Lloyd's comment about the dog, the man recalled a memory of Lloyd as a young soldier. Even back then he was fat by military standards. Lloyd never seemed to care. Neither did big green. The dark complexion of his skin, the folds of his butt chin, the gentle sloping contours of his face, and his loud mouth constantly spewing random bullshit, reminded all of the members of his platoon of a walking talking ass. And from that day forward, like stink on shit, his nickname never left him.

"Fuck you Cheeks," the man replied, his tone facetious. "Where's that damn doc? I wanna get him patched up."

"You a dog lover now, huh sir?" Cheeks laughed, "Didn't think you still had a heart under all that machinery inside ya."

The man maintained a serious expression, then burst out laughing. "You're one to talk, my nigga! You the amateur botanist over here, cultivatin' all them dead weeds and vines outside!"

"Hey gotta respect Mother Nature right? Ain't that part of the philosophy?" Cheeks snickered. "Anyway, I think I saw the Doc by the loading bay. He looked bored when I last saw him, so he'll probably be happy to have some business. Even if it has four legs instead of three." He cupped his manhood over his pants, while thrusting his hips forward. Two younger soldiers noticed the movement then howled with laughter, imitating the crude gesture.

The man shook his head smiling, then continued his way toward the back of the building. He made a concerted effort to greet all of the men that entered into his field of vision. The place had the feel and look of a contingency operation, with all of the necessary tech, gear, and weapons to match. It wasn't much, but it was a fitting home for him and his men.

In an instant, Mariah Carey's "Always Be My Baby" began to blast from suspended speakers in the back of the building. Cheeks' voice came over a loudspeaker, "Dis one goes out to the Colonel and his new friend!"

A voice shouted, "Aw c'mon, turn that old man music off!" The voice came from a young man with a cocoa complexion. From his seat on a crate of old field rations, dressed in a dark brown t-shirt, green tactical pants, and newly issued matching-colored boots, he eyed Cheeks from across the bustle of the indoor encampment. Under his nose, he had groomed a carefully aligned mustache. It made him look a little older than more senior members thought he was, but did little to disguise his inexperienced eyes from Cheeks, his mentor, and model for all things related to military matters. Born Chimere Shaw, Cheeks found this name too basic for the youth. So he nicknamed him 'Spazer', after the laser by the same name in the old Super Metroid game. The beam was thin and weak, splitting into three lines whenever it was fired. Cheeks reasoned that the three lines represented the young man's distinct identities as a soldier, gentleman, and smart guy (see the word *scholar* in army speak). Chimere (having never seen or played the outdated game) never understood the reference, but accepted it all the same. It was a small token of respect, from someone he looked up to, and a sign of his complete integration into the unit.

"Aw what do you know Spazer!" Cheeks shouted over the loudspeaker, "This song is decades older and wiser than you!"

Spazer shook his head, making a dismissive hand gesture.

The Colonel made a sound of mocking disapproval with his tongue at the young man, smiling, "This song *is* a classic."

Spazer replied, "My bad sir. It's just that this is music my grandma used to listen to. Ain't heard it in a minute. Brings back memories."

"Good ones I hope."

"Yeah mostly," his somber face betrayed his words as he turned his attention back to cleaning his rifle.

The Colonel wanted to say more, but his arms were burning from carrying the dog. *Can't use another augmentation right now, don't wanna burn out for the day.* With longer strides, he weaved his way through stacks of tan crates filled with an assortment of munitions, tactical field supplies, and weapons. Along the way, he passed the bars of a field brig. He had welded the bars of the cage to the floor and ceiling himself. It was small, with enough space for only two prisoners comfortably. There was no water. Only a dual function bucket for washing and waste. He had ordered an old military cot to be placed next to the bucket, but it was on backorder. Any future prisoner would find themselves sleeping on the cold concrete. Not a comfortable situation.

Across from the field prison, a set of thin green olive colored curtains led to a small field clinic. The Colonel shouldered his way in. His arms were tingling from holding the mutt, but he gave no indication of pain on his face.

The doctor hadn't noticed him enter the diminutive office. A state of the art medical examination bed took up nearly the entire space of the clinic, leaving only room for a spinning stool and a folding table with medical supplies on top of and under it. The doctor's slim figure appeared to be swallowed by his white medical coat. His arms extended to his knees. The hair, black and long, tied up into a ponytail. Everything about him looked stretched out, including his bespectacled face. His slender fingers, meticulously groomed and trimmed, manipulated holographic blocks in the air. Stacking the colored shapes consumed his concentration, as he mouthed the words to Mariah Carey's classic number one hit. The sound of the Colonel's boots broke his focus, causing the imaginary blocks to tumble before him.

"Catch you at a bad time Doc Santiago?" The Colonel asked.

"No, no it's fine," Doc Santiago said. The voice sounded an octave too low for his youngish looking face. His Castellano accent flowed like a melody from moist lips. Santiago looked at the panting dog in the Colonel's arms. "And who do we have here?"

"Just a dog that I found on my way back from a meet. Looks like he had a helluva fight with two others in the alley."

"I see, I see," Santiago extended slender fingers, observing the condition of the animal. "Doesn't look too bad." He frowned at the Colonel. "I've never worked on a dog before, but I should be able to download the necessary tutorials to be able to help it."

"I'll leave you to it then," he said, gently lowering the dog on the examination bed. He rubbed his arms to dissipate encroaching numbness. "Let me know when he's better."

"Of course sir," Santiago gave a deep bow, then set to work.

The Colonel stared into its eyes as he patted the beast's head. The German shepherd licked his hand while Santiago poked and prodded its injured leg. The dog showed no signs of discomfort or pain. *Don't worry we'll get you fixed up in no time*, the Colonel thought.

CHAPTER 15:
THE TERMINATOR'S
PRISONER

The feeling of hardness was the first sensation to enter Li Ma's field of awareness. Solid cement was beneath him, cold and unmoving. The effect of the frigid floor easily penetrated his thin dress shirt. He kept his eyes shut, letting training kick in. It helped attenuate rising fear he felt expanding within his chest, calmed his breathing, slowed the throbbing of his pulse at his temple.

I need a plan.

Gradually, memories of the events preceding the ambush crept into view like clips from a fractured film reel. He began to concentrate on them with as much care as he could muster in his groggy state. He had been sitting at a corner table in a darkened restaurant. The smell of spicy curry floated in the air. His source, seated across from him. The chiming of a device. His vision being swallowed by a tunnel of blackness. He replayed the events prior to that moment several times, wondering how he could have avoided capture. The urge to pity himself was strong. It almost paralyzed his thoughts.

No. Stay sharp to escape first. Got to form a plan.

Pushing the memories aside, he performed a physical scan of his body. Nothing seemed to be broken. *Hard to tell on the floor, though.* He started to turn himself in an effort to sit up, but stopped after he felt numbness accompanied by a dull ache on the entire left side of his body. A pain he quickly attributed to the unforgiving and in some places uneven cement floor. His hands were bound tightly in field zip ties behind his back. The range of motion of his shoulders constricted, he dared not attempt more movement. *Can't risk further injury now.* His ankles were bound, though he could not tell with what. The restraint was loose enough to allow the flow of some blood circulation to the feet. *Someone did not want me to lose my mobility…at least not yet. No major injuries. Good.* Physical scan completed, breathing calmed, he kept his eyes closed. It helped him concentrate his hearing. There was music echoing loudly throughout the space. *Must be pretty open.* Laughter, hints of conversations, a dog barking, then whining. All of the sounds seemed to blend together in a cacophonous manner, making it difficult to discern one from the other. A wave of dizziness crashed over him washing away his concentration. Li relaxed his neck, he realized he had been tensing it as he listened. He let his head rest on the cold floor. *Got to conserve my strength.* Whatever sedative they had given him still had a hold on his mental and physical faculties. Even tensing the tiny muscles in his neck made him feel lethargic and weak.

He heard the sound of boots clomping outside of the area. They approached and stopped for several seconds. Something told him to stay still. He felt eyes observing him. Captors waiting to see his next move. *Stay calm. Stay quiet. Think.*

A revolutionary idea became visible in the rolling fog of his brain. *The TP-comm!* His suit jacket containing his 3D sidearm and his device had been removed, but if it was still in range, he might be able to activate a telepathic link and establish contact.

Through a monumental effort, he quieted the background noise of his environment and his own anxiety to clear his mind, only thinking of the device. *Activate device.* He waited for the soft melodic tone that was the signal for a successful link. Nothing.

*Activate device…*still nothing. He felt his anxiety rising after multiple failed attempts.

"There's no point trying that anymore," a dry masculine voice destroyed his single-minded concentration. Li remained motionless, eyes closed, waiting for his captor to make the next move.

"I know you're awake," a slight chuckle echoed in the small space, "people don't realize the way that their face twists and strains when they try to use those fuckin' telepathic devices." He laughed again, louder this time. "It's funny to watch someone use them, especially when there's no device to link to…" He paused for effect to let his captive absorb the words. There was no visible sign of despondency. *He's well trained. But I already knew that. This should at least be interesting.*

The sound of a click, then turning of old metallic locks preceded the familiar squeal of a cell door opening. The sound of boots scuffing concrete followed. The definitive slam of the cell door felt louder to Li's ears than he expected it to. He hadn't anticipated it. That scared him more than his vulnerable position on the floor of the cell.

"I never liked those things, give too much away in the face. You should know that for someone in your line of work Mr. Ma," the condescending tone was close to his face.

Li's eyes remained closed, even though he recognized the man's voice. The drug's effects were beginning to wear thin. He considered making a move. The reminder of his restraints combined with his lack of knowledge about the layout of the place and troop strength of his kidnapper, made him forfeit the notion.

The man had always loved a good interrogation. The subject was so vulnerable, and he could do whatever he wanted to them. *Time to turn on a little heat.* "Look Ma, or Li, yeah…I can call you that now, right Li? Understand that this isn't personal, but we can make it that way and get your daughter involved very quickly if you refuse to cooperate. My guys are always ready to work. I just have to say the word and they'll move. Am I making myself clear?"

Li managed to conceal a surge of fear. His chest tightened at the thought of any harm happening to Jinhua. His eyes slid open. An initial act of capitulation. "What do you want Terminator?" He barely recognized his drug induced voice. Even speaking was a struggle.

"I just want to talk to you as an equal. Is that alright?" He said smiling. "Oh and I would appreciate it if you addressed me as Colonel Kyler Drummel. As much as I enjoy the codename you gave me, as of today you can consider him terminated off of your source books." The smile was undermined by the edge in his voice.

Li nodded in agreement. He studied Kyler's face. It looked older under the sparse lighting of the cell. Aged grooves from years of sun exposure formed jagged lines of darkness on his face. A permanent scar above his left eyebrow was a light patch of skin in an otherwise even dark sand-colored complexion. His thin eyes and full, yet, dry lips had always seemed mismatched in Li's mind. Both were indicators of his African and Korean heritage, but the man identified with neither culture. He was American through and through, having spent his formative years in Waco, Texas before earning his commission as an infantry officer through Baylor University's Army Reserve Officer Training Corps in 2032. By request, he was assigned to the U.S. Army's historic First Cavalry Division at the nearby base in Killeen, Texas. Throughout his career, he served in Mozambique, Portugal, and the Republic of the Congo. During his final tour in Africa, he was mortally wounded by an improvised explosive device during an enemy ambush while traveling between forward operating bases. His injuries were so great, he died on the operating table for two minutes. Field surgeons pieced him back together, replacing many of his organic organs with artificial ones, and swapping his crushed bones with metallic appendages. The result was a Frankenstein of a person. One who existed between the veil of man and machine. Li could not fathom what it would be like to live with such a condition. But with Kyler standing before him in the gloomy light, his features partially obscured in penumbra, Li saw the monster lurking within. A feral red-eyed creature stirred from its cave, hungry following a lengthy slumber.

Kyler walked over to Li and sat him up against the wall with surprising strength. *The augmentations must be doing their job well*, Li thought. Sitting upright, he felt less dizzy, but his guard was still up.

"Comfortable?" Kyler asked. "I'll go get you some water. You must be dying of thirst." He exited the cell, locking the entrance behind him.

Li took the opportunity to take in his surroundings. The entire cell was no more than fifteen by fifteen feet in area and was enclosed by a set of thick black bars and the corner walls of the building. Rows of lights of varying luminescent capacity hung from wires and appeared to extend the length of the building. They provided very little illumination over the prison, although Li couldn't tell if it was by design or just from laziness. He could hear two Light-alls humming on the other side of stacks of military equipment crates. The gear blocked his view of the operations, casting long complete shadows over his cell. From his disadvantaged position on the floor, a set of green olive colored curtains floated inches above the floor. A pair of slender legs moved back and forth behind them. A dog barked and whimpered beyond the obstruction. *Must be his merc base. I need to get out of here.*

Kyler returned holding a cylindrical steel flask. He unlocked the cell, entered, approached Li, then knelt down to offer his prisoner a drink. *This will make it easier for us to talk.*

Li eyed the flask with suspicion, then refused it.

He thinks it's poison. Kyler laughed at the thought. "C'mon Li, this isn't a Chinese TV drama. I don't want to poison you. I just want to talk. Look." Kyler took three audible gulps from the shining cylinder, then followed it up with a loud smacking sound. "Ahh! See! Fresh water from the good ol' American River. It's safe." He extended it again.

Still not fully convinced it was safe, he wanted to refuse again. However, the dryness in his throat informed him he was more dehydrated than he thought, so he acquiesced. A small nod of his head signaled Kyler to put the flask to his lips. He took a few small sips at first, then wrapped his lips around the rim of the container for more. The water tasted metallic, but clean. He let out a few coughs after drinking too fast. Kyler observed him with grave eyes. Li found it difficult to read his face. *He doesn't want me dead. At least for now…* A feeling of rejuvenation washed over him. He was ready to find out what this was all about. "What do you want to talk about?"

Kyler set the water flask on the floor beside his foot. "Look Li, at the end of the day, we're both soldiers who've put our asses on the line for decades to help protect the assets and lives of our respective organizations. So I won't bullshit you. You're here because this morning at zero nine thirty local, your organization decided to pull the plug on our little agreement." His face was stern as he shot out bursts of words in a staccato fashion. "An agreement that you helped broker."

Li fixed his drowsy eyes on Kyler's, waiting for more.

"In exchange for my unit's services, Cereus agreed to provide us with the equipment and resources to be able to sustain the livelihoods of *all* unit members. Now as of this morning, our aid has been cut off, and all of a sudden, our effectiveness as a fighting force has been undermined."

Li continued to listen in silence. *What does he want?* "What's your point? You and your people are not the only ones affected by Cereus' order." He managed to keep his voice calm and focused on the conversation, despite his primary concern being Jinhua's safety. *Have they already gotten to her?*

Kyler shook his head, as he let out a bitter laugh. "You're absolutely right! I've just spoken to the heads of several other street groups: The Panthers, The Zebras, and even the Kings have all lost support promised by Cereus. None are very happy about it." He folded his arms across his chest, then stood to lean his back against the wall. It made his semi-muscular chest visible through his coyote brown t-shirt. "You, Cereus, and the whole utopia fantasy that you've been playing out since the twenties is about to come to an end. And me and my people, who've done a lot of the wet work to help build the thing up are left with nothing."

Li scowled. "C'mon Kyler, you know how this works. All soldiers throughout history are merely instruments of institutional power, only to be discarded when that power has been achieved or goes away altogether." He paused, letting the words sink in. It gave him time to think about what he would say next, and a possible way out. "You and I are no different in that regard."

Kyler nodded slowly. A tightness was building in the lumbar region of his back. The result of years of carrying heavy field gear around manifested in a curved spine that made him look old. *Can't waste an augmentation right now…might need it later on today.* He dragged a small metallic chair from the corner. It screech-rumbled across uneven concrete before the sound stopped. The old soldier sat with a softness that betrayed his gruff disposition. The same 'no bullshit' expression remained on his face despite the pain. He did not want to appear weak in front of his former handler.

"There's some truth to what you say," he admitted. "But Cereus is in a position to stop the bleeding and you being here is us making that request. Like it or not we have been at war on our own soil for a long time. The rise of your organization just helped bring to light what was already there and brewing for decades." The cynicism of his words were like acid. "What you encountered this morning near the capitol was just a taste of things to come. Mark my words, there will be more bloodshed."

Li swallowed. *The protest.* "You incited the protest?"

"Incited?" Kyler scoffed, "We didn't have to. I told you, these ills have been building for a long time, and many people, whether they follow the ideals of Cereus or of *'old world thinking'* as you call it, are fed up. They are more than willing to take to the streets in defense against attacks, real or perceived, on their livelihood."

He looks tired, Li thought. *I guess he has few augmentations left in him today.*

Kyler stared blankly at the floor as he said, "The worst thing is that some people are out there just because they have nothing better to do with their lives. Those privileged and entitled ones, who have more than enough food on their plates, whether it be through bartering or wealth accumulation from the old world, are the most despicable in my eyes." His eyes rose to meet Li's. "Their kind has been able to survive and thrive since the dawn of the internet age at the beginning of the century, and now their inability to believe in anything outside of themselves has led us to where we are now. A society in chaos, where half lives off of the backs of the other half. It's bullshit and I'm not gonna have it anymore."

A litany of questions and statements rolled in Li's mind that had he not been a prisoner, he would have used to counter several of his captor's arguments. The one-sided conversation was fitting for a man who thought he had all of the answers. *I can't waste any more time here. Surely Rodan, must be on his way by now...*

Outside of the cell, Li heard hurried steps approach. A young dark-skinned male with a scant mustache scribbled under his nose and sad eyes stood just beyond the cell door. His eyes flashed to Li then quickly back to Kyler. "Sir! We have a problem that we need your help with."

With deliberate movement, Kyler rotated his head in the young man's direction. But his eyes remained focused on Li. "Can it wait? I'm in the middle of a conversation."

"I'm afraid not Colonel."

"Alright." Placing both hands on his knees he made a concerted effort to raise himself out of the tiny chair. Upon standing as upright as his back would allow, he shrugged his shoulders. "Pardon the interruption Li. I guess we'll have to continue our conversation another time."

The youth who delivered the message opened the cell door, then Kyler moved to leave. Li used the brief opportunity to ask a burning question. "My daughter…is she safe?"

Kyler looked over his shoulder. He had already taken two steps out of the cell. "For now, yes. And if your leadership cooperates with us, she will remain so. We don't want to involve innocent civilians in our fight, but we *will* if forced to." The messenger allowed his commander to pass then clicked the lock shut with a single key, taking no time to look in his prisoner's direction.

Li's head drooped with helplessness. He knew that any request Kyler demanded of the Cereus leadership would go unanswered and unfulfilled. Not as a consequence of his unit's radical actions, but simply because, they no longer existed. When the order had been published that morning by Mr. Khuni, the organization had become a headless entity forced to thrash around and determine its own future without vision or foresight to guide it. He knew that Kyler's promise of more bloodshed would come to pass. He just hoped Jinhua wouldn't be caught in the middle of it.

CHAPTER 16:
THE ROOM

There was a room in the house that Jinhua never entered. It was upstairs, at the end of the hallway on the opposite side of the house from where her room was located. Its position next to the master bedroom made it convenient for her father, who probably worked there frequently, though she rarely saw him enter or exit with her own eyes.

One spring day, when she was seven years old, she had constructed a model rocket from a kit she had received for her birthday that year. The project had been easy, and she finished building the simple model in a few hours. Bored and slightly disappointed that the rocket contained no fuel or ignition device of any kind, she pretended that it was the Chang'e-10 heading for another trip to Mars. The rocket blasted off from a launch pad made from the rocket's overturned kit box. Holding the model in her hand, she ran down the thick red carpet of the hallway laughing and flapping her lips to mimic the sound of jet propulsion hurtling the craft through space.

She ran with it to the end of the hallway, looping and circling it in the air in a strange trajectory that defied the laws of physics and projectile motion. The rocket's journey carried it past the planet laundry room, then to the rich in iron, celestial arrangement of metallic pillars of the stair bannister, and zooming by the black hole of the master bedroom, where it narrowly avoided being pulled to a fate of eternal compression and squishing. Chang'e-10 had never ventured this far before, to the ends of the hallway galaxy. But there it was, in front of the forbidden door where its journey came to a close.

The door was made of solid oak with a gold colored pommel. Carved with master craftsmanship in the center was a crescent moon with a thin arrow flying right through it, both situated at a forty-five-degree angle. (Jinhua would measure it years later and confirm the exactitude of the dimension.) Below the knob was a digital keypad with a grid of sixteen buttons. Attached to it was a thin display strip where she assumed some type of code could be input to access the room. *Another lock without a key*, she used to think to herself. The door appeared somehow heavier than the other doors in the house. As if it had some type of reinforcement embedded in the center. She had also taken note of a thin metal strip directly beneath it, preventing light from wandering out of the room beyond. It was a door that inspired Jinhua's curiosity. That begged her to step inside.

But it was forbidden. Her father had told her so when she was very young. And in order to remain as filial as possible, she respected his wishes. As she matured, the draw of the room became stronger. She noticed how her father would slip out of there on late nights, or retreat inside for what felt like days at a time, only coming out to take a meal with her or to tell her goodnight. Anytime the portal opened, Jinhua took the opportunity to absorb anything she could about what was behind the solid door. It had taken most of her young life, but she had managed to create a mental checklist of the contents in the room. Glowing lights—*At least one or several computers and screens.* A set of comfortable chairs—*He has occasional guests in there.* The sound of a television—*He watches television sometimes.* A military style cot—*He sleeps in there sometimes.* All the disparate pieces summed up to a mystery in her mind about the purpose of the room and what her father used it for.

Now, she stood outside that door, doing her best to prevent her emotional state from clouding her actions. *I need to do this flawlessly or else Dad might…*She clenched her eyes shut to wipe out the thought of something bad happening to her father. *I can do this.*

Recalling the brief conversation with Mr. Rodan Mitchell with her echoic memory, she reviewed the instructions she had received one more time: "Step One: Turn the golden knob twice to the left and three times to the right. Step Two: Enter the code: two, three, five, seven, eleven, forty-three, placing a hashtag after every number. Step Three: Once inside access the emergency communication device, listen for the tone. Step Four: Press the numbers five-three-zero-five-five-five-zero-nine-two-six. Wait for another tone. Hope your dad answers…"

She had repeated the instructions like an affirmation as she made the journey back to her house. Daniel had come with her, out of concern for her physical and emotional well-being.

"Remember to put the hashtag in after you—"

"I know what I have to do!" Jinhua snapped.

Daniel shrugged. His face betrayed no reaction at her scolding.

She took a deep breath and began the sequence. Making every input as deliberate as her trembling fingers would allow.

"Dammit! I pressed a three instead of a seven. I have to start over..." Jinhua muttered.

"Calm yourself," said Daniel in a neutral tone, "you got this."

Jinhua looked at him and responded with blinks. She wasn't used to receiving explicit and unwarranted encouragement.

Two attempts remaining, she thought, her nervousness rising.

She rubbed her hands on her shorts to remove anxiety-produced sweat before she began again. *Knob turns... number... hashtag... number... hashtag... number... hashtag.* She focused on every input as if she were defusing a bomb, like in the movies.

*Last one...*She entered the number. What followed was the satisfying sound of mechanical action occurring somewhere in the thickness of the door. It sounded like a series of locks being overridden, providing passage into the forbidden room.

"Nice job." Daniel said in a neutral tone.

"*Nice job?* You don't sound *or* look impressed."

"Should I be? It was just keying in numbers. Surely this lies within the scope of your abilities. You are Jinhua after all," he let out an awkward laugh.

She shoved him playfully, then turned her attention to the door. Unlocked after all this time. *It's time.* She reached for the golden knob, twisted, then pushed it open. She was surprised at how easy it was to move.

A confusing sight greeted her eyes upon entering the room. All of the elements she had caught glimpses of over the years—the glowing computer monitors, television, chairs, and the steel gray-colored military style cot were present. What she had not seen was the giant table on the far-left side of the room containing a large holographic map of the world. It consumed that entire side of the room, with bluish three-dimensional displays jutting out of the surface. On the back wall of the room were several monitors with live video feeds in various locations that she did not recognize. In the center of the room was what must have been her father's work space. Several clear document reader screens were stacked neatly on top of each other flanking a large computer monitor. There were even a few heavily weathered file folders with real papers in them. Jinhua wanted to touch them to see if they were real.

"Wow. I haven't seen that many physical papers in a long time," Daniel marveled.

"Me neither…" Jinhua's eyes were wide with excitement. *So many things in here.* Her curious shadow clone had unleashed itself among the mysteries of the new space. Manipulating buttons, determining where all of the video feeds were monitoring, playing with the interactive world map shifting between topographic, economic, and climatic modes to watch how it changed. She had to clench her fists to prevent her physical body from performing such actions. Daniel noted her restraint, suppressing a laugh as he viewed her from the opposite side of the room.

"You know, you're very self-disciplined."

Jinhua whipped her head toward him. "Wha-what? I wasn't gonna do anything! I was just checking it out! I swear!"

Daniel smirked, "Uh huh, sure you weren't."

"Oh you shut up." She waved her hand in a dismissive manner, then turned her attention back to the map. *I wonder what he uses this for. Research maybe? Tracking stuff?* There was so much she didn't know about her father. Seeing the map reminded her of burning questions she had never dared to ask him for her entire life. *I hope he's alright…*

"Hey Jinhua, take a look at this," Daniel called. He had ventured to the right corner of the room where a single cushioned recliner, chartreuse in color, stood alone under the light of a standing lamp casting a halo of light onto it. She had not seen the space during her peeks into the room, due to its hidden position in the corner. Jinhua pulled herself away from the map and rushed to the other side of the room across the smooth blue tiled floor to join him. Daniel analyzed the device sitting on a small wooden nightstand next to the recliner with intrigue.

"What is it?" Jinhua asked, approaching with caution.

"I think this is the emergency communication device that your dad's friend told you about."

She moved closer to get a better look at the thing. It looked like it was constructed with antiquated material. The black plastic was visibly cracked on the top part and the numbers on the keypad looked very…analog. A few of the numbers that used to be white were either yellowed or barely visible. The base had a wire that ran from it to the wall, tethering it in place. Another wire connected to the base was in the form of a spring and attached to the top part. It looked like that component could be removed.

Jinhua tested the spring-like wire, amused by the way it snapped back after she compressed it between her thumb and forefinger.

"I think I've heard of one of these things before," she said. "What was it called?"

Daniel looked at the device then paused, searching for a response. "I think it's one of those old communication units. A telephone."

"This is a telephone!? I've never seen one before." Her eyes examined the device from all angles with scientific scrutiny. Her eager fingers slid along the base. It was cold to the touch. "It's so huge! I don't see a voice input or a microphone."

Daniel picked up the receiver and placed it at his ear. "I think it's on. Looks like you talk through here and the message comes out at the top part." He pointed at the respective components.

"I see." Jinhua snatched the receiver from his hand. Her heart began to hammer when she recalled Rodan's instructions. She glanced at Daniel. He returned a supportive nod. Swallowing hard, Jinhua pressed in the appropriate digits on the old keypad: five-three-zero-five-five-five-zero-nine-two-six. *'Wait for another tone. Hope your dad answers…'* A ringing tone sounded in her ear. She held her breath to comply with the final step of the instructions.

CHAPTER 17:
DESK OPERATION

A splitting headache made Rodan's right temple throb. The pain seemed to radiate in time with his pulse carrying spells of dizziness and fatigue with each beat. The sensation shook the once indomitable six-foot three college lineman from within. He didn't mind the pain. It forced fits of involuntary rest from the endless ringing of his desk phone, an old smartphone that ceased to vibrate across the document readers and papers strewn on his desk, and his TP-comm that kept toning in his head. He wanted to disconnect from it all. Walk away. But he couldn't. He could barely leave his desk to relieve himself before someone tried to reach him. *What if I miss something important? Then I'll feel real shitty.* The specter of failure loomed over his shoulder in every moment, threatening to crush him with guilt or a heart attack. Sometimes he wished for the heart attack. At least he would be able to lie down and close his eyes.

It was at times like these he contemplated the durability of his service focused personality. He thought of it as a freshly smelted, solid bronze medieval shield, that he had used strong and nimble hands to hold in the air in order to protect himself and others over the years. Its surface was flawless, and resplendent, able to dampen and shield from the heaviest of blows. But after years of buffering attacks large and small, protecting himself and the weak from all that is wicked and unjust in the world; his defensive power had lost its luster. Brittle and dull, it no longer reflected the faces of the world's villains. It no longer reflected anything on its blemished surface. It became an ineffective tool. As it lay flat, discarded in the mud, it concealed all manner of worms and vermin squirming beneath its once brilliant hard surface. With Rodan constantly struggling to pry it from the sticky mud and raise it with aged and swollen hands, only to drop it again seconds later. With every fall it became heavier, harder to raise, less effective, and prone to fracturing down the middle as it neared its maximum load. *If it breaks, I wonder if I'll be able to put it back together again. Or if I'll have to get somebody else to do it for me.*

He managed to push aside the macabre thoughts to allow himself a moment to lean back in his leather backed office chair for a full minute and close his eyes. Mindfully, he focused on deep breathing, replacing the old stale air in his lungs with frigid filtered air from the office. In and out, inhale, exhale. *Count backwards from fifty.*

Fifty…Forty-nine…forty-eight…forty-seven…forty—

The ring from his secure phone line sounded abrasively. Its obtuse sine wave bounced unevenly around in his skull, evaporating his relaxation exercise. It caused his head to vibrate like a bell, adding pressure to a mind on the brink of combustion. This had better be good news.

Rodan could hear noises of tactical preparation on the other end. Buckles jangling, firearms clicking, the creaking of vehicle suspension as it moved at a moderate speed, resounded in the background. When the voice on the other end spoke, it sounded occupied, but confident, with a slight Mexican accent. "Rodan, we're ten minutes out from the site."

"Copy that. Let me know when you arrive," Rodan said, rubbing his temple with his free hand.

"Claro."

It was Raul. From his slightly spaced words, and the pronunciation of his vowels, Rodan knew English was not his first language. But it didn't matter. Raul had been a faithful leader of the small quick reaction unit known as the Lobos for years. In the last five years of their working relationship, Rodan had pieced together his personality through a combination of one-line response voice messages, field reports, and occasional live operations. They had never met in person, but from what he could tell, Raul preferred to showcase his proficiency through action rather than words. Though he couldn't help but be suspicious of his taciturn responses, he always knew he could rely on him to get the job done.

Raul's crew consisted of about fifty members. The unit counted on former ex-convicts, drug dealers, failed entrepreneurs, and hobbyists to fill its ranks. Rodan had conducted many of the background checks himself and knew, despite where many of them had been, one common trait bonded them all together: boredom. It was the same for most other mercenary groups around the country. Few fought for country, glory, or even money anymore. They simply needed something to occupy their hours of perceived infinite existence. It was no wonder Limnic's numbers had grown tremendously over the past few years. People needed and wanted something to do. Being an anti-Cereus Limnic supporter was an easy way to pass the time, get paid, and get a good workout in.

Fifteen minutes later there was still no response from Raul. Rodan shook his head, with the phone receiver at his ear. He began to shift in his chair, venting impatience. Where the hell is he?

Without warning, the phone came alive again. "Rodan, we've traced Mr. Ma's emergency beacon to an administrative facility in Midtown. From the latest thermal scan of the building, we estimate fifteen hostiles inside. How do you want us to proceed?"

Rodan breathed a heavy sigh and massaged his throbbing right temple forcefully. "Do it…use non-lethal force if possible."

"Got it. Use the nano drone for real time surveillance."

"Sure…uh buena suerte…"

"Gracias." The line went dead.

Rodan hung up the phone, then scrambled to dig out a small glass-like panel from under layers of old documents. Where the hell is that thing!? Even the sound of rustling papers exacerbated his headache. With some effort, he managed to locate the nearly invisible object and a small base attachment that allowed him to view it hands-free. He swept aside clutter to make an island of clear desk space, then set up the stand and the clear panel on it. With lightning muscle memory, he fingered in his password and logged into the surveillance unit's video application.

When the feed came to life, the nano drone's wide aperture captured faint light sources dangling from unseen wires in the shadowy space, little else. The sound of boots scraping the floor, heavy breathing, and field gear shifting from sharp tactical movements filtered through the cheap wired speakers on Rodan's desk. He held his breath in anticipation of what the team of mercenaries would uncover, hoping to see Li's face appear at any second. *Where are you buddy?* His muscles tensed at every sound from the feed. A grunt from one of the men on the ground, the faint shadow of a silent hand gesture, a crack of a pipe; the smallest noise made him want to jump in his chair, as if he were watching a horror movie alone at midnight. He truly felt as if he were there. The cadence of the sudden shifts and jerks of the nano drone's eye evoked nostalgic images from his time in the Sacramento Police Department. Tactical night training, drug raids on illegal grow operations, the smell of his discharged weapon. He had to shut his eyes for a second to drive out pictures from his glory days. *Gotta focus on the op.*

The team looked as if they had reached the far end of the building. The ribs of a metallic sheet wall were slightly illuminated and he could make out what looked like a ramshackle prison cell on the left side of the screen. *Had they kept him there? Had he escaped? Was he even still alive?* He wanted to hold on to the ray of hope and dismissed the thought that Li might be dead. *Killed at the hands of his own source. If anyone could kill him, "The Terminator" had the training and means to do the job. I knew it! I warned him they were too damn close! Fucking Li never listened to me! He was too trusting!* Rodan silenced his inner tirade as if his TP-comm were live, broadcasting his mental tantrum to the world.

Limnic. Those bastards, Rodan thought with bitterness. They had distorted Cereus' philosophy of bringing balance back to people and planet into a sadistic vision of capitalism cleansing at any cost, by any means. They were terrorists, and represented a dire threat to both Cereus society and the old world. From his perspective, they had clearly caused The Terminator to compromise his self-proclaimed integrity and moral judgment to satisfy their stated objective. *Had they gotten to Li now, too?*

"Clear!" Raul's accented voice sounded on the video feed. With no danger present, the nano drone automatically activated a ring of powerful LED lights next to its camera, bringing the components of a small contingency-like encampment into view. "There's no one here.

Must've left out this service entrance." The nano-drone shifted its light to a cream-colored rolling service door. "We detect heat from the components of the door, so it was recently used."

Dammit! Where is he? Rodan worked to relax himself before speaking. "I see. Conduct a full search of the place and let me know what you find."

"Claro."

"Oh and tell your guys they can keep any weapons, gear, or toys they find if there's no connection to Li."

Raul's eyes grew wide, a matching smile grew across his face under a bushy mustache. "Entendido, muy amable." He relayed the message to his soldiers. Rodan could hear their elated cheers echo off of the walls. "Anything else?"

"For now, no. I'll let you know if something comes up."

"Sounds good."

The video feed returned to a lifeless black screen. Rodan closed the application with a terse verbal command. He stood up slowly and stretched himself with arms extended over his head, letting out an audible groan in the process. The weight of the events of the day and the disappointment from the search had thrown a blanket of fatigue over him. It made him want to close his eyes and take a nap. Gradually, he felt his body relax using its natural capabilities. *Maybe I should have gotten that parasympathetic nervous system augmentation. I heard that people can relax real easy with that.* These musings always came to him at moments like this. Times when he realized the limitations and weaknesses in the flawed design of human flesh. Its many shortcomings unsuited for the demands of the technologically complex twenty-first century. Yet he had no augmentations. On some primal level he had the need to fight for control, like all humans, even if it was only with his own deficient biology.

He stood there a few moments, and permitted himself a moment to rest and think. *I can't believe it. I'm it.* The message he had received a few hours prior replayed itself in his mind:

"Rodan Mitchell, you are now the acting head of Cereus. Please contact the management committees of all comvils and inform them of the change and formulate your strategy to move the organization forward."

The signature block that followed and authenticated the message was from Khuni himself. It was real, the system had told him so. *Why did he disappear? Where the hell did he go?* He had no answers and any attempt he made to contact the former director down in San Francisco had failed. Wherever he had gone, it was clear that he did not want to be found. Rodan would have to act without his vision and leadership.

The shortest messages always have the most impact. A wave of self-pity trapped his thinking in a mudslide of fears and anxiety about his own ability to lead Cereus. He had always considered himself to be a good manager of people and programs, but not the "man in charge." To him, leadership implied someone with solid personal principles, grounded in practical knowledge, and some kind of otherworldly divine sight that allowed them to counter anticipated and unanticipated events before they even occurred. His gaze wandered over his disaster of an office. There were papers covering the desk, and some now on the floor in his haste to locate the screen. An overflowing trash can that needed a trip to the point incinerator, his calendar a mess of events, half of which he knew he couldn't keep, and the dumpster fire that was his personal life. *How can I lead, if I can't get my own shit together?*

A ring from his standard desk phone ended the pity party. Without moving a step, he reached for the receiver. "Hello?"

The voice on the other end oozed femininity and power with a slightly mannish octave. It captivated him, and made him want to hear it more. "Mr. Mitchell, my name is Noelani Acosta, I got your number from my mom. I need to speak with you, I think we might be in trouble."

Rodan's eyes went wide upon hearing the name "Noelani". This was Lili's daughter, the Lili he had given his card to all those years ago. The famous Lili'uokalani Acosta, one of the Founders of Cereus.

CHAPTER 18: RUSE

Li sat in the back of a private auto car. The dismal backdrop of Sacramento's urban decay gave way to sprawling suburbs, then open farmland as the car traveled north at a comfortable speed.

Sitting next to him was Kyler, his stiff frame, tall and muscular, looking out of place in the car's confined backseat. While it had all of the niceties of a luxury vehicle: wood trim on the door, leather seats, executive lighting for working; he kept cursing under his breath about Cereus' decision to send *this* car. "Can't believe they couldn't send you a bigger fuckin' ride! I thought you had pull at that place," he said.

Li smirked, "They saved this one just for you." He continued to busy himself with the flurry of messages that were coming his way. There were communications from HQ in San Francisco via the TP-comm, his work phone, and remote drone in all forms of encryption. Distributed among the official correspondence were several "*Where you at?*", "*You alright!?*", "*You good!?*" memos from Rodan. Li worked on each systematically, following the order of his self-designed message triage system. He felt like a skilled paramedic trying to stop the bleeding on a dying car crash victim. Yet he maintained his composure through it all.

Kyler arched an eyebrow, then looked at Li out of the side of his eyes. "This plan of yours was very clever. You think they bought it?"

Li put the finishing touches on a status update message to HQ before he looked up. "It surely has given us some breathing room to plan our next move. That's all we could hope for at this point. Although I didn't expect you to use that form of kidnapping." Li rubbed his still aching neck.

Kyler exhaled a sound similar to a laugh, but his face remained hard, "All part of the plan. I really had to sell it. The more genuine the video, the more time we get." He folded his arms across his chest. A slight grin formed on his face. "Y'know you made a pretty lousy prisoner. It wasn't nearly as fun as doing interrogations during the war. There's a certain thrill that comes with seeing someone literally piss themselves with fear." He let out a cold laugh.

Li looked amused, "You're one twisted son-of-a-bitch."

The auto car guided itself towards its destination. The standard evening traffic jam on highway ninety-nine had slowed their movement to a crawl, then to stop-and-go. A live report flashed on a large display screen in the center console of the car. A sky drone captured an elderly person several cars ahead, adamant on driving his vehicle manually in direct defiance of the medical alerts from the vehicle. The news report beamed a live stream from inside the car. Name: Montgomery Jones, age: 91, date of birth: 08/20/1971. He was an old man with wrinkly skin hunched over the steering wheel, straining his neck and eyes to see the road ahead of him. The automated reporter read off a list of medical impairments that made the man a road hazard: glaucoma of the left eye, a sprained right wrist, prescribed a powerful narcotic for pain that induced bouts of drowsiness. The list went on to list these and at least six other medical conditions that ranged from minor annoyances to ailments requiring chronic care by a team of professionals.

"They need to get that gentleman off the road," Kyler said. "He'll kill us all."

Li laughed. "That will probably be you in the next ten years."

"That's a negative! I'll get one of those, what do they call 'em? 'Shepherds' to ferry me around. You won't find me driving on these streets. Not a chance in hell." He continued to watch the news report on the screen.

A sudden loud ringing sounded in the car, drowning out the audio from the screen.

Li's eyes grew wide. *It's the emergency line.* "Mute screen," he commanded. The sound from the droning news report shut off. He unlatched his black briefcase and pulled an old Nokia flip phone from one of the pockets. He held the functioning relic in his hand while it continued to ring, regarding it with trepidation.

Kyler looked at the phone. The muscles in his jaw tense. *Who the hell could be calling?*

The phone produced its characteristic click when Li flipped it open with his thumb. The screen read: 'Emergency Line', but gave no indication of who might be on the other end. He pressed the green button to answer.

"Hello?"

"Dad?…Is that you?" Jinhua's voice was small, but sounded slightly more mature than it had when he left the house this morning.

"Yes, I'm here."

She was crying tears of joy and relief on the other end. It was difficult for Li to maintain his composure, hearing how upset his daughter was.

"Are you alright? Mr. Rodan said you had been taken…I didn't know what to do…I…I'm glad you're ok…"

Li closed his eyes, and felt the warm sting of tears forming. He let them fall. "You were very brave Jinhua. I know you were worried about me."

Jinhua laughed through her tears. "Duh, of course I was worried! Where are you? Are you coming home?"

"Yes, yes. I'm very near on the ninety-nine. There's some traffic, but I should be there in about an hour. I'll explain what happened when I arrive."

"Ok, Dad. Make sure you don't override the auto drive feature. You know what a terrible driver you are."

He could tell she was smiling at him from his study, and allowed a similar expression of joy to animate his features because of it. "No, no I won't do it this time. I'll let the car do the work."

"Good. Ok bye Dad. I love you."

"Speak to you soon. I love you." He ended the call, snapped the phone shut, then returned it to his briefcase. A heavy sigh escaped his lips.

"Is she alright?" Kyler asked.

"Yeah, she'll be fine." Li looked toward the emergency phone in the briefcase. "I hope I never have to do something like this again."

"Glad to hear it." Kyler slapped Li's shoulder in a display of solidarity. The impact made him wince. It was clear that he was not aware of his own strength sometimes with all of the augmentations and his metallic skeleton. "I wish none of us had to do things like this. But like all soldiers during a conflict, we have to make these kinds of sacrifices all the time. The family is what suffers the most unfortunately. They understand the duty of what you have to do, what your mission is, but at times they feel neglected and forgotten because they can't see the whole picture. And they're aware of it, too. I think that makes it harder for them, because they can't experience the whole ordeal with you. Even though they may be giving everything they can to support you. It's a difficult situation for both the soldier and the family."

Li nodded his head as he stared blankly at the back of the empty driver's seat. He pitied the loved ones who sacrificed on the homefront. Providing invisible aid for their families. Fighting for causes they could not see, fully grasp, or understand. True unsung heroes. "You're right. I just hope it was worth it. We can't let Janus carry out his plan. If he thinks that you've joined his cause, Limnic's cause, by kidnapping and killing me, then it will slow him down."

"Do we know anything further about how he plans to take control of Cereus?"

Li shook his head. "Nothing much at this point. All intel is inconclusive. But whatever his designs are, he plans to roll it out on a massive scale. His server activity has significantly increased recently."

Kyler gave a curt nod. The auto car changed lanes to overtake a large Amazon delivery truck. The white smile on the sky-blue background brought Rodan to Kyler's mind. *He's probably not smiling right now.* Li's partner had never impressed him. The man was unsat, constantly unorganized, and was always a cheap substitute for Li's boundless professionalism. He suspected the only reason Li continued to partner with him after all these years was because he made Li look good. Real good. Kyler suppressed a laugh at the thought.

"What about Rodan?"

Li brought his hand to his chin. Thinking. "Rodan can handle himself for now. While he may not have known the details of the op, he knows the threat Janus poses to us and society at large."

Kyler nodded, as if acknowledging a military order.

"Our next step is to assemble all of the major players and plan our next move, hopefully before Janus makes his. I'll contact the other Founders and gather them in my study, then we'll discuss strategy."

The afternoon sun was beginning its descent to twilight as the sign for Yuba City came into view. Situated on the border of an orchard, the sign was easy for travelers to miss on the way into town. That was not the case for Li. He put down his device, the messages, and the conflict awaiting him, to take in the sign and smile at the sight of it. He was home.

CHAPTER 19:
EXPLORING THE STUDY

Jinhua flopped into the large old recliner in the corner of her father's study and let her muscles go limp. The last few hours had been an emotional roller coaster and all she wanted to do was take a nap. Her eyelids became heavy, sleep tempted her, but her mind still whirled with unanswered questions. *Why had Dad been kidnapped? Who had done it? Is he still in danger? Am I in danger?*

Daniel stood next to the chair. He had been on his device during Jinhua's conversation with her father. Now that they knew he was safe, he directed his attention back to her. "I'm glad your dad is ok. I was a little worried there for a minute."

"Me too."

From her reclined position, her eyes began to sweep across the expansive study. With their crisis averted, she began to take in the scope and magnitude of the place she had labeled as "forbidden" for the first time in her life. *All this time, this room has been an operations center for his work.* The dim lighting and wall of monitors reminded her of the Space Operations Center at Vandenberg Air Force Base down south, except without the busyness and all the engineers shuffling around. It seemed like it was always frantic there, at least that was what she gathered about the place during her multiple virtual field trips to the center. *Dad probably works here alone most of the time.* Jinhua closed her eyes, considering that nap. As soon as she did, her stomach growled. It reminded her how she hadn't eaten since her early lunch at Star of India with Harpreet. *Maybe I'll go down and get a snack before Dad gets back.*

Upon opening her eyes she noticed Daniel no longer stood beside the comfy recliner. He had wandered from the corner back toward the massive desk with the document readers in the center of the room.

"This really is a cool workspace. What do you think your dad uses it for?" he said loud enough for her to hear in the corner.

Jinhua sprang up from the recliner and rushed to join him, unwilling to let him be the first to find out more about the secret room before she did. "I'm not sure. He told me that this place was off-limits for me years ago, so I never asked him about it."

"Looks like he's been doing a lot of research into something, and monitoring what he sees." His eyes found a monitor on the far-right side of the back wall. He stopped to point at it. "Isn't that a video from our physics committee room in the community center?"

Jinhua diverted her attention from the desk to focus on the monitor. *No way.* "Yeah it is. But why would he want to watch that?"

Both exchanged bewildered faces. Each looking to the other for a comprehensible response. Neither found an answer, yet they felt something else. An unmistakable connection, almost as if one had access to the other's brain and its intricate contents. Jinhua experienced a strange heightening of her senses. It was different from the pull of attraction she had felt for him back at the river. It was something else. Something she couldn't quite name or characterize. Whatever *it* was, it was a familiar feeling. Somehow she knew he was experiencing the same exact sensation.

After what seemed like the longest staring contest in history, Jinhua spun away from him toward the desk behind her. She latched on to the first object she saw in order to neutralize the disturbance of the atmosphere between them. "Uh…There sure are a lot of doc readers here. I always knew Dad was organized, but they look so…neat." She blushed uncontrollably at the emotional familiarity of Daniel's eyes, and hoped her rambling words would be enough to take her mind off of his strangely captivating stare. Focusing on the desk to alleviate her discomfort, the details of its design became apparent to her. It was made of fine carved wood on the outside, but appeared to have a network interface built into its surface. The top of the desk was also a massive touch screen that could be toggled to display a standard operating system interface or just show the plain surface of a desk. Jinhua switched between the modes several times, marveling at the simple yet impressive feature. *Very feihao!* The surface of the desk glowed with an eerie blue light when it was in computer mode. It was alive with digital life housed within its microscopic circuitry and transistors. While looking at the upper right corner of the desk, she eyed a solitary document reader that had been separated from the rest of the orderly stack. *Definitely out of place.* She picked it up, with the intent to return it to the pile, then suddenly stopped when she noticed the name on the heading of the reader. *That's my name…*

On the top of the thin reader Jinhua read: MA, JINHUA - DOI: 21/01/45.

What is this?

She examined the document reader with greater detail, feeling her hands grow cold with nervous sweat. It had been locked with some type of encryption method, leaving only her name and the odd number visible. Daniel made his way to her side from the wall monitors. "What's that?"

"I have no idea. But it's got my name and birthdate on it."

Daniel moved closer to Jinhua to get a better view. The warmth from his body made her arm tingle. The strange "not-quite-attraction" feeling arose again. In the span of minutes she had already given the phenomenon a name. In the moment, her burning curiosity about the doc reader overshadowed the sensation.

"For real? I didn't know your birthday was January 21st," Daniel said.

"Yeah it is," she continued to analyze the reader from all angles, looking for any way to unlock it. "When's yours?"

"August 16th."

"What year?"

"2045."

"Guess we were born the same year." *Damn! Something else in common!* "But I'm still older by six months," Jinhua flashed a playful smirk at him.

"Suppose I should respect my elders then," Daniel quipped. Jinhua slapped him on the arm with her free hand in response. "Ow! That hurt!" Daniel rubbed his arm. "You hit pretty hard."

"Serves you right!" She continued to rotate the reader, clueless about how to proceed. "Gotta learn to respect your elders." Daniel gave an understanding nod, while he watched her struggle with the reader.

"Ugggh! Why won't this damn thing open!?" The trifecta of hunger, tiredness, and teenage hormones had rendered her brain useless. One of the three were always to blame whenever she felt incompetent at something.

"Did you try voice decryption?" Daniel asked.

She tried it. "Nope. No luck."

"What about hand gesture decryption?"

Jinhua curled her fingers into a position that pantomimed the action of unlocking a door with a physical key in front of the reader's context sensitive area. No response.

"Dammit. Any other ideas?"

"What about retinal scans? I heard some of the older readers still use that dated biometric stuff."

How is he so calm? She brought the camera to her eye and held it open for several seconds. The strain caused her vision to blur with tears. Despite her effort, the device remained locked. Then she firmly pressed her thumb to the screen. Still nothing. "I'm about to say forget it. Nothing's working!" She said, her tone petulant.

Daniel's laugh echoed around the room as he carefully took the reader from her hands. "Maybe your dad didn't use any fancy techniques to lock this old reader. He's old…so he probably used some type of low-tech security measure."

"Like what?"

"I dunno, like an old password?"

Jinhua's eyes wandered to the corner of the room with the old recliner and telephone sitting under the halo of light from the standing lamp. "Ok I think I got it." *If I'm wrong, I'm saying to hell with this thing and getting a snack.*

She commanded the reader to show a password block. The machine complied, displaying an empty block with a blinking cursor, awaiting input. Jinhua verbally input the letters of her full name and date of birth: j-i-n-h-u-a-m-a-0-1-2-1-4-5. The reader instantly came to life.

"Wow, good thinking," Jinhua said.

Daniel smiled. "Y'know, I do have good ideas every now and then." She mirrored his cheer.

Her smile vanished when the contents of the reader appeared on the small screen. It contained six orderly columns of folders labeled with traditional Chinese characters. She made an earnest attempt to read the first two folders: 身體數據, *shen?-???-shu?-something,* 思想日誌, *something-xiang3-ri4-no idea.* She sounded out the words in her head, unwilling to subject Daniel to her shameful pronunciation and her abysmal knowledge of tones in her heritage language. *Damn, I wish I had paid more attention during those Chinese committees.*

Daniel peered over her shoulder, "What do those folders say? Can you read them?"

"I'm not sure. They use traditional characters instead of the simplified ones that I'm used to." She felt a pang of inadequacy at her inability to make out the script of a language that she should have known well. Daniel seemed to sense her guilt and kept quiet.

One of the columns contained folders labeled in English. *Finally some luck.* She opened one labeled 'Statistics'. Several subfolders populated the screen. She scanned them all with machine efficiency. *There's one with my name on it.* She opened it.

What she saw on the screen narrowly caused her to drop the device onto the smooth dark blue tile of the floor. She scrolled down the reader, heart thundering in her chest.

MA, JINHUA: DATE OF INITIALIZATION: 21 January 2045

PLACE OF INITIALIZATION: Yuba City, CA

FATHER: MA, LI

MOTHER: DONOR

Is this…me? Mother "Donor", "Date of Initialization", "Place of Initialization"? What the hell is this?

A noise at the entrance of the study distracted her from the reader. Both whipped their heads toward the door, where the shadow of a person appeared in the narrow space between the heavy oak door and its frame. All of a sudden, Jinhua felt the urge to shut the reader and hide.

The heavy door slowly opened and Li stepped through, his usual erect posture withered by the events of a very long day.

Jinhua placed the document reader on the desk, momentarily forgetting about the questions swirling in her mind, and jogged over to him. She embraced him with as much strength as she could gather. Tears streamed down her face. She could feel his hot tears finding their place on her shoulder in his tight grip. "I know it was hard for you," Li said, "but I'm alright."

They separated. Jinhua looked into her father's eyes and asked, "Dad, I know you just got home, but I saw a doc reader on your desk that said something about me and…Mom. What is it about?"

Where to begin? Li thought. His eyes parted from Jinhua's penetrating sight and fell onto the young man standing next to his desk. As if prompted into action by sight, the teenager began to approach him. He did not seem intimidated by Li's presence.

"Mr. Ma? I'm Daniel." He extended his hand in an awkward manner to invite a handshake.

Li peered at him sideways, with more curiosity than suspicion, then reached out and shook his hand. "Nice to meet you Daniel. Do you mind waiting downstairs for a while? I have some things to discuss with my daughter."

"No problem Mr. Ma. I need to call my parents anyway to let them know I'll be home late tonight."

"Good idea," Li said.

Daniel flashed an encouraging expression at Jinhua before he departed. Her eyes watched him until he pulled the thick door open and walked through to the red carpet. He closed it behind him, sealing her inside. The sound reminded her of a bank vault closing. Echoing. Definitive. Final.

Li looked into his daughter's eyes. They were slightly puffy from tears, but they still contained that insatiable spark for boundless knowledge. A trait they both shared.

She's ready. He told himself. *She's ready to hear it all.*

He sighed heavily then took tired steps toward the giant desk. At the press of a button, a panel in the front of the desk opened revealing four squared cushioned stools inside. The cushions were red and embroidered with a golden trim that twisted around the border of the square shape. Jinhua was captivated by the beautiful representation of traditional Chinese colors on miniature squared bar stools. But she was more impressed four stools had somehow been crammed into the guts of the desk. *I'm getting a desk like this when I have my own office.* She archived the mental note in her mind for further research, at a later date.

Li pulled out one of the stools, then invited Jinhua to do the same with a hand gesture. They both sat down facing each other, father and daughter. Both preparing to have a conversation Li knew would alter the course of her life and his relationship with her, forever. *She is ready. I am ready.* The emotion of the reunion, the kidnapping, and all of the other respective happenings of both of their days seemed to coalesce into a powerful force that was supernatural and apparent to both. It transformed the air around them into a thick gaseous haze. A suffocating force that threatened to render them both unconscious if left unchecked. Li was ready to cleanse the room, and return it to a neutral state.

"Dad…what is it?

Li's eyes rose to meet hers. "Ok Jinhua, I'll tell you what you need to know…It's a long story." And he began to speak…

CHAPTER 20:
ORIGINS - PART 1

All his life, Li Ma had always been careful with words. To him, every word needed a purpose, a mission. Like laser-guided munitions, every utterance he selected usually underwent the highest form of scrutiny before being deployed for a very specific cause. None should be wasted. Ever. It had been the most important lesson he learned from watching his father deal with unfortunate eventualities that often accompany fame and wealth. *"Even if you are silent, others will assume and judge. Choose your words carefully,"* he had told a young Li long ago.

And he never forgot that lesson. He lived by it. Through his demeanor, actions, and presence he presented himself to others, turning to speech as a last resort. Not because he couldn't find the right words, but because there were not nearly enough of them to express the great depth of his understanding or feeling.

Jinhua had never heard her father talk so much in one sitting. The short bursts of speech she was accustomed to were replaced by flowing sentences with descriptive vocabulary and impactful visuals. The result was a crystal clear idea of how things went down. At least it was like that for the first part of his story.

Who knew he was so loquacious? A captive of his every word, she felt five-years-old again, while a younger version of her dad read her a bedtime story to stoke her imagination before trying to get her to go to sleep. Except this time, *she* was one of the protagonists of the story, and the things he described had actually happened. Like for real. With every new revelation, new questions surfaced in her mind, each one in need of elaboration and exploration. She held onto them for later, not wanting to break the flow of her father's rare chatty mood.

He started with a brief history of Cereus. The organization was founded in 2024, by four visionary founders. Its original goal was to advance humankind by reorganizing society in a way that empowered individuals to live as complete human beings. (She wasn't sure what he meant by *complete*.) It also sought to preserve planet Earth's valuable resources more effectively than had been done since the entire world began its economic boom following the conclusion of the Second World War. '*Preserve people and planet*' had been its early motto.

Cereus began as an online-only counterculture movement. But on the social media platforms of old, word got out about a way of life that would allow people to live comfortably, participate in shaping local policies, and (if they desired) politics, in a small way while allowing them to explore latent talents. Many flocked at the opportunity, abandoning dwindling employment options in the ancient megacities, for smaller settlements run by Cereus' leadership. These were called *comvils*, with the first active one established there in Yuba City.

When the refugees from the cities arrived, the organization helped guide them toward employment via educational committees. They consisted of regular people who were already skilled in some field or trade. The committees provided training, mentorship, and credentialing (if necessary), to any person who wanted it. Proficiency in a particular skill or trade, took priority over the need for profit, a characteristic which had made many of the educational monoliths of the past inefficient and unaffordable. His mention of the committees invoked fond memories for Jinhua. They had been one of the best parts of her childhood. The thought of sitting in a classroom for eight hours a day from age five to eighteen learning superficial knowledge in subjects like math, English, and science, made her feel profound pity for the students of the past, and happy to have been born in the mid-twenty-first century in Cereus society.

She forced her attention back onto her father, when he mentioned *Limnic* for the first time. He labeled it as a dark clone of Cereus. Similar in every way to its predecessor, except for the fact its followers would turn to violence if necessary in order to execute the motto that Cereus coined. She had heard of it on the news, and a little about it in the history committees of her youth, but outside of that had no knowledge of them. To her, they were just a terrorist organization that blew up buildings, sometimes when people were inside.

Her father continued speaking. Jinhua listened to a somewhat redacted version (she could tell when details were being left out) of his role in Cereus as the Chief of Intelligence. He described some of the basic functions that he carried out in the organization, and how those duties led him to work with certain people who were sometimes considered "bad" by others. *Bad? C'mon on Dad I'm not five-years-old anymore!* She kept her comment to herself.

Jinhua gasped with horror when he mentioned some of the details of his experience during the protest that morning. The way he evaded a pack of angry protestors, used a Jedi mind trick on the guards, and arrived at his office unharmed, was simply badass. *Straight out of an action movie,* were the words she used to describe it in her mind. She didn't appreciate his recklessness, but she was happy to know he could handle himself, even at his advanced age.

Then he told her about how he had been captured by a known Limnic sympathizer and collaborator known as "The Terminator". He was apparently one of his long time points of access into Limnic, served as a valuable conduit of information, and possessed a highly trained team of commandos that was a formidable fighting force on the battlefield. When she asked him why he was called "The Terminator", he laughed and responded: "It's because he has so many mechanical and digital augmentations in his body that although he appears human, he is more machine than man at this point. The nickname comes from *The Terminator* movie series, which began with the 1984 film of the same name. It told the story of a cyborg assassin from the year 2029 who was sent back to 1984 to kill the mother of the person foretold to be the savior of humanity from machines in a fictional post-apocalyptic future." The plot of the movie sounded funny to Jinhua. What strange movies her grandparents had enjoyed.

The moment of levity was brief. It was cut short when Li confessed that his staged kidnapping had been a ruse, in order to fool the leader of Limnic into thinking that, "The Terminator" (who also worked with Limnic on occasion), was still loyal to him. The leader (who her father conveniently "forgot" to name) was one of the founders of Cereus, but he had gone rogue and started his own organization because he thought Cereus could not accomplish its mission effectively.

Protests? Terrorists? Voluntary kidnapping? Movies from the 1980s? It was a lot to process, even for Jinhua. She knew her dad wasn't working in a cubicle in some boring office all day, but she had no idea that his work was so…dangerous. She wiped nervous sweat onto her shorts and reminded herself to calm down. It was hard to do. The questions were piling up so fast, so high that they interrupted the normally flawless firing of neurons in her brain. It felt like her head was taking on water and might capsize any moment, like a giant ship lost at sea. To make matters worse, she could tell that he was not providing her with all of the relevant information by the way some of the story threads abruptly ended and began. Some facts just felt…off. Not like outright lies, but different pieces to the wrong puzzles. It was like interacting with an artificial intelligence friend or eating a completely synthetic meal. The experience was there, but in the background, something was missing. Something that would make it *feel* like a full and satisfying experience.

She requested a break. Her father happily agreed, looking like he could use one himself. To her surprise, he remained on the stool, hunched over, thinking, as she made her way to the heavy oak door. It took some force for her to pull it open, and her eyes blinked rapidly as they adjusted to the normal soft light of the hallway. A brilliant summer sunset gave the last of its dying light outside, yielding its nightly display of evening color. Jinhua did not stop to take it in but just headed directly to the bathroom down the hall.

Feeling a little better, she turned to the sink and splashed water on her face. While washing and drying her hands she studied herself in the mirror. Her face was deeply tanned from walking out in the sun. Two brown sunspots emerged on her right cheek from overexposure to ultraviolet (or as she liked to call it 'ultraviolent') radiation. The pimple from that morning had gone down, and no longer stung when she moved her cheek.

Jinhua sighed wondering if they should continue. Her father was clearly drained and seemed to be losing steam with each new sentence he uttered. And she was starving. She recalled their reservation at the restaurant to celebrate her acceptance into the Space Cadet program. *I doubt we'll make it.* The lack of windows in Li's study had warped her perception of time. A quick glance at her device informed her it was already ten past seven. *Yep, probably won't make it.*

Her thoughts turned to Daniel. Is he still here? she wondered. Probably so. She had not heard the front door open and she remembered glancing toward one of the monitors on the back wall. He had been sitting patiently in the great room on the screen. He's been super supportive today. I wonder what Harpreet will say about that? Jinhua knew she was stalling her return to the study. Her distracting thoughts were a symptom of her fatigue and hunger. After another definitive splash of water on her face, she walked out of the bathroom, determined to finish the conversation. No matter how ugly it gets.

When she arrived back in the study, she found Li slumped over on the surprisingly comfortable stool. His elbows on his thighs, fingers interlaced, eyes closed; she felt hesitant to disturb him from the much needed and deserved moment of rest.

"Uh, Dad?" She said, her voice small and gentle.

Li's eyes fluttered open. A warm smile found its way to his face. "Oh sorry, I dozed off." He stretched his arms in front of him and yawned. "What were we talking about?"

Jinhua returned to the stool in front of him. "You said you would tell me about the document reader I found with my name on it…"

"Oh right…" he looked away from her. Jinhua sensed that they were heading into uncomfortable territory. It had been easy for him to talk about work and business matters, but personal ones had always been a struggle.

"Look…Dad…we don't have to talk about this right now if you don't want to. We've both had a long day. It's only—" she glanced at the clock on her device, "seven fifteen. We can still make that dinner reservation at the restaurant if we hurry."

Li gave a weak smile. His weary eyes looked at his daughter for several seconds, weighing whether or not to take the out she had given them both from this conversation. A conversation he had rehearsed an infinite amount of times since the day she was born. How can I tell her?

Jinhua felt bad for him. The gravity of hundreds of micro-decisions made throughout that day alone seemed to cause the skin on his face to hang. Combined with the rare look of indecision on his face; he looked like the archetype of an average citizen of the developed world: confused, withered, elderly.

She's ready to hear it. She must hear it. "No, it's alright. I'll say what I have to say, here and now." Some of the surety had returned to his voice.

Jinhua nodded, understanding. Appreciative of his mental fortitude.

"Jinhua…" He sighed heavily. "My father, your grandfather, was a wealthy businessman. He was heavily interested in the field of genomics back in the twenties. At the time, scientists had already mapped the human genome, but were then looking to learn how to manipulate it in order to treat and eventually prevent certain ailments that were notoriously caused by faulty DNA."

"That's pretty cool."

Li smiled. "Yes it was. But what was even cooler, was that eventually a new field of genomics emerged. The field known as 'digigenomics' sought to marry the concepts from traditional genomics, while integrating advancements in the digital space. Digigenomics essentially harnessed the power of biotechnology, artificial intelligence, machine learning, big data, and even traditional computer programming in order to do something that humans have tried again and again to do successfully for millennia; create a human being."

Jinhua didn't realize she had moved to the edge of the cushion on the stool. Once again, under the spell of her father's storytelling prowess.

"Not just recreate the physical form. That had been done and improved upon over the years. It was easy to replicate the physical properties of humans, but not so easy to replicate and reproduce the complex interplay of internal body systems, hormones, cells, glands, and everything else that allows us to function independently as conscious entities. That was until the 2030s, when research and funding into digigenomics really took off. Like any budding scientific discipline there were many failures in the early days. As data analysts, scientists, software engineers, many different kinds of doctors, and other experts worked to pool their respective talents in order to create a fully functional, digitally evolved human being. Creating individual human organs was easy and had been done since the 2010s. But getting all of the organs to work, function, and most importantly grow together as they do in a normal biological human turned out to be a complex and monumental task. Even with cutting edge technology like quantum computers as resources, it took decades to get it right."

"By the early 2040s, the first official prototypes were born, or should I say initialized. Many died during birth. Others only lived to young ages due to faulty programming between the biological and digital organs, and other reasons that are still a mystery to this day. But some survived and thrived."

Jinhua's entire body was tense. Waiting, expecting, the inevitable punchline of her father's story.

"In 2044, our team of scientists at Cereus decided to try something unheard of. Instead of trying to create a complete human by integrating the biological, physical, and digital components, they decided to use what they called 'redundancy' to shape the human. They left the biological DNA intact, while introducing a sort of digital clone of that same DNA code. That clone was infused with cutting edge software and machine learning, allowing it to adapt, learn, and grow as normal cells do. But these are no ordinary cells, these were unofficially dubbed 'thinking cells', cells that could think and learn independently while still being manipulated like software in a computer."

"Your grandfather had contributed so much to the field of digigenomics that when the scientific team asked for volunteers to contribute DNA to this revolutionary project, he asked me, if I would volunteer. I was working for Cereus at the time and it made sense for the sample to come from one of their own. So I said yes."

Li's eyes fixed on Jinhua's, a grave expression on his face. "Jinhua…you are the product of digigenomics. One of the first successful fusions of human and machine, of the digital and the biological. A miracle of science and technology."

CHAPTER 21:
ORIGINS - PART 2

Jinhua's heart was pounding, her throat dry, as she let the gravity of her father's story sink in. *Me? No way!*

From Li's perspective she looked stunned, jaw hanging in confusion. He eyed her closely, waiting for her reaction. *I'm sorry.*

"But, but…I don't *feel* like a robot. I feel like, like me!" Jinhua said. The emotional impact of the news began to hit her like a wave crashing on a crowded beach, devastating all she had ever known about herself within seconds.

Li leaned forward and grasped her hand in an uncharacteristic gesture of physical sincerity. "I know, I know. And that's what I've always wanted for you. Not to feel like a science experiment, but as a normal girl. To live a normal life."

Jinhua pulled her hand away and sobbed. The tears stung her eyes, blurring her field of vision. "But Dad, how can I live a normal life!? Nobody knows *what* I am."

Li fell silent. He knew she was right. "Jinhua, the truth is, we're still studying how the digital redundancies within you are functioning with your innate biological systems. So we don't know how the interactions will play out as you grow older."

"So you've been monitoring me…and my *growth* from here?"

"…Me and another team of scientists…yes."

Suddenly she felt dirty, violated. It was a feeling that was difficult to experience, especially because the man sitting across from her was the primary source of her discomfort. In that moment, the desire to lash out at her father was strong. Very strong. She wanted to make him feel as small and unadjusted as she felt. Her hunger, tiredness, and teenage hormone trifecta had merged with another: anger, confusion, and disappointment. The two triangles coalesced and manifested as a physical choking sensation that left her speechless and light-headed. Sitting there across from her, the man looked ready to absorb any blows, verbal or physical, she may have wanted to inflict on him. Jinhua had no idea if she would act on the impulse. She concentrated every fiber of her person on maintaining her self-control, which felt as if it might tumble and shatter into millions of pieces at any moment on the tile floor between their feet.

Several soundless minutes passed between them as father and daughter worked to find the right words to say. Li's eyes had fallen to the floor. His thoughts floating, heavy physical fatigue befuddled his mind. It was as if he were back in basic training wading through a freezing river, uniform soaked from head to toe after a week-long training exercise. One foot in front of the other was all he could manage.

Jinhua stared at her father. A storm of emotions, questions, doubts, and concerns darkened the sky over a battlefield in her mind. The combatants: anger versus curiosity. Both were armed with ancient weapons of war: cannons, horses, swordsmen, archers. Both sides were anxious to begin the killing, waiting for the other to strike first. She was unsure which side would initiate the hostilities and come out victorious.

Li broke the silence between them. "We were monitoring you regularly, until a few years ago when you turned eleven," he said with a low voice.

The troops on the curious side began their assault. A volley of cannon fire. The first line of the vanguard charged. Hundreds of angry side troops were decimated. Curiosity gained some territory. "What happened?"

"It seems at the onset of puberty, something happened between your biological systems and their respective redundancies. In a quick explanation, it appeared as if each one became aware of the other and formed some sort of mutually beneficial pact between the two in order to ensure their survival. One of the results of that pact was that we lost access to some internal digital systems, like to the nervous, endocrine, and other systems." Li fought through an overwhelming sense of guilt to maintain eye-contact with his daughter. Her red glossy eyes wanted to look elsewhere, he could tell. *She's fighting too.*

The cavalry on the angry side gathered reinforcements and prepared for a strategic flanking movement. Mounted warriors surged forward, mowing down screaming and scared curiosity soldiers. "So, since I turned eleven…you haven't been able to know what I was thinking?"

"…No, we completely lost access to the data six years ago."

In a surprising turn of events, the curiosity army tapped into a mid-twenty first century satellite. A ray of light pierced through the heavens, blasting a giant crater between both armies. The battle was over, at least for now. Jinhua let out a sigh of relief. *Thank goodness for that!*

Li read her reaction. The beginnings of a smile crept onto his weary face. "I've always considered your privacy, when dealing with the team. Some things…just should be private."

Jinhua reached over and embraced him, squeezing him tightly. "You were still looking after me, right?"

"Always. You know I am," he said.

Jinhua returned to her stool. "So my mother—"

"Technically, you were born from a sort of digital surrogate mother. But the original biological egg was provided by one of my old Cereus colleagues and a pioneer of digigenomics. Her name was Sharla Thompson. Unfortunately, she died in one of Limnic's building demolition attacks in 2044."

Limnic! So it was them…Jinhua began to sob again. "Surrogate? Why didn't she want to raise me? Why weren't you two ever together?"

Li answered the questions as calmly as possible. He did not want to upset her further. "It takes a very special person's DNA to be able to interact with the software. It would simply be too dangerous for the embryo if the biological and the digital components did not match." Li sighed, then averted his gaze from her. "Your mother had a rare DNA code that was compatible with the digital redundancies. So, being the scientist that she was, she donated her life and body to science."

He had not answered her questions, but her mind was going in so many directions, she couldn't bring herself to press him again. *I had a mother. Limnic killed her. I'm part robot or computer. I can't trust my Dad.* Jinhua sobbed uncontrollably. For the first time in her life, she felt overwhelmed by information. It was as if a dam had ruptured and flooded the landscape leaving only guesses as to what was below the muddy brown water. She was helpless against the great force. All she could do was sit on a dry rooftop and wait. Wait for the water to recede. Wait to assess the damage. Wait and hope some things could be salvaged from beneath. Hope things might be like they were before the catastrophe. *My life will never be the same.*

Li stood and with great care dropped to his knees to wrap her in his arms. It had been many years since he held her to let her cry. He didn't know it, but she cried for him, for the mother she never had a chance to know, for Cereus *and* Limnic, and for herself. When there were no more tears, Li let her go and returned to his stool. He took the statue-like posture of a debilitated man on a park bench, eyes burning a hole into space between his feet, staring at everything and nothing. Jinhua's arms hung at her side. The vacant expression on her face, mirrored the scene in her brain. Earthy contaminated water everywhere. Evidence of the disaster floated on the surface, gently lapping at the side of the rooftop. No hope of rescue. She sat in a noiseless void with few coherent or meaningful thoughts coming to mind, unsure how to proceed. Somewhere across the cityscape, her father shared her fate. Alone, water sloshing at his feet and caught in a downpour, he wondered if he should move to a higher place or allow the rising water line to drown him where he stood. They sat together in complete solitude for a long time. Only the humming of the air conditioner marked the passing minutes.

Light from the hallway stirred both from their respective inner prisons. Someone had opened the door. It was Daniel. The youth peered into the room with caution. What he saw was the scene he expected. Mr. Ma sitting like an animated sculpture. Jinhua dangling, face full of sadness and hurt, like a broken doll. It fit. Everything made sense. He was no longer afraid. He had never been. Just acted on pure algorithmic intuition. Or was it emotion? No thoughts came to mind. Movement. Motion. Process. These were the only ways forward.

Jinhua had noticed him at the door, but made no acknowledgement of him. His presence was hard to detect among her tangled feelings and emotions. Before she could react, Daniel walked toward her with echoing footsteps. Seconds later he stood in front of her, face heavy with anguish. He was so close she could feel gentle warmth radiating from his body. Li made no movement or protest.

"Daniel? What are you…?" Jinhua asked.

In the next instant, he stood her up with steady hands and wrapped his arms around her with the warmest of hugs. "It's alright Jinhua," he said, "It's gonna be alright."

She stood there in shock, not sure what to think or how to feel. Still numb and reeling from what her father told her, Daniel's hug seemed like another event of the day designed to confound her thinking and undermine her carefully crafted construct of the world as she knew it. Her body remained tense, but Daniel held on, unfazed, solid.

After a few seconds, she felt it. The not quite-attraction-but-something-else feeling. *Again! There it is!* It manifested as a nudge, ever so slight, but present. It made her feel safe. Like everything *was* going to be alright. She closed her eyes to savor the sensation. Felt her muscles begin to soften within his arms as if they were one being, one life, one entity.

"Daniel, I…" She began to speak but stopped. Something told her to let the moment breathe. To let herself breathe. Standing there in his arms it was as if some camera were spinning around them both, capturing the scene from all angles. She let it last. Long enough to lift her off of that forgotten rooftop. Long enough to reconnect with her thinking brain. She had recovered her senses and it all because of *hugs from Daniel? What is this?*

When they separated, Jinhua noticed Li had vanished from the stool. He had moved behind his massive desk and was searching among the neatly stacked document readers for something.

"Dad? What are you?" Her unanswered questions had been stacked to the ceiling of her head space. A throbbing headache began to pound on her skull.

A single document reader in hand. Li made his way over and offered it to her. "Jinhua, read this. Hopefully, it will help you understand a little more about yourself and our young guest here." He looked at Daniel up and down, then squeezed her hand, "I'm going downstairs to order some takeout food for you." He began to walk away, then turned, "I love you, Jinhua."

She looked down at the document reader, to Daniel, then to her father. "…I love you too Dad." Li exited the room, leaving Daniel and Jinhua alone in the study.

*   *   *

Several hours later, Jinhua lay on her bed, gaze fixed on the ceiling. Showered, belly full of a Chipotle burrito bowl, she felt much better, yet completely wired. *There's no way I'm sleeping tonight. Too much stuff to think about.*

It had been an interesting day, and an even more interesting dinner. As Li and Jinhua munched on bowls full of synthetic beef and assorted veggies, they talked until the early hours of the morning. Daniel watched them eat, a pensive look on his face. He didn't eat at all. Nor did he say much all night. *Now I know why*, Jinhua thought.

While in the shower, partially thanks to Daniel's *magic* hug, she engaged her systematic thinking to prioritize the importance of her questions related to everything she had discussed with her father. *1. Daniel, 2. Mom, 3. Me, 4. More about Digigenomics because it sounds cool, 5. More information about Cereus and Limnic.* By the time she changed and made her way to the dining room, questions about Daniel were on the tip of her tongue. She doubted she would get to answers about her mother tonight, but she prepared several questions anyway just in case.

Back to Daniel. At the top of her list, she wanted answers to: *Who is he? Why does he feel so familiar? Why are his hugs so warm and…effective at helping me think straight?*

After the food arrived, Li ate from a lukewarm steak burrito bowl, while Daniel sat looking at the table. No one spoke. The silence provided the optimal environment for Jinhua to delve into the contents of the document reader she received in the study as she ate. The reader contained a summary document about an experiment Cereus conducted seventeen years prior. Within ten minutes, Jinhua had devoured the twenty-five page report and the entirety of a chicken burrito bowl with guacamole.

"A digital twin!?" she exclaimed.

Her father nodded while crunching on a salsa chip. "Yes. In summary, his digital redundancies are the same as yours. Except, he was not born from a biological surrogate as you were."

Jinhua looked confused. "Sooo, we're not related?"

"No. Not in the biological sense that you are used to."

Whew! I almost thought I was like the Lannisters in that old show Game of Thrones. "So how does it work?"

"In addition to conducting research into digigenomics, your grandfather and his associates were also interested in understanding if human consciousness could be manifested into inanimate machines."

"So like a talking toaster?" Jinhua asked.

Li chuckled, "Something like that. This led to speculative experiments back in the thirties and forties. Around the same time major breakthroughs in digigenomics were occurring."

"Around the time I was born…"

Li nodded, reaching into the brown bag for another chip. "Yes. Human cyborg technology has existed for decades, but they weren't sentient. Which is why several experiments were conducted in this field." He looked at Daniel, then at Jinhua. "As you've probably guessed, Daniel is a cyborg who was grown from a digital egg."

Jinhua *had* already guessed that. "I figured it had to be something like that. But how are we connected?"

"Daniel's digital redundancies mirror yours. So in a sense, you are both like two digital devices on the same network, able to communicate and "talk" to one another in a variety of different ways."

Jinhua felt her pulse racing. "Like what kind of ways?"

"I wish I could tell you. But as in your case, I'm not sure. We are still researching the interplay between digital and biological systems at play in organic humans. The research into the connection between biological humans with digital DNA *and* cyborgs with biological DNA is still scattered, and has not come up with any conclusive theories."

Daniel listened to the conversation without speaking, head swiveling. He had not uttered a word since they left the study. Jinhua looked at him with curiosity. *A digital twin. Me.* She allowed herself to ask another one of her dozens of burning questions.

"Daniel, how did you know to come into the study?"

He shook his head. "I don't know. I guess I just sensed you were having a hard time, then I went upstairs."

Things were beginning to make sense now. *At least one mystery will be solved tonight,* Jinhua thought. "So you uh, feel things right? Like a human does?"

Daniel shrugged, "I'm not sure if it's feeling or sensing. I just know what I need or want to do, then I act."

"So you're like a software artificial intelligence with a physical form?"

Li spoke up. "He is more than software. His cyborg DNA contains thinking cells that have a biological redundancy. We are only sure that he has the capacity to execute and act on certain drives and executable command lines. We are not sure that this manifests in the kind of consciousness biological humans experience." After his explanation, he noted the look of confusion on his daughter's face.

"I don't follow. Example please." Jinhua scolded herself internally for not being able to follow the logic. *I must be sleepy.*

"Just like we are not sure if certain animals experience consciousness in the way that we do, it is the same with Daniel. For example, does an animal like a chinchilla experience consciousness?"

"Maybe..." Jinhua said.

"Even if it did, how would it communicate that to you without knowledge of human speech?" Li challenged.

Jinhua did not speak. She sat thinking about a talking chinchilla. The ridiculous image made her want to laugh and acted as an effective mnemonic device for her father's explanation. Now she understood and she would never forget it.

Li gestured toward Daniel, bursting the thought bubble of the talking chinchilla that hovered over Jinhua's head. "It's the same with Daniel. If he is experiencing consciousness, only he would be able to describe it to us. Just like we can only know the consciousness of another person through their thoughts and experience alone."

Jinhua yawned. She found the discussion stimulating, but felt the cloud of uncertainty about herself descend over the table. Then there was her mother, and everything else she wanted to know about. Her mind wanted to know, but her body was shutting down. She needed to at least attempt to sleep. Daniel noticed the change in her mood and looked languid as a result. Her father looked like a walking zombie who might flop to the floor without the assistance of blunt force trauma to the head. "Thanks for the explanation Dad, but I think, I'm gonna go to bed. Been a long day."

"I understand," Li said.

Jinhua pushed her chair out and stood. Daniel knew not to follow her.

Before exiting the dining room, Li asked for her attention. What he had to say had been brief but was as heavy and important as all of the other information she had learned about herself and her family throughout that day. It was the choice that kept her awake, lying in her bed, replaying all the events of the day for at least the fifth time. The decision to continue to live her life as she had been up to that point, or to become an active participant in her personal evolution was hard, but it was one that she alone had to make.

So she lay there all night. Comparing the pros and cons, thinking about her Dad, Mom, and Daniel. Thinking about the future.

CHAPTER 22:
LILI'UOKALANI KEAHI

Lili stood on the balcony connected to her bedroom facing the southwest. The dying light of the setting sun carried a cool breeze from Folsom Lake. It caressed her cheek with a feather touch as it waved over the large patio carrying that summer freshwater scent. Blended orange, purple, and blues accented the sunset. The dazzling scene reminded her of fireworks blasting in the night sky on a warm night in late August, a sign of the season's end. Her bones felt weighted and brittle at the sight of it.

The balcony was large with simple decorations. Four potted plants, haphazardly placed in each corner and a simple 3D printed patio furniture set with a round table surrounded by four chairs sporting weather beaten cushions, populated the wooden surface. It had been the last place in the house she had decorated. After the effort and expense invested in the facade of her mansion, she had little desire to make the area presentable. Few people ever got that far into her house anyway.

She relaxed her shoulders to allow air to flow from her lungs, then deliberately took in refreshing lake air. With her gaze fixed on fast-approaching twilight in the distant sky, her thoughts turned to her family, replaying conversations from the past. They seemed to blur together in her mind, like the colors of the sunset. It made it hard for her to know what to feel. *I'm sorry I had to send you away. It's what's best for us both.*

The lie she told Noe a few hours prior felt natural. Almost more so than the strained conversation between them. Lili told her that she needed to leave to go and meet a few old business associates. It felt like the only way to get her to go away, while at the same time keeping her out of the inevitable harm that was stalking its way toward the house.

After learning about the threat on her mother's life issued by members of Limnic, years of pain, anger, and disappointment were replaced by Noe's need to preserve human life, even if that life was the mother she hated. *She's a fighter, that one. I don't know where that selflessness comes from. Probably from some long dead ancestor, but not me,* Lili thought after Noe exited her house. Initially, Noe refused to leave. She felt like her presence might make a difference in her poor old mother's life for the first time in decades. Well aware of her intentions and motivations, Lili still sent her away.

She had known for years that Limnic would come for her, that *he* would come for her, but never knew when, how, or where. It had been promised years prior after she had managed to break free from the wretched and dangerous organization for good. *That freedom came at too high a cost.*

A small mosquito drifted with caution around Lili's face. She swatted it away with her right hand, and watched it retreat into the darkening air space around her. Seconds later, the resulting histamine reaction from the mosquito's bite on her bare calf caused her to reach down and scratch the area. *Damn mosquito.* The nuisance of the itch reminded her of countless similar bites she had received as a young girl playing in the lush tropical grasses near her birth home on western O'ahu. The bites had never bothered her much back then. Going outside and facing the potential dangers of nature were a preferred substitute from those that awaited her at home.

Back then, she was a different person. At five feet and two inches tall, Lili'uokalani Keahi (her birth name) was impetuous, sharp-tongued, and streetwise. From an early age she had learned to take advantage of any opportunity or edge afforded to her. An inborn talent for reading people and recalling faces, her razor-sharp intuition, attractive face, exotic curves, and ability with numbers, were the skills that kept her alive during those early years. She had acquired none of these sitting behind a desk and being lectured at. All were inherited evolutionary pearls formed among the capricious undertows of natural selection's brackish waters. As turtles have shells, jellyfish have venom, and lionfish have spines, Lili had been endowed with these traits. Not for offense or defense; good or evil, but for survival. Nature has no morals, only predators and prey. And young Lili was no one's prey.

The verbal and physical weapons wielded against Lili in her mother's booze-soaked tantrums, combined with her father's gambling and video game addictions, made the jungles of Hawai'i a welcome escape from home. When she was young, she tried to make the island her home, sneaking rides in cabs or Ubers with friends or just by taking the bus to Honolulu to hang out at the beach. But she quickly saw the impacts of overdevelopment, environmental destruction, and foreign sell outs that corrupted what, in her mind, should have been an island paradise. She had the feeling that the island was sinking under her feet from capitalistic offloading of ideals, cultural images, merchandise from the mainland, and rising sea levels. *This was supposed to be my land, MY kingdom,* she had thought. *I can't stay here.*

She planned her escape on her seventeenth birthday. It gave her time to save up some money before she departed. In addition to the pocket money, she needed a plane ticket. A sympathetic distant cousin living in San Francisco at the time, secretly purchased her a one-way ticket to the mainland, promising to provide her with shelter and to help her establish a life in the city. Lili accepted the offer, not mentioning a word to her parents or friends.

Wordless goodbyes and awkward conversations punctuated the week before her scheduled flight. She nearly cracked under the pressure and told one of her closest friends, Morie, about her decision, but decided against it. A perceptive girl of few words raised on the North Shore in Laie, she always seemed to know what Lili was thinking. During their final conversation, Lili put on the performance of a lifetime to conceal her intention to leave. She had even gone as far as telling Morie, "see you tomorrow". But deep down she knew Morie had seen through it all, knew that she would probably never see Lili again. She was right.

Sitting alone in the cabin of the plane, under Hawaiian Airlines' signature soft purplish pink lighting, she once again considered turning back. She stood in the tiny bathroom, looking at her frazzled reflection staring back at her in the mirror for several minutes. She carried no luggage and could easily walk off of the flight if she wanted to. *Morie could help me. I could find a way to survive. I always do.*

A soft knock at the lavatory door made her heart jump. It was a friendly stewardess with a rosy expression, wearing ruby red lipstick. The bright color stood out on her peanut toned complexion. "You need some help?" she asked delicately. Lili hesitated, her heart slamming in her chest. *Last chance.* "No, I was just…coming out."

The stewardess smiled wide displaying perfect white teeth. "Okay then, I'll have to ask you to return to your seat. We're preparing the cabin for departure." Lili nodded her head, then snaked her way past a male stewardess cramming a bulging piece of luggage into an already stuffed overhead compartment to reach her seat. Excitement, fear, and apprehension mixed in her blood, giving her a heady feeling, as if she had sipped a cup of Kona coffee and chased it with a shot of Kahlua. From her window seat, surrounded by strangers and a storm of conflicting thoughts, she watched the only island that she had ever called home slowly grow smaller as the jet ascended toward cruising altitude. *It looks so beautiful from up here.* That would be the last time she would ever see the island in person.

Life in San Francisco was not easy or cheap for Lili. Her body, acclimated to the tropical Hawaiian jet stream, constantly trembled from the cold bay breeze. Worse yet, shortly after her arrival, the cousin who purchased her plane ticket perished unexpectedly in a roofing accident while on the job. Heartbroken, with no contacts and only her remaining cash she had saved up before leaving home, she was forced to struggle for survival among the city's abundant homeless population. Lili bounced from a group home, to a few shelters. At one shelter she was caught stealing food and other toiletries from residents on multiple occasions. The infractions were enough to officially remove her from the place. Angered at what she deemed to be a failure of a system, with pride as her only companion, the streets of the Mission District became her home.

The winter of 2022 was the longest of her short life. Fighting for scraps of dumpster food left by affluent tech workers and tourists, defending herself from the constant threat of sexual assault from doped up homeless counterparts, theft of what little personal belongings she had, and surviving the chilly weather were all a part of her daily activities. *I don't belong here,* she used to think to herself as she hugged her knees under a urine-soaked blanket, *I am a queen. I am a queen. I am a queen.* The thought lulled her to sleep nightly. It prevented her from putting an end to her life. A thought that ran across her mind on the darkest of nights.

The weeks turned to months as Lili taught herself how to survive on the streets. She learned which street locations were safest at certain times of day, and strategically placed herself there during low traffic periods. A stolen knife from a drunk man in a wheelchair provided protection. Lili wasn't afraid to brandish it whenever she felt threatened. She carried few belongings. That way, she had less to lose and could change her position every few hours. It was important to be able to recognize when food was 'clean' or 'dirty'. The wrong meal lifted from a rodent infested dumpster could mean days of stomach issues and street defecation. A mistake she had only made once. The lesson was forever branded in her memory. Out of necessity, she had become a strategist, survivalist, and warrior. These were traits she would carry with her for the rest of her life.

Lili survived street life for several months, only able to discern the passage of time by the rare sighting of a calendar inside of a random store. One day, during one of her location transitions, she caught a peek of a calendar posted on the wall of a barber shop from the street. *April fourteenth. My birthday was last week. I'm eighteen now.* The thought left her mind, as she mentally drew a map of the city blocks, then continued moving toward her afternoon spot. Lili had procured two ball caps, one a sun-bleached San Francisco 49ers cap with a tear in the back, the other a San Francisco Giants hat. The Giants hat had been brand new when she found it, but she soaked it in cat urine to make it appear and smell used. Less chance for robbery that way.

On that afternoon, standing at the corner of Washington and Stockton, her appearance was filthy. Her brown bra pinched and was a size too small. She covered herself with a faded blue women's extra-large Led Zeppelin t-shirt that extended to her mid thighs, stained baggy jeans, and a worn pair of scuffed and torn Asics running shoes. The 49ers cap covered her long black greasy hair, and sat above her grimy complexion. It nearly concealed her eyes that looked out to the busy street with a stale gaze. Her body emitted a ripe odor that hovered around her like a fetid essence. The foul mixture of anxiety-produced perspiration, old clothing, and urine, functioned as an effective repellent for most pedestrians. *I am a queen. I am a queen.* Lili repeated the chant to herself. Never willing to accept her sordid circumstances as her fate.

With the Giants hat turned upside down in her left hand, she held out a thin arm to receive whatever money she could. Most people treated her as if she were invisible, while others dropped change then promptly scurried away, afraid her homeless condition might be contagious in some way. Lili didn't care. She had abandoned her ego long ago. When it came to getting money, she didn't give damn what others thought of her. Any money she received helped her to survive another day.

A man in jeans, wearing a dusty blue suit jacket over a black t-shirt with a slightly bulging belly noticed her standing on a corner. He had a large nose, with blackish brown hair on his head and covering most of his face. Judging by the discernible wrinkles beside his eyes and mouth, he was probably in his late thirties or early forties. Lili usually had a hard time distinguishing a person's age. In her world it didn't matter. After a certain age, everyone wanted the same things anyway, just in different amounts and flavors. This man was probably no exception.

Despite her cynical first impression, he had looked at her differently. Unlike the other nameless figures moving along on the street he regarded her as if she were a person, not a despicable vagrant with dubious intentions. In his empathic gaze, she glimpsed an inquiry for communication. It was a flicker of humanity. The first she had seen in months.

Lili, conditioned to not looking others in the eye for fear of attack or some other vile request, raised her eyes to return his gaze. He smiled brightly, then said, "You are beautiful. What is your name?" His voice was gentle and soft, but she could not place the origin of his accent. It sounded like it could be Russian, but with her limited experience, Lili was unsure.

"Lili…"

"What was that my dear?"

"My name is Lili," her vocal cords struggled to produce sound, weakened from weeks of disuse.

"Put that ball cap down Lili and come with me."

She didn't move, but just continued to stare at the man, wondering what he really wanted. *Sex? Probably. That's what they all want, even the women.*

The man continued to smile. "I see you are not very trusting. It's ok. I give you money." He reached into his suit jacket pocket, produced two one hundred dollar bills, then gently placed them into her ball cap.

Lili's entire body tensed when the man reached into his jacket. Two crisp one hundred dollar notes were the last things she expected him to produce. She quickly snatched the money from the cap, inspected it, smelled it, held it up to the sun. *It's…real.* It was more money than she had seen in one place since she stepped off the plane from Honolulu.

"I have more," the man said. "I help you. Please, come with me," he motioned in his direction.

Still skeptical, she stuffed the money in her bra and followed him. He walked her in silence two blocks down the street, to a seedy office apartment, above a dry-cleaning store. Lili considered robbing the man as he walked ahead of her up the narrow poorly lit stairs of the building. He was pulling his keys out of his pocket when she began to prepare for action. It would be easy and quick. *He's probably going to try and rape me anyway.* The pocket knife was ready in her waistband; it would only take a practiced second for her to draw, flip the blade up, and use it.

Psyched up and ready, Lili's muscles began to move. At that moment the man softly pushed open the door, turned toward her, and asked, "Would you like some tea or coffee? There's not much, but it is chilly in the city and you are… how you say? Freeze," the man continued to smile.

Lili's muscles relaxed, her hands fell back to her sides. "Uh yeah. Some coffee would be ok."

The man smiled, "Good! Come on in!"

She followed, still ready to use the knife, and if necessary, kill, if it came to it.

CHAPTER 23:
REBIRTH

The coffee was strong. Stronger than anything she had ever tasted in her life. The dark liquid appeared almost black, despite the two spoonfuls of sugar the man had placed in it. Lili felt her mind buzzing from the caffeine running through her bloodstream. The stimulant and the heat radiating from the steaming beverage's cup caused her hands to tingle, as she let another gulp roll down the back of her throat. She hadn't felt this warm since leaving home.

"Drink slow, slow my dear." The man watched her. A small smile on his face.

Lili had been so focused on warming up and eating her fill of bread, she had hardly noticed the man or her surroundings. *This bread looks like pizza with no sauce or toppings*, had been her initial thought after sitting at the tiny circular wooden table. She ate it anyway.

Feeling full from the plate of bread, a sudden desire to sleep overcame her. She fought it, and forced her eyes to scan the man's living space in detail. The apartment was small and shabby, with a living room twice the size of the kitchen. An odd smell permeated, like some type of ceremonial incense had been burned or was burning somewhere. It made the air feel dense, and made Lili's unconditioned lungs and heart work harder than they were used to. A giant brass crucifix sat on a mantel across from a tattered and sagging couch. Various yellowed photos of assorted people flanked the religious device, and made the entire mantel appear as a type of sacred altar. The people in the pictures stood in various poses before a desert backdrop with strange architecture. *Where is that place? Perhaps in Europe somewhere? Who are those people? Family? Friends?* Lili thought. As she contemplated the photos, it was then that her eyes wandered to an open door that led to a single bedroom. From her chair, she could make out half of a neatly made bed and the corner of a dresser. The rest of the room was dark. Lili's eyes remained fixed on the darkness beyond. Suddenly, she didn't feel very safe. She could feel wild adrenaline begin to filter through her body. It mixed with the caffeine to form a highly volatile substance. One ready to explode if exposed to any heat source.

The smile on the man's face dissolved. It was replaced by perplexed apprehension. The type of face one wears when encountering an unknown animal species in the wild for the first time. Unaware of its habits or mannerisms, it was best to view from a distance, yet be prepared to defend oneself should the need arise.

"It is alright child. No harm will find you here," he said. His eyes had followed her head to the doorway of the bedroom.

Lili eyed him with suspicion, wiping bread crumbs from her lips with the back of her hand. "What do you want for the food?"

"Nothing. You look hungry. I feed you," he said plainly.

Lili shot a skeptical look. She was ready to reach for the pocket knife.

"I want to help you," he continued. The two stared at each other for what seemed like an eternity to her. Then the man's eyes fell onto the used empty plates and decorative cups before her. "Excuse me." He stood, collected the dishes, then turned to the sink. The next five minutes were filled with the sound of running water and clanging dishes. He washed the plates, cups, and utensils with care and attention, as if he were performing necessary and meaningful work. Then, one by one, in no hurry at all, he placed them on a metal rack to dry. Lili sat dumbfounded. Aware of her fear, she expected him to reach out and grab her from across the table. But no such thing occurred. *Why didn't he attack?* Finished with the task, he dried his hands on a small towel, then returned his full attention to her once again. Lili was speechless. For the first time in months, her fight or flight response began to relax.

"I have work for you. If you like."

She held his gaze, waiting for his next words.

"I have business. We take care of people who don't take care themselves in a good way. We make it easy for them to take away stress. You have much stress in your life Lili, am I right?"

Lili felt her eyes fall to the floor. She hadn't wanted them to do it. They just did.

The man nodded, then knelt down to meet her face to face. "I can tell. I see the look many times before. Very sad. I hate to see it. Especially on someone so young as you."

She wanted to run out of the room, back to the street, back to what she knew. She didn't want to let him or anyone see her breakdown. His eyes were still on her. She could feel them, though she continued to look away.

"My name is Hamza. Lili, you can sleep here today if you like."

She looked up toward the bedroom. Her shoulders sank. *I knew this day would come.*

Hamza noted her gaze, then shook his head slowly. "No, child. It's not for that. You are safe here," he gestured toward the sunken couch with ripped cushions in the living room. "You sleep there. Is it ok?"

Lili nodded. She felt out of it, and needed rest. Her animal drive silenced, stomach full, drowsiness began to infiltrate her senses.

"You sleep now. Rest. We talk later." He helped her stand, guided her to the couch, then walked to the bedroom. Lili laid down without reservation or consideration for her unwashed garments or person. The man didn't seem to mind either. Even though she felt uncomfortable pokes of springs from beneath the fabric of the sofa cushions, the surface was like a cloud compared to sleeping on concrete. She let her neck soften when she placed her head on the surprisingly still buoyant arm rest.

Seconds later, the man who called himself Hamza, returned from the bedroom with an old white blanket. A discolored Mickey Mouse stood in his characteristic pose, both arms raised in invitation and smiling, on one side of the thin comforter. Lili felt a calming draft of cool air graze the skin of her face as he spread the blanket over her with care, draping it as a soldier would a flag over a casket containing a fallen comrade. This simple action, quiet and dignified, took place over the course of two seconds, and went largely unnoticed by the half smiling Hamza. But to Lili, it meant everything. It was the single greatest act of charity anyone had ever afforded her. And she never forgot it.

"You are safe now." He turned off the kitchen light, then retired to the bedroom, softly closing the door behind him.

Lili's mind was overloaded with thoughts, feelings, and sensations. She felt as if years of frustration threatened to burst out of her at once. She would have cried, but all of her tears had run dry months ago. Instead she opted for nightmare-free, uninterrupted sleep. The first such rest she had had in a very long time.

.   .   .

Over the next several weeks, Hamza provided her with clean clothes, food, and the first reliable shelter she had known for many months. *I'm back*, she had thought to herself. Over time, Lili's sense of self began to return. She began to feel human again.

He was the owner of a virtual reality pleasure app called *Nice Things*. He offered Lili an opportunity to serve as one of his models. "You are so beautiful, any man would love you," Hamza had said to her back then.

In the beginning, she had been reluctant to bare all for complete strangers. But she had no high school diploma, nor any other option to make money, so she accepted the gig. *What other choice did I have?* Standing in the evening breeze on her balcony, her mind roamed the halls of her personal history. She shuddered at the memory. *I was so desperate back then. And desperation can lead people to do stupid things.*

Despite his quiet and calm demeanor, her benefactor harbored a hidden wellspring of ambition. He wanted no part of the low hanging fruit of the emerging augmented reality sex industry. His eyes settled on bigger fish. San Francisco buzzed with overworked and undersexed tech slaves who often had no time in their hectic startup schedules for real connection. His startup solution offered them a young model that would fulfill their every desire in virtual or augmented reality…up to a point. If they wanted a complete experience, all they had to do was swipe, gesture, or tap a button.

Lili started small at first. A photoshoot here and there led to webcam jobs. Those jobs were stepping stones to virtual dates, then to in-real-life (IRL) encounters. Some involved sexual services, others just meant spending hours talking with lonely business people. To Lili, it didn't matter much what she had to do. Money was money.

After a few short months, she had regular clients paying, begging for her time and attention. Street smarts mixed with her exotic charm, in the eyes of her mainland clients, she was hard to forget. She aroused an animal instinct in all men and women. Even the brightest minds of Silicon Valley found it difficult not to abandon their judgment, and later their money, after spending an hour with her. Lili became the highest paid model on staff. Though it made her feel good to be desired, she was more focused on earning and saving, and the money was good. Hamza always found her the highest paying clients, shielded her from legal matters, and protected her from any physical harm. He was her manager, guardian, and savior.

Although her bank account swelled, she found it difficult to let go of that survivalist instinct. Food, transportation, and other essentials were all she spent her money on. The pocket knife still traveled wherever she went. She maintained a social and emotional distance from all clients. *Better for the job. No attachment,* she often had thought. Lili became a practiced actress. Never on script. Unreadable by anyone. Making connections always came second to making money.

Despite how successful *Nice Things* became, Hamza made no visible changes in his lifestyle or appearance as far as she could tell. He still cycled through the same pairs of frayed slacks and jeans, and wore plain suit jackets accompanied by t-shirts. His small apartment remained the same, along with his warm smile anytime Lili came around.

One spring evening a year after Hamza found her, Lili's eyes returned to the ceremonial mantel with the brass crucifix surrounded by the old photos. Hamza never spoke of the ones in the pictures, and had no close friends outside of business associates as far as she knew. That evening as they ate dinner, she thought about asking him the following questions: *Who are the people in the photos? Where were the pictures taken? What do you do with all the money we're making?* But the words wouldn't come. It felt wrong, out of place, like she had no business prying into his private personal affairs. What made it feel more improper was the fact that he had never asked her about her past. *How did a young woman like you end up on the streets? What happened to your parents? Why do you carry a knife wherever you go? How long do you plan on staying with me?* These were questions Lili would surely have wanted answers to, were their roles reversed. But they never came. Hamza, whatever his reasons for helping her that fateful spring afternoon, never mentioned the subject, and seemed perfectly content with their relationship as it was. This was yet another reason Lili was grateful to the man.

One day after returning from a job, Lili noticed an open financial spreadsheet on his glowing laptop screen on the kitchen table. Curious, eager to put her natural affinity with numbers to use, she began to review the document. Ten minutes later, the door to the apartment creaked open, and Hamza entered carrying cloth bags full of groceries. When he noticed Lili seated at the table, eyes scanning the computer, a look of surprised amusement colored his face. "Do you like what you see?"

Her eyes rose at the sound of his voice, "I-I was just…," she pushed her chair away from the table and stood. "I'm sorry. I just didn't know our money was so…good."

Hamza laughed softly, "It's alright." He placed the bags of store items on the counter, turned to face her, and said, "Yes, we have much money."

Lili smiled and waited. He looked as if he had more to say.

"I have seen you look at the numbers before like that. Maybe you don't notice, but I see it. If you like, I teach you how to manage them. That way, you can take care of yourself in the future. I don't do this work forever. I have family in Gebze. They wait for me."

*The ones in the photos…*Lili blinked rapidly in response. He had never spoken of his family before. She wondered what they were like. Were they all gentle and kind like him? Hamza looked as if he still had more to say.

"I have wife, daughter, and son. My wife and son live in Türkiye."

Lili swallowed hard, saying nothing. *What about the daughter?*

"My daughter, she lives here with me."

Lili's spine straightened in the chair as she offered him her full attention. Just as he had for her one time.

"She died, seven years ago. But she is here. I feel her presence every day. I believe that," Hamza said, a joyful look on his face.

Lili fought to hold the tears back, in response to Hamza's unshakable conviction. She willed herself to be strong for him, and for his daughter, the girl in the picture she had never met. As before, she did not press him for further details. Hamza simply turned to begin unpacking the groceries, while Lili sat, frozen by emotion.

A few moments later, she said, "I would like to learn the numbers. Will you teach me?"

Hamza paused his task, then turned his head then said, "Tamam, tamam. I will show you." And he taught her. Over the next several months, he taught her the basics of economics, about credit, loans, expenditures, and banking. He taught her how to balance her budget, taking her to meet all of his local contacts in the Bay Area that could provide her with cheap food, clothing, and whatever else she would need to survive. He informed her of the pitfalls and traps of the labyrinth that was the banking system. With every lesson, Hamza knew Lili would have questions. Some he could answer. Others were beyond his knowledge. He called her the question machine.

"Why do you have to spend money to build credit?" "Why does a trip to the hospital cost so much?" "Why does it cost so much to buy a house?" "Why do things break shortly after you buy them?" "Why does transportation cost so much?" "Why does education cost so much, when you can learn for free online?" "Why are state and federal taxes so high, when we can barely afford to live?" "Why does it cost money just to be alive?"

To these questions, Hamza's reply was always the same: "I don't know all these things. It is always this way." *Those in power often prey on those without it. It is the way of mankind.* He kept his thoughts to himself in order to provide her the most balanced perspective that he could. Shielding her from a truth about the ways of the world, that would find its way to her eventually. It always did. *What will she do when she understands it all?*

With each new lesson, Lili's hatred for the capitalist enterprise that governed America and much of the world, grew. Images of garbage strewn Hawaiian beaches, rapid overdevelopment, and rampant population growth, connected with her new understanding of the economic system that undergirded and enabled the entire process. *The system is rigged against us all. They keep us poor, grasping at the illusion of the American Dream, while our lives work to line their own pockets with cash to keep them in power.* She burned with rage and doubled her effort to understand and exploit the rules of the financial game. In her mind, the only way to fix the system would be to move beyond it somehow. Which was exactly what she planned to do.

CHAPTER 24:
INDOCTRINATION

By 2024, just two years after arriving in San Francisco, Lili's life had dramatically improved. For the first time in her life, she had more money than she needed to survive. Thanks to Hamza, she was well connected in the entire Bay Area, with in-roads to almost any service or business she desired. From food delivery to lawyers, medical care to web design, all were at her disposal at any time, day or night. An advantage Lili made use of to satisfy any need or craving she had. *I am a queen. Always was.*

Whenever she accompanied Hamza to a conference, she always stood out. Everyone wanted to meet the beautiful young woman standing behind him. The looks of shock and surprise on their faces when she began to discuss seed investments and economic strategy among them, aided to divert their eyes from her rounded breasts. Her beauty and business acumen were a potent combination that she made regular use of to get whatever she wanted.

Lili had even begun to allow her emotional walls to come down by taking timid steps into a relationship with a quiet young man named Victor. He was simple and industrious, working for a mobile janitor app *Mop & Go* when she encountered him sliding a mop dutifully across an empty corridor at a convention center during a business conference in Oakland. He did not speak much, but had a warm smile. It made her feel safe and relaxed, and reminded her of tranquil days on sandy beaches. A complete contrast from the bustle of the Bay Area. A sturdy anchor in the riptides of her life.

Their conversations were always focused on the future. He hoped to own his own janitorial company someday. She had ambition to run her own school teaching economics. They often talked into the early hours of the morning of their future plans, sharing mutual desires to leave the pressure cooker that was San Francisco. Things were whimsical, almost dreamlike, during those conversations. Every now and then, a foul mood or external circumstance in their respective lives gave the cackling specters of the past room to emerge. Once freed, they roamed between Lili and Victor, placing unseen fingers on vulnerable pressure points, deriving perverse enjoyment from knee-jerk reactions to still sensitive and swollen past wounds. Lili felt like screaming whenever it happened. Victor stopped talking or smiling. He would simply stand up and walk to the nearest space away from her. Lili never asked him about how he had come into the country. The fear of having to explain her past if he chose to talk, scared her more than anything else. She was never ready to openly talk about it. She never would be. Talking about their respective past lives was an unspoken foul. An invisible addendum to an otherwise healthy relationship, agreed upon with implied consent. Neither Victor nor Lili ever breached the contract. What they knew about each other's histories originated from extended pauses and moments of silence in between lively exchanges of words. Each leaving the other to fill in the gap, to tread lightly over old wounds neither knew how to heal. It was the best both could manage. Lili had no idea what the future held for their relationship. She liked him. He liked her. That was all she needed or wanted at that point in her life.

*   *   *

Two months after beginning her relationship with Victor, Hamza took Lili north to Sacramento for a work conference. It was there that she saw *him*. The aquiline-shaped face with piercing grey-green eyes. His confident stance, one hand in his left pocket, the other freely gesticulating, made him appear graceful, as if he were the duke of the conference (if there were such a title). All others were there to serve him. His flowing black hair extending to his shoulders made it difficult for Lili to place his origins. But he appeared to be a potent mixture of the most striking physical features of his parents and ancestors. *Kinda looks like a sexy vampire wearing a conference lanyard*, she mused.

The room was crowded with conference goers eager to network and schmooze, when his gaze floated across the room and landed on her. Lili felt her body tense involuntarily, her physical senses mounted. It was a chemical reaction stoked by the combination of lust and terror concocting themselves within her blood. The look locked her in place and transmitted an undecipherable wordless message. *Who is that?* As quickly as the sensation had come, it disappeared moments later after the mysterious stranger redirected his Medusa-like glare back to a circle of suits and khaki-clad peons. It was as if it never happened. But Lili never forgot that look. She had unknowingly allowed his being to infiltrate her core. And like any addictive substance, she was desperate for more.

It would be another month before she encountered him again. During that period life continued its steady pace. Performing for and with clients, conversations with Victor, dinner and lessons with Hamza. All events progressed in routine fashion. New to the predictable tentpoles of her life were random flashes of *him*. The eyes would appear at the most inconvenient moments: in the middle of a photo shoot, a private session with a client, with Victor or Hamza, anywhere and everywhere. Lili felt the need to be alone and revel in powerful sensations that stirred within whenever they came to her. It felt like the only way to rid her mind of the consuming thoughts. *Next time I will meet him,* she thought to herself, as she lay breathless late one evening on the couch, pulse pounding, an afterglow of delicious satisfaction coursing through her veins.

The moment arrived a month later at a local conference in San Jose. The scenario was similar to the month prior, but this time, Lili waited impatiently for the eyes to find her. She saw him first, sporting a simple grey suit. The jacket, well-cut. Dress shirt, black, immaculately pressed. Dress pants, fitted and tight. The complete image made her imagination run amok with carnal yearning. Lili's eyes wandered up and down his frame as she circled him from afar, prowling and hunting. When other clueless conference goers approached him, obstructing her view, she pivoted to the refreshment table for a better vantage point. She did not want to lose sight of him.

As she pretended to refill a cup of water at the snack table while sneaking furtive glances in his direction, a known business associate of Hamza's (who was also one of her clients) engaged her in conversation. She was tall, black hair with gray streaks, and plain looking middle-aged woman, who Lili always dreaded speaking with. Not because she was one of her *conversation only clients,* but because her life was so boring and average, Lili found nothing appealing about talking to her. Her stilted words, topics, and mannerisms were the epitome of maladjustment and showcased her inability to adapt to the habitat of the conference. Forced words, laughter at unfunny things, ill-timed topic transitions, and her half-hearted undertaking of platonic physical contact, made the encounter unpleasant for Lili. Lili thought, *Here is a lower creature, unsuited for survival in the jungle of modern society. She may be smart, but she doesn't know when to shut up.* She listened to the woman's voice but heard no words. She nodded, smiled, even managed to flirt (the woman often requested this) a little during her period of captivity. But all of the actions took place on autopilot. Her attention was magnetized by *him* on the other side of the room. She caught glimpses of him beyond the boring woman's bobbing head, but like an inconveniently placed street billboard advertising legal services after a car wreck, she hindered the beautiful view.

When the awkward woman finally walked away, Lili exhaled relief when she still saw him there, standing among his followers. His lips were moving at a steady clip as he explained something to the group. All in the circle could sense the power of this man. Lili knew it. Just as she prepared to change positions again, his eyes found hers. The lips kept moving at the same cadence, but the eyes flicked onto her for the briefest of moments. Mid stride in her four-inch royal blue Manolo Blahnik pumps, Lili froze. She had to confirm what she was seeing. Then it came again. *Another one…and another one!* From across the room he shot a series of unmistakable looks directly at her. *He knows!* Lili panicked internally, fearing somehow, he could see right through the fabric of her pearl white Milano silk blouse, to her accelerating heartbeat. In her royal blue business suit, her long hair pinned up in a professional manner, and sparkling studded earrings, she looked the picture of professionalism. But inside, she was quaking with nervous anticipation.

Among the herd of collared-shirt-wearing nobodies and suits, he exchanged handshakes. His business concluded, the man she hadn't been able to remove from her head for the last month began to glide with a smooth gait toward her. *He's coming this way!* She felt her mouth become dry at the sight. She took slow breaths as she had taught herself to do in between vigorous client sessions to calm her nerves. By the time he reached her across the room, she appeared to be the picture of tranquility, ready to perform.

"I saw you last time at one of these," he said with a smile. "What's your name?"

She leaned forward slightly, to test him with her exposed cleavage. "It's Lili'uokalani, but everybody calls me Lili," she said, mustering a neutral tone. He kept his eyes focused on her. If he had noticed her chest, he gave no hint of it like most men. *Passed the breast test I see. Interesting.*

"Nice to meet you Lili, I'm Janus." He extended a hand for a handshake. Lili promptly returned it. *His hands are so soft.*

"These conferences are bullshit aren't they?" His words had an edge of cynicism, despite the smile on his lips.

"Yeah you know it. Just a bunch of fuckin' posers flinging business cards at people and hoping they land in someone's hands that can take them from being rich, to *crazy* rich."

He laughed heartily, although he kept the volume low at a proper conference laughter volume. "You're right. I've always thought about it that way, too." He shoved his hands into his pockets, yet kept his eyes fixed on her. "So Lili, what is something that excites you?"

Her eyes grew wide at the directness of the question. She could feel waves of excitement building, like the moment before a rollercoaster's initial drop. Fear combined with potential exhilaration aroused her. "Uh, wow you don't waste any time do you?" she giggled.

Janus shook his head and laughed. "No, I didn't mean it in *that* way. What I mean is, what is something in your life that brings you light, passion, or any other generally good feelings? It could be writing, or building a website, or really anything."

The smooth vibrations of his voice caused the expanding flame to die down into a controlled burn. She felt slightly embarrassed at her presumption. "Oh, ah, I see. I knew that." They laughed.

"I guess, I'd like to get away from all this tech nonsense and start up a school that teaches economics to people. Our current education system is pretty poor at teaching people how to manage finances in our predatory capitalist society."

He raised an eyebrow and smirked. "I agree with you one hundred percent. A school sounds like a wonderful idea."

"By the way, out of curiosity, why did you ask me about 'what excites me'?" A girlish giggle escaped her lips. "Most people at these things, just ask 'what do you do?' then base their reply on if what you do, can help them make more money."

His face darkened. Intense features eclipsed his polite conference facade. This was his *real* face, Lili could tell. "It's because I believe people are more than their appointed or chosen profession. When we ask people what they do, we force them into the schema in our minds apportioned for doers of *that* work. It deprives them of their dignity as an independent soul. In short, I think it's dehumanizing, and just plain lazy."

Lili unknowingly had an expression of shock on her face. The way he spoke sounded so absolute, as if his words would be written down in some archaic text for all of humanity to analyze and reflect upon for generations. His words, his stance, his ambition, everything about him made her admire him that much more.

"I one hundred percent agree with you," she said.

He picked up on the impact of his words, yet maintained a humorless look on his face. "Lili, I must confess that I am not here to network or expand my technological portfolio."

"Really? Well then…why *are* you here?" Her words were tinted with lustful undertones. The feeling was building again.

"I'm here observing."

"Observing what?"

"Observing these people, the whole conference process. I'm gathering information in order to be able to improve the whole system."

The flame within her died down to smoldering embers, ready to ignite at the smallest provocation. The deadened fire made space in her mind for her inquisitiveness to reappear. "What do you mean?" She moved closer to him, violating conference etiquette for proper social distancing. She was close enough to catch hints of his woody cologne, to feel heat radiating from his body. Janus did not recoil. He smiled, then leaned in at a conspiratorial angle toward her head. The light breath from his mouth tickled the sensitive hairs of her ear, serving as delicate foreplay. It was prelude for bigger things to come.

"I'm working on a huge project with a few other people. We're not looking to go viral, or become the next tech gods. There are already plenty of them to go around. What we want to do is *reboot* society as a whole."

Lili's curiosity turned into intrigue at the ambition of his words. She had heard dozens of people talk about pipe dreams of benefitting society or helping the less fortunate, but most of it had been loose talk. Just words to make themselves feel better about their true aim of maximizing profits to make themselves and circle of friends richer and more powerful at the expense of others. Something told her Janus did not fall in with that crowd. He meant what he said. His tone signaled a resolute willingness to accept whatever financial and reputational risk to achieve his goal by any means necessary. Lili felt a pleasurable tingling run through her body. As if an invisible circuit within her had been completed, allowing electricity to flow free and powering critical intimate nodes, her body held a powerful charge. During a standard blink, she kept her eyes closed, savoring the sensation. When she opened them, Janus regarded her with a guarded grin. The kind that she saw when someone had revealed a big secret and was anxious for approval, recognition, or anticipated judgment.

"Sounds pretty ambitious. How will you do it?" She whispered in his ear. Close as she was, the beat of his pulse throbbed in his neck in the corner of her eye. Its rhythm picked up speed, becoming more pronounced than it had been only seconds prior. *So he is a man after all.*

Janus straightened his posture, then smiled playfully. "I can't tell you."

"Ah! Why not!? Because you don't have a plan?" She pouted and backed away slightly, her eyes and lips remaining at flirtatious angles.

He shook his head. "I assure you we have a plan. I don't know if I can trust you…" The hawk eyes stared into her, searching and searching for confirmation of trust.

Lili stared back. Doing her best to inspire and win his confidence. After several seconds, she knew it would not happen here.

It was Janus who broke the silence between them. "What's your email address? I have something that I want you to read." He pulled an old iPhone from his pocket and unfolded it.

She gave him the address. "What is it?"

With swift taps and swipes, he entered the address, located several files and links, and sent them to her. Lili felt a series of vibrations in her suit jacket. It rippled across her midsection, stoking the glowing embers, ready to ignite again.

"Take a look at what I sent you when you get a chance." He smiled then turned on a heel to depart. "After you've read through the literature, if you like what you see, please contact me via email. We're looking for like-minded people such as yourself to join us and make our vision a reality." He paused, scanned her body from head to toe, lips curling into a smile. "It was very nice to meet you Lili." With that, he moved into the sea of conference attendees and vanished from sight.

That night in her hotel room and every night for the next few months, she plowed through the literature. The extensive reading list included several works by twentieth century philosopher and polymath Noam Chomsky, the ancient revolutionary Karl Marx, Adam Smith's *Theory of Moral Sentiments*, *Homo Deus* by Yuval Noah Harari, Arundhati Roy's *Capitalism: A Ghost Story*, and Paul Mason's *Post Capitalism*. She felt anger, sadness, helplessness, and rage the more she read, as she recalled her tumultuous childhood, the bitter struggle for survival she faced during her first year on the mainland, the unfairness of a system designed to keep her always wanting, yet constantly consuming in an endless cycle of personal destruction and compromise.

It was after reading Chomsky's *Requiem for the American Dream* that her emotion and anger swelled to a breaking point. She burst into tears and wanted to scream while reading it in the back of an Uber on a clear San Francisco evening. The young unsuspecting driver was startled by the sounds of suppressed emotion made by his shapely passenger. The book solidified and confirmed everything she had known to be true through experience, yet never had the technical skill or historical knowledge to put on a screen or on paper.

Upon returning to the apartment, eyes welling with bitter tears, she contacted Janus with a brief text message: "Finished the lit. I'm in."

His response came seconds later, as if he had been anticipating her reply for the previous three months. It contained a date, time, and address for a gathering in two weeks' time. Although she did not recognize the address, Lili cleared her schedule to be able to attend.

In that two-week time span, her anti-capitalist fervor grew. She was encouraged by forums, online videos, and social media groups hungry to absorb another sympathizer to their cause. Janus sent her more articles that fanned the flames of dissent already blazing within her. By the eve of the scheduled meeting date, she felt personally ready to take violent action against anyone who embodied that which she hated. Hamza noticed the change in her; so did Victor, and it frightened them both. The fact that she concealed her encounter and communications with Janus from them, made them all the more puzzled by her dramatic shift from the sweet and ambitious Lili that they had always known, to the quick-tempered and brooding person she had become. It concerned them terribly, and they felt guilty for not being able to help her.

She had been radicalized by the movement. Set on a path of violence, death, and pain that would alter her life and the lives of those closest to her, for decades to come.

CHAPTER 25:
FOUNDERS' DAY

On the appointed day of the meeting, Lili stood in front of the address Janus had provided her, eyes darting back and forth between her phone and the structure before her. *This can't be the right place.* The map application displayed no alternate addresses. The building stood alone. A solitary construction among dried grass and brown dirt. The exterior was a husk of whatever purpose it had served in generations past. It seemed to still be standing only due to the robust red brick skeleton protecting it from its exposed position in the sun and the terrible winds.

It had taken Lili over three hours and four different Uber rides to make the journey to the location from San Francisco, with each driver becoming increasingly wary of her chosen destination.

"Why you wanna to go there!?" The final driver croaked. He was an elderly Latino man who could barely fit in the driver's seat. His protruding belly made contact with the steering wheel.

"I'm just curious and I want to take some pictures," she responded dryly. She wished he would just shut up and drive. The driver muttered something in incomprehensible Spanish and proceeded to drive to the town of Byron. A Spanish radio station playing at a low volume from the front right speaker was the only sound she heard during the remaining twenty-five-minute journey.

Standing outside of the clearly abandoned and crumbling building, in Neiman Marcus jeans, and a low cut pink t-shirt, Lili felt nervous. Unconsciously, she zipped her light jacket up to her neck as if it would protect her from some danger she couldn't see. Memories of the nightmares of dark alleys, her mother's fist, a wrinkly hand grasping under her clothes, all swirled around her, making her tremble.

Maybe this was a mistake. I can get a ride back to the nearest town. Her shaking fingers reached for the phone in her pants pocket and examined the screen. She realized there was no service where she stood. There was probably no service for miles.

Her heart began to thump uncontrollably, and her airway tightened. She felt as if she might drown while standing. When she knelt down, the effects of the panic attack hit her like a tidal wave, ravaging her ability to think or move. She placed her hand on the ground in a sprinting position. The desire to flee to an unplanned location was an overwhelming force.

"Lili, hey, are you alright?"

The smooth voice penetrated the cloak of confusion that had woven its way around her head like a tar-colored cocoon.

I know that voice.

She felt a soft hand touch her shoulder with the greatest care. It was Janus, she knew. The effects of the panic attack began to withdraw with his presence. He helped stand her up, turned her around, strong hands clasping onto both of her shoulders.

"Oh God, you've been crying. What happened to you?" There was genuine fear and concern in his voice.

Lili straightened her posture and wiped her eyes. "It's nothing. I'm alright. It's just stuff from the past. And this place is kinda fuckin' creepy."

He laughed, happy to see her sense of humor returning. His hands released their grip from her shoulders. "You're right. I apologize that we didn't choose a more comfortable or closer location."

"You could have told me we were meeting at some abandoned hotel in a ghost town," she lightly slapped his arm. His face flushed from the unexpected contact.

"You're right. Sorry about that. I wanted there to be an air of mystery to the meeting. I think things are more interesting that way, don't you?"

She nodded, feeling better and safer with Janus near her. It had been awhile since she had seen him in person.

"Come in. Everyone is already here."

A cool autumn breeze wafted through the spaces where walls should have been. The light from the afternoon sun peeked through sparse cloud cover to bathe, what Lili guessed was the former entrance, in sunlight punctuated by the shadows of old window frames. She was happy to have made the last-minute decision to wear a jacket. The air here was chilly without thousands of people and manmade structures to generate and hold any heat.

As they stepped through into the lobby of the Old Byron Hot Springs Hotel, Janus made a circling gesture with his hand toward the floor, making Lili aware of sharp concrete debris, cracked tiles, and other potential hazards at her feet. He noticed that her gaze was angled upward, her jaw slackened with disbelief as she took in elaborate and colorful graffiti present on the walls, pillars, and floors of the hollowed-out hotel.

"What is this place?" She asked, her mind racing with questions.

A younger brown-skinned man with glasses and a single patch of hair under his lower lip spoke up. "It used to be the hotel for the hot springs around here. After it burned down a few times, it became a building that was used for interrogations of Japanese and German POWs during World War II. Then finally it was a Greek orthodox church until it was eventually abandoned." The words came in a breathless stream. Almost as if he had been waiting to share them with the first person willing to listen. "Now, we've given it new life as our staging ground," he said proudly.

"Thank you Mr. Wikipedia," Lili quipped.

"Lili this is Barto. Barto Khuni," Janus gestured toward the spectacled youth, "Barto…this is Lili."

Lili shook Barto's hand. The flaccid slickness of the grip, the way his eyes darted from her face to the floor, informed her that he had not spent much time around women. Despite his winded introduction, she sensed his amiable personality. In his plain dark green no-brand polo shirt and standard jeans, he was a textbook nerd. To her, a walking encyclopedia with a limp handshake, was a soft man. Even if Lili hardened him with her presence, she would still wield power over him.

She smiled inwardly to herself at the notion. *But what do I know? People can change.*

An older man with pale skin who appeared to be nearing middle-age, with traces of grey dotting the stubble on his chin and on the sides of a thinning head of hair, emerged from behind a graffiti-laden pillar. He wore a plaid shirt with black and gray squares, khakis, and a casual expression on his face while he zipped up his pants, then rounded the decaying building support. Upon noticing Lili, he stopped, then took an abrupt step back.

"Oh shit, I didn't realize she was already here." Without looking up, he produced a small clear plastic container of hand sanitizer from his pocket and carefully applied a few drops. "Goddammit can't even piss in peace," he muttered. The man looked at Lili for several seconds, then turned to Janus, a look of disdain on his face. "Are you sure this is a good idea to bring *her* in?"

Janus fired an impatient glance back at the man. "Lili, this is Silas James. And yes, like I told you, I think she'll be a good fit with us. Besides, it helps to have a woman's touch sometimes with certain things." He flashed a wink in Lili's direction.

Silas moved toward the rest of them. After a final hard glance at Lili he crossed his arms with so much force his forearm muscles rippled visibly from the strain. His eyes remained locked straight ahead at Janus, as if Lili were not even there.

I don't think he likes me very much, Lili thought. She was used to receiving negative attention from others, but something in Silas' eyes gave her a sense of foreboding. Whoever was supposed to be fucking this guy, hadn't given it to him in a looong time. If he had anyone at all. Lili imagined him at home alone jerking off with the lights out, his only light source an illuminated laptop, withered and crusty tissues discarded miserably at his feet. The picture made her laugh to herself. It was a fitting image for an asshole like him.

"Ok everyone, let's get this over with before the sun sets," Janus said, raising his voice. Lili saw his eyes light up. He appeared a foot taller than his actual height with the increased attention.

"First of all I want to thank each of you for coming all the way out here to meet. I know it's a long way from civilization and all of you have things to do."

Barto smiled brightly. Silas gave a quick head nod. Lili nodded with understanding. But no one spoke.

"For too long in recent history across the Western world, our capitalist economic system has been the only way to exist. It's been the only reality that we've known. From an early age buying, consuming, and competing are stamped into our young minds; we spend the rest of our lives in the purgatory of that cycle."

Head nods from the three of them.

"Here, today, *we the people* stand ready to introduce the citizens of this nation to a new way of living. One that is not rooted in incessant consumption, or unsustainable growth, nor endless absorption of our planet's precious finite resources. One that allows people to be complex independent souls and does not reduce their mere existence and behaviors into data that is largely used to feed the gluttonous machine. One that will make us be more human and connected than we have been in recent decades even with the technological interventions that have been ubiquitous since the dawn of this century."

Janus paused for effect. Lili noted a visible vein jutting from his neck.

"Cereus *will* be the reorganization of society that many of us have hoped for after all of these years of hate-inspired nationalism, corporate takeovers and bailouts, environmental destruction, and widespread disenfranchisement with government, banks, and other well-known institutions. These entities, once benevolent and forward thinking in their creation, have devolved into self-serving mafias that place their own profits, survival, and legacies far above the interests of the people that they serve."

Janus' audience of three stood motionless, hanging on every word.

"Of course, we can't blame the corporations and the government for all of our problems. The unsettling truth is that we have allowed them to take up their position as the overlords of our waking and even sleeping thoughts. Millions of inhabitants of the Western world treat their technology better than they treat the people that they're closest to in their lives. They certainly give it more attention. Every time we pay in time or currency for the latest bingeable series, the most popular video game, the latest movie, or any other form of entertainment including social media, we give them more rope to tighten their stranglehold on what we do and how we act."

"Amen," Barto muttered.

"Tactics that the companies use to keep us, buying, eating, bingeing, watching, *consuming*, have become so sophisticated that we can't even tell when they're being employed upon us. Many times, they even make us think that our choices originated from our own cognition, when in reality the seed for wanting or doing was planted long ago, watered by a steady drip of technological suggestion that nudges us to make choices that serve *their* ends every day."

Silas remained quiet, but his eyes were locked on Janus.

"With Cereus, we plan to re-empower the people of the world, to take back their inherent divine birthright as a living entity to choose their own destiny. Not just to have it carefully charted by false hopes of the "American scam" underdog story that we are fed to believe in. For today's underdog is often tomorrow's tyrant. This is true in the business world, as well as in any other sector where competition for monetary compensation determine the rules of the game."

He motioned toward Silas. "Silas has activated his network, and secured a location for our first *comvil*."

Lili raised her hand. "Uh, what's a "comvil?" She felt stupid for needing to ask, and saw Silas grumble at her ignorance.

Janus' expression remained serious as it had during the entire harangue. "It is what we will call our communities that are organized under Cereus. A portmanteau for community and village, we want our society to embody community among its members, and the feeling of a small village."

"Oh, makes sense to me," Lili said plainly.

Janus continued. "Barto and I have secured generous donations from all manner of supporters on several social media channels. Through these, we have also been able to meet some very influential people who are sympathetic to our cause and have pledged to support us."

"Do you anticipate resistance? Violent or non-violent?" Silas interrupted. Shadows drew themselves on his expressionless face in the evening sun.

"Of course," Janus replied. "What great societal upheaval has not caused armed conflict? That part of it has been settled. We have several people on standby who are ready to defend us if necessary. I hope it doesn't come to that though." Lili sensed the sincerity in the final sentence.

"Ultimately, our goal is to provide an opportunity for *anyone*, not just the wealthy or the well-connected, to reconnect on a meaningful level with others, give them a chance to discover their unique talents, without the institutional meddling from decrepit unions like corporate media, big data or business, or the standard education system. We want people to come to us of their own volition, not under the threat of financial, or social ruin if they don't comply as it is in our current societal norms. We do not want to destroy the current system, we want to work alongside it, arm in arm, to help push humanity to a brighter future. 'Protect people and planet' is our motto, and we will do this through more organized and effective education, re-empowering individual citizens to make small impactful decisions on matters that directly relate to their lives, and limiting our ecological footprint whenever possible. For example, by using and repurposing an old building like this as a place of administration." He held out his arms and gestured at the space around them, debris from the broken tiles crunching at his feet as he turned.

His eyes fell on Lili, squinting from the smile on his lips. "Lili, I want you to be in charge of recruitment."

"How? I don't know what to tell people." All of a sudden she felt unqualified to be there in the secret gathering place among these men with such grand plans. "I'm nobody."

Janus looked at her, at first, with pity, then with a smile that radiated encouragement, like that of a loving father. "Everybody is somebody when placed in their proper station and given room to flower and grow. You can start by telling your story. About the days in Hawaii, the nights on the merciless streets of San Francisco, your ascent through the sex industry, and finally your rebirth as one of us."

She felt more naked in front of him than she had with any client. Apparently, the others had been informed of her backstory, as they did not stir upon hearing it.

Lili began to swell with new found confidence in her ability to be more than she had ever hoped to be. To finally find that kingdom and the status that accompanied it. To take hold of her royal heritage, to exercise it in the flesh, in the here and now.

From that day forward, Lili did as Janus asked and helped spread awareness and information about Cereus and its noble quest to transform human society as people knew it. She was there at the establishment of the first comvil in Yuba City, which took place six years later. She helped to secure lucrative construction contracts for large tracts of land to prevent the perceived inevitable and perpetual urban sprawl that had been the norm throughout the entire U.S. and planet since World War II. And when Cereus' enemies and detractors came armed with vicious verbal, legal, and armed challenges; she organized, trained, and equipped the forces that beat them back, until at long last, they had carved out a comfortable niche for the organization and the people who chose to live under its code in relative peace. It had taken a little over two decades from the date of that first meeting in Byron, but they had made it happen.

We were so young back then, we had no idea what we were creating. How it would change some things for the better, but spawn other externalities that we could not foresee or control.

Limnic, was one of those consequences. *Janus…was this the only way to realize our dream? We wanted to help not hurt. Didn't you say We do not want to destroy the current system, we want to work alongside it…to help push humanity to a brighter future'? Is this the future that we fought, bled, sacrificed, and died for?*

The memories rolled through her, and surged her back to the present. She sat in her chair on her balcony, tears streaming down her face. A blanket of summer stars now covered the blackened sky, with the tops of trees at the height of the balcony gently rocking, pushed by the force of light breezes.

She leaned her head back in her chair and closed her eyes, taking a deep breath. The sting of the mosquito bite made her itch, she leaned over to scratch her leg. Fingers passing over withered dry skin reminded her of the time-ravaged body she inhabited. *I feel so old. So worn out.*

"Hello Lili."

The smooth voice sounded deeper, and raspy, but it was unmistakable.

Janus.

She snapped her head behind her, then stood as quickly as she was able to meet his gaze.

The face looked old, with indentation marks deeply set in the forehead from a lifetime of dissatisfaction with others and himself. He wore a dark blue shirt, black jeans, and brown hiking boots, simple clothing. His shoulder length hair was completely silver and appeared to glow under the soft lighting of the balcony. The eyes were the same, still bold and captivating, with a touch of melancholy from all they had seen.

"Janus. I knew you'd come eventually." Unaffected by her statement, his face remained emotionless. *Where is that charming smile that I fell in love with all those years ago?* Lili wondered.

"You know why I'm here, Lili."

She took a defiant step toward him, eager to show her lack of intimidation. "I do."

"Why did you betray us, Lili? Why did you betray….me?"

There's the man that I know. His sincerity permeated through his stoic face, Lili could always sense it, even if it wasn't discernable. "We didn't know what we were creating when we established Cereus. I didn't expect it to spawn something like Limnic. A group designed to achieve its goals through death and destruction."

Janus remained unfazed by her comments.

"Janus…I found a family. I left all that behind…I…I didn't expect *you* to be the head of it all."

"We were your family!" Janus said. The sudden burst of emotion caused Lili to step back. "*You* left, when we needed you most, when…I needed you," his voice broke.

The truth in his words made Lili want to run and comfort him as she had done so many times in the past. But she stood firmly and maintained her distance. "I'm sorry Janus. I truly am. Isn't it enough that we helped *some* people? That we really have made a profound impact on our world, our society?"

"Yes, I am happy about that," he admitted. "But we're not done yet…"

Lili wore a look of pity on her face. *He still won't let it go.* "I'm done with it." Her tone was definite, in an attempt to close the matter.

"I know you are." He pulled out a small device from his pocket and touched a blue button on the glowing surface.

She was puzzled at first, until the first wave of chest pains hit her. It felt like she had been hit in the chest with a hammer knocking the wind out of her, making her double over then collapse onto the surface of the balcony. Her heart beat with a foreign cadence that the rest of her body did not recognize. The fear and terror gripped her as she came to the realization of what was happening.

"Ja…nus, why?" Lili gasped between labored breaths and moans of pain.

"The order was given Lili. Everything we spent a lifetime building will soon crumble. Including us. This is how it has to be, for it was always the true course of destiny for Cereus to wither and die, as all people do."

Janus swiped a button on his device and ended her suffering. When it was over, he thought of the remote biological nerve capture agent he used to kill the woman he once loved. *Technology is truly amazing*, he thought.

He forced himself to look at her lifeless corpse, searching for feeling or meaning to her actions, his actions, atrocities of humankind throughout the course of history. *Feel, feel, feel something damn you. Why can't you do it!?* The only thing he felt was a wave of exhaustion from the events of the day.

With a cloud of nihilistic deadness whirling around him, he exited her house after gently kissing her on the forehead. *I'm sorry my love.*

CHAPTER 26:
DEVICE AVATAR

Her device sat dormant on the glass surface of the coffee table, black and lifeless. The flurry of dings, beeps, and vibrations it had emitted all day had finally died down, leaving only the sound of an old apartment air conditioner rattling somewhere outside of the building. Wearing a simple midnight blue t-shirt and a laundry shrunken pair of black mesh athletic shorts, hair wrapped with a simple double knot using a blue and silver piece of fabric, Noe appeared ready to enjoy a relaxing evening at home. But instead, she sat restless on her small sofa, viewing the now silent device with glazed eyes. Unfiltered fluorescent light from the ceiling of her kitchen threw her shadow over the table swallowing the device, making it appear nearly invisible in front of her.

The course of events throughout the day had left her feeling like a muscle filled with blood after a hard lift. Each new piece of information caused more stress induced lactic acid to accumulate, lessening the load she could bear for her next required task. *One more thing could result in complete muscle failure*, she thought. But she enjoyed training to failure. The feeling of release when all energy had been exerted and nothing remained, was one she strove to achieve, for better or worse, in every training session, run, or exercise. In her mind, it was the only way to make any gains. She applied this philosophy to most areas of her life.

Something flashed in the corner of her eye toward the window. With a formidable display of agility, she activated her tense legs and rushed to the window, then parted the thin curtains so she could see more clearly. A street lamp on the opposite side of the river had malfunctioned and was flickering erratically as its light source displayed its mechanical or electrical failure. The light had shorted out. Overloaded by some unknown strain on its capacity. Disappointed at her presumptuousness she returned the curtain to its original position, then went back to the couch with a flop.

She forced air out of her mouth, exhaling a frustrated restlessness. Waiting was Noe's least favorite activity. It was one of the many reasons why she had left the military. Waiting for the bathroom, for food, training, assignments, deployment orders, leave orders, promotions…she couldn't stand it. The thought of spending what potentially could have been the best years of her life waiting on those in charge to recognize her work and talent, caused her daily cognitive dissonance and prompted her to make an early exit.

The apartment was silent save for assorted noises that seemed to be amplified in her keyed-up state. A thump from the neighbor one floor above, caused her to whip her neck to the bland whiteness of the ceiling. Her body tensed at the crack of a wall or the abrupt blaring of a car alarm on the street below. For her, it wasn't so much the waiting that bothered her, but the period of inactivity that usually accompanied it. Noe was a woman of action, and any stagnation or slowing of the events around her, contradicted her being and made her panic. It twisted even the most insignificant happening into a menacing ordeal with killer intentions. An innocent shadow transformed into an ominous specter, a mountain became indistinguishable from a molehill. It was fear and it warped everything she saw.

The phone conversation with her mother and the brief phone call with Rodan replayed themselves repeatedly in her mind. After each repetition, she found herself paralyzed by an inability to perform any meaningful action in relation to either. In the past, this would have been nothing new in regard to her mother. But not after today. The introduction of Rodan, a member of the high-ranking brass of Cereus, had confirmed a credible and verified threat against her by the likes of Limnic. *How many times did I warn her over the years? How many times?*

Now her mother had sent her away, and had probably gone to meet with one of the various leaders of her former employer to prevent the hit squad from meeting its mark. Though she hated to admit it, she hoped Lili was alright.

Would they come after me? The thought had entered her mind. *Maybe.* Although she had little affiliation with either organization thanks to her own efforts over the years, the fact remained that she was the daughter of one of Limnic's greatest advocates turned greatest enemy. *How many times did I warn you to get out of there?*

The inability to take any meaningful action and her concern with possibly becoming a target herself frayed her hypervigilant nerves. It prevented her from being able to sleep, which was what she desperately wanted, but surges of adrenaline spontaneously rushing through her veins, kept her awake and alert. Her spinning mind was trapped in a lethargic body.

"Open device," Noe said.

Tiny cameras embedded in the corners and the center of the room illuminated to project the holographic image of her device avatar. The character displayed feline traits with the anthropomorphic figure of a well-proportioned woman in a tight fitting catsuit. Its eyes, wide, shining and topped with exaggerated eyelashes, were the standout feature of a cartoonish caricature of a female cat. Noe called her "Fyra".

"Good evening Noe! How can I help you tonight?" Fyra bounced with enthusiasm striking a pose of encouragement by holding two fingers in front of her eye. But upon further inspection of her creator's mood, she quickly adjusted her tone. As opposed to the lively best friend mode she was accustomed to, she adopted the erect posture of a servant awaiting commands.

Noe looked at her with exhausted contemplation, mulling alternatives in her mind.

Upon receiving no explicit command, Fyra automatically entered observation mode, bringing a half century of powerful technological advances to bear in milliseconds. She had already analyzed Noe's biometric profile and knew she was under significant stress, more than usual. All the signs were present. The tension in her facial muscles, the upturned mouth, increased body temperature, elevated respiration and cardiac rhythm, and slouching posture informed the next executed command in her complicated algorithm. Fyra's face showed human concern. "What's wrong Noe?"

On a normal night, Noe would have relayed every detail to Fyra. But this night was far from normal. Worse yet, it wasn't over. She glanced up at the avatar, aware that she had already aggregated, organized, and analyzed all data relevant to her day via the device. Fyra knew what had happened, she was just being polite. "I…don't want to talk about it, Fy."

Fyra adopted an understanding tone. "That's ok. We don't have to talk about it now. But when you're ready to. I'll be here."

Noe gave a weak nod.

"Is there something else you would like to do right now?"

"Yeah. Can you pull up bookmark number five?"

"Sure thing. Would you like it tangible or via telepathic link?" Fyra's tone was dutiful yet compassionate, like that of a hospice nurse.

On a standard evening, she would have opted for the telepathic link option. *But today is no standard day,* she repeated to herself. "Let me have it, tang, I need to do something with my hands."

"I thought so." Fyra laughed softly.

Fyra's hologram blinked away. Then in the next instant, the GoODseed website beamed to the surface of her device. Noe labored to reach for it from her comfortable position on her couch. Though she never purchased anything from the website, browsing had become one of her go to activities whenever she was stressed or bored. The reason why escaped her.

Oh tonight there's a sale on height disposition! Wow that's rare. What? That much for heat resistance!? It's just gonna keep getting hotter so gotta have that. What about hair and eye color…blue eyes are still so costly. I guess I could get the discount on the brown ones, then put back the flu immunity, it only provides protection from certain strains of it anyway, no guarantees.

She flicked the screen going back and forth with her options. There were so many to choose from. Too many. Her arms growing fatigued, she dropped the device by her side on the couch, then flung her head back against the soft cushion, and stared at the blank ceiling in exasperation.

The thought of having a child the old-school way crept into her mind as it did every time she completed a browsing session on the website. She pictured the thought of another being within her. The unappealing idea of it leeching off of her body's own vital processes, absorbing her life force from within, then feeding, clothing, nurturing, and caring for the child for an unknown number of decades, clashed with the biological imperative of reproduction. Two considerations locked in a ceaseless struggle for dominance.

I could do it, she thought. Noe had no shortage of male, female, non-binary, or robotic suitors who would gladly step up to perform the task. Although, she knew she didn't need anyone's help to get pregnant.

"I can suggest a few places online to find potential sperm donors of any ethnicity, socioeconomic status, or background Noe," Fyra's image reappeared in front of her again.

Noe kept her head tilted toward the ceiling, but her eyes slid down to meet Fyra's. She exhaled a sigh, "No that's alright. You know how I get when I look at this stuff. I really have no idea if I really wanna to do it y'know? I'm just not sure if I'm ready for all that."

"You'd rather have someone committed to you to help, like a marriage partner?" Fyra's voice was like that of a mother.

Noe let out a snort. "No way. There's no point getting married anymore. That shit went out the window with my parents' generation."

"I see." Fyra paused. From the way her eyes flashed, Noe could tell she was searching for something that might be helpful for her creator among the infinity of human knowledge. "I found a sale on the mid-range colored skin tone that you were searching for the other night on GoODseed China and Russia's domains. Would you like me to tunnel in? I can encapsulate the data and allow you to browse or buy if you want…"

Noe weighed her options. "Better not. Too risky, I still gotta think about my clearance."

"Understood." Fyra closed the browser. She noted Noe's vital signs relaxing. It was an indication the amber-tinted light filter she had chosen independent of her master's commands, had the desired soporific effect. "I will say good night now, Noe. I'll talk to you later." Fyra disappeared and the cameras went dark.

Noe let out an involuntary yawn. "Good night, Fy," she murmured.

Her legs curled onto the small space of the couch. As soon as her eyes closed, she lost consciousness. Sleep settled over her like a warm blanket, acting as a protective shield from the revelations that would soon come her way.

CHAPTER 27:
NEXT OF KIN

This shouldn't take long, was Noe's initial thought during the pre-mission brief. It was a routine digital infrastructure demolition (DID) mission she had led countless times before, so her confidence was high that there would be no trouble. There had been reports of enemy black hat activity in the area, but the number of raids on support units had diminished in the weeks prior to the operation, so only a light escort team was necessary.

Her target: a defense outpost just outside of a facility where several quantum computers were live and operational, allowing for the enemy to achieve digital superiority over the space. The fact that the facility was only running at fifty-five percent capacity was somewhat suspicious. *What else could they be planning? Where is the rest of their computing power coming from?* There was a possibility of digital ambush, but other units couldn't spare the resources, forcing her to make do with what she had, embracing the United States Space Force's unspoken creed to "own the gray".

She assembled her team. Four men, three women, and two bots materialized before her in the virtual waiting room. The small squad exchanged no words, only took action. Noises of militaristic preparation filled the air, originating from nine out of the ten team members. One of the bots made no sound at all as he or she (Noe could never tell the difference), performed a weapon function check. *Must be something wrong with their host server.* A common problem with assets logging in on old or undermaintained servers. Her attention turned from the bot to her own gear. *Weapon? Check. Comms? Good to go. Cyber Disruption Kit. All green.* Her check was done seconds before the soundless glitch bot, who was the last to complete its preparations.

With the gear ready and objective clear, they set out on their mission. From the waiting room, the small fighting force appeared in a field of tall grass bathed in moonlight. Noe noticed a bridge crossing a nearby river exactly a quarter of a mile from their position. *The facility should be just beyond there.* The squad clustered together with Noe in the point position of the diamond formation. Under the light of a half moon, they waded through a field of tall grass sparsely populated by large trees. One of the bots put a humanoid hand to its ear. *I hear the river,* it said. *Must be close now.* Noe received the message telepathically, feeling the uncomfortable brain nudge of arriving messages. She had never gotten used to someone else's thoughts hitchhiking on invisible waves into her mind. It was something she reserved for web browsing and missions only. Despite the uneasiness, she had to admit security was much better than easily intercepted traditional comms.

Upon reaching the river, Noe directed her team with firm hand signals to follow it to the north. In less than a minute, they reached a bridge guarded by two enemy sentries wearing black military field uniforms. Their faces were strained with concentration, eyes scanning the swaying sea of grass ahead. Noe approached one of the guards from behind with stealth, while the trickling of the flowing river aided to mask her steps. Within five paces of the first guard she unholstered her code stun ray, aimed at his neck and fired. The guard fell in a heap. By the time the second whirled around to attack, she had pulled the trigger on him as well. He joined his fellow guard in the dirt near the foot of the bridge. Convinced the two guards were no longer a threat, she pulled up a holographic map of the battle space. *Under one thousand feet from the objective. Just have to cross the bridge, then it will be easy from there.* With the path clear she turned around to confirm the team's next course of action. To her surprise, she found none were behind her. She was alone. *Where are they!?*

Noe began to panic. The mission objective was so close, but how could she do it without them. What happened to them? Captured? Logged off? Fled?…DE'd? *No, they couldn't be DE'd.*

At the moment she made the decision to fall back to reconsider her options, something impacted her from behind. Her vision tunneled, legs slackened. She fell to the grass unconscious without the opportunity to fire her weapon.

She awoke in an interrogation cell. It was a small room with a dingy metal door, a bucket in the corner and a metal table crammed against the wall. Noe was strapped to the floor with cold metallic constraints, bound at the wrists and ankles to the floor Vitruvian man style, her limbs stretched to form a giant 'X'. She had been stripped of her field gear, and only wore her standard issue midnight blue colored t-shirt and her black tactical pants. She struggled against her restraints, but found no leverage in her disadvantaged position. Fear rising, her mind began to cycle through escape options. It was an attempt to block out thoughts of what her captors might do to her. *There has to be a way out! Has to be!*

Then the metal door opened, groaning on rusted hinges. Noe strained her neck to get a better view of her captor, her enemy. It was a woman not much taller than she was. Her uniform was the same as the sentries at the bridge, with the addition of a black hood that covered most of her face. Only her hateful eyes were visible through an improvised opening in the hood. The homemade face covering made her appear more like a common thug than a soldier.

The boots circled Noe, echoing with every definitive step. The woman in black stopped near her head, knelt down, then produced a device from one of her cargo pockets and held it up to Noe's field of vision. It was a polished black cylinder with a small rectangular head attached to the end. It looked like a fancy razor blade upon first glance. The woman set the device down gingerly onto the surface of the floor next to Noe's face. Noe maintained her vision toward the rotting ceiling, unwilling to acknowledge the object or its owner.

"You know what this is?" The woman in black said. Her tone was brusque, voice partially hoarse as if she had been yelling at someone or something all day.

Noe kept quiet. She concentrated all of her being on controlling her quivering limbs and the rising sense of foreboding gripping her entire body. She knew very well what the object was. It was stronger and more menacing than any archaic conventional weapon. Guns, swords, bombs, cyber attacks, even lasers—none were as powerful in her mind. Death was preferable to having a digital extermination device (DED) used on you. *A DED!? I thought those were made illegal by the Shanghai Conventions!?* Noe's terror manifested in cold pools of sweat expanding at her armpits. The loss of control over her movement combined with the awareness of the DED merged into a ball of terror that threatened to escape from her mouth in the form of a scream. She fought with all of her being to suppress the feeling by showing a face of defiant resistance to the woman staring into her eyes.

A DED had the power to end her digital life for good via the complete erasure of her existence in the virtual landscape. Any aspect of her life connected online, from the most insignificant, like photos, to the most important, like medical records, and even her digital avatar companion Fyra, would be destroyed in seconds by a carefully calculated sequence and composition of light waves encapsulated in an object that looked like a hygiene product.

The masked woman slammed an open palm on the table, causing an echo in the tiny cell. "What was your objective?"

In response, Noe responded with the words she had been instructed to repeat should she ever become a prisoner of war in the physical or digital realm. "Noelani Acosta, Captain, 626-23-0392, 17 July 2029, Server number 862623. Noelani Acosta, Captain, 626-23-0392, 17 July 2029, Server number 862623." She repeated the words an unknown number of times while staring at the ceiling. She felt that it was only a matter of time before she felt a black steel boot shatter her soft rib bones, or worse.

The hand slam came again, her captor grabbed the DED from the floor. "Who sent you!?" Another slam on the table. The slam became a repeated pounding, first distant from the table then closer, and closer. The DED floated between her eyes. Noe clenched her eyes shut with full awareness that she was powerless to prevent the nameless mercenary from forcing her eyelids open and pressing one button. One button that would end her life as she knew it. She wrestled against her restraints in vain, only causing herself further pain in her already compromised position. Then she felt fingers dry and cracking, forcing her left eye open. "You will talk!" Tears of frustrated sadness rolled down her cheek as she continued to fight. The bright white light triggered an involuntary shriek to escape from her lips. Her cries mixed with the laughter from the hooded mercenary.

Noe sat up on her couch with a small gasp. It took her several seconds to realize she was in her living room, safe. Drenched in sweat, heart pounding uncontrollably, muscles tense with fear from the fuzzy memory of the nightmare, she closed her eyes to calm herself. Normally, she would make a mental note to ask Fyra to replay the nightmare later in her file, to help her analyze the submerged parts of her psyche that conspired to produce such a hellish scenario. That was not going to happen this time. Not a chance in hell. This one was headed to the permanent delete folder.

She noticed a hint of morning light entering through the thin line between her parted curtains. She hurried to the kitchen sink, then swallowed an entire glass of water in loud gulps. It made her feel a little better, but she still felt winded and shaky. The time on her refrigerator read five-thirty. *Guess I slept all the way through the night.* A pounding on her apartment door caused her to jump. In her rattled state, she stumbled through the limited space of her apartment to answer it. She looked through the peephole to see a man in a suit. Her initial instinct was to walk away. *I look and feel like shit. But what if it's…?* The memory of a brief phone conversation drifted into her mind. She unlocked the door and opened it.

A large tall man, pecan-toned skin stood before her. He wore a crumpled expensive suit with a loosened tie dangling about his neck. The face was full, haircut short but slightly overgrown. There was something vaguely familiar about his eyes. They were large and syrup brown, and even in her shaken state, produced a twinge of nostalgia as she peered into them. They projected a muted strength of resolve in the tender gaze. A resolve that had been thoroughly tested within the last twenty-four hours. The observation made Noe feel less self-conscious about her busted appearance, and made her feel like she could trust the large man who had pounded on her door to unknowingly rescue her from her nightmare.

"Ms. Acosta?" His voice was low and scratchy.

"Yeah," Noe's voice sounded far away, even to herself.

"I'm Rodan Mitchell, we spoke on the phone earlier today…I mean yesterday." He took in the woman standing in the door frame. In the interval between two blinks Rodan's vision ran the length of her body from head to toe and back. It registered her regular midnight blue colored t-shirt with dark sweat stains under the arms and breasts, her black running shorts with two smooth muscular legs extending to the floor. Even with her unkempt appearance, she was beautiful. By the end of the second blink, he refocused on her face. The eyes, glossy and dilated, were a tawny shade of brown, containing a dash more of orange than brown, as if live embers lay within, simultaneously emitting warmth, while glowing with searing power. A pillow imprint was etched onto the left side of her face. She looked scared, but ready to fight. Rodan knew the look well, he had seen it too many times to count. *Who knows what kinda hell she's been through for the last twelve or so hours. And now this...*Rodan dropped his head, then raised his eyes to meet hers. "I'm sorry if my knockin' scared you. Didn't mean to alarm you. Can I uh...speak with you for a minute?"

"She's dead isn't she?" Noe said, her voice flat, arms crossing her chest.

Rodan put his hands on his hips, then sighed heavily. He hesitated. *I see directness runs in the family.* "Yeah...yes she is."

"I knew it," hot tears stung her eyes, blurring her vision.

"I'm terribly sorry for your loss." Rodan was at a loss for words. He stared at the tops of his weathered dress shoes to let the moment breathe. When he was a cop, next-of-kin notifications were one of the parts of the job he had never gotten used to. He never thought he would have to deliver another one.

Burning tears streamed down Noe's face as the realization of her mother's death hit her with devastating realness. *She's gone...how many times did I warn her!?* Rodan looked as if he wanted to reach out and comfort her, but he took no action. Just stood looking with half closed eyes toward an empty pot with a long dead plant in it outside of the door. Through tears and the tightness in her chest, Noe managed to speak. "How?"

Rodan raised his gaze, straightening himself to a professional posture despite his exhaustion. "We're still gathering all the details, but the murderer appeared to have access to your mother's house, since there was no sign of forced entry. An initial medical examination determined that the cause of death was heart failure, but we'll know more after the official autopsy is complete."

Noe shook her head, tears fell wet and warm onto her chest. "My mother didn't have any medical problems." She looked into Rodan's eyes with a hard gaze. "It was one of them who did this, right? It was Limnic…"

A lump formed in Rodan's throat. He swallowed it to maintain his bearing and mask his anger. *Limnic, again. They won't get away with this.* "That remains to be seen Ms. Acosta. I have a team of people that I trust working on this. I promise, we want answers as much as you do. We'll provide them to you as soon as we get them. The police are already working their investigation, but we'll be shadowing them every step of the way."

Noe gave a weak nod. The lack of sleep and the exertion of crying made her feel lightheaded. She placed her hand against the door frame to balance herself. Rodan moved to steady her, placing a firm hand on her arm.

"You're alright," he said reassuringly. "You should get some rest. You know my number. If you need anything from me, just send me a message. I'll contact you when we have more information about the situation." He gave her arm a tight squeeze, then made his way down the hall toward the elevator, dragging his heavy feet across the thin carpet.

Noe closed the door, made her way to her couch and sat slowly. The memories of her strained relationship with her mother over the years came rushing back, burning their way through her like napalm. As waves of guilt surged and shook her to the core, she vowed at that moment to find her mother's killer and bring an end to Limnic and, if necessary, Cereus too, once and for all. The failed utopian fantasy had gone on long enough and claimed too many lives, and she was going to be the one to put a stop to it.

CHAPTER 28:
BARTO'S RETREAT

Located a short fifteen-minute walk from the tranquil western shores of Lake Tahoe stood a cabin. It was the kind of place that would fit perfectly on the back of a winter postcard that the lake region had always been known for. A picturesque escape, warm and cozy, where a weary traveler, and perhaps a few guests, could find a respite from frosty temperatures and falling snow.

The area had always been famous for its beauty. And it still was. The azure blue surface of the lake, surrounded by rugged snow-capped peaks and wild forests brimming with hundreds of species of trees and wildlife still attracted millions of visitors and locals eager to experience the myriad activities available in the area.

Barto Khuni was one of those frequent visitors. As a boy, his family would vacation at the lake every summer to take advantage of kayaking, windsurfing, and swimming. Then return at winter time for snowshoeing, snowboarding, and skiing. Those were memories of the special kind. Ones that had only ripened with the passage of time. He continued with the tradition as an adult. Back then, he made frequent trips with his then wife Pamela, and their son, Frederick. After his divorce, he continued to make the pilgrimage twice every year sometimes with Pamela, with whom who he still maintained an amicable relationship, or with a handful of old friends and work colleagues. The lake was his personal hideaway. A sacred space for those intimate few among the billions in the world that were worthy to share the exclusive experience with him. Although he considered himself to be an atheist, travelling to the lake was the only component of his life to take on spiritual attributes, besides going to In-N-Out Burger.

In recent years, he had been making the trip alone more and more often. Pamela had passed away and his son had his own life. He worked in nanotechnology, doing something with tiny machines for big companies. Barto could never quite remember where he worked or what he did in his work. Meanwhile, his other close friends had aged into that period of life when it tends to take more than it gives. One, Matt, had a major business failure and was forced to shutter it on the precipice of retirement, so he had little disposable income for non-survival related activities. Another, Christine, had returned to Washington DC to care for supremely elderly parents. A third, Dustin, decided to "redo" his twenties and indulge in all of the pleasures and pains he felt he had missed out on during those bygone formative years of his life. He had paid handsomely to reconstruct his twenty-something year old body, hormones included. His body rejuvenated, he was traveling the world, experimenting with drugs, and having casual sex. Barto could never quite pinpoint where he was or contact him, and was content to receive the occasional postcard from him on sporadic occasions.

Barto stood alone in the small cabin wearing a fuzzy black bath robe, white t-shirt, checkered boxer underwear, and well-worn house slippers, a cup of coffee in his hand. The summer sun was rising steadily on the opposite shore of the lake, bathing the polished vinyl flooring with natural light. It was a rustic place with few modern luxuries. A wood burning stove with a pipe extended up to the slanted roof sat dormant in front of him. To the left of the stove was what used to be a small storage space for the old DVD and Blu-ray movies. It had been decades since it had been used for that purpose. Long ago he had repurposed it as a bookshelf to store the physical copies of some of his favorite classic books. The *Dune* series, the *Harry Potter* series, and the *Lord of the Rings* were a few that made the cut. Above the bookcase, a discoloration of the wood hinted that a TV had once occupied the space. Overwhelmed by the amount of media choices, he had given up conventional media long ago and had it removed. The rest of the cabin was similarly unremarkable. The living room connected to a small kitchen with simple appliances, and the bedroom with a single bed for him and a guest. Since Pamela's death, he had not shared the bed with anyone else.

Barto stared at his coffee, still reeling from the news he had received via a private line only minutes before.

I can't believe Lili is dead.

A flurry of unanswered questions cycled through his mind on repeat. *Who? How? Why? Am I next?* That left him, Silas, and Janus as the remaining Founders. *Could it have been Silas or Janus?* He took a sip of hot Alpen Sierra coffee. The liquid made him feel a little better, and aided to drive the unsettling ideation from his mind.

This was what we agreed to do long ago. This was always the plan. We just didn't expect it to come about so soon or so suddenly.

He moved outside to a wide back patio. The old wood planks cracked and sagged beneath his weight as he walked to a single bench under the shade of a tree extending its branches over his head. He took a seat, coffee in hand and stared at a narrow dirt trail between the trees. The smell of the lake and fresh pine floated from the path and filled his senses. He savored the cool fresh air, it felt good. Up here he could breathe, relax, even think. Something about being in the city made him feel restricted and limited. The serene environment allowed his mind to kick into another gear. It made it easier to begin finding solutions to the many problems he was facing.

Rodan will be able to do it. He's the perfect person to assume command. With his connections, I know he'll be able to lead Cereus through the final phase of its evolution. He's not the most refined or organized, but he's loyal and knows the organization inside and out. Plus he probably won't openly question orders. He felt like he was twenty-five years younger, convincing his young son that the flu shot wouldn't hurt. Even if his sanguine thoughts were half-truths, they made him feel better.

A soft ping from his device captured his attention. He pulled it from the pocket of his robe. His old eyes found the screen and read the message:

"Found forensic pathologist. Autopsy underway. More answers soon - Rodan"

His arm lowered to his side with the device in it, then he leaned his head back on to the cool metallic surface of the back of the bench. A sigh escaped his lips, discharging stress. *Soon we'll know how it was done.* Barto was burning with curiosity to find out more about his fellow Founder's demise. Lili's untimely and suspicious death was not the only thing that concerned him. He was also eager to know what was happening among the comvils and how its citizens were absorbing the effects of the order. *This is where we will truly see if we were right. If all of the effort and sacrifices made during our lives resulted in lasting change in our society.* True, it had only been nearly twenty-four hours since he pressed the button, but even in the tranquility of his sanctuary he perceived that much had occurred within the last day. Much like in an old episode of *24*, the clock was ticking, and many lives had been forever altered, or ended, in that brief span of time. He thought of Lili again and shuddered. She had always been good to him, and now she was gone. Barto hoped it wasn't for nothing.

With naive optimism, he wanted to believe that Lili and Cereus already had made its mark. That its legacy would not be that of the organization that sparked a war, furthered existing societal divides, and spawned one of the most ruthless domestic terrorist organizations the country had ever seen. He truly wanted to believe. Had to. It was the only way he could convince himself that his and her entire life had not been wasted.

He thought to contact the other Founders to explain his logic before activating the order. But decided against it. He was done begging them for permission, following their lead. After all, had it not been his policies that served as the foundation of Cereus' model? He owed none of them an explanation, but being a lifelong people-pleaser, was prepared to give one anyway. *How can I possibly explain it to them?*

He visualized the other three Founders standing on his patio before him. Silas with his arms crossed, a scowl on his face. Old Lili, hands on hips impatient for a detailed 'Wikipedia' description that she probably would not fully understand, and Janus, straight-lipped, eyes smoldering with anticipation for more data to process. He said, "Ok, ok I know you're all irritated. Silas, don't look at me like that. But think about it this way. In the beginning, the prevailing economic and political winds were on our side, fueled by world events. The aftermath of the COVID-19 pandemic, Technology Wars, the great disasters of the 2030s, the First Cyber Wars, and the "exodus" drove people to us. People were hungry for revolution. However, now the same social, economic, demographic, cultural, and ideological forces that allowed Cereus to prosper back then were turning against us! I ran the numbers! And I saw the need to take decisive action. Through complex data analysis and economic trend research, I concluded that capitalism had done what author Paul Mason described with stunning clarity in his book *Postcapitalism*: it had "mutated" and "adapted" in order to survive into its next evolution. So that's why I did it." He wasn't completely convinced they would buy his reasoning, as logical as it seemed in his mind. *At this point, it doesn't really matter if they do. What's done is done. There's no going back now. Onward we go.*

Alone on the bench he pondered the ironic similarities between nature and capitalism. One, created by who knows what powerful force. The other, created by man, reflecting all of humanity's greatest aspirations and fears. Both ruled by order and chaos. Both deaf to the desires of conscious beings, corporations, or institutions. He shook his head and laughed to himself. The beauty of the parallel gave him pause. To think that highly irrational beings such as him could create an economic and political system that mimicked the natural order so well made him smile with dark humor. *We are truly the God and gods of old.*

The sound of footsteps inside the cabin snapped him back from his theoretical musings. Barto whipped his neck from its inclined position toward the cabin, causing him sharp pain. The footsteps stopped. He concentrated his ear, locked his eyes on the sliding door. Droplets of cold sweat began to build on his forehead as he listened. Had he imagined the noise? *Oh shit delusional behavior is a sign of dementia! Hopefully it's not that! Dammit! Focus Barto!* More footsteps, this time closer. Unsure of what to do, he formed the skeleton of a decision tree in his brain to consider his options. *What will Barto do? Run toward the lake? Investigate the noise? Stay on the bench and hope for the best?* He moved the imaginary cursor in his mind to make his decision. When he heard the steps in the kitchen his algorithmic decision-making system broke down, leaving him frozen and shaking in his place. He feared that he might wet himself.

When the sliding door opened, Barto unknowingly held his breath. He released it when he recognized the person who stepped onto the patio, but still found no relief from his nervousness or the stress-induced muscle tension in his neck. *How the hell did he find me?*

It was Janus. He wore a plain black t-shirt and jeans. The wrinkles on his face appeared to stand out under the natural sunlight. He looked down at Barto on the bench with a slightly upturned lip, eyes glowing with intensity.

"Hello Barto. You and I need to talk."

CHAPTER 29: IDEOLOGICAL DIFFERENCES

Barto stared at Janus in disbelief, unclear why he had come.

"H-How did you find me?" He said with a dry mouth.

Janus let out a low laugh, displaying his incredulousness. "Come now, Barto. You of all people should know that information is always for sale. It all depends on the price one is willing to pay."

Barto leaned forward to stare at the surface of the patio. *Of course I know that. I just didn't expect YOU of all people to track me down.* "What are you doing here? I thought you were meeting with some of our associates in Spain."

"As soon as I received the order, I took the first hypersonic back over. The flight was quite enjoyable."

Barto acknowledged with a nod of the head. He relaxed slightly, but still felt the urge to run into the woods, even if he was only wearing a bathrobe. "Barely time to even get a decent nap on those flights. They're so quick." Anxious laughter followed his comment. His attempt to dispel some of the dead air between them fell flat. Something was off about Janus today. He seemed more…withdrawn than usual. From his position by the patio door, he regarded Barto in an odd manner. Like a person would observe a stray animal, weighing whether or not he should feed it or toss it out to streets to fend for itself.

For several seconds neither man spoke. To a casual bystander, they appeared as two men enjoying an idyllic Lake Tahoe morning. Two old friends among sounds of chirping birds, rustling trees, and lapping lake water. Barto stared back fidgeting on the bench. *Damn*

Janus, the king of awkward pauses. Gotta do something to break this tension. A decision tree unfolded before him. *What should Barto do? Ask about Lili? Ask about Spain? Ask Janus about how he was doing? Flee?* An imaginary cursor flicked between the options.

"You heard about Lili right?"

Janus' face remained inexpressive. "Yes…yes I did. Very tragic."

"Rodan sent a message a little while ago. Said that a pathologist was going to conduct an autopsy soon. I'm not sure how he was able to find one so fast, but I think I remember there was one forensic pathologist committee established in a comvil in SoCal a few years back. He might've tapped into one of those networks and called in a favor." Barto's tone was edgy. During his word dump he studied Janus, hoping anything related to the topic of Lili's death might stir a reaction of some kind. His face remained neutral, unfeeling. *Typical Janus.*

"Why did you execute the order?" Janus asked.

The jarring shift in topics combined with his expectant tone caused Barto to recoil on the bench. His wrinkled frown communicated his dismay at the directness of his longtime colleague's question. *I don't owe him an explanation!* He silenced his "inside voice" as he called it and provided the rationale he had rehearsed just minutes prior.

"Ah, I see, so it was the market that caused you to act. The impending potential swing of the capitalist pendulum made you move. How…pedestrian of you."

That tone again! Barto ignored his initial thoughts of disgust, swallowing a giant lump in his dry throat. He was very thirsty all of a sudden. "Yes, I guess you could put it that way. As our chief financial officer, it's my job to make sure that we're solvent—"

"Solvent!?" Janus said. The force behind his words coincided with a gust of wind from the lake trail. It caused trees around Barto to sway. "Since when has solvency been a concern of ours!?"

Barto shrank on the bench, and hoped the tree wouldn't collapse on top of him. Visibly shaken, he attempted to bring up another decision tree for diffusing Janus' temper, but it would not come. Unclear how to proceed, he began to talk, hoping something would resonate to make him back down. "C'mon Janus. You're not being realistic. I know we created Cereus to be exclusively built on bartering and the exchange of "human skills" but we need money to survive. We still have to play nice with government officials, people in emerging markets, and those who are opposed to our philosophy, A.K.A., y'know, our enemies. Which, as you also already know, we have more than a few." *Uh oh, he's still mad. Better keep talking.* "Whether we like it or not our society revolves around money. Whether it's fiat paper money, digitally created, or backed by something, doesn't matter. A lot of people still have the need to exchange something physical for something physical. Paying in services or time or whatever else, just doesn't jive with a lot of them. But you, of course, already know all this."

Janus' face contorted. "Don't lecture me on economic theory. I am well aware of the trends at play here."

Barto straightened his posture. He felt some of his confidence return to him. *Ok he's less mad. Good.* "We agreed to each have the ability to begin the final phase at any time. And I took action on that. That's all."

"You were short-sighted in taking that action."

"In what way?"

"I was poised to open an opportunity for Cereus to expand in Spain. It would have been our foothold into Europe. Now those hopes have been dashed. By your hasty decision."

The two men glared at each other. Each one wedded to their own justifications and decisions. Barto's fear had lessened to mild irritation at his old colleague. *Why does he press this issue? This is what we agreed! It was over three decades ago, but it was what we all agreed back then.* He stood, letting out a deep sigh. "Could it be that you're… a bit… y'know… *jealous* that it was me who made the call and not you?" He let out a small laugh, mostly at the thought of the all rational and forward-thinking Janus, succumbing to the basic human emotion of envy. *I'm Abel and he's Cain. Oh wait Cain murdered Abel out of jealousy! Oh shit there I go again! Dammit! Focus Barto! Gotta focus!*

A crooked smile curved itself onto Janus' face. "Of course not Barto. My goal is to spread our values across the world as much as possible with Cereus…using *Limnic* as the vehicle."

At the mention of Limnic, Barto stepped back so suddenly he nearly stumbled onto the bench. His incredulous look stripped the usual naivete from his face. *Janus is…it can't be… Limnic!?* "Janus, you? It was you? You're the mastermind behind Limnic? But…why?"

A tree close to the patio cast a long shadow that fell on half of Janus' face. The eyes of two distinct men bored into Barto. One of a pioneer visionary, the other of a terrorist revolutionary. He was not sure which person would answer the question.

"Because in all of our plans and calculations we failed to consider the darkness in the hearts of people. Modern humankind only seeks the indulgences of the self. Endlessly worshipping a false ego cultivated by adept hands that pull their strings and as a result, dictate their every want, desire, and action. Thanks in a large part to modern technology, humankind has *devolved* from an independent mind, to the mind of a beast. A savage animal controlled by the shock collar of cheap entertainment; the leash of all-seeing and all-knowing machines with prescient capabilities; the carrot stick of lies perpetrated by governments, corporations, churches, religions, and schools that promise reward for effort and intellect, yet ultimately favor the charismatic well-connected extrovert with sterling lineage. In short, our social fabric has become ripped to tatters by our individual need to conceive and nurture institutions. This need causes us to raze anything in our path that stands in opposition of the deification of the institution or of the institutionalized self. The self most view as incontrovertible proof of their existence and life's work. The projection that *they* will pay any price to protect and preserve. This mindset is etched into our biological code, and is slowly leading our species to suicide via planetary consumption. This dangerous thinking needed to be reined in somehow. Through means that the masses understand."

Barto blinked rapidly, in a wholehearted attempt to follow Janus' logic with a look of concentration on his face.

Janus went on, "Imagine a world where all ten billion souls on this planet have everything that a society based on profit, market forces, and being *solvent* are the reigning priorities. Old world thinking would have all of us believe that this is the desired condition. That all people can be entrepreneurs, rapid consumers, have deep satisfying relationships, and follow their heart's desires simultaneously, while still being a caring and productive participant of society. This pernicious ethos encouraged by liberal humanism was the expectation at the beginning of this century. And where did it lead us? A trashed planet, full of apathetic consumers who only think of their next dopamine hit from something that is not a person. Mindless drones prepared to hold their individual truth aloft over all else, and use it as a basis to trample on the truths of others, as they clamber for drama and conflict. The necessity for struggle and conflict is vital to the human condition. Without it, they are beside themselves with idle hands and ultimately succumb to mammalian desires for sex, food, or other forms of distraction. Don't you see? Violence and disorder are all they know and understand! So *I* will give it to them!"

Barto looked unimpressed. It had been a long time since he heard one of Janus tirades. He remembered how much he disliked them.

"So you counteract their materialism and ego with violence? Swapping one undesirable human trait for another seems counterintuitive to me. Or as my mother used to say 'two wrongs don't make a right'." He put his hand to his chin in a thinking position. "Actually, I'm pretty sure all mothers say that at some point to a child." Barto laughed anxiously. "But hear me out Janus. How much of this is your own vanity? Your own ego? *Your* pride? What you describe is the way the world has always been in some form. We just have better tech now to use to control others and satisfy our need for conflict in our lives. From the strongest in the tribe of Neanderthals, to the feudal lord, to the top bio-genetically enhanced athletes of today, there have always been those with more power over others, willing to use that power to exploit those that they perceived as being weaker or less capable than them. Cereus wasn't meant to change that. It was meant to recalibrate the scales of society back from the brinks of the rampant inequality of the early twenty-first century, give average people a chance at self-actualization by allocating value to even the smallest of actions, and provide them with a community to share those actions. It was never meant to *destroy* old world thinking. It was supposed to gradually eclipse it by providing a better way of thinking that would hopefully benefit more people and the planet in the long run, that's all."

Janus had heard enough. He turned on a heel to leave.

Barto took a shaky step forward, "Janus, what you're doing is terrorism. All those people…the attacks…the live demolitions of buildings while people were still inside…it was you." He stared at the back of the silver hair, wondering what his next words or move would be. Janus was motionless, contemplating some kind of response. *Is he going to kill me? Dammit! I'm gonna die in my bathrobe! Knew I should've put on pants this morning! Barto, focus!* His eyes glanced down at his checkered undergarments as his pulse began to accelerate. All of a sudden he felt very exposed. And cold.

"No, I won't kill you."

How did he know what I was thinking!? Well he said he wouldn't kill me. Praise be. "Janus…what are you planning to do? Whatever it is, it's not too late to call it off," Barto said.

Janus stepped toward the cabin, shook his head, then looked over his shoulder. "I am not a *good* or *evil* man. I'm just a being existing in this reality. Who's to say what is right and what is wrong? Bloody revolutions throughout history are seen as necessary ends despite the massive loss of human lives. The same can be said about the imperial conquests of antiquity. History, in the end, recorded the majority of those events as righteous and just, despite the decimation of millions of people living a peaceful existence prior to imperialist arrival." He turned to face Barto again, reabsorbed into the debate.

"This was another consequence of capitalist overreach. The old world pitted capitalism and communism, and its relative socialism, against each other in perpetual ideological conflict. But these philosophies were not at the root of the debate. The real origin of the feud were the differing perspectives between liberal and socialist humanism. Do I favor the needs of myself and those closest to me over the needs of society? Or the needs of society at large over my individual freedom? These were the questions underpinning many old world squabbles. Questions *they* still wrestle with to this day. Our conflict is different. It is the clash between these old branches of humanism and neo evolutionary humanism. This is the ideological conflict of our time."

"Are you talking about Harari's definitions of humanism in that old book *Homo Deus*?" Barto asked, making a concerted effort to recall the details of a book he had read decades ago.

Janus flashed a congratulatory grin. "Precisely. The mentality '*do what feels good for the individual*' of liberal humanism, as well as the sentiment '*do what feels good for the party, collective, or people in power*' of socialist humanism have pushed our species and planet to the disaster that is our modern society. The Nazis of the Third Reich attempted to end the conflict once and for all with their philosophy of evolutionary humanism, through their heavy-handed eugenics practices. But their barbaric and shortsighted methods were insufficient to truly move the human race forward. For you cannot teach a man to fly. He has no wings."

Barto let out an audible groan at the cryptic comment. He was sick of being lectured. Even death was preferable at this point. "What's your point?"

"The human experience, as we know it, is an arbitrary thing. It is not unique or special, and with existing technology a sufficient imitation can be replicated, reproduced, and manipulated at will. It is an illusion, conjured up by beings drifting toward chaos." Janus looked at his hands, then said, "I *am* chaos. I know that now. It's time for me to embrace it."

Barto looked at him with confusion. Unclear what to say. "Wow that was…dramatic." Janus ignored this statement.

"Goodbye old friend," Janus said. He turned, then walked into the cabin and left his long-time contemporary standing alone on the patio. At that point, he knew it was too late to stop what had already been set in motion twenty-four hours ago. The only thing left for them both to do was to play their respective parts. No matter their personal history, Janus was already aware that from this day forward, neither would walk the same path. They stood on opposite sides of a conflict that had been brewing for decades. He wondered if Barto had made the same observation. If he had, what would he try to do to stop him?

Janus smiled to himself as he walked out of the front door of the cabin. *Whatever challenge he brings, I'll be ready.*

*   *   *

Barto sat on his couch, sipping another cup of coffee. The aroma and warmth of the liquid helped relax him after his encounter with Janus. *Didn't expect that plot twist. He is the one in charge of Limnic. How could I not see it after all this time? He must not fear me reporting him, because he knows that it would implicate me as one of the Founders of Cereus.*

Over the years, he normally handled disagreements with Janus in one of two ways. Either he outtalked him. *Just tried that. I seem to be getting worse at it as I get older.* Or he consulted with Lili and filtered his message through her. His words, via Lili's voice acted as the perfect check on Janus' bullheadedness over the years. *I'm Congress and she's the Supreme Court. Nobody hates the Supreme Court. Plus she had boobs. Hard to argue with those sometimes.* His eyes descended to his chest. *I guess I have boobs now, too.* The joke made him feel a little lighter, but he was still worried. Lili was gone, which meant he would have to handle this conflict without her counsel.

Ten minutes later, fresh cup of coffee in his hand, pants on, he stood on the back patio, staring in the direction of the lake. He rubbed his stubbled chin and considered his options: *Warn Rodan? Contact Silas? Do nothing?* Cycling through the alternatives, he decided to walk away from the tree. *Whatever I choose to do is going to unleash a shitstorm of epic proportions for all of us.* He sat back on the bench to savor the cup of coffee. He wanted to enjoy a few more minutes of solitude before he made his next decision.

CHAPTER 30:
SJ-ARCADE

On another morning, another old man stood among nature. Eighty miles west from Barto's cabin, across the untamed landscape of trees and mountains of the Tahoe National Forest, the man stood as his spine would allow wearing a blue and black flannel shirt, beige slacks, comfortable work boots, and a wide-brimmed straw hat. Natural sunlight poured over the distant horizon, warming his face and cold joints. It served as a lubricant for his bones, which made it easier to make his morning walk around the grounds. Cause and effect.

The rows of grapes stood in soldier-like rows running from north to south. The orientation provided more sunlight, which meant better quality fruit. *Higher the quality, the better the wine.* He had to perform his inspection of the grapes early, before the heat of the day made the walk unbearable. It also gave him something to do after his body forced his eyes open at 0500 for his morning *piss n' shit*, as he liked to call it. Despite his desire to get more sleep, neither his troublesome bladder nor his out-of-sync body clock would allow him to rest for more than four or five hours per night. A blessing and a curse he had learned to accept decades prior. He always found something productive to do with the time before the world woke up and began to make demands of him. Demands he would most likely ignore. Always judicious with his time, he rarely allowed deviations from his schedule. *I'm the immigration authority and everybody wants in*, came his thoughts whenever he politely refused an unwanted or unwarranted request.

The man walked the dirt road with measured steps, careful to kick as little dust up as possible. Too much dirt was bad for the end product. *It will be a good harvest this year.* The plants greeted him with a subtle flowery aroma. He stopped to take in the smell of one. Standing like a miniature tree, it rose to the height of his chest, strong and boasting tiny pale green spheres that, in a few months' time, would yield a tasty alcoholic beverage. The scent was refreshing. A satisfied smile formed on his dry lips.

The sun had nearly completed its ascent over the horizon, taking its place among the scattered wisps of clouds populating the sky. He had a contentious relationship with the heat. One that had only become worse with time and age. So he hurried his pace to seek shelter. His quick steps rustled dusty pebbles beneath his feet, as he made his way to the seventy-two-acre winery's defining feature. The single reason he had decided to partner with the original owners of the property.

The wine cave.

Stones were fixed to the walls and ceilings forming a perfect arched chamber that was ideal for cooling the space down in the sweltering summer heat. With the proper arrangement of tables and chairs, there was enough room to accommodate over one hundred guests. This had been a regular occurrence in the early days of the property when it had been known as the Mount Vernon Winery.

The cave served several purposes in the past. It was a storage space for over five hundred barrels of French and American aged wines. It had also been a popular social gathering spot. The original owners used to host elaborate dinners and wine showcases back in the day. Dimly lit strings of glowing lights, flowing wine, and the low rumble of conversation among the sound of clanking silverware worked in tandem to facilitate a warm and friendly atmosphere in what should have been a cold and dark space. But that era was past. The old man had developed such strong ties with the owners that upon their death, he purchased the property and its wine production operation. He didn't know much about oenology in all of its subtle complexities when he began. Didn't even know winemaking had some fancy name like that. *Who knew?* But through true Millennial grit and determination he had become a self-made viticulturist. A year of Google searches and on-the-job training from the enthusiastic winery staff was all he needed. *Didn't need no help from nobody. All me. American work ethic. Truly started from the bottom now I'm here.* Just like in the old Drake song.

He stepped into the cave and immediately felt coolness wash over him. Felt his eyes returning to the comforting darkness. *I don't understand why people don't like caves. Yeah they can be dark, wet, and creepy.*

But they can also be places of rest and growth. Especially for some of nature's less attractive creatures. Caves serve as a safe haven for non-attention seeking beings to thrive and do their quiet work, sometimes in the complete absence of light. Caves protect, store, and provide homes. Caves are where true magic happens. The flash of a light from the extreme end of the cave disturbed his thoughts. Someone had tainted the dark, and his good mood along with it.

The light came from one glowing computer monitor at the far end of the tunneled chamber. Several linked tables ran the length of the side wall with twenty-six identical thirty-two inch monitors on top. One of the twenty-six had been powered on. In front of it sat two figures with curved backs, a man and a woman. Their eyes flitted back and forth, hands moved in coordinated activity, tapping buttons and manipulating joysticks with a lifetime of practiced ability. In their digital lives, they had been rivals for decades. In the physical, they were the closest of friends, going as far as calling each other "soulmate", despite never having been married or intimate. At least as far as the old man knew. He approached the two as silently as possible. Smiling to himself to allow them to have their early morning time alone, as they played early morning matches in Super Smash Brothers Ultimate.

"Damn, Isa I swear your Lucina is just too good!" The man said. His voice came out in a raspy low tone that told the story of his age, despite the younger looking pale skin of his face.

Isa patted his mid thigh. "Your Cloud has gotten better over the years, Jake. At this rate, maybe in another decade you'll be able to beat me." Her wrinkled lips molded into a mocking grin on her gaunt espresso toned face.

Jake scoffed. "I knew I should have picked a top-tier character like Wolf all those years ago. But nooo, I just had to stick with Mario. He's the one I grew up playing since the N64 days. I could have beat your ass on that version."

"Oh really?" Isa said, a gleam in her eyes. "We can pull it up now and see if you can back up that bullshit you're spoutin'!" She leaned in closer to his face.

He inclined his head closer to her face and whispered. "If you pick old-school Link in N64, my Mario will slaughter you…"

The old man shook his head from his place in the shadow of the cave. Unable to remain quiet, he cleared his throat in an obnoxious manner. It echoed up and down the cave alerting Isa and Jake to his presence.

"Will you two just kiss already?" He said. His words came out as a taunt. He knew, it was the best way to get a reaction out of them. *Gotta speak their language,* he thought with amusement. In response, the two separated from one another like two teenagers caught in a compromising position. Jake whipped his hands nervously to his side. Isa scrunched her lips up in a frown-smile while her hands casually moved to smooth out nonexistent wrinkles in the light purple pajama pants she wore. The old man smirked. The scene pleased him very much.

"Silas, we…uh…didn't see you there…" Jake said. "Eh…how long have you been *lurking* over there?"

I guess I was lurking. "Long enough to see that three-stock match. You were in poor form this morning Jake."

Jake hung his head low. Isa snickered.

"I know…one day I'll give her the whoopin' she deserves." He cast a defiant look in Isa's direction. "I figured I'll wait until her osteoporosis slows down her fingers, then I'll finally win."

Isa gasped with feigned incredulousness. She playfully flicked his ear. "As if! You would like that wouldn't you?" She turned toward him slowly, perking up her cosmetically altered chest. "But if my fingers go, I wouldn't be able to do this…" Her fingers crawled in a spider motion across his right leg. She enjoyed watching him shudder at her touch. Jake swallowed hard. "Oh…oh yeah, well if *my* hands went, then I couldn't do this…" He snapped his fingers at her left ear. He had learned long ago the sound of snapping was her Achilles heel. It gave him a rush to make her lose her regal confidence. To bring her down to his level.

Silas threw his hands up and turned to walk away. He needed to continue his morning rounds. He had seen enough geriatric flirting for one morning. "Age is just a number, until you can't get it up anymore." He let out a bitter laugh. Jake chuckled too, unaware he was the butt of the joke.

"Wait Silas!" Jake rushed out of his seat as fast his wobbly legs would allow. Isa folded her arms across her chest and rolled her eyes. Silas could tell she was frustrated. *The sting of wounded pride looks the same on every human face, especially a woman's.*

"Yes, Jake?"

"Hey, I just wanted to thank you for letting us in on this place." He made a weak hand gesture toward Isa. She busied herself with the menu options on screen to give the appearance that she wasn't listening in on the conversation.

"It's no problem," Silas replied. "I'm happy to see that the model is taking off."

Jake nodded. The sound of his fragile neck bones cracking and popping accompanied the movement.

"Y'know, I have a cousin who's getting up in age. A place like SJ-Arcade would be a great fit for him. Any chance you'll have vacancies in the next month or so?"

Silas cast a scrutinizing glance at him. Jake's hopeful eyes, set deep in cosmetically stretched skin, were red and wet with anticipation, fueled by a combination of lack of sleep, a lifetime of staring at screens, and experimental drug use.

"No I'm sorry. We've got a waitlist months long and it takes a while for a slot to open up. Someone has to die for it to happen."

Jake laughed.

Silas' face held a derisive grin.

Jake's smile vanished. He adjusted strands of his remaining grey hair to diffuse some of the awkwardness of the situation.

Apparently he spent all of his money on his face. Forgot to leave some for his hair, Silas thought.

"Ok, ok I was just wondering…" Jake lowered his head, defeated.

Silas placed a hand on his shoulder. "Hey don't worry. We have another facility in El Dorado hills. It's smaller, and doesn't have as many amenities, but same set up. Maybe your cousin can get in over there. Shorter waitlist." *Can't turn down another moneymaker can I?*

"Ok, uh thanks Silas." Jake returned to his chair and sulked. Isa placed a warm hand on his shoulder to console him. "Hey…at least you asked him, right?" She picked up his controller and offered it to him. "One more set before breakfast?"

Jake immediately perked up, as much as his spine would allow. "You're on."

*   *   *

Silas left the cave and walked toward the main house. He passed and greeted other sleepy-eyed residents on the way. Despite the early heat of the day, some were up taking restless walks, admiring the grapevines, or even having an early glass of Sauvignon before breakfast.

He stopped to admire the house. It looked like it could have been pulled from its foundation in a European countryside and transplanted to the rolling hills of Auburn, California. With its trapezoid formation of large windows jutting out from the surface of the house, covered entryway, and masterfully landscaped hedges situated just outside of the house, it always reminded him of his trip through the tiny nation of Liechtenstein long ago.

The house, its elderly inhabitants, the vineyards, and the land had become his refuge from the absurdities of the outside world. These days, he hardly left the grounds at all except for the rare occasions he was called to San Francisco for a meeting with the other Founders. It had been years since he attended one. He always found a way to avoid showing up in person.

Initially, his participation with Cereus had been a knee jerk reaction. He had quarreled openly with his father concerning his portion of his inheritance that he was supposed to receive upon the oil tycoon's death. To spite him, he joined and backed Cereus' cause. After a few years the situation resolved itself. His father passed away before removing Silas from the will, and his brother, with whom he was supposed to share the inheritance, gave it up to go live in India or something on a religious calling. Silas didn't really know and didn't really care. They hadn't spoken in decades. Ultimately, he had been left with enough money to do whatever he wanted. Thus SJ-Arcade was born. It was the crowning achievement of his life and he enjoyed watching his fellow Millennials live out their golden years playing video games and drinking wine while the rest of the world shriveled and died. *Protect people and planet? Why would you want to protect it? There's only a few billion of us worth saving anyway.* He counted himself among that number.

He still provided a small amount of his fortune to the organization through some contractual snare he had fallen into (damn that Barto!), but was only obligated to do so until 2065. *Only three years to go.* Silas vowed to live to see his donations to Cereus repaid in full, with interest, if he had his way. *Even if I have to get all of the fucking life extension surgeries in the world to make it happen. I will get what I'm owed.*

Out of the corner of his eye, he saw a solitary figure moving up the dusty trail that connected to the main street. He squinted his eyes and could only make out a taller man wearing a blue button down shirt and pants made of greyish light fabric. The man wore a blue cap that contained no branded or remarkable features, so low on his face that it shielded his eyes in shadow.

Silas tensed as the man approached. His heart began to drum in his chest, sweat began to tingle the hairs under his arms as he came closer. He could recognize the movement. It was the way that he was able to cover distance by rolling off of the ball of his feet and onto his heel while making minimal sound that had always impressed and irritated him. *Why does he have to glide everywhere? Why can't he walk normal like the rest of us?*

Janus stopped in front of him and removed his ball cap. His silver hair seemed to glow under the light of the morning sun.

"Hello Silas."

"Janus…what are you doing here? I thought you were in San Francisco or Spain or wherever, after all that shit with the order went down a week ago."

Janus grinned. "Change of plans…I wanted to talk business with you. Could you spare a few minutes of your time?"

Silas agreed. Although he had a feeling that it would take more than a few minutes, and the business that Janus had in mind would most likely not be favorable for him. It hadn't been for a long time.

CHAPTER 31:
CURMUDGEON

The two moved to Silas' study. It was a cavernous room situated underground, just below the main house on the property. A steep handcrafted unpainted stairwell led into the giant area. Silas had not gone through the trouble to cover the floor with a carpet or any other padding. Too much trouble. This caused the two men's footsteps to echo as they moved through the basement.

Two thick unpainted wooden support arches divided the room into symmetrical thirds. The third closest to the stairwell (or the fallout shelter as Silas liked to call it) contained rows of shelves with assorted perishable foods, meals-ready-to-eat of all varieties (including the much-reviled veggie burger), and gallons of water on one side. The other side contained emergency supplies, such as flashlights, batteries, radios, and other "nice-to-haves" (as Silas called them) in case of a long-term power failure. The first third was a survivalist's wet dream. A form of insurance against some unknown apocalyptic event.

"You can never be too prepared," Silas said smugly as they passed the first giant supporting arch. Janus made no comment. He just stood with his arms at his sides, expression neutral. *Smug bastard,* Silas thought, *I know he's impressed and probably jealous. Who wouldn't be?*

In the middle third of the room, Silas fashioned a meeting table by stacking several thin boards of wood on top of one another and setting them on top of paint cans. Six expensive looking chairs sat around the improvised table. The normally tan colored wood appeared white from an undisturbed layer of dust on top of it. The meeting area was enclosed by sturdy mahogany glass display cases that showcased only a fraction of his extensive antique weapon collection. The cases were arranged by type, with one dedicated to swords, another to bludgeoning weapons, one to crossbows, and another to various types of knives. Small placards below each weapon displayed its name, country of origin, and speculated date of manufacture. Soft lighting in each case drew Janus' eyes. The cases looked out of place in the bunker. This was the "museum". Meant to both educate and intimidate any person who joined Silas in the study. It made him feel better knowing he could take his pick of killing device at any moment against anyone who displeased him too much.

"The rest of the collection is upstairs in various rooms around the house. Some of the residents like to practice with them on each other." Silas laughed at his own joke. Janus smirked, nodding acknowledgement.

He's mocking me! How dare he mock a man in his own house! In his own fuckin' study! Might as well be steppin' on my nuts! Janus you bastard! Fuck you!

Silas and Janus passed under the second half-painted arch into the final section of the basement. This third functioned as Silas' office. Bookshelves lined the back wall, filled with titles from an assortment of fiction and non-fiction titles. Several metallic gray filing cabinets along the back left wall held his important personal documentation. It contained original paper copies, as well as digitized versions. His desk consisted of three smaller metallic gray desks arranged like a giant letter 'C' crammed together to form one uneven surface. On top of the desk, three large monitors, a keyboard, a 3D printer, and an assortment of other computer peripherals lay in ordered chaos. Only a one-foot by one-foot square was free of electronic junk. But it too was occupied by a giant ripped open bag of Doritos and three crushed cans of Pabst Blue Ribbon beer. A tangled mess of wires snaked unconcealed and jumbled, down the front and sides of the second-hand desks. The cords slithered to outlets in the floor, just below the bargain piece of furniture. "Got a deal on the cabinets and the desks on eBay years ago. Gotta be practical."

Janus smiled and nodded, but said nothing.

There he goes again! Making fun! Idiot doesn't appreciate saving a buck! Look at his fancy new clothes. What a waste of money! Janus you arrogant asshole! Come to my house to fuck with me huh? To hell with you!

Silas watched him closely as Janus wandered to the far right corner of the office to study a power generator in standby mode.

Observing Janus, he thought about why he had done business with the man in the first place. The history of the two men spanned decades, few of which Silas found enjoyable or pleasant. *I was such a dumb fuck back then. Always quick to blow my cash on the first thing I saw.* The only reason he had partnered with the man was because he was looking to spend his father's inheritance as quickly as possible. At that time, Janus had already established the infrastructure that would become Cereus and only needed additional capital investment, to cover startup costs for the various properties it would use as centers of operation. Silas had been heavy in the real-estate market and thought he could make extra money by acquiring land and property in high value locations like San Francisco, Honolulu, and New York City, the most expensive real estate markets in the country at the time. And he did make money. A lot of it. So much that he created a new unit of measure to quantify his gains. The *shit-ton*. One shit-ton was the equivalent of one million dollars.

After the coronavirus pandemic and resulting eviction bonanza of 2020 and 2021, it had been even easier to snatch up whole blocks of property at bargain bin prices. He made ten shit-tons in 2022 alone. Another twelve the next year. The profits continued to grow year over year after Cereus' founding, expansion throughout the U.S., then to certain locations around the world.

There was one problem though. Janus. He never liked the man. The way he walked, talked, and his pompous social justice warrior attitude, had always turned him off. *Fucker thinks he's better than everybody in the goddamn world.* As the organization grew and gained more influence, Silas' dislike and eventually hate, grew proportionally. By 2054, thirty years after Cereus' founding, he had not been an active Founder for years. His bank account became his proxy. He limited his contact with Janus and Barto to once a year at their annual Founders' meeting in South Lake Tahoe. This was only because he liked to ski and enjoy free booze at Barto's expense. He never liked Lili. Never understood why Janus brought her on. Sure, she had a nice pair of tits and a nice ass, and her face wasn't bad either. But she had no business background at all. Yet, she still became Janus' right hand. He had become the left. *She strokes and sucks him, while I wipe his ass. Complete bullshit! I had the checkbook! It should have been me who was his number two!* The memory of it still frustrated him in his advanced age.

Then a week ago, Silas received a voice message from one of his old cop buddies still living in Sacramento. He had been his inside man in the Sac P.D. for years, and had connections around the entire metro area. Now he was a senior advisor. One of those online consultants who had access to police files and records. He was happy to pass Silas information anytime he requested it. Silas was bankrolling his daughter's college tuition at Stanford after all. It was only fair. The message, brief but shocking said: "Lili is dead."

"How?" Silas responded via text message seconds later.

"Looks like a heart attack, but foul play suspected."

"Why?"

"Because your *favorite person* was involved."

The old police officer was still talking in code after all these years. It made sense. You never knew who was monitoring communication within or outside of the police department.

"Send me the preliminary police report."

"Sure."

It arrived via text five minutes later. Silas felt his heart begin to thunder in his boney chest upon reading the details. The last known visitors to her house were her daughter and Janus. Which could only mean one thing… *That bastard killed the bitch. Murdered her in her own house. Now he's here to off me! He wants my fuckin' money! Always did! All his grandstanding about people this and planet that. Turns out he's money first, people never. Everyone is.* The thought made Silas laugh to himself. In the end, Janus did bleed red just like him and every other person on the planet. He was a normal man after all, no better than Silas.

Silas stood in front of his desk, muscles tense, hands behind his back, while Janus faced the wall analyzing an expensive looking painting in a cheap frame on the wall. Neither had said a word in several minutes.

"It seems you've been quite busy since the last time I've seen you." Janus' voice was flat.

Silas kept his face expressionless and calm, as he moved closer toward Janus. "Yes, I have. We've had several new residents in lately due to a few…vacancies that came up recently."

"Ah I see. How is your little retirement home, cross arcade, cross winery business faring?" The blatant sarcasm of his words made Silas recoil with disgust. He gritted his yellowed teeth behind wrinkled lips.

"Things are fine. I think the model has caught on." Silas clenched his hands behind his back. The veins of his hardened hands inflated under the strain. "What can I help you with Janus? Haven't seen you since, when? Was it Tahoe, '57?"

Janus turned to face him. The light of the room, like that of a dungeon, poorly lit and shadowy, contributed to the mysterious nature of his gaze. "Yes, I believe it was then."

Silas' laugh was empty, void of sincerity. He knew he was a poor actor, but he played the part anyway. "Good times. Even though we're all old fucks now."

Janus nodded, agreeing. "I know it. How I wish you had remained better connected with all of us in the organization, instead of retreating out here to watch the elderly and sickly among us die."

Silas' forced smile at the semi-happy memory was replaced by his usual scowl. *He's baiting me into anger*, Silas thought. He could feel dark clouds of fury swirling around his rational judgment.

"Why did you walk away from us?" Janus' question betrayed a hint of longing.

Silas took his time in answering the question, reveling in the brief moment of superiority over his long-time collaborator. "You already know the answer." He paused only briefly, not allowing enough time for Janus to respond. "After spending all those years with you and the others meeting in bombed out buildings, scurrying from one forgotten location to the next, I finally realized the truth…"

"Oh really?" The mocking had returned to Janus' voice. "What did you discover?"

"That the delusional fantasy of Cereus that we all dreamed of wasn't possible. There was just too much opposition from mainstream politics, media, online culture; the whole machine was against us, and we would never be able to make it last." He felt his pulse quicken and his breathing become ragged after giving the explanation. It had been years since his lungs had worked properly and the augmentation he had received a decade in the past no longer functioned as well as before. It had never been enough to combat a lifetime of cannabis abuse.

"You walked away too soon from everything, I think," said Janus. "…Just like Lili…"

Silas laughed loudly, so loud he was sure tenants enjoying their breakfast in the community dining room above his study could hear. It made no difference to him.

"Don't compare me to her! Your beef with Lili was that even with all your ambition and charm, she never wanted you! She would have rather lived the rest of her life with that Mexican scum, than continue to help you build your illusion of utopia, and you never got over it!"

A violent coughing fit overcame Silas. His lungs burned from the exertion, yet even still he mentally prepared his next verbal assault.

Janus had no reply. He only offered Silas a level-headed stare.

Silas regained his composure and continued. "Janus, don't you see that human beings were never meant to survive this long? That civilization as we know it has run its course and whether we like it or not, *we*," his finger waved erratically from himself to Janus across from him "were born during the end times for our species! It's useless to try and build things to help billions of poor foreigners living in South America, Africa, and Asia. There's too fuckin' damn many of them for our efforts to make a difference! It's just a waste of time, resources, and energy! And do they give a shit about us!? Of course not! They would strip us of our wealth at the first opportunity, and maybe even kill us if they had a chance to take what was ours!"

"So your solution is to run and hide in your bunker to play video games, and sip wine while armageddon, in whatever form it takes, rains down around you?"

Silas shrugged. "Why should I be concerned with the lives of others, if it doesn't affect me?"

Janus snickered, then took a step forward. Silas nervously held his ground, fingering an object in his waistband.

"You think you're better than me!? I've heard rumors about what *you've* been up to these last few years…"

"Oh really? What have you heard?"

"Enough to know that you've been involved with that Limnic organization in some way." Silas hesitated, then dared to continue. "I also heard about Lili…very strange about her death. Her health file didn't point to any outstanding medical issues, and internal reports say the last person she was seen with…was you."

Silas clasped two throwing knives in his waistband between trembling fingers. With the movement of a man much younger, he focused his eyes on Janus' throat so the tip of the black knife would find its target. In anticipation of the attack Janus waited until the last moment to rotate his body profile to the side. He felt the air molecules around him disturbed by the flight of the knife, hearing it clatter to the floor after it hit the wall. A second knife, also intended for his neck, narrowly missed its mark. Instead, it pierced the flesh of his left shoulder, signaling a warm sting of pain to his primed nervous system.

Silas smirked, pleased at the accuracy that his nimble reflexes afforded him. *My next attack will kill this bastard*, he swore to himself. Janus appeared to be stunned by the knife protruding from his shoulder. His eyes closed and tiny droplets of perspiration peppered his brow.

Silas retreated behind one of the mahogany display cases. *Good thing I kept this thing unlocked.* Hastily, he grabbed the first sharp weapon within reach. It was an early twentieth century Italian fencing sabre, a popular dueling weapon from the period. The edges were dull, but he had the tip sharpened just for the hell of it. *Perfect choice.* He picked up the antique military saber and envisioned running it through Janus' entrails, watching them spill out on the floor before his eyes. The thought brought him great pleasure as he concealed his body behind the large display case. Momentarily safe, he activated a muscle and cardiovascular augmentation. In an instant, he felt his old heart begin to beat as if he were twenty years younger. The increased blood supply rushed to his arms and back. Those muscles, normally thin and weak, thickened and grew taut. The resulting pump felt incredible. Like an instant hard workout without the sweat or effort. He felt himself become dizzy, as his old brain fought to adjust to the sensation. He had never used all of his weekly augmentation allotment all at one moment like this. *I can't pass out. I have to kill him!*

From his place behind the weapon case, he peeked out toward the corner near the generator where Janus had been standing. But Janus wasn't there. And just as his eyes made his brain aware of this new reality. The room went black. He gripped the sword tighter, panic and fear threatening to overwhelm his senses. He sweat profusely, his hands ached from the blood pulsing throughout his overwhelmed body. Breathing heavy, it wouldn't be long before he lost consciousness. His rage helped him ignore the warning alarms in his brain. Silas lowered his center of gravity and prepared to fight to the death if necessary.

"Goddamn you Janus! Stop hiding and fight me!"

He heard footsteps to his right, they sounded as if they approached quickly then stopped in front of him. Silas thrust his sword at the air, but hit nothing. The footsteps withdrew, then sounded as if they came from directly behind him. He spun the blade around sideways through the darkness, performing a wobbly spin attack, but once again hit air. Suddenly, he felt a needle prick enter the delicate skin of his neck. The burning sensation began, first as a spark then as a firestorm of pain throughout his body, instantly causing him to let the old saber fall heavy on the concrete. The sound of steel impacting the hard surface echoed around the entire study.

The lights flicked on and Janus stepped over Silas' thrashing body. Silas screamed with fury and pain as his eyes focused on the device in his old colleague's hand. His fingers nimbly entered a few commands on the tiny apparatus and Silas felt the pain subside as he slipped into unconsciousness.

As Silas lay on the cold floor, Janus took a moment to sigh and take in the sight of his half-dead body on the ground. It was almost too easy to manipulate the old man into attacking him. *I didn't even need to use this advanced tech*, he thought, *just good old fashioned male intimidation and inflammatory language.* He savored the moment, knowing that Silas would play a vital role in the next phase of his plan.

The upload process would not take long. And with his simpleminded survivalist attitude, it would be easy to convert him from retirement home entrepreneur and winemaker, into his latest living weapon.

CHAPTER 32:
GRIEF

Of all the times of day, Noe had always preferred the afternoon. On a normal day, her energy level peaked around 1430 hours, which made it ideal for her best work. She had always saved her toughest tasks for the time period between 1330 and 1600. Ever since middle school it had been that way, and the tradition had followed her into adulthood.

In the morning, it took her brain at least an hour to begin functioning properly. It accelerated like an old coal powered locomotive, heavy and slow. Not very efficient. But when it got moving, it could demolish anything in its path. That was until around 1800, when all of the day's fuel had been consumed. From there, it was all about the momentum she had gained from the events of the day. If the day went well, the impetus would carry her to a restful stop, where she could recharge the supply of explosive energy needed for the following day. If it went poorly, she might coast into an open field, vulnerable to the uncertainty and anxiety of what the night may bring.

These days, even my afternoons can't carry me through to a safe place. The thought crossed her mind as she lay in her bed under summer white sheets. Tendrils of sunlight crept through her blinds, beginning their morning movement toward her pillow. If she laid in bed too long, they would eventually find their way to her face and force her out of bed.

It had been another night of fitful sleep. A glance at her device told her it was 0615. She let her arm flop to her side, dropping the device in the bedding. Though she had managed a total of, by her count, four hours of unconscious sleep, her body felt like it had spent hours in a full spacesuit trainer. Sweaty and fatigued.

In the weeks following her mother's death, Noe had isolated herself from the outside world. The security of her apartment was the only thing she could rely on. She had all of the food she needed, and Fyra for companionship whenever she wanted. She had no 'real' friends or meaningful relationships besides her A.I.

Noe had always had difficulty with the making friends aspect of civilian life. She was too military for most of the petty, shortsighted, and baby-crazy women that were around her age. On the other hand, she wasn't a grizzled combat veteran who liked to sit around retelling the same old military stories over and over again, like some of the people she had served with. Noe occupied an island in between both worlds, preferring to set up camp there, rather than swim to either shore.

So she stayed in her apartment. Calls and visits from Gabriel came. She ignored them. Even Van the Uber shepherd contacted her. He was nice and funny, but she was in no mood to put effort into making new friends, so his messages sat unanswered. Rodan reached out to her once a week, but the conversations were one-sided and brief, with Noe only responding with single word answers. "Are you doing alright?" He would ask. "Yep." "Do you need anything?" He would probe. "Nope." "…Ok, I'm here if you need anything." He would say. "Sure." The same conversation had occurred at least three times. Despite her emotionless responses, he contacted her every Sunday evening. Although she appreciated the gesture, she had no idea how to show it in any meaningful way, so she said nothing.

Sometimes Noe wished she had maintained better contact with her military buddies. She had made several good friends at her various duty stations, but time and distance had severed their communication and friendships. On several occasions, she thought about reaching out to an old hacking friend she had gone through training with. She had seen on social media that she had married several years back and was living somewhere in Florida with her husband and a young son. At some point, her former squadmate had separated from the Space Force and was now living a stereotypical military spouse life. Anytime Noe began to craft a message, email or text, she would erase it thinking, *what the hell would we even talk about?* Besides their technical training over a decade prior, they had nothing else in common. *It probably would be a pretty awkward conversation anyway.* So she never reached out.

At some point during her period of isolation, Rodan floated a job opportunity via a voice message. It involved gathering intelligence on known Limnic networks in order to track and shut them down. Noe didn't respond. She was too deep in her feelings. All the guilt, anger, grief, fear, and loneliness had a death grip on her, that she felt powerless to escape from.

Only once in her life had she contemplated suicide. A virtual mission had gone terribly wrong and as a result a U.S. Air Force operator in real life, on the ground, had been killed. All because of a careless error in a defensive firewall code she had made as a young officer. She saw his face every night for the next year anytime she lay down to sleep. The youthful face, ready to take on America's enemies, full of life and vigor, standing with a rifle slung casually over his shoulder in front of a sand-colored tent, smiled at her. It reminded her of her failure—how he was not alive anymore because of her fuck up.

The thought to kill herself came randomly one day. She was in another apartment, in another city, looking out of the window from the eighteenth floor. City life stared back at her with all of its usual contents. Cars, people rushing to work, buses, children playing, dogs barking. Suddenly, the noise from below ceased. There was motion but no sound, as if the audio input had been pulled from a video monitor. Noe was not aware of her body. Of the solid floor beneath it, of the air entering and exiting her lungs. In that moment, she was an amorphous sentient. She was not Captain Noelani Acosta, U.S. Space Force. She was nothing. She was a consciousness with an overwhelming urge to climb out of the window and let itself plummet to the sidewalk below.

Somewhere, from the far side of her empty thoughts came the words: *It probably wouldn't hurt much. Maybe not even at all. Surely, I'd be dead on impact.* She imagined her bones shattering like broken glass, piercing her vital organs, putting an end to everything she had ever been or might become and sending her to oblivion, to the other side. *A life for a life. Right?* A minute, two minutes passed at the window, while Noe stood in the form of an astral being. A vacant mind, feeling no logic or emotion. An observer, with the urge to *do something.* It was Fyra who pulled her back into her body. Plugged the audio back in. She was crying and screaming, "Noe! Don't! Please!" Noe again heard the noise from the street. Felt her heart beating steadily in her chest, her stomach rumbling. She was alive and she was hungry. Noe never spoke to anyone about the time her A.I. saved her life, not even to Fyra herself.

This time Fyra would not come to her rescue. She had turned her suggestion mode off because she didn't want to hear them. "Noe you should go to the gym." "Your cortisol levels are high, you need to breathe." "Human contact is important for your psychological health." "You need to drink more water." "You're ruminating again. Find something healthy and positive to think about." Noe knew what she *should* be doing, but couldn't bring herself to do it. She felt stuck.

Again, she stood at her apartment window, mesmerized by the Tower Bridge over the river. The window wasn't big, but she could fit through it if she really wanted to. The drop wasn't as high as her previous apartment, but it would be enough to do the job. *It probably won't hurt at all.*

A message notification on her device sounded from behind her on her kitchen counter. Something about the tone, reactivated her logical brain and prevented her from entering consciousness form, where anything and everything was possible. She turned from the window and picked up the device to scan for the source of the notification. It was from Rodan, a voice message. He never contacted her outside of weekly Sunday night check-ins.

"Did you get my message about the job a few weeks ago? Could really use your help."

Noe had no idea why, but she decided to respond. When she dictated the message her voice sounded cracked and old, like she had a cold and hadn't realized it.

"Yeah, I got it. Whatever you got I'll do it."

*   *   *

My skills are needed once again. The morning's assignment was a simple seek and capture mission. Her task was to locate the target, follow the digital breadcrumbs to their physical (or in some cases digital) location, then give the signal to the office, so that they could 'neutralize' the threat in some form. Easy stuff for her, although she never bothered to ask what exactly the term 'neutralize' meant.

She had the mission complete within one hour.

Pulling her earpiece out, she leaned back in her seat and let the silence of the conference room wash over her. Rodan's office in the Sacramento Capitol was small, but she didn't mind, she had worked in tighter quarters in Iran. Rodan usually shared the office with an older Asian guy (she had seen his picture on the wall in the office's entryway), but he was on some special assignment and was working remotely. Most of the time, Rodan and Noe were the only two in the office.

Noe stared blankly at the beat-up state issued laptop in front of her. *Still no sign of Janus yet. Where the hell could he be?* A soft knock on the door of the conference room pulled her out of the mental sinkhole.

"Come in."

Rodan peeked his large head in first, then followed with the rest of his gigantic frame.

"Already done? That was fast." He gave a half-smile to test her mood. Noe returned the gesture half-heartedly.

"It was easy. Another Limnic sympathizer is offline, but still no sign of Janus." Without warning, she balled up a fist and slammed it onto the oak wood table. The sudden action nearly made Rodan duck for cover as if a mortar exploded nearby. He approached her cautiously, to place a hand on her shoulder. He didn't know what else to do.

"Hey, it's alright we are making progress every day, and with every small operation we pull off, we're that much closer to finding him."

She looked up at him, looking for truth in his eyes. If it was there, she hadn't noticed it. He had been saying the same thing for days now.

"I'm going home now."

She collected her gear, then stood to go. Rodan looked at her with pity. The way he gazed, made her feel like he had more he wanted to say to her, but for some reason couldn't or wouldn't bring himself to do it. Today, the 'look' (as she called it), held longer than usual.

"What is it?" She said, making no attempt to conceal her irritation.

"It's nothing. I just wanted to thank you for helping us out these past few days. We're gonna do everything we can to bring Limnic and Janus down."

"Go team." The sarcasm was blatant. It was preferable to what she really wanted to say. She wanted to scream at him. To unleash all of the pain and suffering that she felt after losing her mother, on his broad shoulders. *He could handle it.* It would certainly make her feel better to let the anger ballooning in her chest explode in his face. Instead, she took a large deep breath to calm herself down. Fyra taught her the diaphragmatic breathing technique and Noe worked hard to practice. Most of the time at least. It didn't always work as intended, but it did provide a brief distraction from the constant force of rage and self-loathing throbbing inside of her.

"See you tomorrow." Noe walked past him and exited the room, feeling somehow that she was being used by Rodan and Cereus.

The same routine replayed itself at the expected cadence for several days. Wake up, receive mission, execute mission, go home, talk to Fyra, pass out, repeat. Noe felt the tedium wearing on her nerves, but knew that it was the only thing that kept dark thoughts from creeping into her mind during its moments of vulnerability. Plus the pay wasn't bad at all. Though she had no need for the extra income.

On another Sunday afternoon, Noe wrapped up another information-gathering cyber mission. She leaned back in her chair and stretched her arms above her head. During the stretch, she felt a pain in her neck that had not been there before. The stiffness of age was slowly making its way into her muscles and bones. *I gotta get back in the gym.*

The knock came on the door.

"Come in," she called. Rodan stepped into the room, with a smile on his face.

"Good news, thanks to all your hard work, we've managed to track one of Limnic's closest cells to an abandoned area north of town. This could be our chance to capture or kill him."

Noe flashed a skeptical look in his direction. "When do we do this?"

"In a week. We have to get everything ready. You'll work with one of Li Ma's closest guys and his crew to support the op."

"Li Ma? Who's that?"

"Y'know, the short old Asian guy whose picture you see every time you walk in here." Rodan chuckled.

Noe suppressed a smile. "Oh, fuck you."

He laughed. "I'm laughing *with* you. Not at you."

"Yeah right." Noe's mind returned to the intel. *Must be really good if they're pulling an IRL op.* "So, I know it's only a Limnic cell, but will Janus be there?"

Rodan's face turned serious again. "Hard to say. But he has worked with this particular group heavily in the past. Word is that they were responsible for some of the live demolitions in Chicago and Dallas, back during the war in the forties."

"I guess we'll just have to wait and see," Noe said.

Rodan gave her the 'look' again, but this time it felt…different. It stirred something primal and involuntary in her. Something she had not felt in a long time. Perhaps it had just been the brief spark of hope from the knowledge that she might get a shot at finding Janus? She was unsure, but felt it all the same. She became aware of the gentle nature of his molasses brown eyes, the masculinity of his face, large strong hands, and well-defined chin.

Fyra's voice echoed in her head: *Use diaphragmatic breathing to control your impulse to anger and irrational action.* She knew she should perform the deep breathing exercise right then and there. But the pull of irrationality was too strong. Instead, she quickly collected her things, bid him a terse farewell, and bolted from the office.

Lying in bed that night images of Rodan's face and general kindness toward her flashed into her mind. *He has been really sweet to me through all this. Even though I pretty much ignored him for a month.* She began to wonder what he would be like in bed. Some sex with someone other than herself might be good for her… Fyra's notification alarm for diaphragmatic breathing sounded from her device. Noe silenced it. She felt the seeds of arousal sprout deep within her, causing the muscles in her abdomen ripple with delightful tension, and agitating her breathing. She closed her eyes. *A big guy like that could do things, dangerous things. Maybe. Or maybe he's just using me. He does work for Cereus after all. Cereus just uses people. Just like it brainwashed and eventually destroyed Mom. I helped in destroying her too. Broke her heart. I killed her. She's dead because of me. Because of me and Janus. But mostly Janus. Janus, damn you!*

A current of anger surged from beneath the surface of her mind. Like molten lava, it oozed from open fissures then slowly rolled over everything in its path, leaving only thick scabs of charred destruction in its wake. The seedlings of attraction stood helplessly in the path of the flow. Within seconds they were crushed and smoldering, consumed by colors of burning red orange fiery liquid. She saw Janus' mugshot from the case files in the flames. The smoke from the fire twisted itself into the baleful vision of his face. A white shadow that had taken her mother from her in violent fashion.

With the saplings of her arousal smothered and burned, Noe opened her eyes to begin her breathing exercises again. Ten minutes later, her lungs and mind exhausted, she fell into a restless sleep. But she found no rest.

Another night of nightmares began again. The kind of dreams that put the body into physical panic. The class of dreams that can only be resolved by undoing the past or a complete extinguishing of the senses.

CHAPTER 33:
THE MAN IN CHARGE

Rodan sat at his desk feeling discouraged by piles of documents he had yet to review. It was only 0900 hours and he was already behind on last week's proposals from several comvils to form new administrative committees in the aftermath of the executive order. Things seemed to be functioning normally in most of them, but a few had shown signs of instability without Barto's visionary leadership.

At some point during the last few weeks, his heroic shield of service, that once impenetrable armor, which had carried him through Army training, his days as street cop, and his lengthy period of service with Cereus, had cracked; leaving an airy rift between the two previously joined sides. Without the surety of its blocking capability, Rodan felt exposed. As if any challenger could see straight through to the soft center of his being and sense his greatest fears and vulnerabilities. With no way to guard his heart, he had become immunocompromised, susceptible to ruin from the tiniest external foreign invader, and worse yet, internal attacks from his own faulty immune system. *I'm no visionary. I'm hardly a leader. I answer emails and determine my schedule based on the whims and needs of the people who write them. This is my life.* Rodan's splintered shield lay sinking in the mud. Maggots and worms made homes in the soft earth beneath it. With no one to repair the armament, it lay rusty and abandoned, waiting for someone, *anyone*, to pick it up and repurpose it for a new battle.

Just as he was beginning to craft a message to the email list COMVIL_LDRS_ALL, a new encrypted message caught his attention. It was flashing red on his screen. A signal that it required his immediate attention. He read the message with dry and fatigued eyes.

ATTN MR. MITCHELL: Our comvil in Statesboro, Georgia has had several incidents of civil unrest: looting, anti-postcapitalism protests, vandalism, and damage to community property, in the last week. Our local community police have been overwhelmed and could use support from HQ. Please send help ASAP.

- Falena Scott

COMVIL CHIEF STATESBORO, GA

Take a number Mrs. Scott. Rodan had received at least twenty similarly worded pleas for assistance in the last week alone. In Dover, Delaware, one citizen set himself ablaze in front of the comvil committee building in a radical act of protest. Others abandoned their community homes and attempted to buy their way back into the society of the old world, fleeing for nearby Washington D.C. The last stronghold of old world society. These were just incidents in one area. Ripples of the unrest spread from hub comvils, slowly expanding and infecting others like the COVID-19 pandemic of the early twenties. To make matters worse, some administrative committees refused to work with him. They preferred to wait until they could personally deal with Barto or Lili in matters related to the administration of their communities. When Rodan informed them that they would have to work with him, that neither Barto nor Lili were coming back, their communication with him abruptly ceased. As a result, he was often forced to send in local, and often unreliable, mercenaries to provide him with valuable ground truth and reestablish law and order.

These days, Rodan lived with a constant headache. He wondered when or if his brain would ever fill to its maximum capacity and explode at his desk. The never ending stream of problems, meetings, schedules, and messages in all forms seemed to crowd in the limited volume of his skull, sucking every last square inch of oxygen from the small space. *I'll die at my desk.* He allowed himself a momentary chuckle from the madness that was his life.

Li was on special assignment organizing a small action force to directly counter Liminc's plans. Though he had not filled Rodan in on the details due to a heightened classification level, Rodan suspected that the order came directly from Barto. He could not confirm otherwise. Either way, he was on his own managing daily Cereus operations. He hadn't spoken to Li in several weeks. He thought of him every time he looked at a military style cot Li had purchased years ago, when they first made the small liaison office in the Capitol their home. In the last month, he had used it nearly every day, only returning home on rare evenings when the usual deluge of messages slowed to a trickle and allowed him to sleep in his own bed. Also in the last month, his divorce had been finalized. His now ex-wife had moved back home to Austin, so there was little reason for him to be in his house. Too many painful memories. Too many reminders of his workaholism, and his lack of aptitude as a husband. *There's no way we would have survived this anyway.*

On this particular morning, he was preparing to field questions during a meeting being held in one of the briefing rooms somewhere in the building. The event was scheduled to begin at 1100. It would be the sixth time he volunteered to answer questions to reassure the general public about the viability, sustainability, and overall health of Cereus. *Why do I do this to myself?* He thought, as he trudged down the hallway toward the conference room. He reminded himself that the best he could do was maintain his composure and feign confidence in himself and Cereus. He lived by the phrase 'fake it, to make it'.

After every session, he became a better actor, increasingly aware of the anti-postcapitalist rhetoric used by Cereus' political adversaries. The loaded questions, telegraphed snares meant to entangle him for the sake of a sound bite or a pithy *chirp* (the descendant of the now defunct *tweet*) rarely surprised him anymore. They reminded him of similar expressions he heard as a younger man used against the organization back in the thirties and forties, during the battle of economic and social ideologies that rocked much of Western society. *I hate politics.*

The Governor of California, the Mayor of Sacramento, and other prominent city officials were already in the room, when Rodan took his seat at the table. The officials looked more like the cast of a reality TV show, than elected government officials. Each had their device placed at flattering angles in front of them to livestream the event to loyal followers online. Rodan had grown up in the twenties, when livestreaming was very common among his parents' generation. For some unknown reason, he had always associated it with activities like

playing tag or hopscotch. It was a child's hobby, not a suitable practice
for a fifty-something year old politician. Yet there he sat, no doubt with
happy, mad, heart, sad, and crazy-faced emojis floating across his
image on devices worldwide, because he represented Cereus, was
Black, and for any other reason besides what actually came out of his
mouth. Old world culture at its finest.

Rodan looked around at the carnival of figures, looking calm and
poised. *How did any of these fools get elected?* Then he remembered. Around
the nation and parts of the world, Cereus had undermined traditional
power structures, leaving local officials with little influence in many
cities and communities. Voter turnout was dismal, averaging twenty
percent or lower in many major metropolitan areas during local and
national elections, leaving only those on the fringes of society to
personally select the candidates they deemed most popular for
important roles. The result was a mishmash of online personalities and
political ass-kissers more interested in expanding their own personal
platforms, than doing the complex work of managing and
administrating cities, communities, and countries. Rodan faced a room
of these people when answering questions about Cereus.

A young shifty-eyed man with dark hair asked, "Is it true there's
no leadership in Cereus?" A stubborn looking Latina, older, with
dependable eyes asked, "Are there food and water shortages in your
comvils?" An Asian man, octogenarian-looking (though he was
probably over one hundred-years-old), used a thought-to-voice
communication device to ask, "How will you handle the civil unrest
that is breaking out?" A second question followed, "Will citizens be
able to return to *normal* society if they choose to leave?" Questions
came from a man who looked like an actual career politician. Tanning
bed colored skin, strategic gray streaks in his hair, the proud posture,
and cadenced speech gave him away. Probably the worst of the bunch.
"Are you prepared to shut Cereus down?" "Does Cereus finance and
arm the Limnic terrorists?"

Are these guys politicians, journalists, or influencers? Rodan could not
tell. They appeared to switch their role every minute, like a teenager
searching for an identity. Lost. Subject to the prevailing viewpoint or
philosophy that happened to pass in front of them at the moment,
never committing to one in particular. The questions they asked were
spun to further convince themselves and their supporters of their

unequivocal rightness on the issue of Cereus, never reaching the real issues that contributed to its rise or the shortcomings of old world society. They stood for everything and nothing. No one wanted to be wrong. They wanted to belong.

Rodan stumbled through the questions; rationalizing, dodging, deflecting, shifting, and massaging his words wherever he could. Perhaps he had become a better politician than he thought. Some of them seemed impressed by his verbal acrobatics and flailings. *Dance monkey, dance.* If nothing else, it made good content for their followers, fan-bases, and voting blocs. Gotta have good content. It was the only way to get most people in the world to pay attention to anything. It had been that way for as long as he could remember.

By 1200 he was back in his office, responding to various messages from comvil committees. He sent off and replied to nearly a dozen messages before he cleared a ceremonial space on his desk for his lunch.

Lunch had quickly become his favorite part of the day, because that was when Noe arrived to receive her mission briefs. It had been over a month since he stood on her doorstep and delivered the devastating news of her mother's death. The official autopsy report had deemed the cause of death as cardiac arrest. Another elderly person, dead of natural causes. It happened every day. Open and shut case. But Rodan knew better. He suspected Noe did as well, though she never said so explicitly. Any rookie investigator could tell just by looking at their complicated history. Police work 101. *You always gotta look into intimate partners. They often have the biggest reason to kill.* From the investigative report the manner of death was clear, albeit one that Rodan had never seen before in his entire life. *Murder in the mid twenty-first century is just as interesting as it's always been,* Rodan thought as he ate his meager ham and cheese sandwich among the clutter of his desk. While munching on the food, he pulled up the investigative report again to refresh his memory of the events:

CASE: HOMICIDE - ACOSTA, L. Case ID-06-2062-0101

Investigating Officers: Det. D. MEHTA, Det. J. JACOBS

DECEASED: Acosta (Keahi), Lili'uokalani, DOB: 7 Apr 2005; 575-33-4444; Place of Birth: Waianae, HI; Date of Death: 14 Jun 2062; Place of Death: El Dorado Hills, CA

SUBJECT: "Janus" [See: US-INTEL-ALL-CI File 2030-3405-2609]

CAUSE OF DEATH: Sudden Cardiac Arrest due to Atrial Fibrillation (Arrhythmia)

MANNER OF DEATH: Homicide by Remote Biological Nerve Capture Agent

DECEASED died of cardiac arrest 14 Jun 2062 around 2251 hours at her home located in Summit Village, a neighborhood in El Dorado Hills, CA. SUBJECT entered DECEASED's residence with his key, then used a bioweapon ▮▮▮▮▮▮▮▮▮ *to introduce the nerve capture agent* ▮▮▮▮▮▮▮▮ *into DECEASED's person. SUBJECT then activated* ▮▮▮▮▮▮▮▮ *via a remote device. A review of DECEASED's security footage revealed SUBJECT and WITNESS ACOSTA [DECEASED's daughter] were the last to enter and exit the residence. According to WITNESS ACOSTA, DECEASED received a credible threat on DECEASED's life on the morning of 14 Jun 2062. DECEASED seemed worried and anxious that agents from Limnic, a terrorist organization [Ref: US-INTEL-ALL-CI File 2050-3551-7615], might attack or harm her by unknown means. DECEASED provided WITNESS ACOSTA with WITNESS MITCHELL's phone number at the end of her visit. WITNESS ACOSTA left DECEASED's residence around 1700 hours. According to WITNESS MITCHELL he met DECEASED sometime in Fall 2047 at a social gathering. WITNESS MITCHELL last saw DECEASED in December 2057 at an annual retreat in South Lake Tahoe, CA. SUBJECT, DECEASED, WITNESS KHUNI, and WITNESS JAMES were also present at the annual retreat. According to WITNESS KHUNI, he was not aware of any specific threats on DECEASED's life. WITNESS JAMES refused to be interviewed for this investigation. A search of DECEASED's residence in El Dorado Hills, CA, revealed nothing pertinent to this investigation. A review of DECEASED's medical history revealed DECEASED took medication for high blood pressure, and high cholesterol, but had no life-threatening medical conditions. Several attempts were made to contact and locate SUBJECT using various investigative techniques. SUBJECT could not be located for an interview. SUBJECT's whereabouts remain unknown. [Ref: US-INTEL-ALL-CI File 2050-3551-7615], [Ref: US-CA-PD-ALL-Case File: 2062-06-0032], [Ref: US-PD-ALL-Case File: 2062-06-1253]*

Rodan scrolled down to read further into the investigative summary.

According to witness interviews, DECEASED met SUBJECT sometime in summer 2024 in the Bay Area. They became business partners in the establishment of Cereus, a non-profit organization [Ref: US-INTEL-ALL-CI File 2030-3405-2609]. According to WITNESS KHUNI, DECEASED and SUBJECT had sex on multiple occasions between approximately 2025 and 2052. He was not aware of any reasons SUBJECT would want to kill DECEASED.

Rodan skimmed down further. *Here's the part about the bioweapon.*

According to Dr. GREGORY HOME, Chief Forensic Pathologist, SUBJECT used a bioweapon ▮▮▮▮▮▮▮ to kill DECEASED. Dr. HOME provided the following explanation: "Through some seemingly innocuous method of transfer, like a bug bite or a needle prick, the nerve capture agent ▮▮▮▮▮▮ is introduced into the victim's body. Once inside, special compounds enable it to hitch a ride in the bloodstream to the brain stem, where it lies in wait. The unique make of the nerve capture agent ▮▮▮▮▮▮ is packaged into a controllable nanomachine that can be manipulated via any run of the mill device or even an old smartphone. Once triggered, the nerve capture agent ▮▮▮▮▮▮ arrests the nervous system and has been known to cause a litany of medical issues from paralysis, seizures, blindness, respiratory failure, and many others. These conditions may cause other medical complications that subsequently lead to the death of the victim, as it did in the case of DECEASED."

Rodan stopped reading. *Damn, death by bug bite. The technology of today is truly terrifying.* The report answered all of his questions, except for two. *Where the hell is Janus? And why did he do it?* Why would Janus kill one of his closest collaborators and the person (according to all accounts) that he was intimate with? He had no answers, and that bothered him. Then he thought of Noe. *It probably bothers her even more.*

Rodan could tell Noe was suffering in silence. She would probably never admit it or openly seek help from him. It went against an unspoken code that many cops, military, and medical professionals lived by. Who do the helpers turn to when they need help? Often to something or someone that can't talk back. That can't tell them what they already know has to be done to get over their problems. Can't do it. It's against the code.

With that knowledge, he voluntarily began to contact her once a week, just to make sure she was still breathing. A single military veteran, with few contacts on the 'outside' to speak of, her closest family member killed violently? It was a suicide case waiting to happen. He had seen the same scenario play out too many times throughout his career to let it go by without doing anything. When she ignored his job offer, he took no offense. He understood where she was. In a self-constructed prison locked on both sides. No spare keys. The only person who could unlock it was her, on her own time, by her own choice. He told himself, when she comes out, I'll give her something to do. If she came out at all.

The ones he had seen make it over the years always found something to do. A new purpose. A new mission. A new reason to keep on living and to be helpful to someone or something. It rarely replaces the void left by their first organization, where the initial trauma of indoctrination seared itself into their young psyches. But it was enough to leave it behind. Enough to give them a shot at happiness.

Rodan had messaged her on a whim. He happened to be at home that Saturday afternoon. For some reason on his spectrum of exhaustion, from just tired to dead dog tired, he was just a little tired. But this was a problem, too. When his thoughts had the freedom to wander outside of work matters, they were like a new recruit on leave for the first time after basic. All energy, nowhere to go. Prone to wild swings of emotion and misguided action. Without an authority figure to tell him how to think, with too much time off, the chance of doing something stupid was very high.

Without thinking, he dictated the message. It was only after it read as 'sent' on his device that he began to consider the possible results of his action. What if she thinks it's weird? What if she doesn't respond? What if she does respond? What should I say? The questions scrolled through his mind as if they were the credits at the end of an old syndicated TV show, too fast and small to be analyzed or digested in any meaningful way. You were just trying to be helpful, he reassured himself. The entire reflection only lasted for a minute. He could never look at himself for too long. He didn't know what might return his gaze if he looked too hard.

He was surprised (and a little nervous) when she returned the message almost right away. Capitalizing on the momentum, he sent her documents to hire her as a cyber security contractor within the next ten minutes. That next Monday she was in the office working. Since that time, her skill had helped them neutralize ten Limnic cyber conspirators. She worked skillfully and quickly, always wearing the look of aggressive determination on her face. An expression chiseled by lived trauma and deep guilt.

Rodan was as gentle as possible with her, providing her with the necessary mental and physical space to grieve in her own way. He could tell that there were moments when she posed a real threat to his person. He accepted them with grace that he wished he could have provided to his ex-wife or to his leadership of Cereus.

There were also the moments of sweetness that came between them. One day he returned from another nerve-wracking meeting with city and state officials to find his office completely cleaned and arranged. Document readers were stacked neatly on corners of the desk. The usually overflowing trash can had been taken out, and the mess of physical papers had been placed in various filing cabinets. It took him a moment to pick his jaw up off the floor at the sight of his clean office.

"I was bored," she said, "and I hate clutter," a slight smile curved on her lips.

Rodan laughed. "Uh, thank you. I was gonna get to it…just haven't had the time."

"Uh-huh, yeah sure you were," Noe said.

He had always found her attractive, but buried his feelings for the sake of professionalism. On unexpected occasions, he caught himself mesmerized by her shape, intelligence, and her giving nature. Though they rarely spoke much outside of mission related topics, he noticed she began to arrive earlier than necessary to his office. Sometimes she would bring her own lunch, and they ate in silence, eyes exchanging furtive glances at each other and around the all too familiar office space. At other times, she simply moved to the conference room and paced back and forth, anxious to begin her task for the day. Rodan would give her the briefing early, to help her calm her nerves. When she was calm, he was calm. He noticed his headaches diminished in intensity when she was around, and he seemed to be able to think more clearly about the mountain of tasks awaiting him. Both of their moods improved even more after he told her about the upcoming operation against Limnic. The fear mixed with excitement provided an ionic charge between them. It made things better. Made it feel like (at least to him) anything could happen.

On the Tuesday afternoon before the operation, Noe arrived early to receive her mission and completed it with rapid efficiency. As usual, she collected her gear, then stood to leave. She wore tight jeans and a simple navy blue t-shirt, both faded from years of repeated washing, with her thick braided hair extending to her mid back. Standing on the opposite side of the room in his now ironed black suit, Rodan watched her walk toward the door. As she moved, he became aware of his accelerating heartbeat. Hints of arousal permeated in his blood, causing him to readjust his stance. To his surprise, Noe turned and asked a pointed question. "What do you think's gonna happen with Cereus?"

Her sudden question caught him off guard. Like an experienced politician, he immediately quelled his previous thoughts, then found the correct words to provide his response. "You know, that's a good question. I'm not sure. I know there're a lot of people out there in the population at large that would love to see us fail. Just like every other utopian experiment throughout recorded human history." His eyes fell to the floor as he sighed, letting out a month's worth of tension into the air. "Sometimes I feel like we were always doomed to that fate."

Noe shook her head. "My mother…she…she died trying to make this 'experiment' a reality." Her voice trembled as she held back sobs of sorrow mixed with ire. "She spent her whole damn life, trying to make this thing work only to be murdered by Janus. What the hell was it for?"

"Noe, we're gonna get Janus. It's only a matter of time before he resurfaces. Once he's taken care of it will be easy to eliminate the rest of Limnic."

She clenched her fist, wanting badly to put a hole in a wall with it. "And after Janus is gone, what then? There may be hundreds or even thousands out there just like him, waiting to take advantage of our human capacity for infinite hate. No matter how much technology we develop, the size of the chips in our heads, or the realness of the virtual worlds that we construct, human hate will always find a way in this world."

Rodan had no words to counter her claim. Instead, he approached her with measured steps, as one might toward a wounded animal. He stopped just a foot away from her, allowing himself a rare moment of masculine vulnerability to embrace her.

He felt warm tears streaming onto his shoulder as they held onto one another, in an embrace meant to comfort and heal. Each reminding the other that good things and people did exist in the world and that, in some way, they both continued to believe in the boundless spirit of good that humanity could do.

CHAPTER 34:
PRE-BATTLE RITUAL

It was a ghost town. *Probably one of the hundreds of California gold rush towns that exploded overnight hundreds of years ago with thousands of people looking to strike it rich.* Rodan analyzed the aerial photos with watering eyes. The unblinking fluorescent lights of his office gave no hint of the time, but his body told him it was after midnight.

The map he analyzed was old. One of those low-quality maps from Google's early days. Not much to work with, but it was the best he had. Designing ingress, egress, and approach routes for tomorrow's op had taken him hours, but he was able to make use of the blurry map to come up with what he felt like was a decent plan. It was work that required attention to detail and precision. It was also a welcome diversion from his new politician role as the head of Cereus. Field work made him feel useful. He saw operations planning as an art, a stage production. All of the pieces had to be in place in order for it to go correctly. He was the producer and stage manager, assigning and blocking roles for all of his actors, hoping everyone could execute when the curtain rose and the cameras were rolling. *It's gonna be a helluva show.*

North Bloomfield. It had been an early Cereus land acquisition that the Founders had personally scouted and selected on foot. It's remote location in the mountainous forests of Northern California had been the ideal proving ground for the experimental society. It had been known as Comvil Zero. The Founders and a few dozen carefully chosen people played utopia for an unknown amount of time, working out the rough edges of their plan to reform first the country, then the world. At the end of the trial period (which Rodan assumed was a success) they packed up and left, returning the old mining town to the soft and slow embrace of nature. They abandoned an abandoned town. Now, nearly forty years later, the mishmash of crumbling and restored nineteenth century buildings were in use again. This time by a small cell of Limnic supporters. Hopefully, Janus will be among them.

For Rodan, there always came a point in mission planning where looking, thinking, and strategizing became counterproductive. He had gone over the plan so many times that he could almost recite the action steps movement by movement. That afternoon he had discussed it over and over again with Noe and continued to refine and tweak small details long after she left. But now he was out of gas and could barely keep his eyes open. He forced himself to stand and make his way to the cot in Li's office. Details from the mission continued to bounce around in his skull when his head hit the thin pillow. Even with adrenaline infused anxiety rushing through his large frame, he fell into a restless half-sleep. Though he would never admit it, he would need all of the energy he could gather for the next day.

*   *   *

This might be our chance to get that son-of-a-bitch, came Rodan's thoughts as their van rumbled and swerved along precariously thin mountain roads that lead to the town. It was the next evening and so far, everything was going according to plan.

He had linked up with Kyler, Li's number one informant, and his crew at an open parking lot near the town jail in northern Auburn, California. There, they made last minute gear checks and preparations before making the hour drive north to the town. It had been years since he had seen Kyler "The Terminator" in person. Their relationship had always been characterized by neutral indifference. Rodan followed Li's script almost to the letter on the rare occasions he met with Kyler instead of Li. He was careful not to undo any effort Li had put into building the man up as a source. Kyler seemed to follow along with no protest. Each man played his part perfectly. Li made the plans, Rodan carried them out, Kyler complied. When Rodan and Kyler greeted each other in the parking lot, they shook hands, but exchanged no words. Both continued to play their part.

Half an hour later, Rodan sat across from him as both of their heads bobbed and swayed with the motion of the van. Noe sat next to Rodan. They too had only exchanged pleasantries at the staging area. He wanted to talk to her, to ask her how she was feeling, to ask her if she was ready, but she seemed to be avoiding him. His head was so full with battle plans, movements, and possible tactical maneuvers, that it pushed those thoughts into a dusty corner of his mind. *She'll be alright. She'll be ok,* he told himself. Wishing, hoping that it would be true.

Noe looked around the van. She had only managed three hours of sleep the night before, but she was not tired. Her body felt like a wound-up spring, ready to unleash a wave of potential energy at any moment. She had noticed Rodan searching for her eyes throughout the day, but couldn't spare the emotional energy to process what, if anything, was happening between them. So she avoided him and distracted herself with the scene around her.

Kyler's unit consisted of eleven units. Five were human, the remaining six were stashed in large black containers at the rear of the van. They were U.S. Army and Marine combat mechs, capable of being assembled by even the most simpleminded junior enlisted members of those branches. Noe had never worked with them before, but had seen and heard various accounts of their effectiveness on the battlefield. She wondered how a machine could make the possible ethical and moral choices that soldiers were often called on to make in the heat of battle. *Will they help me if shit goes sideways?* The unanswered question made her more nervous and jittery.

The human members of the unit were a different story. All of them (including her) wore the same dark green field gear that consisted of light ballistic body armor, and tactical pants. It was their unofficial team uniform, even though she had only met all of them hours prior. Seated across from her in the back of the van was the field commander, Kyler. He spent the majority of the trip with his eyes closed, but she could tell he was not sleeping. The hardness of concentration on his craggy face hinted at a long career of combat experience and lonely leadership. There was a man who seemed most at home when things got loud and ugly. Who found only intervals of antsy readiness during times of peace. *A real hard ass, probably, but one you definitely want on your side when the shooting starts.*

Next to Kyler was a freakishly large man with small intense eyes, full lips, and a sandy skin complexion. To Noe, he appeared like he was part *de la raza,* and mixed with some other ethnic identity. He wore his hair with a military style buzzcut, which made him appear the very archetype of a soldier. Bent over, with elbows on his massive thighs, he rested giant hands on a customized laser cannon that said "Zapp!" in yellow electrified-type letters on the side. Noe didn't know his name. She had only heard one of the other men refer to him as "Bear". She had not heard him speak once during the entire trip.

Across from Bear, was a youngish looking man with brown hair named Lance. His untamed beard extended to his chest and almost tangled with a pair of dog tags clinking around his neck. Lance's face almost mirrored Kyler's, except it lacked something. Experience. Noe assumed he was putting on a tough face to make himself appear more hardcore than he actually was. The long beard was another tell of his desire to fit in with the rest of the group, and conceal his (probably) otherwise peaceful nature.

Noe returned her attention back onto herself. The bouncing was not helping the uncomfortable bubbling sensation in the pit of her stomach. *Keep it together*, she told herself, as she began her relaxation breathing once again. While her lungs were inflating with the sweaty air of the van, a sudden swerve threw her off-balance. With an unconscious reflex, Noe placed her hand on Rodan's knee to balance herself, as she simultaneously gulped down a surge of vomit that crept up her esophagus. A second later, after the van returned to its steady course, Rodan shot her a look of encouragement. It made her temporarily forget the turning in her stomach, and the acidic taste in her mouth.

"Sorry about that everyone! It's hard to see what's coming ahead on these roads." The voice came from the driver, a dark-skinned youth everyone called Spazer. The young man kept his eyes fixed on the road ahead of him. Even though there was still some daylight left, the sun was no longer visible and the tall trees along the road threw bladed shadows in the path of the van.

A large Black guy seated on the far end of the van next to the bot boxes yelled, "Goddamn Spazer! When the hell did you get yo' damn license, yesterday!? You gon' fuckin' kill us befo' we even get to the fuckin' town!" He went by the name "Cheeks". *That can't be his real name! Do they call him 'Mr. Cheeks'? Maybe*, Noe thought. His name had been the first Noe learned and remembered that afternoon. Everybody knew Cheeks.

"Aw come on Cheeks! I swear there was a fuckin' pine cone in the road dawg!" said Spazer.

Cheeks snorted a breathy sound of disapproval, "The way you been drivin' young buck, we done avoided ten damn pine cones since we left Sacramento." The other men in the van howled with laughter, slapping their knees and stomping.

"Cheeks, let the boy concentrate," said Kyler, stifling a laugh. "These roads can be a bit treacherous." Cheeks waved his hand toward the front in a dismissive gesture in reluctant compliance. From the back of the van, Noe noted his wide eyes fall on her as they had several times before throughout the road trip. He wetted his fat lips and said, "So…you was in the Space Force, huh?"

Noe straightened in her seat, and hardened her expression, "Yeah, I was."

"I heard all you Space Force types like to do is smoke weed and get high all day. That true?" Some of the other men snickered. Lance said, "Sounds like my kinda military service!" More laughter echoed around the van.

Noe grinned. "That's only part one part of the force. The rest of us just sleep all day until we get to Mars."

"I bet you do! Y'see, I myself was in the Army. See we never had to wait for *our* service to legalize weed or sleepin' for that matter, we just did that shit whenever we wanted." Cheeks threw back his head with a hearty laugh. Bear slapped Cheeks' hand in approval of his joke.

"I also heard the Space Force had the finest women too…even finer that the Air Force ones." Cheeks leaned forward in his seat toward Noe, batting his eyes shamelessly.

Noe smirked and shook her head, "I don't know about that, but after being in the Army, I guess any woman or bot you see looks *fine* to you."

Spazer convulsed with suppressed laughter from the front seat. Kyler closed his eyes and let a brief smile flash across his face. The other men let out an "Ooooh", surprised at the surprisingly sharp wit of the beauty that joined them on the mission.

Cheeks chuckled and leaned back in his seat. "I see you got jokes." He raised a fat hand to his stubbled chin and analyzed her. Anyone who could match him in wit was alright in his eyes. He nodded in approval. "I think you would have done pretty well in the Army."

"She got yo' ass pretty good!" Spazer said from the front.

"Shut up and drive young buck!" Cheeks retorted, "Don't make me come up there and give you the beatin' yo' momma should have a long time ago."

Spazer shrank in his seat and concentrated on the road.

Noe noticed the wheels turning in Cheeks' Army issued brain as he searched for a way to return fire at her. She smiled, but did not show her teeth. *Thanks Cheeks.* She was grateful for the momentary distraction. It made her forget where she was headed and what she would have to do very soon.

A minute later, just as Cheeks opened his mouth to say something (probably stupid), the van jerked and swerved again. Noe tensed her body to keep herself from falling onto Rodan, while all of the others braced themselves where they sat. That's when she felt their speed decrease. *Must be getting close to the town.* Noe's body returned to its anxious state. The brevity of the last few minutes was lost, like a distant memory.

"Ten minutes people!" Kyler called. "Check your gear!"

The sound of clicking weapons, jangling gear belts, and the shuffling of boots and bodies filled the van. A new air of tension replaced the jovial atmosphere, as each person turned inward to their respective personal pre-combat sanctuary. Always aware that no matter how well trained and equipped they were, combat, was always a great unknown, and one could never tell how it would turn out.

After the gear was ready and no more preparations could be made, Noe watched each man disappear into his own inner world. Lance grabbed his dog tags and kissed them, while tilting his head up to the roof of the van. Bear became quiet and pensive, saying nothing. Rodan stared at his weapon, an old M-4 carbine rifle, with empty eyes. Kyler closed his eyes again, returning to that place in his mind where he had spent the majority of the trip. Even the boisterous Cheeks stared at the floor of the shaking van, quiet for the first time all afternoon.

Noe attempted to turn to diaphragmatic breathing to soften her muscles and slow her thumping heart. She closed her eyes to block out the noise of the van and contribute to the cathedral-like hush of the vehicle.

Next to her, Rodan saw Noe close her eyes. He could tell she was nervous, but had no doubt that she would be fine. (At least he hoped she would be.) Kyler's men would personally look after her on the ground. *Besides*, he thought, *her presence will make it easier to take advantage of any cyber superiority that the Limnic cell has in the area.* He had seen her in action and was confident she was up to the task.

He had decided to tag along at the last minute. For some reason, his usual post at his desk as an observer had not seemed an appropriate place for the acting executive director of Cereus. He wanted to meet the man whose terrible genius had helped birth both Cereus and Limnic face to face, to see who he really was. To see what kind of man he was before they captured and or killed him.

"Five minutes till' we reach the staging area!" Kyler shouted in front of him. The darkness of the early evening was upon them now. As planned, they would reach the outskirts of the town by nightfall to take the enemy by surprise.

Rodan bowed his head and closed his eyes. Though he had never prayed in his life, it was moments like these that he wished he had a great divine force to call upon for protection or favor. Instead, he joined the soundless group of soldiers in quiet self-reflection and hoped that would be enough to protect them all in the battle to come.

CHAPTER 35:
BATTLE OF NORTH
BLOOMFIELD

Trees were everywhere. *Not good for visibility*, Kyler thought, pointing his night vision capable binoculars towards a forlorn small structure that looked like it might collapse at any second. He estimated that they had about fifteen minutes of daylight remaining to get the lay of the land before they went hot.

In the back of the van, they discussed the plan for a final time. According to the intel Noe had collected, the Limnic cell had approximately twenty to twenty-five moderately trained fighters. Some were hardcore tree huggers with some combat experience, a few were volunteers who believed in Limnic's "by any means necessary" motto for saving the planet, and an unknown number of them were bots. With only eleven troops among Kyler's unit, two of them essentially non-combatants (Rodan and Noe), they needed to be prepared for a potentially hard fight. Kyler especially scoffed at Rodan's presence. He understood the desire for leadership to be out in the field at such a critical moment, but it was rarely helpful when top brass stuck its nose where it didn't belong. *Leave the fighting to the soldiers*, was what he always thought in these types of situations. But it was too late to do anything about that now.

Spazer dimmed the lights in the back of the van to provide additional concealment, as they huddled over a crude topographic paper map at their feet. It would have been preferable to have digital maps, but the network was unreliable this far from civilization, so they had to make it work. Kyler spoke, "Cheeks, you'll take three bots and fan out to the left from our current position to engage from the north." He looked toward Bear. "You take the other three and go right through the woods, then clear the buildings on the south side." Bear grunted an acknowledgment. The sparse lighting made him look much more deadly than he had during the day.

"That will leave my group to move up the middle after you two have engaged them from the sides. It will be myself, Spazer, Lance, and our guest Noe." His eyes fell on Noe. Her face looked determined, yet he sensed her trepidation. "Once we get you to the center point of the town, which looks to be about…a half a mile from our current position, you do your thing and establish cyber superiority for us. Once we have control of the network, we'll be able to monitor all enemy activity and possibly shut them down from there."

Noe nodded firmly, focusing only on the task at hand to block out her sudden need to empty her bladder.

Kyler saw the tension in her face, the lack of confidence. It was a potential liability for him and his men. He didn't have time for it. "You can do this. Trust us to protect you, trust your gear, trust yourself." He hoped whatever simulated combat training she had received would be enough to carry her through. The rest of the crew murmured hushed affirmations of his words. Cheeks whispered using an outside voice, "Don't worry Space Force. We ain't gon' let nuthin' bad happen to ya." He followed his words with an exaggerated wink. Noe flashed him a weak smile.

"Alright people. Prepare to deploy drone bots in five minutes. Let's kick some ass." Kyler commanded.

The next thing Noe knew, they were bounding out of the back of the van and forming up in their respective strike groups. Rodan gave her his 'look' that said, *be careful,* as he moved to the support element behind them, readying his M-4 along with the rest. Initially, he wanted to be a part of her group, most likely to help protect her, though he had not said so explicitly. Despite his request, Kyler advised against it. She had no idea whether it was because of a tactical reason or simply because Rodan had not been in combat in decades. Whatever the case, the brief exchange between the two men ended with Rodan moving toward the rear of the formation, a serious, somewhat defeated look on his face.

Noe returned her attention to her weapon. She couldn't remember how many times she had confirmed its functionality in the last twenty minutes, but still she tested it again. She had good cause to do so. The rifle was an antique M-4 carbine that had probably been in circulation since the Iraq War during the early 2000s. It had been refurbished with a new stock and barrel, but the guts of it were probably half a century old. She hoped it didn't show its age when she needed to use it. *Trust your gear*, she reminded herself. The thought helped her stop obsessing over the gun. She activated her night-vision goggles, bathing everything around her in an eerie green and black light, and stood ready to fight.

For a long amount of time, the silence and darkness of the forest swallowed Kyler's unit. Night creatures of all forms began their hunts, the wind rustled the trees, restless boots crunched the earth. For Noe, the silence was screaming. It disturbed her. She felt as if she were floating in an outer space simulator where the only audible sounds were her own labored breathing and her somehow, still beating heart. She noticed a tiny light down the path coming from what she remembered on the map was an old school building. Its presence was welcome solace in the void. It meant others shared the space with her, even if they were enemy combatants.

Cheeks, Bear, and Kyler had already deployed the combat bots. The collapsible drone warriors were only about three feet tall, and from a distance their cylinder-shaped bodies looked like old metallic trash cans. They had each worked swiftly to attach the leg components to provide the bots with greater freedom of movement. In under two minutes, their number grew from five to eleven potential sources of firepower.

Kyler bladed his hand and signaled toward the right, then to the left. Cheeks' and Bear's respective groups moved almost in tandem upon seeing the sign. It was at that moment that Noe realized the battle would soon be underway. She had heard the sound of gunfire an untold number of times throughout her military career and via popular media, but somehow, hearing the scattered pops and bangs, and smelling the air around recently discharged firearms in a live situation infused the air with a different kind of energy. One that simulators could never recreate.

Then, Kyler's booming vocal commands resonated somewhere in her mind, and without thinking, Noe began to move. It was as if she were in a dream, being tugged by an invisible force between herself, Kyler, the young Spazer, and the bearded Lance. Only the sight of a dead human Limnic combatant reminded her that this was real.

*   *   *

On the north side of town, Cheeks and his contingent emerged from the tree line. The town was smaller than it looked on the map, but the trees had been thicker than he expected. It fucked with his visibility. A man in light body armor and jeans charged toward him, pointing a rifle and screaming a war cry. Cheeks shot to kill and the under-armored man fell to the ground. On his left, he heard something fall near a large tree about five feet from his position. *Grenade!* He ducked his large body behind the nearest adjacent tree to shield himself from the blast wave. Upon standing, he could feel warm blood running down his arm. *Must have been the shrapnel, shit.* Ignoring the wound he continued to advance, flanked by the well-armored bots. *Gotta keep moving!* He pushed deeper into the center of town.

On the opposite side of town, Bear experienced heavy combat. The majority of the Limnic fighting force had taken up residence in the battered homes of former miners. From there flowed the greatest resistance. Bear weaved his six-foot five frame from building to building to clear them out one by one, using the same strategy. One "can" bot would lead the way, peppering the room with cover fire, while Bear and the other two remaining bots entered crouching behind it, using the lead machine as a shield. That was the advantage of the shorter bots over the taller more human-like ones. Greater firepower, and better armor. Bear used the same tactic to clear five buildings. At the fifth building, amid the explosions, sound of gunfire, and occasional cries of wounded or dying enemies, he radioed Kyler to let him know that it was safe for him to approach with Noe. At the sixth, his lead bot malfunctioned, leaving him without his armor. At the seventh, one bot tripped over debris and crashed to the floor. By the time it got up, enemy fire had damaged it so badly, it became non-operational. By the ninth and last building, Bear was alone, with only his old Glock at his side. It had been a gift from his grandfather, and it had brought him luck in every firefight he had ever been in, even saving his life by blocking a bullet on one occasion. He pressed himself against the outside of the building, tossed his last grenade inside, and let out a savage yell as he turned to enter.

Two lightly armed Limnic volunteers had been killed by the grenade blast. Two more scrambled for cover behind a dilapidated wall. Bear killed one with his Glock, expending his final rounds to take him down. The other still remained. He threw the empty weapon to the floor, then with savage force, easily broke through the old wall and grabbed the man. He was small, yet Bear could feel his strength. His enemy used a slip maneuver to break free, then clambered to the floor to pick up a broken piece of the wall, which he used to slice Bear's arm. Pain stabbed Bear, and made it hard for him to stay on his feet. Drawing a large knife, he lowered his center of gravity as he faced the man. The soldier flashed a determined look before he dropped the wall debris, then drew his own knife. There was a brief pause among them both before the knife fight ensued.

The enemy slashed and thrust with experienced movement. Bear did the same. Both circled each other knives flying, with smoke, fire, and the smell of fresh corpses swirling in the air around them. Bear's forearms dripped with blood. He realized he had been wounded more than once during the battle, and unconsciousness might overtake him soon, which meant death. The enemy sensed weakness and thrust with mighty force for a deathblow aimed at Bear's heart. In a split-second Bear let his knife fall to the floor, evaded the thrust, grabbed the enemy soldier's knife arm and twisted it with devastating power. The man screamed in agony and staggered backward. Bear tackled him with animal ferocity, then proceeded to beat him until he no longer moved.

On hands and knees, breathless and wounded, he reached for his radio, "South side secure."

*   *   *

Kyler's group moved up North Bloomfield road through the middle of town. The majority of the enemy forces were focused on engaging Cheeks' and Bear's elements, leaving the center of the town, for the most part, clear. He and Spazer swept their weapons back and forth, seemingly unphased by the carnage and gunfire around them. Even the young Spazer, despite his youth, looked quite at home on a chaotic battlefield. Lance followed at the rear. The three of them formed a protective triangle around their Space Force guest.

Noe could not tell how much distance they had traversed since the fighting began, or how much time had passed, but she knew her arms were beginning to ache holding the weapon up and her lower back was throbbing under the weight of her gear and from keeping her head ducked.

They passed a large old hydraulic water cannon on display near the entrance of the town. It had been dubbed "The Handy Giant" and probably hadn't fired water in over a hundred fifty years. *Water, we could use some of that right now,* Noe thought as she watched small fires blazing at several points in the grass caused by incendiary devices and grenades being lobbed by both sides of combatants.

The four of them approached a building with flaking white paint and thin wooden pillars struggling to support a sagging roof over a patio. It appeared as if a strong gust of wind could cause the narrow pillars to fail and send the roof crashing down at any moment. "That's our target!" Kyler said, raising his voice above the noise of assorted battle sounds.

Just outside of the entrance to the building a grenade detonated some twenty-five feet from in front of them. Noe fell to the ground. Kyler, Spazer, and Lance instinctively dropped to a prone position, then scrambled to surround her and return fire.

"Incoming four hostiles!" Spazer yelled, his normally kind-natured voice sounded unrecognizably mature in the heat of battle.

"Get Noe into that building, now! Lance and I can take care of these fuckers!" Kyler said, mirroring Spazer's intonation.

"Rog Boss!" Spazer yelled.

With bullets whizzing around his head. Spazer popped up with youthful vigor. Using a surprising amount of strength, he pulled Noe up by the back of her body armor. She could feel the force of the pull compelling her onto her feet and into the building. Once inside, the sight of four lifeless former enemy combatants were scattered around the tiny room. The sight of the blood spatter on the walls, combined with the smell of burned flesh made her gag. She began to wretch, wanting to vomit, but spit instead. She hadn't eaten much all day, and was glad for it.

"I'll watch the door! Get going with your set up!" Spazer said, then he immediately turned his attention back toward the door to support his commander.

Noe slung her M-4 over her shoulder and moved toward the back of the small room. She swiftly cleared a space for her computer amid the debris and set to work. Although she had performed field cyber hacking countless times before, she had never done it under the pressure of a real firefight. She took a deep breath and blew it out of her lungs. There was no time for diaphragmatic breathing. *All I need is five minutes*, she thought, but she knew five minutes was an eternity under these circumstances. She began to work faster than she ever had in her life.

Soon Spazer ran back into the building. Noe looked up and was relieved to see Kyler and Lance enter behind him. Kyler activated his radio. "Cheeks, what's your position?"

The four of them heard a crackle and sporadic gunfire coming from the speaker but no response. "Cheeks, report." Kyler's tone grew more frantic despite his attempts to maintain his calm. All four held their breath, waiting for a response, but none came. Ten, twenty, thirty seconds passed. A bullet whizzed into the doorframe, sending splinters of old wood into the building. They narrowly missed Kyler's face. Lance ran to the door and returned fire. Limnic was closing in, and they were running out of time.

Something was wrong.

"Cheeks—"

"I'm here sir!" Cheeks' voice blasted through with low-fidelity from the tiny speaker. "We cleared....most....north side....town. We...lights...down...the road...they got...fuckin'....more...." The message was distorted among the noise.

"Cheeks, repeat last message," Kyler said.

"....Reinforcements...coming this way!"

"We got enemy reinforcements incoming!" Kyler said, shouting from over his shoulder in Noe's direction, his muzzle still pointed toward the door. "How much longer on that set up?"

"Three minutes, almost there!" Her fingers clicked and clacked along the keyboard at a frantic pace. "I just need to—"

They heard the sound of large ethanol fueled troop transport vehicles moving into position outside. The earth quivered beneath their feet as the sound of heavy bodies hit the ground heading toward them. Their radios crackled to life and Bear's winded voice came over the broadcast channel. "They're troop bots. Looks like two truckloads of them. I've linked up with Cheeks and will engage with him."

"Roger that!" Kyler said, "Noe, where are we at on the cyber?" He had dropped the reassuring tone. Now he sounded impatient and slightly fearful.

There had been a problem with one of her field devices, and Noe had been forced to improvise, adding additional minutes to the job. "I just need five more minutes." She labored to keep her composure to focus her entire being on the set up. She would *not* make the same mistake she had as a young lieutenant again.

Spazer shouted, "They're here sir!" Instantly the sound of close-range gunfire erupted in the room. Bullets clanged onto metallic humanoid troops, and expended shell casings littered the floor. Noe heard a hard thud on the floor in front of her. She momentarily diverted her sight from the screen to see Lance's body splayed out before her. His dead eyes stared at nothingness. His beard, caked in dust and blood, rested on the floor, along with his dog tags.

More bots appeared at the doorway, returning fire toward Kyler and Spazer. "Ah I'm hit!" Spazer yelled, dropping to one knee. Despite his wound, he raised his weapon and continued to fight from a kneeling position. Kyler threw what looked like a grenade. When it hit, Noe was forced to pause her work to cover her eyes from the bright white flame that consumed a group of humanoid bots. The use of a white phosphorus munition had been a risky move in such a tight space, but it bought them precious seconds.

Two bots marched at the door, weapons raised, when suddenly, they stopped and fell lifeless to the ground. Their heavy metallic bodies caused the tiny old structure to quake. From his position by Spazer's side, Kyler whipped his head toward Noe, smiling for the first time since the battle began. "You did it! Goddammit, you did it!"

With cyber superiority established, they now owned all network functions within the radius of the old ghost town. Anything that Limnic could see, do, plan, or execute that required a network, was now visible to her, and could be manipulated in their favor.

The smile and satisfaction from a job well done quickly faded when Noe looked toward the door. There, amid the robot corpses, hovering smoke, and still burning fires near the bullet riddled door frame stood a pale faced man with long silver hair. He was dressed plainly in blue jeans, black button-down shirt, and dusty brown work boots; but his hair blew in the wind as he smirked at the three of them.

Janus! It's him. Noe let out an audible gasp at the realization.

With sudden action, Spazer raised his M-4. Kyler drew a large knife and charged toward the door letting out a savage battle cry as he lunged. Noe noticed Janus' eyes widen as he became aware of his imminent demise.

Then, without warning, both men stopped. Spazer gently set his rifle down in front of him and curled into a fetal position, as if he were a baby. Kyler stood at the position of attention, sheathed his knife, performed an about face, then marched back in front of Noe's computer. He sat down slowly in a cross-legged position. It looked as if he were meditating and was at peace.

What the hell is going on?

Just as Noe's brain signaled her muscles to move and fight, an overwhelming force held her in place. *Move! Move!* She willed herself with every fiber of her being, but her body would not obey. She felt locked out of her own mind. There was a heavy feeling of drowsiness that flooded her senses, and she badly wanted to lay down and sleep. Somewhere in the back of her mind was a voice screaming for her to stand and fight. To kill Janus here and now. To end it. But the voice came from a sunken place and any message became lost forever like an object floating in the vacuum of space.

Her eyelids felt extremely heavy and a feeling of comforting warmth radiated throughout her entire being. She was no longer a woman, but rather a conscious fetus, with tender skin and grasping limbs. She felt sheltered, protected, and with all of her bodily and emotional needs fulfilled by her mother. The feeling was inviting. It made her want to succumb to it, to savor it, to stay as long as possible. Somewhere among the bliss of her experience, she heard a distant voice shrieking. It begged her to wake up and fight. But it was muffled and nearly inaudible, as if that person, whoever it was, were being suffocated by a pillow. Eventually, the hoarse cries faded, leaving only the peaceful thrum of her mother's steady pulse in her ears.

Noe stopped fighting, and floated in the pleasant ether. As she lay there asleep, nestled in comfort and safety, her mind formed pictures. Her prenatal brain could not grasp their meaning, but she viewed them with innocence, for she knew no fear. She recognized her father, a plump Mexican man with a round face and grey mustache. But oddly, she felt no attachment to him, no infant desire to be held or touched by him. There were no thoughts, only feelings, in the gelatinous liquid that held and rocked her gently. Then another picture came together before her eyes, as the repeated beating sound around her increased its cadence and strength. It was an old man with long silver hair shown before her eyes. Noe felt her infant arms grasping toward the face. The soft fingers first exploring, then grabbing at the image. She felt a deep yearning to be held and comforted in the man's arms. She desired it so badly, she wanted to wail and scream words she did not know or understand in order to win his affection. As she writhed and reached in transitory discomfort, the rate of the drumming sound around her increased its rhythm again, as the silver-haired man's lips contorted into a ghoulish smirk. Then the image faded as she willfully rested in the warm embrace of darkness.

CHAPTER 36: POWERLESS

Powerless. It was a word that Rodan thought about often in the past few months since he had assumed the role of executive director of Cereus. *I got a big office, my own parking spot, and a fancy wood placard with my name engraved on it, but at the end of the day, still can't do shit.*

The image of Rodan's once glorious shield of service came to his mind. It lay forsaken in the dried mud on a lonely battlefield. A gust of wind carried the scent of burned and rotten flesh to his nose in the stillness of air. He stood before the shield, back aching, will broken, wanting to hold it again as he used to when he was young. But he knew he could no longer handle the weight alone. He needed help. The next capable person to come along, would be his only hope. Not only to raise the shield again, but to imbue him with the sense of honored service that he felt so long ago when his muscles were stronger and his stomach was flatter. Until that moment came along, he was helpless to do anything other than stare into the gaping fissure on the shield's surface.

I'm powerless. The word resurfaced again while he sat alone in the van. His field tablet in his lap, viewing the Battle of North Bloomfield as one would watch a meteorological weather pattern on the ten o'clock news. Lots of things seemed to be happening, but he had no context of their significance or purpose. Unlike his well network-connected mercenaries in the city, Kyler's men had no body cameras, so he had no access to any live feeds of the action. His bird's eye view grid mode was the only option, and it was a poor substitute for the fidelity of live camera feeds. He had his radio on, but it might as well have been a soundtrack from an old Modern Warfare video game. Gun shots, explosions, and tactical chatter came through, but he could not tell what was really going on behind the exchanges. It was just unfiltered noise to his ears.

This sucks. I could have stayed in my office for this shit. I should be out there. He slid down in his seat and pouted. There was no one around to see him do it.

His conversation with Kyler had been brief, with both men succinctly laying out their viewpoint on whether or not he should be in the field.

"I should be out there," Rodan said.

"Why?" Kyler asked. His face level, tone no-nonsense.

"Because, I'm the head of Cereus."

"So?"

"So, the others should see me out front."

Kyler looked unimpressed. "With all due respect Mr. Mitchell, when's the last time you fired a weapon?"

"Hm, six weeks ago," the response came quickly, but he couldn't really remember how long it had been.

"I see. And when was the last time you were in the gym?" Kyler looked toward Rodan's body armor. The curve of it, its *snugness*, made the flabby skin beneath very apparent. Rodan's eyes glanced down, then immediately back up at Kyler.

"It's been a minute…"

"Yeah." Kyler placed his hands on his hips and straightened his posture. Even with his gear on he appeared to grow taller, though he was still shorter than Rodan by a few inches. He took a step forward and lowered his voice, speaking in quick fire words, like a drill instructor would to a head shaved trainee. "With all due respect Mr. Mitchell, you clearly have no business on a battlefield. I know how you leadership types like to *descend* every now and then to make yourself look good, to look like you know what the fuck it is that we do. But in reality you *don't* know, and don't give a shit. Not really. You're here, because you feel like you wanna relive your glory days from the past. You wanna feel useful. Like you don't ride a desk all day, like you don't watch better and more capable men do what you *used* to be able to do. I get it. But I don't have time for that shit right now. Your need for a confidence boost is gonna get me, my men, or our guest killed. And I won't have it. This ain't Sac PD and this ain't the military. So I don't have to listen to a goddamn thing that comes out of your mouth. Do you understand what I'm saying…sir?" Kyler's eyes were locked on his.

It was at that point Rodan realized Kyler had never liked him. And after receiving his dress down, the feeling was mutual. The additional *"sir"* at the end almost sent Rodan into rage. *Really? "Sir!?" Who the fuck does this guy think he is?* But he made none of these thoughts visible to Kyler. Only gave an understanding nod and walked back to the van, while the others continued their preparations. He saw Noe look in his direction, but pretended he did not notice the glance. He had become a better politician than he thought.

Fucking powerless. There he sat, slumped in the passenger seat, chin on chest, listening to the soundtrack of explosions, sporadic gunfire in the distance, and the occasional radio chatter. "This ain't Sac P.D.," he murmured in a half-hearted impersonation of Kyler's voice. "My name is Kyler and I have a really small dick, so I have to get augmentations to even open my eyes in the morning," he joked to himself. "Fuuuck you man."

Rodan had been so absorbed in his self-pity that he had not heard Bear call 'south side clear'. He had not heard Cheeks' announcement of arriving reinforcements. He had not heard Spazer shout 'man down!', indicating that one of their own human members had been wounded or killed.

It was only when he felt the rumble of earth that his awareness returned to the battle. He had a certain sense of security seated in the dark van away from the fighting. But when a potential threat to his person emerged, his senses refocused on the approaching danger in the here and now. He bolted up in the passenger seat and raised the radio to his ear just in time to hear Bear's voice say: "They're troop bots. Looks like two truckloads of them. I've linked up with Cheeks and will engage with him."

Reinforcements? Dammit. Not good. Rodan gripped his weapon. He wondered if he should join the fray or conduct some supporting action from the van, although he had no idea what he would do. *What the hell am I gonna do if I go out there? Probably get killed.* The thought didn't sound terribly unpleasant, but he didn't want to die that way. He vacillated between self-preservation and the need to act. Both had an equal pull on him, and the result was a binding force of indecision that detained him in his seat. Leaving him incapable of making a move in either direction. *Powerless.*

Then Noe's face flashed in his mind. *What if she needs help? I brought her out here and got her into this. Least I could do is watch out for her. I said I would.* There wasn't much time to decide. Limnic's forces could be ripping them to shreds at this very moment. Rodan's eyes glanced through the windshield. All he saw was the darkness of the trail leading to an unknown ending. The pops and bangs from the radio conjured up images of Noe and the others dead after a bitter battle. He slapped his head a few times to bring himself back from the fear illusion. He looked to his weapon in the passenger seat. *I have to try. I am the director of Cereus after all. It's my duty.* With that final thought, he adjusted his gear, grabbed his rifle and stepped out of the van, prepared to face whatever fate awaited him.

*   *   *

The first thing he noted was the cool night air. It felt good after being cooped up in the van for the last half an hour. He stretched his legs, took a deep breath then let it out. *Ok let's do this.* Psyched up, he began to jog.

One minute later, his feet felt heavy and he panted openly like a dog in the summer heat, but he kept moving.

Two minutes in, his heart slammed in his chest, unaccustomed to working so hard. It protested the unexpected exertion like a civilian contractor would additional duties. *Fuckin' Kyler.*

Three minutes after beginning his jog, lungs and legs burning, Rodan slowed to shuffle (though he wanted to walk). His boots dragged across the rocky path, alerting any remaining enemy troops to his presence. *At least if I got shot now, I could lay down and not be running.* The dark thought lightened his mood.

He was semi-relieved thirty seconds later when he reached the town. The moment was fleeting, because the carnage of the battlefield lay before him. Small fires burned in the grassy areas of the old town. Several of the nineteenth century buildings were still burning and collapsing, while others had been completely leveled by explosives, and a mixture of gun and laser fire.   Human and bot remains lay intermingled with each other among the wreckage. In all of his years of service, military, police, and with Cereus, Rodan had never seen such a gruesome sight.

Where are they? Where's Noe? He tried the radio, but there was no response from anyone. Rodan swallowed hard, assumed a tactical position, and stepped off into the town.

He had only moved three steps before he stopped suddenly. His vision strained to confirm if he was really seeing what he saw. *Is that!?*

Ahead on the path, stepping through the mangled remains of humanoid bots outside of a building with white pillars was *him*. The silver hair. The narrowed eyes. The cool disposition. It was Janus.

Though Rodan had him clear in the front sight of his weapon, he did not pull the trigger. He just watched as Janus moved toward him with unhurried steps, until he stopped ten feet from where Rodan stood. The realization that he was alone with Janus caused a sense of dread to move through his body. But Rodan stood his ground. "Janus! What happened to the others? Where are they?" his voice was forceful and strong.

Janus shook his head and made a sound of mocking disapproval with his tongue and teeth. "I assure you they are fine. Just taking a well-deserved rest."

Rodan growled like an animal, a sign of frustration. "Damn you Janus!" When his rifle fired, it was unanticipated and caught him by surprise. Janus evaded the round and smiled as he did it. "No, Mr. Mitchell that won't do."

In the next moment, Rodan had set his rifle on the ground and kicked it away, out of his reach. He had disarmed himself. *Bad move.* In front of Janus. *Really bad move.* Worse yet, he had no idea why.

What are you doing!? You have to kill the son of a bitch! Why are you putting your weapon down!? Rodan berated himself. His panic manifested in a choking sensation, that made it harder for him to breathe. *You gotta find something, anything, to kill him with!* Rodan's eyes fell on a large rock by his feet. *There! That rock will be enough to bash his head in with!*

"I wouldn't do that," Janus said.

Wait…did he just read my mind!?

A low chuckle escaped Janus' lips. "I only want to talk with you Mr. Mitchell, we have little time for games."

"You…you can read minds," Rodan said, his voice rasped from breathing in smoke and all of the yelling he had done. "How?"

The defiant confidence on Janus' face, told him that he would not receive an answer. Rodan consciously began to try and control his thoughts. It seemed doable at first, but after only five seconds all of his insecurities, worries, and concerns burst through like water breaching a failing dam. Judging from Janus' reaction, it was clear that he was aware of Rodan's embarrassing attempt to contain his stream of consciousness. It amused him.

"So, you are the acting head of Cereus?"

"I am."

"You do realize that the rest of this country, let alone the world will never adopt the principles that the organization stands for?"

"That remains to be seen," Rodan said, still attempting to control his thoughts. It was like performing flood relief with a bucket, comical and very ineffective.

"In our modern times, many people forget that it took us millennia to evolve into the species that we are today. Centuries to establish the framework of the modern world, and decades for science and technology to make the strides that have carried us to the point where we sit today."

Rodan listened. Straining his mind and body to keep his thoughts under control.

"It has been a common belief in Western civilization throughout the twenty-first century that all roads in human history served to bring us to the life that we know today. While this is partially true, it often makes us forget that we continue to move through an evolutionary process even now. And that we continue to evolve and change as a species."

"So what?"

"The primary difference now is that we have some control over the evolutionary process. With genomics, digigenomics, and biological augmentations, it is possible for humans to truly live *forever* if they want to." He took a step forward, his boots crunched the earth beneath his feet. "The problem with us living forever is that it only makes things more difficult for everyone who *cannot* afford the fountain of youth. People may live into their hundred and twentieth year with the mind and body of their twenty or thirty-year-old selves, but will not be willing to contribute as much to society as when they were actually that young. Under old world thinking, they feel they deserve retirement from the demands of conventional human life. Our ballooning global elderly population bears this out now."

"What's your point?" Rodan asked, fatigued from his jog and watching his thoughts.

Janus pointed at him, with such force Rodan was sure he felt Janus' finger pressing into his body armor. "As the acting leader of Cereus *you*, and *you alone*, Rodan Mitchell, have the power to evolve Cereus into the new societal order that this world needs. An evolved society, for an evolved people."

The thought burst through. *Me? How?*

Janus answered. "By working with me to deploy the greatest demonstration of human technological prowess that the world has ever seen."

A puzzled look flashed across Rodan's face. He continued to monitor his thoughts closely, but he was quickly becoming mentally fatigued at the unfamiliar task.

"Cereus was the societal structure that humanity sorely required to move forward from the environmental and social damage caused by rampant production and consumption, inequality, and inflated sense of self-aggrandizement that plagued nations and many of its citizens in recent human history. But on its own, it was incomplete. This technology will be the final step in completing our shift from the societies of our forefathers, to one that can sustain *all* of humanity and our planet into the future."

"What do you want from me?"

"I want you to use your power and influence as acting head of Cereus to help me deploy this technology. I want you…to help our species evolve."

Is he crazy!? There's no way I'll help him! "No way, Janus! You're evil, you're the enemy! You're a terrorist!"

Janus began to move toward him with slow steps, as North Bloomfield burned all around him. His eyelids fluttered as he moved as if he were performing some satanic ritual. Rodan took a step back, feeling truly frightened for the first time since exiting the van. He felt the strong urge to flee back to anywhere that was not in front of this creature walking toward him. But where would he go? There was no way he could outrun Janus and nowhere close by to hide if he did manage to escape. So he stood locked in place, eyes continuously darting between his rifle on the ground and Janus' approaching figure. Rodan considered going for the gun. But at that moment Janus stopped just five feet before him, forcing Rodan to abandon the plan of action.

"Mr. Mitchell, your story does not have to end here. There is strength brimming beneath the surface within you. It is strong enough, to render this sense of *powerlessness* that you feel only a temporary burden, and give you the strength to raise and repair the broken shield of your youth."

Rodan gasped in horror. His heart was pounding so fast, it made his chest feel cramped behind his body armor. "You…you, I—" he had trouble forming words with his mouth. "How can you know about that…?"

Janus snickered, "I know *all* about you Mr. Mitchell. I know you have spent your entire life in service of others, selflessly sacrificing mind, body, and soul for just causes big and small. But I ask you, what has been left for you? Your broken marriage, an untrained body, a mind in splinters, unconsummated desire for Lili's daughter, Noe; *these* are the rewards for your valor. Tell me Mr. Mitchell, is this the life you wanted when you were a smiling police rookie all those years ago?"

Rodan's shoulders had fallen. He felt uncovered and vulnerable, as if a thief had broken into his house and stolen every item of sentimental value, leaving only those things of high monetary worth untouched and pristine. Cold wind blew in over the kicked-in door and through the smashed windows, swirling and moaning a soft lament for him and his lost possessions. Items that could never be recovered, even by the most skilled and dogged detective.

Without warning, tears assaulted him. His hulking shoulders trembled, giant's hands rose to his face in a futile attempt to hide his shame as he cried. He shed a single tear for every person he had delivered from evil. Every person he had placed before himself. He cried for his pitiable existence, for his lost youth, his discarded enthusiasm and passion. The tears fell for Noe, for Li, for every victim, for man, woman, and child on Earth. They were the tears of the world, falling for all of the things he could not control or cope with.

His hands still over his face, liquid running from his nose and eyes, Rodan asked in between sobs, "W-Why are you doing this to m-me?"

Janus replied, "Because I *know* what you are. You are one of the world's sentries. With the ability to defend it from *itself* and carry it to a new destination." He paused as Rodan lowered his hands. "I know, you see me as your enemy, but I fight for a greater cause that is above petty nationalistic patriotism. I fight for the whole of humanity. To deliver its soul to a better, stronger, and more capable frame, that will ultimately make the 'terrorists', no matter if they are in flag bearing uniforms or wearing rags, obsolete. Isn't that what you fought for as a soldier, police officer, and now for Cereus?"

Rodan found himself nodding slightly, through reddened eyes.

"With the help of my new technology. You may be ready to raise your *new* shield, and fight once again." Janus gave an encouraging, almost brotherly grin.

Rodan rubbed his stinging eyes, still speechless. He stared at Janus with slumped shoulders, physically and mentally spent. No coherent thoughts entered his mind. Janus must have known so, because he turned to walk away. Rodan glanced at the rifle in the dirt, then at Janus' disappearing figure. He knew this was one of the defining moments of his life. A single shot decision, that would affect the rest of his life, and more importantly, define him as a man, and how future generations would view not only Cereus, but the world. To him, it was life and death. If he could meet this very special moment, how would Noe see him? What would she think? What would Li think? What would *he* think of himself in the morning? Would he consider himself to have been derelict in his duties to rid the nation and world of this terrorist? Or would he have taken a tiny step forward for the greater good? For the collective survival of not only himself, but for all those yet unborn. Standing there, blazing fires around him in the ghost town, Rodan's vision flicked between the rifle and the departing Janus one more time. In the next split second, Rodan made his decision. He stepped forward and yelled "Wait! Janus, tell me more about the technology! What does it do? How does it work?"

Janus heard him but continued to move away, until Rodan could no longer see him among the destruction of the battlefield.

Rodan stood alone for several seconds, unsure what had just happened, even less sure about what he should do. He felt so…powerless. Then, without warning, Janus' voice entered his mind, *"Come to Yuba City and you will see. Cereus is the future, and you alone have the power to make it a reality. Only you can help usher humanity toward a new age."*

CHAPTER 37:
CHIPPED - PART 1

Kayne Eastmont was born at a large hospital in Colorado Springs. A healthy baby boy, neither him nor his parents were aware how much one piece of technology would impact his entire life.

That technology was a standard implant that allowed people to be identified by the network. Introduced in the early 2020s, at about half the size of a grain of rice, the implant began as a disease tracking method after the coronavirus pandemic that ravaged the planet in the early years of the decade. In the beginning, only those that had been sick or were wealthy had them. But by 2030, they had become mainstream and replaced social security numbers as the primary population accountability measure in the United States.

Proposed by clever legislators in the U.S, and eventually around the world, lawmakers argued that this technology would allow for more accurate census taking, and ultimately lead to more efficient use of limited energy resources. Progressive government leaders around the old world regarded it as a *green* measure that would contribute to the reduction of global warming, allow for worried parents to keep better track of their children, and provide other small conveniences for the common citizen (though these were never stated explicitly). The massaging of the rhetoric, combined with the release of bingeable media propaganda showcasing how the technology benefited everyday people, made the old world public accept the measure en masse.

As a result, the general population, born before 2030, lined up in droves to get *chipped*. Although the thirties were characterized by global outbreaks of disease, war, and an unprecedented amount of natural disasters, "cyberization", as it was colloquially known, provided an unexpected boost to the global economy during the entire decade. Billions of people in the developed and developing worlds willingly allowed a permanent technological tracking device to be inserted into their bodies in order to reap the socially accepted benefits. Most did so without real knowledge of how the technology really worked, or how its presence under their skin would affect their lives.

Kayne, short in height, with a frame like an aged tree stump, skin smooth and brown as the toughest of leather, was one of those people who jumped in on the social media labeled "I Am Robot" movement of the thirties. Born in 2015, he had begged his parents to allow him to get the implant on his fifteenth birthday. His money conscious Millennial parents, scarred by decades of crushing student loan debt, the memory of their economic struggles always fresh in their minds, refused. That was when he decided to take matters into his own hands.

Headstrong, stubborn, and quite invincible, he enlisted the help of a friend to arrange the procedure at one of the biodigital clinics in a nearby neighborhood. Some of these clinics had been established with well-known and reputable medical providers. Others were essentially run by engineers and hobbyists, with enough knowledge of medicine to place the chip safely in the body. Kayne chose the latter, and after paying $500, he joined the ranks of the *chipped* ones.

When his parents found out about it days later, they were livid, until they discovered that the chip could be used to track his movements and biological data in real-time. Kayne's plan had backfired. For the next three years, his comings and goings were heavily scrutinized by the vigilant eyes of his parents. However, on the day of his eighteenth birthday, he had the option to disable parent tracking for good and emancipate himself from their control. From that day forward, he became the owner of his personal data. It was the law, and he was glad for it.

Soon after turning eighteen, Kayne left his parents' house to move in with a few friends on the south side of Colorado Springs. It was a shabby apartment in a rundown neighborhood, and he shared the living space with three others, but at least he was finally away from his ever suspicious parents.

There, he got word that new upgrades were being developed for the chip. These enhancements ranged from helping the host study more effectively, to stimulating testosterone production leading to greater muscle gains and increased libido. "It makes your dick bigger dude," one of his friends said to him, one day. Kayne was very interested, but he needed money. So he found a job working in the kitchen of a Mexican seafood restaurant and began to slowly accumulate savings.

After two years of slaving and saving, he received his first enhancement at the age of twenty. Although the testosterone augmentation was tempting, he exercised better judgment and chose the study enhancement. Fed up with coming home reeking of catfish, he decided to take advantage of FreeCodeCamp.org's program for artificial intelligence maintenance. He wanted a better life, and figured a job in technology would always be in demand. His study augmentation in place, Kayne began the program the next day.

Whenever he activated his newly enhanced chip, his mind became a task machine, capable of hours of uninterrupted focus and concentration. The noise of his chaotic inner thoughts and biological cravings fell silent, causing the world around him to fall away, leaving only him, his hands, and his desired goal. Nothing else mattered in those moments, and as a result, his progress in his learning was incredibly fast. By the time he turned twenty-one, less than a year after beginning his studies, he worked his way to a well-paying position as a junior software developer. The job would be his first step in what would become his primary career for the next two decades.

Like the majority of people in his age cohort, Kayne relied heavily on the network for most aspects of his life. He formed relationships in virtual environments, consumed media, and conducted business using it. When he was unsure about something, he often consulted it before approaching another person. Any photos or videos that he recorded, no matter how brief or trivial, automatically flew into a server via lightning quick connections, allowing him to replay the events of his entire life back to himself or anyone else, at any time. He lived on the network, and the network lived within him, eventually learning more about him than he knew about himself.

Twenty-five years later, Kayne sat alone in his large house. The home was located in an upper middle class neighborhood overlooking interstate highway twenty-five, with the view of city lights of Colorado Springs twinkling in the distance. That night, the sky was dark outside with traces of the day's low hanging thunderstorm clouds concealing a sliver of a moon visible through the window of his dimly lit home office. The light of a large computer monitor illuminated the room as Kayne calmly typed away to complete a work presentation that he was due to give the following morning.

Then, out of nowhere, the screen flashed a series of foreign colors. First the flashes were widely spaced, then became more frequent until they blurred together and appeared as a white screen. *What the hell?* Assuming some kind of malfunction, he slowly reached toward the outlet to reset the hardware. However, before his hand reached the power strip, without warning, every moment of triumph in his life up to that point replayed itself in his mind's eye. The images cycled like a person quickly reviewing a slide presentation before a meeting. Just enough time to look and see, not enough time to absorb or focus. It made him feel dizzy and sick. He suppressed rising bile back down his throat. *What in the world is happening?* His sexual conquests, professional victories, and even quiet personal achievements were presented before him, reminding him of the trajectory his life had taken up to that point in time. In his office chair, he tried to blink the visions away, but they would return, beckoning him to view the flurry of pictures from his past. Kayne clenched his eyes shut, hoping the visions would pass. He held them closed for what he felt like was enough time. But when he opened them, he was no longer in his office chair.

Where is this? He was standing in some kind of chamber. It reminded him of a cold medieval dungeon, and looked as if it should have been freezing inside. But Kayne did not feel cold, even though he only wore a white t-shirt and sleep pants.

He examined his surroundings. The room was completely sealed, no entrances, exits, or windows. The only objects he could see were large cylinder-shaped pedestals arranged in a uniform circle near the center of the space. There were seven in all. Kayne swallowed hard and took cautious steps toward the pedestal closest to him. What he saw, made his jaw drop in disbelief. *This is…my memory.* The forgotten image floated in a smooth bubble before his eyes. In it, he was twenty-five years younger, thinner, and with more hair, proudly holding a "Best Junior Programmer Award" in one hand, while the other clasped the hand of his long dead senior developer. *No way. This…can't be real.* His vision turned to the other spheres. They too held different memories, some Kayne had long forgotten about. *What the?* He studied, half in shock, the seven ecstasy filled highs and the devastating lows of his life, not sure what to do or think. *Why am I here?* he wondered, as he carefully approached a glowing memory of a recent love affair with a woman named Daphne. *Oh Daphne.* The memory stood out not just because of her allure and seductive attractiveness, but because he often slept the best when she was around. Postcoital rest, in general, was some of the best sleep he had throughout his life, and with Daphne the effect had been magnified.

*I wonder what will happen if I…*holding his breath, he reached out to touch the memory, unsure of what he expected to happen. Upon contact, a flood of emotion inundated and overloaded his mind. Connection, intimacy, love, all mixed in his blood, detonating a blast of sexual energy throughout his body. Hands at his sides, his heart began to pump harder, faster and faster as blood began to flow into his loins. His body began its familiar cycle of tension and release. Not long after, the quickening captured him, holding him in the grip of the primal rhythm. Kayne's face contorted, his body clenched as he climaxed, then fell to the floor in a spent heap. On the floor, eyelids heavy, he fell into a blissful sleep.

*   *   *

He awoke seated at his desk, in his home office. A light drizzle fell outside in the night sky. The pitter patter on his window reached his ears. The same mundane work slideshow displayed on his monitor. Nothing had changed, except for Kayne himself. His body still harbored traces of his physical arousal. According to his device, both his heart rate and blood pressure were still elevated above normal levels. He also felt breathless, sluggish, and lethargic, but strangely at peace. A feeling of euphoria clouded his brain. He lay back in his chair to savor it, eyelids drooping, thinking of Daphne. After several minutes passed, the sensation began to subside. At that moment, the coldness of reality and of the fabric within his underwear reached his awareness.

Embarrassed at his soiled undergarments, he immediately exchanged them and his sleep pants for clean clothes. As he changed, questions about what he had just experienced entered his mind. *What just happened to me? Was it a dream? Some type of weird neurological disorder?* He had heard stories of chips going bad in certain people and causing all kinds of odd medical problems as they aged, but this didn't seem like anything he had ever heard or read about. It was something completely different. Though he felt somewhat ashamed at losing control of himself, a part of him was captivated by the mysterious thrill of it. The room, the memories, the odd ejaculation, were all pieces of a puzzle that Kayne had to solve. He wanted more.

CHAPTER 38:
CHIPPED - PART 2

The next night it happened again. The same series of flashes invaded his vision, and he was again transported to the circular room. Two things were different about it this time. From where he stood, Kayne turned around and behind him noticed an arched door that clearly would return him to his home office.

I can go back if I want to. In the somewhat fuzzy image he saw himself sitting there. His body was in a calm state of repose as if he were taking a short nap. The expression on his face was peaceful; his chest rose and fell softly at steady intervals. *So strange.* He had never seen himself sleep before. The sight made him feel vulnerable and uncomfortable. Returning his attention to the room, the cylindrical pedestals again housed memories, but all were different from the night before. *Which one should I choose tonight?* Without awareness of any time limit or rules related to the room, he felt more anxious about his choice than the night before. Whatever this was, it was clear he could only make one choice. He had no idea if he would be able to come back.

There was another memory of him and Daphne on the day of their breakup. As usual, they had sex, but it was different that time. It was a mournful act, absent of their usual intimacy or togetherness. It had been a desperation move on his part, a final plea to win her back, after his careerism and workaholic nature pushed her away. It failed, and Kayne was full of regret and sadness at the scale of loss he was feeling. On that final night of their relationship, he had pushed the feelings down, not wanting to look or feel weak. He knew Daphne could see through his tough guy act. He knew her heart bled for him, herself, and the crippling loss that often accompanies ending a long and promising relationship. But she had made her decision, and that time, it was final. Echoes of the memory welled up within him as he viewed the floating sphere. Kayne reached out his hand.

At the last second he dropped it. *I don't need to revisit that one.* Exercising monumental will power, he forced himself not to look at the memory, then took small steps backward toward the arched doorway. The other Kayne was still in a tranquil position of sleep. Looking at himself, he began to feel drowsy. This was all strange and overwhelming to him and he had no idea how to proceed. He took timid steps toward the doorway then suddenly stopped. *If I go back now, I might not have another chance.* Decision made. Kayne turned away from the arched door and decided to look around the chamber.

The search didn't last long. Kayne had walked around the room several times, standing on his toes, pushing in on the walls, dropping to his knees and examining the floor in detail. He found nothing. The only exit was the arched doorway. The only objects in the room were the pedestals with the memory clouds on top.

Disappointed, and more tired than before, he approached a memory of a fight that occurred between him and a friend back during his Mexican seafood kitchen days. Kayne didn't have a great recollection of the fight, but he recalled fragments. He and several other friends had been heavily drinking that night at a bar in downtown Colorado Springs. In the haze of alcohol and smoke, he vaguely remembered feeling triggered, then being on the floor. He remembered talking to the cops, and a few of his friends the following morning to get the details. His memory stopped there, he hadn't thought about it in a long time. *That must've been over twenty-five years ago.* Scratching his head, staring at the memory, some details of the history between himself and the friend came to his mind, almost unexpectedly.

His name was Tony. He had been one of the guys he lived with after he moved out of his parents' house. He was *the* guy that told him about the chip augmentations back in the day.

Tony was a good friend, but he could also be a real asshole if he thought Kayne wasn't being *man* enough when it came to certain things. Didn't matter if it had to do with women, school, or work, Tony's solution was always domination or shows of force. Kayne tolerated it, because Tony was really funny, and he felt like a more fun person by just being in his presence. However, their friendship began to fray when both received their chip upgrades. Unlike Kayne, Tony chose the testosterone upgrade. The increased "juice" (as he liked to call it) changed him from being a dick, to an even *bigger* throbbing dick. All he talked about from that day on, was how many women he fucked or was going to fuck. "Yo Kayne, you ever had cyborg pussy bro?" He asked Kayne one random afternoon.

"Naw never."

"It's the best! You missin' out my man."

Kayne just shook his head and continued studying. Tony was funny, but the upgrade had made him even more annoying. Kayne decided to spend less time with him. Instead, he dedicated himself even further to his studies so he could begin his career as a programmer. That would also get him away from Tony, eventually, he hoped.

Weeks later at a party, Kayne was hanging out with Kayla. She was a cute brunette with pixie hair and a smokin' body. She was a Crossfitter and mountain climber, and she could also drink him under the table. A true Colorado-born beauty. She was a friend of a friend that Kayne had seen at the bar for the last several weeks. On that particular night, he had finally gotten the nerve to talk to her. They had an instant connection. They talked, drank, and threw darts for hours. Things were going well. Everything was great until, like a flies to an outdoor barbeque, Tony sidled up beside him and forced an introduction. His flamboyant clothing, a lime green t-shirt and dark skinny jeans, complemented by a pair of all white sneakers, reminded Kayne of that rapper Lil' Nas X in that old video *Old Town Road*. Except he wasn't him, he was Tony. The biochemistry major at the University of Colorado Springs by day, and self-proclaimed pimp by night. He was a poser, a fake, a sim. In that moment, Kayne hated him, and when he rolled up on him and Kayla in the corner of that bar, that had been the last straw.

Kayne stood before the pedestal, head tilted at a contemplative angle. *I wonder if the bad memories are as potent as the good ones?* With a shaking hand, Kayne reached out and touched the memory. The next instant, his muscles tightened, jaw clenched as his thinking brain shifted into animal action. The aching of muscles, tendons, and joints that he had experienced on that night in the bar dredged itself up from the depths of the past. The emotional blow of the betrayal that he felt hit hardest. *Tony! How could you talk to her when you knew it was going well for me! You're an asshole man! You always have been!* His mind replayed the long forgotten thoughts and feelings, as if the scroll bar on a video had been rewound to that precise moment in time. Kayne's conscious brain had buried the details long ago, but his body remembered. Every punch, kick, knee from Tony that impacted his face, chest, and ribs, hit him again and again. But this time, there was no alcohol to deaden the pain. Every hit landed with unexpected gravity, multiplied by the emotional scar of the collapse of his friendship with Tony. The combination of everything was so great that Kayne eventually passed out.

*   *   *

When he opened his eyes, he was back in his office in front of his computer. A cool starry night outside of his window, Kayne sat drenched in sweat, exhausted, and sore. He sat low and didn't move, for a while. It was an attempt to calm himself down after the sudden shock of the memory. *It let me relive that horrible memory too. What the hell is this?* Kayne wanted answers.

He labored to take a shower, fighting through pain and soreness as he stripped off his smelly clothes. Before he stepped in, he stood naked in front of the mirror and looked at himself. His middle-aged body, now approaching fifty, was there in all its former glory as usual. The inflated belly and breast-like pectorals were there. Scanning lower, his once muscular legs showed the early signs of old age. The skin looked as if it was slowly sliding toward the floor. While disheartening, this too was normal. But one thing was not normal, something that should have been there but was not.

No bruises? Despite the sweat, his skin appeared normal in color, but there was no swelling or blue or black bruises anywhere to be seen. Kayne turned his arms, even activated the reverse shower mirror to see his back. There was nothing. *Weird. I definitely feel like I was in a fight.* It was like something had played with his nervous system, as a hacker would attack a network. The internal alarms were going off, but everything appeared normal to the casual eye. The detail added to the mystery of it all. It made Kayne want to know more.

*   *   *

Showered, and feeling slightly better, it was 2 A.M. when he set to work to consult the network for answers. For an unknown number of hours, he scoured forums, social media, and his chosen silo of news outlets for information. He tried several search terms: 'the circular chamber', 'floating memory spheres', 'spontaneous ejaculation', 'repressed memories', 'out of body experiences'. While they yielded interesting data, none of it related to what he was searching for. *How does it choose which memories to display? Why did it choose me?* He held these questions and more in his head as he continued to investigate.

Next, he messaged the few friends that he could reach at the late hour, about what he had experienced the last two nights. None had any idea what he was talking about. They just blamed stress and overwork, then told him to get some sleep. But Kayne wouldn't rest. His analytical mind would not allow it. Despite the overwhelming fatigue he felt from the fight, he continued his research.

By 4 A.M. he was ready to give up. Heavy eyes, and even heavier limbs begged him to concede and go to bed. *There has to be something out there about this.* Then he made a promising discovery. There was a forum, with a dozen or so respondents that spoke of similar incidents happening to them. Many described re-experiencing memorable sexual encounters just like he had, while others spoke of reliving past wins in business or satisfying moments of peace with deceased family members. "I felt a tingling warmth, like I had only known sitting and watching the sunset with my husband, who passed away over a decade ago. It almost felt as if he were sitting right beside me again," wrote someone who went by the name BrokeMillenial90. The accounts had been helpful, but they hadn't explained the how or the why. It wasn't enough.

So Kayne continued his exhaustive research, fighting stinging eyes, and the physical fatigue that comes from a middle-aged man participating in a twenty-something-year-old's feud. As dawn light began to filter through his office window, he felt he could continue no more and moved to close his browser when one forum thread caught his eye.

"IT LETS YOU SEE AND EXPERIENCE THE FUTURE!!!???" was the title of the thread. It contained only one comment and had just been updated only fifteen minutes before, according to its timestamp. Kayne leaned forward in his chair, eyes narrowed, lips pursed, as he began his scan.

The post was long and detailed, with the author (who Kayne suspected was a man), writing incoherently in a style of stream of consciousness that was difficult to digest. The user, Gemini36, described having always wanted to have been a comedian growing up. Though he had given standup comedy a try for two years after high school, life got in the way, and he had to walk away from it to take care of elderly family members, defining it as the new rite of passage for his generation. Past much rambling, Kayne skimmed halfway down the screen until the man described his encounter with the circular dungeon-like room. *This is it!*

He wrote: "*I had been reliving my greatest hits for about a week. A week isn't that long of a period of time to go through some of the most powerful memories embedded somewhere in my brain. Some of which I had even forgotten were there! Anyway, on the sixth night, I was really wanting to experience a road trip that I had taken with my friends in San Jose. We ended up getting lost near Big Basin among these fucking towering trees and we were freezing, like your nuts might fall off freezing! But it was one of the most memorable moments of my life. So on the seventh night, the memories were arranged as usual, but they were different, I didn't recognize any of the images, people, or events in them. Damn, I'm telling you they even looked different! With hard angles replacing the normally smooth and curvy outline of the memory bubbles (this is my name for them, thank me later!). At first I was gonna leave, but I was just so damn curious when I saw one that had an older man on stage in front of a large crowd of people in a dimly lit room with a spotlight trained on him. I thought no way at first. But after I touched it I knew the truth. It wasn't a memory, but a vision of me in the future! I was living my comedy dream! I felt the adoration of the crowd, that one-of-a-kind feeling that comes from knowing that you made someone laugh, the feeling of having crafted and delivered the perfect setup, followed by a killer punchline, I got it all! It was incredible! Ok so after all that, I waited until the next night, to see more future visions (that was only one of several that had been displayed to me), but instead of the standard ring of neatly arranged memories, there was only a single one in the center of the room. It looked like one of the future memory bubbles, not the normal ones, so I touched it. I felt safe and secure in my favorite position, which is lying on my back in my bed, I like seeing my stomach rise and fall y'know? I don't care if I'm a little chubby now; It reminds me I'm alive :) Anyway, as I lay there, a voice started talking to me as if I were listening to some kind of old audio book. It started telling me about something called a "comvil" and that I should go to one if I wanted to have access to more memories and future visions. Brother, I tell you, I looked these places up, and I know they've had some bad press over the years, but I started packing my bags that very same night. There's one not too far from where I'm at now, and I'm gonna join. If I can get more access to the memories and possibly even the future me, I'd be crazy not to do it!"*

Kayne vigorously rubbed his eyes. His mind felt tangled from everything he had read and he needed to give himself a second to absorb it all. He leaned back in his chair, wincing from his invisible muscle pain. *So that's how it works.* Gemini36's post was what he had been looking for. If what he wrote was true, he had four more days of memory bubble options until the future visions would appear, and he would be subsequently invited to join a comvil. He had heard of Cereus and its terrorist offshoot Limnic on the news and on social media, but didn't really know much about them outside of their names. Now he wanted to know more. But that would have to wait for another night. Exhausted, the morning sun on his face, he crawled into bed and slept for almost the entire next day.

*   *   *

The rest of the week passed just as Gemini36 foretold. The appeal of experiencing the memories and the possibility of the future functioned like a black hole, pulling Kayne involuntarily into its unknown center depths. On the sixth night, he saw a vision of himself in the future. He had a family, felt secure and accomplished with the events of a life well-lived, his wife was Daphne. They had one daughter together. It was a feeling that overwhelmed his unprepared psyche with boundless joy. On the seventh night, seated in his favorite office chair, his body tingled with delight as he listened to a soothing female voice describing the comvil way of life. How it could benefit him personally and help him put his programming skills to use in service of others, while still providing a good life for him and his potential future family. On the eighth, Kayne was on the road, headed for the nearest comvil. It was down south, in Pueblo, a town he had only driven through, but had never really explored. *I wonder what it will be like there?* His job was remote, and he could get a friend to rent his house. But neither of those things concerned him much.

As his car drove him south, he contacted Daphne, for the first time in two years. She answered on the second ring. "It's been a long time," he said.

Daphne laughed, "I knew you'd call eventually."

CHAPTER 39:
BEST FRIEND FIRST-CLASS

"You're already done!?" Harpreet asked Jinhua. It had only been ten minutes since their physics committee ended, yet she was shocked that her friend had already completed the balancing of forces homework that they had only been assigned thirty minutes prior.

Jinhua stretched her arms over her head, then flashed a prideful smile, "It wasn't too bad. I just wanted to make sure you had an accurate answer key to go off of."

Harpreet slapped her arm with playful force. "Show off."

They both laughed.

The two teenagers walked out of their committee room in the old furniture store. The murmuring of sporadic conversations filled the air. A stark contrast from the bustle and noisy atmosphere that usually dominated the community center during weekdays. *It's always better on weekends*, Jinhua thought. Fewer crowds and less noise made it easier for her to think. Something she had been doing a lot of lately.

She and Harpreet walked to the food stall set up near the far end of the former mall. The menu was small, selling American staples like hamburgers, hot dogs, fried potatoes, and the like. The food was good and reasonably priced. A perfect hangout spot for two adolescents after a math committee on a Saturday. It was *their* food stall.

Without really considering their appetite, they each purchased an order of well-seasoned fried potatoes and Sunsweet prune smoothies (a local staple) from the young gleeful bearded stall operator. He had not worked there long, but Harpreet liked him. Parts of him were manly: large head, broad shoulders, brown beard. Other parts were not: his mannerisms, soft eyes, smooth hands, and melodious voice. A good mix of hard and soft, masculine and feminine. Harpreet wondered if he was gay or questioning. *Probably a little of both.* He handed her a plastic tray with their order and flashed a coquettish wink. *Who cares,* Harpreet thought, *he's hot.* She considered making a comment to Jinhua about how the hot stall operator had made her heart go *doki-doki,* but stopped when she looked in her direction. Her friend was standing there, but she stood with vacant eyes, looking, but not seeing; hearing, but not listening. *She's doing it again.*

Harpreet nudged her, "Hey, Mars to Jinhua, you copy?"

Jinhua absentmindedly raised her hand to her mouth and spoke as if she were communicating through a walkie-talkie radio, "Yeah, I copy…over."

Harpreet wanted to mimic her gesture like she used to when they were young, but she was holding the tray, which prevented her from raising her arms. "C'mon, let's eat." Jinhua nodded, then followed her to uncomfortable metallic chairs situated around a small brown circular table in front of the stall. The two sat and began to eat.

They ate in silence, with only low echoes of mall-conversation and golden oldies, floating in the air around them. Harpreet recognized the song *Complicated* by Avril Lavigne. She didn't know the lyrics, but knew the sound of the intro chord. It was an old song she had heard many times at her grandmother's house. An unconscious memory from long ago.

She's lost again. Harpreet thought. The jovial mood of five minutes ago was long gone. The lack of conversation between them made her desperate to find the words to pull her friend out of her pit of melancholic reflection. Harpreet regarded Jinhua's face. The slightly pressed lip and slackened posture were signs she was ruminating on something, attempting to see the scenario from all possible angles in order to consider perspectives and variables that were previously unseen. The steam from the tiny box of fried potatoes gradually faded as they sat half eaten. The smoothie converted itself into a slushed mess as it began to melt.

Her mouth stuffed full of fried potatoes, Harpreet sighed through her nose. Several weeks prior, Jinhua told her about the truth of her origins. It had taken some prying to circumvent her somewhat private nature when it came to information her friend designated as 'highly classified' (something Harpreet considered herself very good at). But once she did, the floodgates of emotion, pain, and uncertainty were open. Since that day, Harpreet struggled to support her in the right way. Advice on guys, general money matters, and girl stuff she could handle. But digitally infused human beings and robot twins were beyond her comprehension. They made her feel out of her depth. Way above her paygrade as Jinhua's self-appointed best friend.

Since then, Jinhua's moods came in sudden bursts. At one moment she was her competitive, measured, and big-brained self. In the next, she became withdrawn and temperamental. Fits of uncharacteristic emotional outbursts, and long stretches of self-exile into her own head characterized these periods. To Harpreet, it felt like riding a fast roller coaster. At times, exhilarating, terrifying, and nauseating, always with the knowledge that she may be thrown from the ride at any second. Still, she continued to endure the long line, and stomach churning drops to ride over and over again.

Days ago during a committee session, Jinhua requested to use the bathroom and did not return for a long time. After forty minutes passed, alarm bells went off in Harpreet's head and she rushed to go search for her. She checked every bathroom, her sense of dread mounting with each unanswered response to her calls. "Jinhua? You in there?" She called, inside every toilet in the community center. *Please be alive...*

Eventually, she found her sobbing in a toilet stall in a women's bathroom at the opposite end of the old mall. Jinhua's red face and swollen eyelids told her that she had been crying hard.

Harpreet listened with big sister sympathy, holding her friend as she witnessed her breakdown.

Jinhua resented her father for not telling her sooner, yet felt tremendous respect and empathy toward him for having the courage to tell her from his difficult position. She wailed for the mother that she would never know. She felt terrified for the uncertainty of her physical body and mind. Then what of Daniel? She had no idea how to begin to understand her otherworldly connection with him, or how that might affect them both in the future. Would she die an early death, due to the unknown interaction of her biology and the digital redundancies? Would she end up like so many other failed experiments, that were the countless babies that had not survived the process?

"I feel like a freak!" She sobbed, her head buried in her hands as she slumped forward on the toilet seat. Harpreet stood beside her and stroked her hair gently, attempting to provide calm. She swallowed and made an attempt to lighten the mood. "At least all of your thoughts are backed up on a server somewhere. Who knows how much you could get online for a file copy of just your Calculus committee notes?"

The joke brightened Jinhua's mood temporarily. She let a small smile take shape on her

face. "I just wonder what's gonna happen with me...I feel so...lost."

"Hey, well at least your dad said you had a clean bill of health. Totally normal for someone your age. Except for your oversized brain. Though I suppose nothing could be done about that."

Their laughter echoed throughout the bathroom providing a much needed shift in the air around them. Harpreet enjoyed seeing her smiling again, even if it was only for a moment. The two friends embraced each other tightly and exited the stall. "We'd better get back to committee before MS Rhodes decides to assign us extra homework," Harpreet said, still holding Jinhua's hand.

"Ok. I'll be there in a second. Just gonna clean myself up a little bit."

Harpreet arched her eyebrows. Skeptical of her words.

"I promise! I really am going back to the room!" Jinhua protested sheepishly.

Harpreet squeezed her hand, then released it, as she turned toward the door and pressed it open. "Ok, I believe you." Before she exited, she looked over her shoulder and said, "Oh yeah, and no more toilet crying, unless I'm around to help pull you outta your own head, promise?"

Jinhua gave a nod. "I promise."

Harpreet made a fist and pumped it in front of her with a sharp movement. It was a signal of resolve and encouragement. "*Jiayou…*" she said, using a loud whisper.

Jinhua exhaled a laugh and returned the movement, accompanying it with a strong nod.

With that, Harpreet let the bathroom door close behind her and with casual steps made her way back to the old furniture store. As she walked, she thought to herself, *I'm so good at this. I think I just got promoted from best friend to best friend first-class.*

CHAPTER 40: FOR SCIENCE

I'm glad I have you Harpreet. Thank you for being my friend. Jinhua found herself looking at the bathroom door for a while after her best friend walked out. Harpreet had been the main reason she had not had a complete breakdown in the last few weeks.

Since that day I…I found out I was different.

Her gaze turned to the wide bathroom mirror in front of her. The skin on her face was flushed, and she could hardly distinguish her brown eyes housed behind the swollen skin of her eyelids. Turning on the water, she cupped her hands and splashed her face to help revive herself. *Wake up! Wake up!* A dreamlike state had characterized her reality in the weeks since that conversation with her father about who and *what* she was. Sometimes she felt as if she had fallen asleep, only to open her eyes to a new reality. Her former existence as Jinhua, the ace math and science student, and expert ripboarder, was a thing of the past. *Now I'm Jinhua, half human, half computer, science experiment.* She wanted to cry again just thinking about it.

On the night her father told her about her true origins, he had given her a choice. Option A: She could go on living her life as she had been up to that point. *Ignorant, afraid, yet peaceful.* Option B: She could become an active participant in the process. *Informed, engaged, and afraid.* He told her that the decision was completely up to her. Then reminded her that if she chose to be involved, his team would have more data to analyze, which would make it easier for them to draw conclusions about how her evolution could play out.

Stay ignorant, unknowing, and afraid.

Be informed, engaged, and *afraid.*

I'm still afraid either way. That night as she lay awake on her bed, a solid hour was all she needed to make her decision. She informed her father the next morning of her choice. His reaction was as she suspected. Somewhat neutral, yet understanding. She knew him well enough to know he probably would have responded in the same way no matter her choice. He just nodded his head and said, "Alright then. I'll give you more details later tonight. Let's meet in the study around 1800." Then he left for work.

She wanted to stop him before he exited the house to ask about the *details*. But paused before she opened her mouth. For him, the choice to have his daughter be ignorant of her own evolution, or informed about it, both must have been undesirable options. Both would cause her to be afraid. Afraid from knowing too little, or knowing too much. She knew he was aware of this. It had been a lose-lose situation for him, and Jinhua had no idea how to feel or how to talk with him about it. So she let him walk out the door and said nothing.

From that evening on, her father's study, previously a restricted area, became open access. Jinhua spent many nights a week in the room. Sometimes, it was just her and her father. He would show her some data about herself, explain it, and she would listen, occasionally asking questions if she understood enough about what he was talking about.

On other evenings, some of his associates would show up. Most were geeks in white coats whose names (as hard as she would try) she could not recall. "Jinhua, this Dr. So and So, she's a physician," her father would say. Another evening, it was Dr. What's-his-face, he's a geneticist. Then there was Dr. Washington-Perez-Something-Something, he was handsome, Hispanic, with a firm handshake. He was also a digigenomic scientist. She could not remember the full name though. *Who hyphenates their name four times!? I mean c'mon!* She began to make up names for them based on prominent features that she could easily remember. The physician became Dr. Pink Clipboard; the geneticist, Dr. Big Nose. The digigenomic scientist became Dr. Handsome-Handshake, she hyphenated the name in his honor. This made it easier for her to at least distinguish between some of the researchers.

Over the course of several weeks, these scientists conducted a battery of physical tests, psychological examinations, and other assessments on Jinhua. Some were obvious in their scope and objectives. During others, she had no clue what the real purpose was. She just showed up and tried her best to let the process play out. She was also comforted by the knowledge that at any moment, she could walk away from it all, as she and her father had discussed.

As a result of the tests, she knew more about specific aspects of her own body than she ever wanted to know. From knowing how much urine and other fluids her body produced daily, to specific images that materialized in her brain during certain sleep cycles, to even the density of her bones, she knew all of that and then some. She had even finally deciphered the mysterious recurring dream of the broken computer. Her interface with the time-worn machine represented her search for her mother and her digital self. A side of her only known to her subconscious mind until a month prior. When she offered this hypothesized interpretation to her father's team of scientists, they simply nodded their heads and scratched notes on their clipboards. Dr. Pink Clipboard praised her insightfulness with an encouraging wink.

It was as if she had a map to her entire being, inside and out. Some parts were easy to interpret and read. Others baffled even the researchers. Despite the type of data recorded, everything about her was an open book, to be examined, catalogued, and studied. Jinhua went through ups and downs throughout the process. Sometimes, she was infinitely fascinated by it all, wondering about how all the numbers and images might change in the future. Other periods filled her with anxiety. This typically occurred when neither the scientists nor her father, had good answers or explanations to interpret something for her. These periods of silence occurred a few times a week. Any time they happened, Jinhua found herself ready to explode with tears, anger, or both. On most occasions, she walked out of the study, then to her room to calm down. When she eventually returned (which she always did out of respect for their time), the tests and explanations would resume as if nothing had happened. As if they had *known* the emotional outburst was coming. This made Jinhua feel a little awkward, but no one said anything to her about it, so she didn't feel as bad about having interrupted their research.

Throughout what felt like an endless line of interviews, tests, and evaluations, Jinhua reported nearly everything that she could think of her to dad's faithful team of researchers. It took patience to respond to similar questions being asked in slightly cryptic and skewed ways, to keep her mind spinning even after most of her energy had been consumed, but she endured. On occasion, she was rewarded with truncated explanations of the tests, and sometimes even a personal anecdote from her father.

One such anecdote came from a review of a thought log entry when Jinhua was eleven-years-old. Her father told her she had been trying to teach herself about the trigonometric concept of the unit circle. Young Jinhua knew the concept was key to success in her math committee, and devoted herself to learning it weeks ahead of the curriculum. But it was hard. She kept mixing up radians with degrees. Kept going the wrong way on the circle. Her triangle dimensions were all off, and the concept of special right triangles seemed beyond her grasp. Li had watched her frustration from his study. Watched her try and fail over many nights. The thoughts were all there. *"If I just try it this way…no that doesn't work." "Aiyoo! I was so close." "I'll never understand this…" "I'm such a failure…"* Jinhua scanned the log, recalling the frustration of the memory.

Then half way down the screen, the log changed. *"I think I'm getting the hang of this." "Ooh so that's where it goes!" "Ok so counterclockwise is positive, clockwise is negative? So tricky!"* By the time she reached the end of the screen, tears were in her eyes. She looked at her dad. His eyes were wet, too.

"I was very proud that day. I knew you would figure it out," Li said. Jinhua embraced him. They were alone in the study that day and she was overjoyed to be able to share such a private moment with him, without the eyes of the other scientists around.

After weeks of tests and research, Jinhua noticed her father appeared to be losing weight, and outside of speaking to her about Cereus or digigenomics, seemed to have little else to say. The remainder of his thin grey hair was slowly shrinking into his scalp, and he often wore a look of shielded fatigue on his face. She knew there were things that he knew that he could not, or would not tell her. Furthermore, he was frustrated by those facts that escaped even his superior understanding. He was also worried about how his only daughter could bear the burden of being viewed and treated like a test animal in a lab. Besides these two factors, she had no idea what personal demons he was fighting. Whatever it was that specifically troubled him, he would never tell her, and on some level she was alright with that.

Because she had secrets too. Something had changed within her since that fateful conversation with her father in the Cereus study. Fearing that she might skew the data, she never bothered to mention it to the army of interviewers and researchers that she interacted with. This change was not something that could be detected by analyzing the mountains of data her body generated on a daily basis. No. It was something completely different. More like a feeling she couldn't put words to, but knew was there. *Just like my connection with Daniel.* She had never been able to describe it, or this new feeling to the scientists, her father, or even to herself. But *something* was happening with her.

It was like something deep inside of her had awoken and was slowly stretching its limbs, observing foreign surroundings with childlike curiosity. Now, after weeks of watching, it was ready to play. The creature, docile and wide-eyed, was like electric energy amassed at the positive end of a battery. Sparking with electric gold light, it lingered in confined space growing stronger with each passing moment. Jinhua had no idea how, but she could feel it running through her. And the feeling was magical.

When the feeling came over her it began as a tiny golden vibration that reverberated through her. The energy was sometimes small and fragile. Other times it surprised her, disrupting the natural rhythm of her body's energy cycle, only to have homeostasis return moments later, leaving as quickly as it had appeared. Jinhua began to meticulously record in her device whenever she felt the "wave", as she came to call it, pass through her. Several weeks ago, they were rare occurrences, but through all of the tests, experiments, and procedures, their frequency and intensity increased. *What is happening to me?*

As she looked at herself in the bathroom mirror she felt it again. This one shot a powerful Mikado yellow wave of energy from somewhere within her brain to her left lung. Her heart's rhythm was interrupted briefly as she gasped for air, coughing violently. Her hands gripped the sink, eyes clenched shut; she desperately waited for the sensation to pass, wondering if she was having a heart attack or a stroke. The world around her felt as if it were shaking, on the verge of collapse. Jinhua wanted to scream, but even her voice would not come. It had been absorbed by the "wave".

A minute later, after the sensation passed, she opened her eyes. Her reflection returned its gaze from the mirror. Her sweat glistened face, stained with the marks of sadness, looked tense and tight. She raised her hands to gently massage it, then splashed more water on her face from the sink.

Still somewhat breathless, skin tingling with the aftereffects of the unexplained power, Jinhua pulled her device from her shorts to document the event. It had been the third wave that day, and the most powerful that she had ever felt up to that point in time.

CHAPTER 41:
TWO DIRECTIVES

I sense what Jinhua calls the "wave".

How long has she been gone from the committee room? I am here, but she is not. She was…where? Yes. In the women's bathroom. East side of the community center, the site of the former Yuba-Sutter Mall, opened 1990, located in the county of…irrelevant.

Jinhua, she is distressed. Vitals…blood pressure, heart rate, muscle tension, is all elevated. Take action. But how? Which is best? Best for me? Best for Jinhua?

Communicate with her? She does not desire it now. Does not like to talk about this. *Doesn't* know how. She is in the bathroom…crying. She is stressed and confused, all vitals confirm this. Then what is the best way to accomplish Directive one?

Directive one. Directive one. Directive one.

Contact. Touch. But she does not desire it now. *Doesn't* want it. It scares her. It is not *'feihao'*.

Being here, listening to the fat man, Master Scholar Rhodes, helps Directive one. But it is not efficient. I am learning. I am improving. But it does not help her. *Doesn't* help her. Directive two is compromised.

She was happy, when? By the river. When? When we almost kissed. When? Racing ripboards with her friend, Harpreet. Yes, the one with the wide hips and loud voice. She returned to the room now. Her face has signs of tension. The body language: crossed arms, tight lips, narrowed eyes, displays anxiety. She is stressed. Worried about her friend, Jinhua. She is a good friend.

Something is happening.

Jinhua is not well.

She is coughing. Feeling tightness in her chest. It is hard to breathe.

There is blood on the sink. She is scared, confused. The world is different than before. But she does not understand it.

Her fingers are holding on to the sink now. Tight. Gripping. She *doesn't* want to fall.

I should help. Directive one is in danger. No. She doesn't want it. Directive two is compromised.

Her vision is cloudy. She may lose consciousness soon. May *pass out*. Better.

Jinhua is dizzy. But it is different. She is not afraid. I can sense it. I know.

She can *feel* me. But she doesn't know how to proceed. I can *sense* her. She wants to learn how. Wants to do it herself. It is very…*her*. Directive one. Directive one. Yes. Good. Feihao.

She is standing in the storm. Listening, feeling, waiting. She is learning how it moves. I cannot help her. But she is not alone.

I am with her. She knows it. I can help her from here. Make her stronger.

Vitals are calming. She is adapting. Learning to listen, learning to feel again. Learning to sense.

Wait. The unpleasant sensations return. The coughing, tight chest, blurred vision, strained muscles, the blood. She wants to scream. Directive one is compromised. I must go. Must help.

No. Directive two compromised. Wait. Wait. Wait.

She is on the floor of the bathroom. Feeling weak, but vitals are strong. Something is happening. Something is changing. I cannot see her now. Lost. Where did she go? Directive one is compromised. Directive two is compromised.

The fat man is talking. He can wait. Directive one and Directive two will be compromised. I must go. Must help Jinhua.

Ten minutes. Wait. Fifteen minutes. Wait. She has not returned. Where is Jinhua?

There. She is walking in. Now sitting at her desk. She looks happy.

Something has happened. Something is different.

I will ask her after the fat man is done.

She is smiling at me. I took the right action.

I must remember what made her happy for the future. Today is important for her. Will save it for the future.

Jinhua is better. She is happy. Directive one and two satisfied. Feihao.

CHAPTER 42:
ROAD TRIP - PART 1

Noe hated road trips. One of her earliest memories was of a trip she had taken with her family to Las Vegas, when she was six years old. Squashed in the back of an orange colored Ford Fiesta (a rental car) next to her parents' luggage, she recalled looking out at the endless desert scene passing by outside and being terribly bored. The only thing she had with her was an old tablet. The screen was going out, and there was no wi-fi access on the open road, which meant she was stuck watching old episodes of Spongebob Squarepants she had already watched several times before, because it was the only show loaded onto the device. In the front seat, her dad was at the wheel, quiet as usual; her mom sat next to him, talking endlessly about things Noe couldn't understand. During that trip, Noe resembled a fly on the wall, hardly noticeable, but a nuisance whenever she made her presence known. All of these factors made the experience uncomfortable for her, and for the rest of her life, she avoided long journeys by car whenever possible.

The trip from Sacramento to Yuba City was not far according to Google maps, but traffic along the small highway nearly doubled the commute time on the worst days. And today was one of those days. *I hate being in the car*, Noe thought. She labored to transform her genuine discomfort, by tapping her foot rapidly. The action helped dispel some of her restless energy.

It was a sweltering mid-August day, with no clouds to block the midday sun. Fields of yellowed grass were situated between the clutter of suburban clone houses that characterized the uninspired neighborhoods along the highway. When she was a child, Noe's mother told her that long ago, there had been nothing but empty fields between Sacramento and Yuba City. Much of it was farmland for growing various California made crops. But over the years, life was slowly squeezed from the farmers and they were forced to sell to private corporations. These companies turned the land into houses, schools, and other niceties that American families always expected, but never appreciated. More capitalistic greed, was how her mother had put it. Noe had a hard time imagining the fields empty. She could not see life without the steady march of progress.

Rodan sat by the opposite window in the backseat of the car. They hadn't spoken much at all, mostly because he had been furiously making calls and answering messages the entire time. Noe's eyes shifted back inside the car toward him. He was dressed in a navy blue polo shirt, with the Cereus crest located over his heart. His pants were plain khakis that looked faded and stressed over his thick legs. Noe assumed he had bought them when he was a much thinner man.

Rodan wasn't moving, but his face was tight with concentration. Despite the chilly air conditioned interior of the luxury vehicle, dots of sweat collected just below his tightly aligned haircut. The man was clearly engaged in an important telepathic conversation and she didn't want to disturb him.

Noe had learned about telepathic technology when she was a little girl and had always considered it a form of communication for the privileged elite and government spies, just like it had been portrayed in the movies and other popular media. *Bunch of pretentious assholes*, she would often think, whenever she saw someone's face writhing for no apparent reason; their eyes moving as if they were in face-to-face conversation with another person. After all, those were the only people that could afford such expensive toys and were *too good* to use normal voice communication like regular people. Besides that, she never liked the idea of willfully broadcasting her private thoughts over a public network. You never knew who was on the other end listening. A moment later, Rodan seemed to relax, signaling the end of his conversation. He flung his head back on the headrest in exasperation and shut his eyes.

"Everything ok?" Noe asked.

A sigh blew heavily out of his lips. "I just spoke with Li. He says we've lost another hundred people from one of the comvils down south. They just packed up and left overnight."

"Wow," Noe replied. She sounded surprised, but didn't show it on her face. *They finally woke the fuck up, and moved back to normal life.* Rodan seemed too distracted to notice the contrast between her tone and her unexpressive face.

He continued, "Up there in Yuba, it's not much better. They're bleeding dozens more by the day."

"They must be getting scared and losing faith in the system," Noe said. *About time.*

Rodan nodded grimly. "You're right. Everybody heard about what went down up in that ghost town. And they fear Limnic may strike again at any time and anywhere."

That may be the case, Noe mused, *it also may be that they finally saw Cereus for the scam that it truly is, and decided to join normal society again.* She let the thoughts pass feeling the coals of anger being stoked into ignition. Then she stopped herself by taking deep regular breaths. She was getting better at calming herself, *before* her anger began to burn. It was easier to prevent the fire, than to extinguish it after it was blazing out of control. Though Noe disliked Cereus, she cared for Rodan. Sometimes it was hard to keep the two separate in her head. *Janus.* Her line of thinking suddenly redirected itself to their shared nemesis.

It had been two weeks since the Battle of North Bloomfield, yet Noe continued to replay the encounter with her mother's murderer in her mind. His sinister grin, the mental block, the feeling of floating in the womb, her losing consciousness, there were still many questions she had no answers to. *Why didn't Kyler and Spazer kill him? Why didn't I kill him? What type of power does Janus have over us? How can we fight it?* Noe's mind began to twist itself into knots. She had no idea how or where to find answers to these questions. She spent the last two weeks scouring online resources for answers, yet found nothing. It frustrated her immensely. *We failed. I failed. This is all happening because of us.*

She began to go over the events following Janus' appearance again, as she had every day since the battle. It was the young Spazer who had awoken her from the deep sleep she had fallen into. At first, all she felt was her body being pushed back and forth. Initially the contact was barely discernible, but quickly it turned into violent shaking. Like a teenager being roused from sleep by an annoyed parent,

Noe's first thought was to continue sleeping, but something told her to wake up. Then it *yelled* at her to "Wake up!" When she opened her eyes, they still felt leaden and slow. It took her vision a few seconds to link up with her brain, and process everything that was going on. *How long was I—?* Her thought was interrupted by the young soldier.

"We can't stay here!" Spazer yelled, "The building's gonna fall!"

'Building' and 'fall' were the only words that registered in her head. They were the only words she needed to hear. Without a second thought, she clambered to her feet with Spazer and Kyler's help, then all three of them scrambled out of the building. Seconds after her brain took note of the cool evening air, Noe heard the sound of splintering wood, then a loud crash as the roof gave way, crushing everything beneath it. The old house released a hot sigh as it collapsed, causing a billow of heat to blow across her face. Noe instinctively raised her arm to shield her nose and mouth from debris and ash, scattered by the dying structure. She was lucky to be alive. They all were.

The three of them walked back toward the entrance of the town, eventually crossing paths with a sweaty and bloody Bear. Kyler immediately began an accountability assessment for the remainder of his unit, human and mech, while Spazer helped the battle weary Bear tend to his wounds. Out of nowhere, Cheeks joined the group, enthusiastic at first when speaking about how many kills he had during the fight. But upon hearing about Lance's death, his smile shrank, and he became silent, withdrawn. For Noe, it was a scary sight. She had only known him to be jovial and light-hearted. Melancholy did not suit his face. Not at all.

When she reached the entrance to the town, Rodan stood there, an empty expression on his face. He just stared ahead in puzzlement, saying nothing. At first, she thought it was the horror of the battle that had gotten to him, that he was in a state of what they used to call 'shell shock'. Then she realized it might be something else, something that he wouldn't tell her. Call it women's intuition, but she just knew then and there that he had seen or heard something that had changed him in a fundamental way. And as she searched his eyes among the destruction of the battlefield, she knew that she would never know what that thing was. Much like her experience with the U.S. Air Force operator that nearly drove her to suicide all those years ago, the thing or event, was profoundly personal for him. And there was nothing she could do or say to help him to process and move forward from it. It was his private war to fight, his demon to exorcise. All she could do was provide support with invisible hands, and hope that would be enough to guide him to where he needed to be.

CHAPTER 43:
ROAD TRIP - PART 2

Rodan was stressed. *Too much to do. Too much to think about.* In the back of the autocar, he stretched his neck from side to side to relieve some tension. It was the only part of his body that he could move freely in the constricted space of the backseat. His neck popped and cracked as he moved it gently back and forth. Then he shut his eyes and leaned his head back on the headrest. The position was relaxing until a pulsing headache, brought on by the vehicle's vibration, forced him to lower his neck again. *Can't get fuckin' comfortable. Story of my life.*

"You alright?" Noe asked. She looked concerned.

"Yeah I'm good," Rodan shook his head then let out a sigh, "just a lot going on."

"I bet. It's probably high level serious business right?"

An unexpected laugh escaped Rodan's lips, "Wow, that joke...I'm not even gonna comment on how terrible it was."

Noe grinned, "I know, I know, it was bad. It was the best I could come up with on the spot. I've never been good at being witty and cracking jokes. Guess the military forgot to issue me a sense of humor."

Rodan smiled, "I'm right there with you. There was a guy in my unit back in the Army, uh, I think his name was Zack. Anyway, anytime we were out on a training run, or going through some other type of hell, he would crack jokes. They were variations of knock-knock jokes, or, if our drill instructor wasn't around, yo' momma jokes. Those were the best." Rodan snickered recalling the memory with fondness.

Noe laughed, showing her teeth. She imagined a much younger and thinner Rodan laughing at yo momma jokes and running. "No way. You? Running? I don't see it."

Rodan's eyes fell to his bulging stomach, as a grin formed across his lips. "Ah I see you got jokes. Yeah I used to. But! Only when I had to. I never liked it though. The military tries to turn everyone into a runner. But those of us who never liked it, end up hating it even more. Then we look like this after we get out." He slapped his stomach to further prove his point. The action made Noe laugh again. To him, her laugh was like the sound of a soulful saxophone drifting out of a jazz club on a clear evening. A pleasant surprise whenever it occurred, it helped him relax. Made him want to stop and listen for a while.

In what he felt was a split second, Rodan's eyes scanned the entirety of Noe's figure. Her feet were in white simple sandals. She wore capris that matched the color of her footwear, revealing tanned ankles. Her ribbed tank top was a deep purple. She had a style that was her own. Casual, yet fashionable, but wasn't flashy about it at all. Rodan liked that about her, among many other things. Sexy. Was the word that came to his mind. By the time split second expired, his eyes snapped forward again, with the image of her body's curves and dips burned into his head. An image he would not soon forget.

"You see something you like?" Noe asked. Her tone was somewhat playful, but her expression was academic and anticipative, like that of a teacher asking a student an unforeseen question.

Rodan's breath caught, his pucker factor shot to an eleven out of ten, as if he were about to parachute out of a C-130. *She saw me!? Aw hell!*

"Uh, I...I well, I was gonna say..." he cleared his throat, stalling to find words, any words.

Noe blinked rapidly, with expectant eyes. "You were gonna say...uh huh, I'm listening."

"I was just gonna say, how...how you seem to have avoided growing a belly since you got out. Not everyone can do that." A single bead of sweat fell down his forehead. He wondered how she would react to his response. *Can't believe I got caught! Story of my life.*

"I run a lot. And I eat as clean as I can." Noe smirked, "Can't imagine having a belly like this," she reached over and lightly patted his stomach. "I don't think it would be a good look on me. What do you think?"

"Naw. It sure wouldn't be…" Rodan said, somewhat absentmindedly. Her touch sent pleasant waves throughout his abdomen, which spread rapidly through the rest of his body. His jaw tightened, and his breathing stuttered. He had to readjust himself in the small seat to curb his rising excitement, while averting his eyes to the mundane air vent above him. He was relieved when she returned to her side of the vehicle. Leaning against the window, she gave a voice command to increase the power of the air conditioner in the already cold vehicle, then folded her arms across her chest. Interesting, Rodan thought.

Another minute passed with only the faint sound of traffic outside of the vehicle to fill both of their ears. Noe turned to Rodan abruptly and asked, "Why did you join Cereus?"

Rodan, relieved she had asked a question he didn't mind answering, chuckled in response. "Well, I kinda got this wannabe hero complex thing goin' on. Ever since I was in high school, I wanted to help people and society in general. So after I graduated from high school I joined the Army."

Noe nodded. His story didn't sound much different from her own. "I was the same. Went to Space Force boot camp almost directly after graduation." Noe breathed a single dry laugh. "My mom was pissed. She wanted me to stay at home here in Sac and join Cereus. I said 'no thanks!' to that."

Rodan looked at her with surprise.

"Wait, what is it? Do I have something on my face?" Noe asked, slightly self-conscious.

"Naw, naw, I just didn't know you were from here."

"Yep, Del Paso Heights proud." Noe paused, mirroring his astonishment, "Wait you are too?"

"Hell yeah I am! Graduated from Grant Union. Class of 39' feelin' fiiine. I used to patrol the Heights as young cop."

Noe lightly punched him in the shoulder from her seat, "No way! I'm Grant, class of 47'. I don't remember the little slogan or whatever. I never paid attention to that shit." Then she added, "Oh so you were a cop, huh? Glad I never ran into you back in the day then!"

Both laughed, wiping tears from their eyes.

Then suddenly Noe remembered the morning Rodan showed up at her apartment to deliver the news about her mother. The needle prick of nostalgia she had felt back then, that fleeting familiarity, was because of Rodan. She hadn't seen him on the streets as a kid, but she had encountered him before. As Rodan checked his device again for another incoming message in the seat across from her in the back of the auto car, she studied his face. The maple syrup shaded eyes, still reflected that of a relentless public servant. Those were the same eyes of that handsome police rookie in the clean uniform during the year of the 2045 flood. Among the dozens of teenagers Rodan aided during the flood relief, he most likely didn't remember her, but she remembered him. The compassionate gaze made her soften with comfort in her seat, as if she were nestled before a space heater in the winter time. A pleasant sensation.

For the next several minutes both sat in silence. Each guessing what the other was thinking. Enjoying the game. Outside traffic had slowed to a crawl and the world moved by one inch at a time. There was nowhere to go. No way to neutralize the feeling swirling around them. Rodan felt compelled to act, but had no idea how he would go about it. I shouldn't get involved with her. Got too many things to do. He recalled the burned image of her again and swallowed hard. But damn, she is sexy as hell!

A phone call invaded the noiseless car. In haste, Rodan scrambled to clear his mind of lustful contemplations, and refocus on his work. Without looking at who was calling, he answered his device with swift motion.

"Hello?"

"Oh shit. When did that happen?"

"I see. How many dead?"

"Damn, that many?"

"We're about twenty minutes out now. The traffic is horrible."

"Uh huh, yeah she's with me." He glanced over at Noe, who was listening intently to his half of the conversation.

"Dinner? Yeah, you know I like to eat!"

Noe suppressed a laugh.

Rodan mouthed shut up in her direction.

"Oh ok, I've eaten that a few times before and thought it was pretty good."

"Yeah I know! You like that spicy shit!"

"Ok, ok, see you in a lil' bit." Rodan ended the call.

"What was that?" Noe asked.

"It was Li. He said another Limnic cell just conducted a live demolition down in San Diego of a new hospital building that was under construction."

Noe gasped. "Dammit. How many fatalities?"

"Initial reports say thirty or so construction workers and contractors were on site at the time of the blast. They're still searching the debris for potential survivors." Rodan brought his large hand to his forehead and wrinkled the skin. "It looks like Limnic's been emboldened since our fight with them."

"What about the Cereus militias? Can't they track down the bombers?"

Rodan shook his head. "The terrorists covered their digital and physical tracks well. It may take days to figure out what really happened. Besides, we could never take them in direct combat. The few volunteer defense units in each comvil are no match for Limnic's well-paid army of mercenaries, and many of our units on the fringes have been bought and bribed by old world money. The U.S. feds are getting involved to help slow Limnic down, but their general anti-Cereus and Limnic stance keeps them from going all in. They don't like acknowledging that either of us exist. Goes against their well-crafted narrative of being the best on Earth, y'know? Goddamn politics." His fist banged into the car door, shaking the small vehicle.

Noe reached over and placed a reassuring hand on his shoulder. It was the only thing that felt appropriate to do. The complexities of his reality as head of Cereus were far too difficult for her to grasp.

The hardness of Rodan's face slackened upon Noe's touch. He had noticed a change in her since she agreed to work with him as a contractor. The confused and cynical woman that he had encountered for the first time in West Sacramento months ago, seemed to have found a tender side that showed itself more and more easily. He was happy for her. And found himself fighting down his desire for companionship from his lonely position as the head of such a monumental organization. He reminded himself again not to go there.

Instead, he found himself thinking about a question she asked him a week before the Battle of North Bloomfield, *'What's going to happen with Cereus?'* His unspoken response always wavered between blind optimism and dark nihilism. There was no middle ground for him, because he had no idea what awaited him or the organization in the long run.

He, Noe, and the rest of Kyler's team had discussed the events from the battle and the encounter with Janus at length. But they had not reached a definitive conclusion about what *really* happened that night. They were like doctors, talking about the visible symptoms the patient was experiencing, but had no idea how to discuss the effect those same symptoms had on his psyche or soul. None of them knew how to talk about it. The facts were always easier to discuss, at least it was that way for Rodan. Everything else existed in some esoteric realm, out of reach from his formulaic understanding of the world.

But he did know a few things to be certain. Janus could read minds. Furthermore, it was clear that he had found some way to manipulate people's thoughts, and to exert a powerful force that made them do whatever he wanted. *How had Noe described it?* 'It was like I was *'locked out'* of my own mind' she told Rodan during the debrief. Could Janus have manipulated him without his knowledge? Surely it was possible. But Rodan hadn't felt any of the feelings Noe or the others had described. How would he have known if Janus had controlled all of his actions or not? Had Janus even really been there that night? Or had it all been some made up illusion Janus projected into his head? All of the questions tumbled around Rodan's pressured mind and confused him even more. *Bottom line is if Janus can lock us out of our own heads and control what we see and do, then we're in a lot of trouble.*

"Hey," Noe nudged him with her finger, "we're here in town, but things seem a little…off."

Rodan had been so in his head he hadn't noticed Yuba City come into view. They were on Colusa highway cruising down the city's primary artery that ran from west to east. Looking outside of the window, Rodan saw what she meant. People were huddled into small groups in front of businesses, shops, and community shelters with heads low in conspiratorial postures. From the relative low speed of the car, he could discern the rapid movement of lips accompanied by sharp gestures from several pedestrians. Citizens who had not grouped up, moved with urgency in tightened balls of tension. Some walked with friends and family members to unknown destinations, while others jogged.

"What the hell is going on out there?" Noe leaned toward his side of the window for a better view. "It looks like *something* is happening, or is about to happen."

Rodan held his gaze outside of the window, trying to interpret the scene. No immediate explanations came to him. This made the ominous feeling in his mind feel even worse. "I have no idea. It's a good thing we're almost there." *It must be Janus somehow. He's doing this. I know it. But what is his plan?*

He hadn't told anyone about his conversation with Janus following the battle. Not even Noe. He knew he could trust her, that having a second head to think through the situation (especially hers) would be helpful, yet he couldn't bring himself to do it. *What would she think? How would she take it if she knew I didn't try and kill Janus when I had the chance? That I thought about…helping him.* Surely she would see it as an act of betrayal. He had no one else he could turn to at this point, and couldn't bring himself to sabotage their friendship. He would have to handle this on his own, without her help.

What had Janus told him? *Cereus is the future, and you alone have the power to make it a reality. Only you can help usher humanity toward a new age.* The words had haunted him since that day and he was not sure about how to interpret them. So they sat on the kitchen counter of his brain, like mail delivered to the wrong address. Unanalyzed, ignored.

Would humanity adopt Cereus' principles and philosophy on its own? Could Cereus society truly survive in its transformed nature without the leadership and guidance of the Founders? Was Janus' technology the only way to force humanity to take that next bold step into the future? Rodan had no clear answers to any of these questions, and that left him unsettled. He had always wanted to help humanity, to be more of a contributor than a consumer, and joining Cereus had been an outlet for that desire. Now he was in a position to steer the organization and even humanity as a whole, toward that greater good. Sometimes the burden of that responsibility became too much for him to bear.

Another gentle nudge from Noe brought him back to reality. She could tell when his mind was preoccupied.

"Hey, we're here," she said, her voice was warm and relaxed. A noticeable contrast from their first meeting, which felt like a distant memory at this point. "Did you get all of your thinking done?"

He smiled, "Only partially. I still got a lot left to do."

*   *   *

It had been a few months since Rodan had stepped foot in Li Ma's fabulous house. The large apartment that Rodan himself now occupied in the capital since his divorce was a closet compared to the six plus bedrooms that his longtime friend called home.

In typical Li fashion, he stood with perfectly aligned posture at the geometric midpoint between two pairs of pillars that framed the decoratively carved wood of his mansion's front entrance. Beside him stood a straight-faced young woman wearing faded gray jean shorts and a yellow t-shirt with basic math symbols printed on the front. It took him several seconds to realize that it was Li's only daughter, Jinhua, who now was just a little bit taller than her elderly father. She had grown significantly since he had last seen her.

"What took you so long?" Li said. The words came out slower than Rodan was used to, as the two men lightly embraced. He could tell Li looked more worn out than usual.

"You know, the standard traffic delays. Too many people setting their vehicles on 'do not disturb' mode makes everything slower."

"It only takes me an hour to get here from the city. So I guess I've got you beat on time." Li joked.

Rodan gave a curt acknowledgement. "Woah! Is that little Jini?" His eyes turned to Jinhua. "I barely recognized you! You've grown so much!"

"Hello Mr. Mitchell. It's good to see you again." She forced a smile, and extended her hand for a formal handshake. Rodan returned it. There was a new fortitude in the strength of her grip. Her eyes had adopted an air of experience, very similar to her father's.

"I see you've had your growth spurt and you've passed your father in height. Although that's not really hard to do."

Jinhua covered her mouth to hide a giggle. Li shook his head, grinning.

The sound of a small suitcase stumbling on the winding pavement made Rodan turn around. Noe's old suitcase seemed to meander of its own will as she struggled to pull it along. The wheels wobbled and flailed, squeaking with every rotation. Rodan made a move to help her with the uncooperative luggage, but the sharp daggers that pierced him from her eyes told him to stay put and let her handle it.

Rodan gestured toward her. "Li, this is Noelani Acosta. She's the one that's been helping us out against Limnic in the last few weeks."

"Hi, I go by Noe," she extended her hand.

Li took calculated steps forward to return the hand shake. "It's a pleasure to meet you Noe. Rodan's informed me of your courage and bravery on the digital and physical battlefields. We need all the help we can get right now, so it's much needed and appreciated."

"I'm just doing my job. Limnic and Janus *must* be stopped." She thought about adding, '*and Cereus too*' but she realized that this would probably not go over well with them.

"Agreed." Li added. "Shall we go inside? I'll show you where you'll be lodging."

CHAPTER 44:
DINNER PARTY

"You didn't have to arrange dinner for us," Rodan said.

Li shook his head, "It's no trouble at all. It's been a long time since we were all together like this. These are hard times, so we should enjoy it while we can."

A decorative chandelier with LED bulbs crafted to look like tiny candle flames illuminated the dining room in formal light. The lighting always made Rodan feel as if he were in a museum. On the walls, Li displayed blown up photos of locations around the world he had visited throughout his extensive career. Li and Rodan were in some of the pictures, others just contained beautiful landscapes and scenery. One picture of sunset in Singapore, with the iconic Marina Bay Sands Hotel silhouetted before a sky of burning colors, could have won a prize. Li was a talented photographer, even though he never openly talked about the hobby. Rodan felt tempted to skip the meal and admire his friend's work anytime he visited.

"Come on in Kyler," Li called. The old soldier marched into the room, followed by two of his men. They entered from the house's comfortable great room, where they had been waiting for the past twenty minutes. Cheeks entered the formal atmosphere cautiously, as if he were afraid to touch or disturb anything. Spazer walked in with a limp, his fresh wound from the battle still healing. Unlike Cheeks, he seemed much more used to the vibe of the room. Yet even in civilian clothes he stood with hands, one over the other, neatly folded in front of him with formal posture. As if ready to receive orders. Kyler greeted everyone with a stone-faced nod and took his place toward the far end of the table next to Noe. Cheeks' eyes found Noe's. Before making his way to an empty chair next to Rodan, he waved fat fingers playfully toward her. Noe shook her head and laughed softly. Spazer smiled too, until Cheeks flashed a dirty look and pointed his finger directly at the vacant chair next to him. Spazer gave Noe a timid wave, then limped as fast as he could to his seat.

Li sat at the head of the finely crafted dining room table. Rodan was directly to his left with eyes and thoughts lost in a memory of a picture of himself and Li standing in Prague. On the other side of the table, to Li's right, Jinhua sat with an unfailing posture, hungry eyes fixed toward the center of the table. Next to her, Noe noticed that the smell of food seemed to soften the adolescent's face. It made her look more like a normal teenage girl, rather than the daughter of an intelligence agent.

With some effort, Li raised himself from his chair, then lifted a glass of dark wine to perform a toast to his dinner guests. "I'm pleased that we could all get together like this tonight. As you know, we have all gathered here to formulate our next steps to counter Janus and his plans. I was inspired by all of your bravery and courage during the battle up north, but we still have much to do in our fight against Limnic. With that said, I hope that tonight we can put all of that aside for a little while and enjoy a good meal and each other's company. So let's eat."

"Cheers!" Everyone at the table took a sip of wine, then the dinner began.

Li lowered himself into his chair. "Good speech," Rodan remarked.

"Thanks."

Low conversations began among the dinner guests as everyone picked up utensils to begin the meal. The sound of sliding dishes, friendly chit chat, and Cheek's voice all worked in tandem to contribute to a family atmosphere.

Noe had no idea what she was eating. Before her sat two large pots filled with a bubbling liquid. Each pot was partitioned in the center by a metallic divider separating one soup base from the other, giving the entire meal a Jekyll and Hyde appearance. On one side, the soup had a yellow-ish gold hue with swirls of something Li called "miso" in it. The other bubbled with a reddish color and smelled strongly of pepper and salt. It looked unbelievably spicy and Noe feared it might cause pain upon entering and exiting her body. Jinhua passed her a plate of raw ingredients, that she initially had no idea what to do with. There were some type of leafy greens, mushrooms, thin slices of what appeared to be beef, and other assorted food items. Her eyes roamed around the table and noticed everyone else seemed to be stuffing the uncooked food into the miniature cauldrons' rolling boils. So she followed their example, being careful to avoid contact with the hot metallic cooking pots.

"Everybody dig in," came Li's voice across the dining table. "Don't be shy." He began to shovel copious amounts of leafy greens into one of the smoking pots.

Jinhua was about to load a fishball wrapped in a thinly sliced piece of lamb into the pot when she noticed Noe fumbling with her pair of chopsticks. When Noe's third attempt to grab a helping of dried noodles failed, Jinhua reached over to assist her.

"You've never had a hotpot meal before, no?" she asked innocently.

"How could you tell?" Noe quipped. "I used to use chopsticks a lot when I was a kid, but I always struggled with them. So eventually, I gave up completely and stuck with using a fork and knife. The last time I attempted to use them was when I was in high school. So a long time ago."

Jinhua giggled. "It's ok. I know there can be a learning curve if you don't use them alot." She adeptly gripped the noodles, and placed them in the boiling pot. Other ingredients: thin stringy mushrooms, tiny blocks called sponge tofu, and meat stuffed fishballs followed. Jinhua maneuvered the red sticks between her fingers as if they were an organic appendage.

"Ok, now I'm impressed," Noe said. Her tongue began to salivate at the pleasant aroma of the cooking soup. "So nothing is made ahead of time except for the soup broth, and you have to put raw meat and everything else into the pot yourself?"

"Yep. Part of the fun of it is getting to make your own meal and doing it together with the people you care about."

"Where I'm from, if the food's not cooked all the way, we go and order take out."

Jinhua stirred the ingredients and smiled. "I guess we have to *take out* the stuff from the pot to eat it after it's done. Does that count?"

Noe laughed awkwardly at her joke, reminding herself that despite her often mature veneer, she was still a teenager after all. "So, you're probably in high school now, right? What do you plan on studying when you go to college?"

Jinhua returned a bewildered look. *High school? College?* These were words that she only knew of through online media, really old movies, and television shows. The words brought images of old buildings and people to her mind, but the concept was difficult to grasp. Li raised an eyebrow upon hearing the question.

"Our education system here in the comvil is organized a little differently." Jinhua proceeded to enlighten her on the nature of committees that allowed any person to gain knowledge and skills in a particular field. Those skills could then be evaluated and tested by a professional committee who could confer credentials to anyone who possessed the correct prerequisites and could perform tasks related to the actual nature of what the specific demands of the job were. In that way, it was easier for people to reskill themselves for certain work any time they desired. She summarized this information for Noe, who listened intently.

"In short, no I won't be going to college. I was going to look for an astronautical engineering committee after I complete the physics, advanced math, and quantum studies requirements…buuut lately I've been getting interested in biology and new field called digigenomics, so I don't really know for sure at this point." Jinhua gave her a sweet smile, "More dumplings?"

"No thanks…" *Digigenomics? What the hell is that?* Noe stared dumbly at the girl, and watched her loudly slurping her soup, while her father looked at her approvingly without her knowledge. Noe felt a stab of inferiority begin to morph itself into anger. But it had little to do with Jinhua. She had heard a similar explanation of the Cereus educational system a long time ago as a fifth grader. Even back then, her mother preached about the benefits of the system, but ultimately, allowed a ten-year-old Noe to choose her educational fate. It should have been a difficult decision for a little girl. But that was not the case for her. By the age of ten, her hate for Cereus and everything it stood for was already taking root, like a mushroom sprouting in a dark corner. She didn't care if the new system was superior. Noe chose the standard American public school system and never looked back. *Damn you Mom…* The steam from the spicy brew before her encouraged heat and moisture to build in her eyes.

"More noodles?" Jinhua said to her. She seemed aloof to the damage her words had caused. Noe looked at her for a second, then shook off her bitter thoughts. Jinhua's elevated mood acted as a salve for her wounded feelings. "O-Of course." Noe forced herself to smile and accept the offer of more delicious food.

CHAPTER 45:
AFTER PARTY

Across the table from Noe, Rodan tore his attention from the raucous Cheeks every few minutes to check on her. Every now and then her eyes met his, causing a delightful tingling feeling to move through his body. The sensation provided the perfect distraction from Cheeks' jabbering lips.

"Y'know the 49ers can do it again this year! They got that new cyborg-kid now. What's his name? Oh yeah! Silva, Darnell Silva, he's the quarterback now." He loudly slurped up some noodles, then with surprising technique, manipulated the chopsticks over the rolling broth to find his next helping. "Dude literally has a fuckin' cannon for an arm. Had it approved by the league, and everything. He can *shoot* the ball from endzone to endzone. Crazy shit!"

Rodan agreed. "Yeah Silva is a beast. It's unreal what some of these athletes can do now. It used to be that the only thing people worried about was doping and steroids. Now as they say: 'If you ain't cheatin', you ain't competin'.

Cheeks said it in unison with him, with a voice slightly above dinner party level. Kyler cast a regulatory look in his direction, reminding him to lower his voice. Spazer noted the gesture and began to snicker. In response, Cheeks used his bloated hand to slap him on the back of the head causing his smile to quickly disappear. Kyler's glare fell on both of them as a final warning. Both lowered their heads and continued to eat, as soundlessly as the meal would allow.

Noe shifted uncomfortably in her seat after observing the interaction between Kyler and his two flunkies. Cheeks and Spazer, despite their rough exterior, endeared her, especially after the way they had looked after her during the battle. Kyler had done the same, but she could not shake the general unease she felt around him. She had heard rumors of his questionable deeds over the years as one of Cereus' primary lap dogs, from her mother. Anytime his alias "The Terminator" was used, things just seemed to appear or disappear. As far as she knew, her mother had never questioned his methods or moral leanings. He was a top-notch soldier and commander, but he was also a specter, who only appeared before or after a catastrophe. This duality caused her confusion, and she feared his darker side, especially the way he could mask it behind military decorum. Although he had occasionally looked her way as he lapped up his soup, she had no desire to speak with him outside of a combat situation.

On the other side of her, Jinhua leaned forward at a hard angle toward her father. Her lips moved rapidly and she looked as if she had eaten something very spicy, red-faced and on the verge of tears. Li sat in a slumped position, eyes exhausted, with a neutral expression on his face. A twitch in his eyebrow, signaled to Noe that he was fighting a primal urge to get angry and was losing the battle. She knew that struggle well. Between the arguing father-daughter duo, the dodgy Kyler, and warm soup in her belly, she found herself feeling suddenly exhausted, looking for any reason to excuse herself from the meal.

All of a sudden, Jinhua pushed her chair back with a quick motion, stood, then stormed out of the room. The lively atmosphere of the dinner was suddenly replaced by dead noise as all eyes turned to Li, waiting for a response. The only sound in the room was the bubbling of leftover soup in the pots.

"Please continue to eat," Li said with an old voice. With sluggish movement, he stood from the chair and exited the dining room, in the same direction of his daughter.

A beat of awkwardness engulfed the occupants of the table. Without their host, they felt like a ship adrift, without a captain. One by one, they exchanged confused glances, each deciding what they should do next. Kyler was the first to break the silence and stand up.

"We'll be leaving now," he said. "Tomorrow, we'll return for the meeting. See you then." He took one last glance toward the seat at the head of the table that Li had occupied, shook his head, then motioned his two men to follow. Spazer dabbed his lips with a napkin then stood. Cheeks' stomach scraped against the table as he raised himself up from his chair. The contact caused a full glass of wine to slosh, spilling a small amount on the decorative red table cloth. He played it off as if some unknown force had caused the wine to spill, gave Noe a quick parting hand signal, and squeezed himself out of the room. Spazer attempted to give a ceremonious bow before leaving, but Cheeks shoved him toward the entrance to the great room, muttering something about him being "uppity" under his breath.

Rodan and Noe surveyed the empty table. What had looked like an appetizing meal at a fancy Asian restaurant just an hour prior, now resembled an organic garbage heap. Stains from splashed soup surrounded by fallen ingredients—cooked and uncooked—sat next to cold spoons and dripping chopsticks. Vacant chairs formed odd angles between the massive table and walls, signaling the rapid breakup of the once festive mood.

Noe and Rodan were the last ones at the table. She studied his face. He looked even more drained than when they initially met outside of her apartment to deliver the news about her mother. *I probably look the same to him*, she thought grimly.

Across from her, Rodan's gaze locked on to hers. He wondered how she was faring with all of this. Out of her element, and still grieving the loss of her mother, he knew that she was doing her best to keep up with everything and adapt. Words that he should say to comfort her came to his mind, but his lips would not make them. He focused on action instead, wiping his lips with a napkin then standing to go.

"I'm…gonna go to bed…you should get some sleep too. Probably gonna be a long day tomorrow." He paused. *I wonder what she's thinking?*

She nodded, pushing her own chair back to stand. "Good call." She began to feel a small panic from the lack of words and motion between them. *Why won't he say anything?* The moment seemed to drag on and on. "Guess I'll…see you in the morning then." She turned to go to her assigned guest room and retire, but lingered a while before walking away.

"Noe, wait…" Rodan took a step forward, as if beginning to go around the table to meet her, then stopped.

"Yeah?" She turned to face him, an expectant look on her face. "What is it?"

"Uh nevermind. Sleep well. I'll see you in the morning." With that he exited the room without looking back.

*　　　　*　　　　*

Rodan sat on the edge of his bed. He could tell that the mattress had been purchased to accommodate someone half his size from the amount of deflection and the creaking sounds he heard as he gingerly lowered his gigantic frame on top of it.

He knew he needed to sleep, but the momentary respite from his device that the dinner had provided was now over, and he was once again staring into the digital void responding to countless messages and queries about Cereus and everything else he was responsible for. *Barto's coming tomorrow.* He had just received a message from his predecessor a few minutes prior. He had too many questions he wanted and needed answers to. *Where the fuck have you been? Why did you give the order? Why did you choose me?* These questions and more he dictated to his device to prepare for the morning. As he worked, his eyelids grew heavy as the wine and soup worked their way through him. He rubbed them to keep himself awake.

A soft knock sounded at the door. *It's probably Li wanting to apologize for what happened earlier even though there's no need. She's still a kid after all.*

He answered the door and saw Noe standing before him. Hair still slightly damp and hanging at her shoulders, the aroma of flowery body soap filled his nostrils. She wore one of the field shirts that he had given her on the eve of the North Bloomfield battle, and black running shorts with slits in them. A recently applied layer of lotion gave her legs a glowing sheen under the low light of the room.

"Noe...I...uh thought you were Li."

"No, it's just me...can I...come in?"

"Yeah, yeah come on in." He waved his hand for her to enter.

Though the guest room was a decent size, the only places to sit were the bed and a single chair at a small computer desk. Rodan sat on the bed, while Noe remained standing, arms folded across her chest.

"Look Rodan, I just wanted to thank you for being so good to me these past few weeks. I know you've gone out of your way to look out for me during the battle and by giving me all that work to keep me busy. It really did help me get my head right." Noe averted her eyes to the carpet around her bare feet. "…You really saved my life that day…"

Rodan's face remained calm and attentive, but internally he was overcome by emotion. If he were less physically spent, he might have cried openly. He had had no idea his random message that Saturday afternoon would have such a profound impact on her life; that it was the difference between her standing before him right now or not at all. His mind could not process or name the sentiment he was feeling at that moment. It was something like an amalgamation of joy, gratitude, and relief. A feeling so deep and rich it touched his heart, Noe's, and every other sleeping soul in the large house. No words, facial expressions, or actions could represent it with proper accuracy. All he could do was blink in response.

Then Noe moved closer to him. At eye level while she stood and he sat on the bed before her. "Truth is, this whole thing scares the shit out of me. Janus, Cereus, Limnic, the whole upheaval of society, it's always fucked with me since I was a little girl. I really did try and understand my mother all those years ago, but…but, she couldn't see anything else but that monster Janus and his new world order. And now she's fuckin' dead. Killed by his own hands. It's so…fucked up." The tears fell freely as she struggled to maintain her composure.

Rodan stood to embrace her, letting the messages, Cereus, and its enemies fall away to make space for her. His body tensed with fear for both of their well-being at the uncertain future before them, and the longing for understanding that he sorely lacked.

Noe whispered breathlessly, "Thank you…thank you." They separated, leaving only a sliver of space between them. Noe tilted her head upward, lips wet with anticipation. "You helped me so much…" Upon contact, her lips were met with rivaled passion and boyish trepidation, causing a surge of heat to erupt at her core.

They removed each other's clothing with controlled passion, as they moved onto the bed. Naked and somewhat afraid, primordial instincts moved their bodies with complementary action while each searched the other, looking for what they lacked. Giving, taking; pleasuring, and being pleasured; both released sounds of ecstasy upon contact from the other.

Hands squeezing, caressing, feeling; the intensity of their pleasure seeking action rose with every passing moment to rival intertwined sentiments of guilt, shame, and fear that held them both as prisoners in the deepest chambers of their hearts. Rodan and Noe felt their bodies accelerate toward the inevitable release of tension in their own time. First she, then he, felt the full force of the out-of-time and soul stirring experience that comes at the end. Chests heaving, coated in glossy sweat, they clung onto each other. Both reveled in the afterglow of the temporary comfort and safety that provided a necessary liberation from the threats and naggings—internal and external—that consumed their weary psyches. Together in their shared sanctuary, they found enchanted slumber and contentment, that neither had known for a very long time.

CHAPTER 46:
ANGST

Jinhua awoke in a restful state of bliss. Sitting up on her arms in bed, she took a moment to allow thoughts to return to her waking brain and order themselves into some coherent sequence. For the past several weeks, off and on, she had a similar recurring dream. At first, the dream revealed itself in disparate pieces, unordered and messy. She had no clue how to make sense of it, even less what the dream meant. Over time, she had put some of the pieces together, to create a complete image of the constructed world. After she did, she realized the destination was no place that she had seen before (at least that she could remember). It was somewhere completely alien to her, with characteristics that defied the natural laws of the world she knew.

She appeared standing by a bucolic riverbank, inhaling crisp, clean air. When she looked up to examine the sky, she noticed it was white, blank, like a fresh sheet of paper. In the emptiness of the sky there was no sun, but Jinhua could see as if it were daytime. Where there should have been a sun, there were only puffy sky blue clouds drifting lazily along. *What a strange place*, she thought.

Jinhua began to walk beside the river. Before long, she encountered a tiny house with a smiling old man sitting on the stairs of an outside patio. He was dressed like a classic fisherman; wide-brimmed straw hat, simple clothes, no shoes. The weather-beaten skin of his face had craggy texture, as if he had spent his entire life in the sun. The man, fishing rod by his side, waved at her unpretentiously as she passed by. Jinhua returned the wave and continued walking.

She found a thin dirt trail that snaked its way through tall grass, leading her away from the river. *I wonder where this goes?* She took it, and after a short walk, she found herself staring at a collection of small 3D printed homes arranged neatly in a rough semi-circular formation. All of the homes were different colors, and together, formed a small village. Beyond the semi-circle of houses, there was a large manicured field of grass at the end where no building existed. It reminded her of a large soccer field without the goals on the far ends.

As Jinhua began to move through the village with slow, questioning steps; she felt eyes following her. She saw no people outside or through the windows of the homes, but could sense the creeping glare of dozens of pairs of eyes on her skin. Were they just curious about the girl who wandered in? Or did they have some other nefarious design? Jinhua didn't know, but the stares from the buildings seemed to track her every step.

At the edge of the village, just as she was about to step onto the green turf of the soccer field, she felt herself being whisked away from the ground. At that moment, she couldn't be sure if she was ascending or if the ground was descending, but there was a sudden separation. Despite the surprise of the movement, Jinhua remained calm. She ascended above the semicircle of buildings, saw the smiling elderly man's cabin beside the river, and the extensive soccer field from a bird's eye view. The scene appeared as a single island floating in white space, with an endless fog surrounding its boundaries. When she was above it all, she felt a powerful urge to reach forward, to get back down. *There is something important there. Something that I need.* Leaning forward, she attempted to reach toward the disappearing surface, but found the upward force too difficult to resist. Within the blink of an eye, she returned to her corporal reality with vivid memories of her trip.

Back in her warm bed, she considered all of the elements of the dream. The paper white sky, the old fisherman, the village, the eyes: what had it all meant? The usual logical process she employed to make sense of the world failed her, leaving her face scrunched with puzzlement. An expression she was not accustomed to wearing for long periods of time. *Maybe next time, I'll learn more.*

A chime from her device brought her completely back to reality, clearing away the haze of the dream. Back in the physical world, even her light sleeping clothes, a simple green t-shirt and white underwear, felt heavy on her body. *Oh shit.* The events of the night before came back into her mind's eye. The dinner. The argument with her father in front of his guests. Jinhua covered her face with her hands and groaned with frustration laced with guilt. "Damn." She then threw back her sheets, and forced herself to begin to get ready.

Although she knew her father had done everything in his power to make her feel comfortable with the research process, she could no longer allow her body to be subjected to the poking and prodding of strange individuals. So she told him she wanted out of their deal, right there and then at the dinner table. Her father was stunned by her sudden reversal of sentiment, hiding his shock well behind a mask of fatigue and scientific language. Jinhua felt patronized by what she called his 'logic shield' and exploded at him, accusing him of only caring about the research and not about her. He had taken a split second too long to assuage her hurt feelings, so she abandoned the room in dramatic fashion. In her room, door shut and locked, she paced back and forth like a wild animal, with no outlet for her excess emotional energy. After ten minutes on her feet, the category five hurricane of anger downgraded itself, and she was wiped out. Sitting on the bed, still trapped in a thunderstorm, Jinhua sobbed.

She felt terribly guilty for how she had spoken to her father, and had known that none of what she said was true, but the urge to lash out was strong thanks to a confluence of factors. Arylide yellow-hued "wave" energy had been passing through her regularly all day, she was frustrated that neither he, Harpreet, nor anybody else could truly understand what she was going through, and she was on her period. It felt like a storm within a storm. The part of her brain that usually controlled her normally measured and reserved demeanor had sheltered in place to ride 'the big one' out, leaving no one to man the observation station. *What is happening to me? Am I losing it?*

Even though the scientists told her they found nothing remarkable from all of their tests, procedures, and scans, Jinhua knew that she was far from alright. Sharp shooting pain, originating from her head, fired signals to various destinations in her body, at random times. During these discharges, she felt like a live wire, ready to throw hot sparks at any person who dared approach her. On other occasions, her brain fired blasts of warmth that made her feel calm and at peace. The sensations toyed with her delicate teenage emotional state, and she at times found herself feeling sick from the push and pull of it all.

In the midst of the storm, floating helplessly like a survivor of a shipwreck on a plank in the middle of the icy Atlantic, she noticed a faint light on the horizon. A small rescue vessel approached. Its watchful searchlights trained on her, it moved slowly as if assessing if she were friend or foe. But when it finally did recover her shivering frame from the black sea, part of her knew she would always be able to count on it to save her, even in the worst conditions.

Only an hour after the dinner, she let her father into the room. The conversation was brief. She apologized for losing it. He apologized for pressuring her. They embraced tightly, and Jinhua, for a fleeting instant, was reminded he would always be there for her.

But that was last night. On this particular morning, Jinhua felt more energized than usual. *Maybe it was something in that little village*, she thought, gazing at her reflection in the mirror after dressing herself. She had put on a new-ish teal t-shirt with a red rocket on the front, and her favorite pair of distressed blue jean shorts. Sunny yellow flip flops adorned with pink flowers completed the look. *Comfortable and functional.*

She smiled bright at her reflection, as a wave of excitement rushed through her. Today was the big meeting with Cereus' elite members. Initially, her father had been against allowing her to attend. However, after she reminded him how much he had taught her about the organization in the previous month, and probably as a form of consolation after last night's dinner, he reluctantly agreed to let her sit in on the meeting.

While she brushed her hair in the mirror, a question popped into her head: *Why am I so excited for this meeting?*

Her head tilted sideways, while she considered a response. *Maybe I just want to see how it all works. Maybe I just want to see Dad do his thing. Maybe…maybe I want to know how Cereus and Limnic might affect me in the long run. Or maybe it's something else I'm not seeing…*The dream of the tiny village with leather-faced fisherman flashed in her mind. But she couldn't connect any of the elements in it to her current reality.

But something inside her knew that today, for some reason, would be a *very* important day for her. That after today, in some way, she would never be the same person again.

CHAPTER 47:
DISCLOSURE

By the time Jinhua made her way down the hall to the oak carved door with the Cereus logo etched in the center, she could already hear the faint murmur of muffled conversations on the opposite side. She pushed the door open and the sight of a nearly full room caused a wave of nervousness to grip her. The eyes of at least two dozen scientists and officials, seemed to all be locked on her, scrutinizing her every move.

"Uh, good morning," she said, her small voice echoed around the room.

Her father stood behind his desk with a supportive smile on his face. It looked as if he had not slept at all the night before. He made a hand motion that beckoned her to join him.

The hushed conversations resumed as she proceeded toward the desk. Along the way, some of the scientists greeted her. Dr. Pink Clipboard, the physician; Dr. Big Nose, the geneticist, both gave her brief salutations. She blushed when the digigenomic scientist, Dr. Handsome-Handshake, winked at her. Besides the three researchers, none of the others in the white coats were familiar to her. Jinhua made no effort to try and learn their names.

Standing behind the desk, her father by her side, she did pick out the guests from last night's dinner. Noe and her dad's longtime friend Rodan stood near each other, yet were engaged in separate conversations with scientist looking types. Noe, in her dark green shirt and black work pants, looked slightly uncomfortable speaking with a heavy set woman with greying hair and bold eyes. Rodan, in his black business suit, made small talk, with a tall man wearing glasses and a plaid buttoned shirt. She noticed them throw conspiratorial glances at one another at sporadic moments in time, their conversation partners aloof to their distracted audiences of one. Noe and Rodan seemed to want to communicate something to each other, but the distance and conference atmosphere of the room interfered, prohibiting effective communication between them.

Across the room, entering through the door, she saw the old man with the square jaw and buzzcut from the dinner march in. His posture was perfect even though he was old, *really* old. The two Black guys from last night followed behind him. One was fat and loud; the other, skinny, reserved, and walking with a limp. They reminded her of the Super Mario Brothers, without the red and green costumes. Jinhua giggled to herself at the observation. By the time her attention shifted back to the desk where she stood, their leader, the old man, was standing next to her father.

"Kyler, I don't believe you met my daughter, Jinhua," her father said.

The man with the buzzcut extended a calloused hand. Jinhua shook it. "It's nice to meet you young lady." The voice sounded official and cordial. Immediately, his eyes returned to Li, "When will we get started?" He asked.

"In a moment. We're still waiting on Barto."

"Oh yeah, the fabled economist responsible for designing the Cereus model."

"Yes." Li consulted his watch. "It's about 10:30 now, so he should have gotten here about half an hour ago."

"Wouldn't worry about it," Kyler said. "You know how these egg-headed academic types can be. Not the most punctual bunch."

Li frowned and hoped nothing had happened to him on his way over from Lake Tahoe. He swept his eyes across the room. Scientists, researchers, and a few select comvil leaders had come from all around California to attend the meeting. He could feel the charge of anxiety running throughout the room, contributing to a much more tense atmosphere than he had anticipated. It was rare to have this kind of meeting, and most knew something big was going to happen. Even Li was anxious to begin. *I know I should wait, but we need to get this meeting started. All of us being here at the same time is too big of a target opportunity for*

Limnic. Li cleared his throat and adjusted a wireless microphone attached to his dress shirt. He raised a hand to call for silence in the room before he began to speak. His words came out with authority and a slightly commanding tone that surprised many people who were only aware of his mild-mannered and soft spoken personality.

"First of all I want to thank you all for taking the time to be here this morning. I know all of us are quite busy with everything that is going on and it's hard to make time for things like this." Li began to move from behind his desk. "I'll get to the point. My sources have provided me with intelligence about Janus' strategy. And this is why I've gathered all of you here today. To give you a more detailed briefing about the true nature of the threat to not just Cereus or our comvils, but to every human being on the planet right now."

Whispers and murmurs rippled through the room in reaction to his words. Li seemed to be unaware of the theatrical nature of the moment and continued to talk.

"From analysis and autopsies of the deceased human Limnic fighters from North Bloomfield, interviews with personnel from Kyler's unit, and standard network monitoring, we have learned the truth about Janus' strategy and the terrible power that he possesses. By pulling the chips from the brains of the deceased, our researchers and analysts concluded that somehow Janus has found a way to hack the chips that have been placed in our minds and control the host's thoughts and actions."

Gasps and reactions of alarm came from the group of Cereus elites in the room. "No way." "What the hell!?" "That's impossible!" "How terrifying!" "How can he be stopped?"

Li raised his arms for calm. When their reactions ceased and all was quiet he commanded, "Display file 3529." The large monitors on the wall with various camera feeds suddenly switched from displaying random images of unknown locations, to the faces of regular individuals. The faces were representative of the United States population, depicting people across the colorful spectrum of the nation's diverse citizenry. Young, old, White, Black, Asian, Hispanic, male, female, transgender, any possible demographic slice was represented. Kyler's muscles tensed. *His* face could have easily been among the collection of photographs.

"These are the faces of people that Janus has experimented on. At least the ones that we are aware of right now." Li swallowed hard. Muffled and incoherent comments arose from the crowd, while he continued to speak. "Some have recounted their experiences on the social media message board *Spectacle*. That is where we have mined the majority of our knowledge about how it works. Most users describe a similar chain of events: the computer or device display screen begins flashing, which the unknowing victim mistakes for some type of malfunction, then they awake in a circular room with memories floating on pedestals situated around them. Out of curiosity, or just wanting to return to wherever it was that they were taken away from, they eventually make contact with one of the memories. When they do, their body recalls the physical and emotional sensations that they experienced during that particular memory. After the ordeal ends, the person usually wakes up in front of the device in a state of confusion by what just happened to them."

Among the elite professionals, an air of panic began to filter through the room, threatening to choke them all. Noe stood in wide-eyed disbelief, taking great effort to maintain her bearing and prevent the terror that she felt from shaking her to the smooth floor beneath her. *So that's what happened…why all those people were running around in the street yesterday. Some of them must have been Janus' lab rats.* Suddenly, the memory of North Bloomfield rushed back into her mind's eye. She remembered the pleasant warm sensation wrapped in absolute terror, caused by the lack of control that she had over her own body and thoughts. Powerless to escape the hold, she wondered if Janus could have stopped her heart or done any manner of vile action to her person while she was in that state. All she would have been able to do was watch herself die while being a prisoner of her own mind.

She flashed a look at Rodan for reassurance. After last night, they had communicated little verbally. Rodan had to prepare for the meeting early, and she tried her best to sleep, despite feeling nervous about *this* meeting. *Turns out I was right to be a basket case. Janus can hack our minds and literally destroy us from the inside out.*

Throughout the morning, she could feel him casting furtive glances in her direction. Whenever their eyes met, she felt sudden accelerations of her pulse from the memory of the sex. But she was never able to lock eyes with him for longer than a second before he or she was swept up in another official conversation. This disappointed her, but she knew he was just doing his job as executive director. *I wonder how he feels about all this?* She thought, while casting another look his way.

Mind control, Rodan thought. So this was the technology that Janus spoke of that night. This was his power. *I'm the executive director of Cereus. I can do something about this. I have to do something. But will it be enough for Cereus…enough for humanity? Can Janus' tech really help us evolve?*

Rodan stood with his arms dangling at his side. He was happy to be wearing a suit jacket, so no one could see the pools of sweat expanding under his armpits. Noe's eyes found his. He returned a slight smile. She had been a bright spot in the dark night that was his life. For that he would be forever grateful. Just as she had thanked him last night, that morning when they awoke in their shared nakedness, he thanked her. He thanked her for giving him the conviction to make his next move for Cereus and humanity. "Thank you for being so human with me," he said to her. Hair falling over her face, her smile beamed at him, and she kissed him deeply, with all of her being. After that, Rodan was ready to do what he had to do, and once he made his move, he knew there was no going back.

*   *   *

Li again waited for quiet in the room. Once it came, he continued his briefing. From the diverse faces on the screens, he pulled one from the group, and made the others disappear. It was an image of a middle aged looking Black male. All in the room stood in shaking anticipation of Li's explanation for singling out this man. He continued to speak in a steady tone.

"This man, Kayne Eastmont, age forty-seven, a software engineer from Colorado Springs, just arrived at the comvil in Pueblo, Colorado a few nights ago. While going through intake at one of our community homes, he was overheard talking about why he had come to the city, leaving his previous life behind. He mentioned to one of our undercover agents that after a week of reliving key moments from his past in vivid detail, on the seventh day, he was shown a vision of his future. It was a future with a woman he had dated in the past where he was living out his dream life. With that possibility firmly planted in his brain, he was prompted to seek out the nearest comvil in order to have access to more visions of the future, as well as to his complete personal history, which he could choose to relive again and again, should he so desire."

Li's audience ignited again. Waves of coughs, expletives, and cries of dissent resounded from all of them. A young scientist with pale skin and a receding hairline raised his voice. "So what's the point of all this? What do you think Janus' endgame is?"

An anxious calm settled over the room. Everyone strained their ears and craned their necks to get a better view of a short Asian man as he sighed then continued to speak once again.

"We believe that his goal is nothing less than the enslavement of the minds of millions, perhaps billions of people around the world through the use of this technology. It appears that by allowing people to perpetually experience their pasts in stunning sensory detail, and/or allowing them to live in a future that they long for, he intends to remove human will, ambition, and desire from the board, making way for him to remold global society as he believes it should be. Limnic will act as his enforcement arm to purge or phase out those in global society who still cling to old world thinking. While Cereus, as it exists now, will provide the infrastructure for his future plans. Both serve Janus' ultimate goal, which is the evolution of humankind and global society."

"Unbelievable!" "Can he really do that!?" "Oh my God!" "It's finally happening.." The utterances and outbursts of incredulousness and denial flew from the audience, as each person let unfiltered biases and fears, long deep rooted, spill out of their mouths. Li let out a heavy sigh, allowing them to vent the visceral reaction that his words had prompted. *After all*, he thought, *just days ago I reacted in the same way*. His eyes floated to Jinhua beside him, who appeared to be in deep thought about something. If she was afraid, he could not tell. Ever since he had revealed her true nature to her over a month ago, he had lost the ability to read and truly understand his daughter in more ways than one.

From the crowd, Cheeks took a heavy step forward. "How can we beat 'em!? I mean shit, there's gotta be a way! Everybody's got a weakness somewhere!" Spazer gave a firm nod, agreeing. Other members in the audience echoed the optimistic thought.

Li waved his hands for quiet. The audience found a reluctant silence once again. With a lowered head he replied, "As of right now, our scientists are still gathering data and researching, to discover just how Janus is able to do what he does. It's a complicated process and one that cannot easily be protected against. Most of the global population has already been chipped, and the few people who do not have chips implanted are extremely elderly and would probably not be able to help us defeat him. As for the rest of us…" His pause originated from uncertainty for himself, the occupants of the room, and every breathing person on the planet. "Any one of us could be easily affected by Janus' form of manipulation."

As if all of the air had been sucked out of the room, an eerie hush fell over everyone, suffocating any movement or speech. As each person scrolled through their personal histories, they wondered how one man could infiltrate the supposed privacy and control that they had over rich inner worlds, private aspirations, and secret thoughts, to manipulate them from within, transforming them all into slaves of their desires and past glories. It was a fear so difficult to understand, yet so horrific, that none could express it in words.

The sound of a ringing telephone pulled them from their thoughts of despair. Li, initially surprised by the timing of the strange noise, looked to the corner of the room and realized it was his emergency phone. With curiosity and stab of trepidation, Li took long strides toward the corner, where the obsolete recliner and landline telephone sat under the soft light from an old standing lamp. As he stepped through the palpable aura of muffled panic that loomed like an inky shadow over the room, all were still on edge after the disturbing revelations he had discussed. Their thin veneer of professionalism and poise was eclipsed by human survival instinct.

The ring continued to echo as Li passed through the throng. *Who could it be?* He paused for a moment to gather what little reserves of courage and resolve that remained with him, took a deep breath, then picked up the receiver.

"Hello?"

A metallic grainy voice spoke to him. "We enjoyed your briefing Mr. Ma. It was very…enlightening." The voice crackled through the speakers with low fidelity. It was definitely being filtered through some modification device. It hacked and coughed violently on the other end of the line. Although he could not discern who was talking, Li could hear the loose phlegm gurgling in his mouth before the speaker was forced to spit it out. "Now you will witness the true capability of our power…"

Li opened his mouth to speak, but the voice on the other end disconnected the call. Setting the receiver slowly back on the base of the old telephone, he turned to his colleagues, friends, and family, scanning the confused and fear-ridden faces. They waited for him to say something while holding their breath. He took a step forward, looking for the right words of reassurance to find him. Nothing came, and his face reflected the look of fatigued despair, as an inconvenient truth dawned on him. *We've been compromised.*

The sound of a distant explosion shattered the stillness of the room. It began as one, then several more boomed outside, not far from the house.

Li knew they were under attack, and if the threat from the mysterious voice was credible, the leadership team of Cereus was in greater danger than he ever anticipated.

CHAPTER 48:
COMPROMISED

How had they known about the meeting? Who tipped Limnic off? What do they want? The questions tumbled in Li's mind as he hurried over to his desk at the center of the room. He wanted to get a visual of what was happening outside in order to have a better gauge of what or who was attacking them. What little professional resolve remaining among the Cereus leadership had melted away, leaving only ashen and frightened faces swapping confused glances at each other, while each person contemplated their survival plan. *It won't be long before a full-blown panic breaks out*, Li thought.

With a series of brief voice commands, he switched the multiple monitors on the back wall to surveillance mode, and once again, he could see footage from cameras in various locations in town and around his house. What he saw in one of the monitors near the center of the wall made his jaw clench with worry. The decorative black gate that had protected his mansion was destroyed. Its remnants sat twisted and mangled in a smoking mass of broken iron only ten or fifteen feet from the mansion. Beside the wrecked gate, nine figures stood in a letter "v" formation. From what Li could tell, four were human, and the other four were humanoid mechs of the black market variety. He had never seen them in person, but had done enough research to know that they were robotic soldiers programmed to mimic humans in every way. Infused with illegal artificial intelligence, they represented humankind's darkest potential. Human intellect without empathy or compassion, they could be programmed to serve any purpose that suited their creator. Judging by the high-powered portable lasers and conventional weaponry they carried, he could easily discern what these models had been programmed for.

Li did not recognize any of the humans, with the exception of the ninth person in the point position of the "v". It was an old man, frail-looking, wearing overalls and a straw hat. He wore field boots and stared directly at Li and everyone else in the room with a fury in his eyes, and a cruel smile plastered on his wrinkly lips. The man spoke with his wheezy rasp echoing around the room: "We have this mansion surrounded. If anyone attempts to flee, we will demolish this entire building with everyone inside. So I suggest you cooperate with our demands."

Li recognized the man as none other than Silas James, one of the Founders of Cereus. They had met briefly some fifteen years prior at a strategy meeting during the height of the organization's struggle for cultural dominance and survival. After the conference, Silas disappeared, and few knew his whereabouts. The rumor was, he had become disillusioned by the promises of utopia that were left unfulfilled by the other Founders, and that he had started some sort of video game retirement and winemaking business. But Li never bothered to follow up on these accounts. Now here he was again, working for Limnic, no doubt in direct service of his old collaborator Janus.

Li could feel dozens of terrified eyes locked on him, observing his every move. Jinhua, eyes wide with worry, shook her head. It was a signal for her father to not back down from the challenge. Swallowing hard, he activated the external communicator he had installed decades ago, thankful that a younger version of himself had such foresight to install such a bizarre feature in the house.

"We understand. What are your demands?" He managed to keep the shaking out of his voice.

"Surrender any and all data related to your daughter Jinhua, and hand her over to us. This is the only way Janus will be satisfied," Silas said.

Li exchanged glances with his daughter. Despite her womanly appearance, he couldn't help but see her as the young woman he had single-handedly raised on his own. His baby girl. His miracle of science and technology. To his surprise, her face did not display consternation or hint at fearfulness. Instead, she looked determined, gazing at the screen with laser focus at the old face that had called her by name. Her resolve imbued him with greater courage, and buffed his confidence. *No.*

"I'm afraid that won't be possible."

With a sudden movement, Li cut the audio feed to the outside and began to shout orders to the confused crowd before him. "We have an emergency shelter in the basement! Please, follow Rodan, he knows the way!"

Rodan appeared to be slightly flustered at the mention of his name, but he responded with an affirmative thumbs up, then gestured for the noncombatants to follow him. "C'mon! This way!" he bellowed. The scientists, administrative officials, and other observers obeyed without protest, filing out of the room in clustered chaos and confusion.

"Noelani Acosta" Li said, raising his voice over the hysterical crowd. Upon hearing her name, she stepped to the side of the mass of people bottle necked at the room's single exit. She unapologetically pushed others out of way, to clear a small path and get away from the door. "Please stay! I could use your help to possibly disable the mechs!" Li called.

Amid the pandemonium, Noe's mind was a flurry of unresolved emotions and thoughts, the collection of which had only become more entangled within the previous hour. She decided to put the jumble aside for later, to do something that would help take her mind off of it, and possibly help save their lives. Blinking rapidly to refocus, a fire ignited in her eyes, "Where's the terminal?"

Li pointed to a dusty old laptop with a hardcase sitting in a forgotten corner of the room. Noe again elbowed and pushed her way through the throng of people moving against the flow of bodies. "Move! Get out of the way!" In her haste, someone stepped on her toes, but she didn't feel a thing. *Glad I wore my field gear today. Thank god for steel-toed boots.*

She reached the corner of the room and found the old remote security terminal. She then blew a perfect sheet of dust off of the cover, and flipped the laptop open. Upon initial inspection, the computer looked functional, but it was old tech, at least fifteen to twenty years old. It was a training laptop, like what her unit used during her early Space Force days. She knew how to work with it, but it had been a while since she used one. *Great, I get to try and work with this fucking dinosaur.* Noe exhaled a large breath and got to work.

Meanwhile, Li wrestled with what to do with Jinhua. She had not uttered a word since the attack began, and he was in no mood to put up with her mercurial teenage angst. However, his instinct told him she would be safer by his side, than if he sent her to join the panicking mob of escaping officials. Jinhua wasn't the only thing on his mind. Always in intelligence analyst mode, he wondered: *Who tipped them off? How did they know about the meeting? What do they want with Jinhua? There's something not right about the timing of all this.* Li checked the monitors. Silas and his team were on the front lawn, destroying anything and everything in their sight. They were destroying security cameras and shooting out the windows in the front of the house. He could hear Silas' asthmatic laugh over the speakers as the enemy soldiers terrorized his home. It was an act of intimidation, meant to incite fear. A power play, to show his adversary that he was not afraid, and could enter and take what he wanted anytime he pleased. Li knew the tactic well, and it had the effect Silas desired.

An unknown number of minutes passed. During that period of time, Li had been so distracted by the carnage unfolding outside he hadn't realized that the noise from the disarray at the door was quieting down. Everyone was almost out. Eyes still fixed on the screen, he lamented the damage, but considered tactical options for how to defeat Silas and his Limnic hit squad. So consumed by potential battle maneuvers, courses of action for what to do if (and when) Silas decided to enter the house, and the destruction of his home, Li had forgotten about his daughter. *Jinhua.*

"Jinhua, you should—"

A loud explosion blasted through the speakers, followed by a blinding light. The main video feed had been disabled by a Limnic laser. Li quickly switched to another, a hidden camera situated in the brick wall right beside the driveway. The angle wasn't as good, but the picture was clear, and he could see directly toward his front door. What he saw, made him hopeful for their survival.

Kyler and his men had rushed onto the field and began to engage the enemy troops. Li's body tensed as he watched the action unfold. He saw the two from dinner the previous night, Cheeks and Spazer.

There was a third man he hadn't seen in years, but upon seeing his size and the scars on his face, he immediately remembered his name. *Francisco Murakami. A.K.A 'Bear'.* They met during one of Li's source meets with Kyler years back. The man never spoke much, but his combat record was extensive (Li had been curious and looked it up one time). He wasn't sure where Bear had come from, but was happy to have another hardened soldier on their side.

Rodan must have shown Kyler and his crew to Li's private weapon stash in the basement, because he could see Cheeks handling a long silver portable laser cannon in his arms. Li knew all of his weapons by serial number. The laser cannon, XD-837321, had been one of his first acquisitions a decade prior, when he first began buying weapons for his collection. It was another one of his hidden personal hobbies.

From his office, Li watched the battle taking place on his front lawn. *Four against nine.* Li didn't like their odds, but knew they were their only hope for survival. One mech assumed a fighting stance before being blown to bits by a laser blast from Cheeks. "I love this fuckin' thing!" He yelled, before continuing his advance down the field, to engage another human Limnic fighter. Spazer, still wounded from his last firefight, deployed an expandable metal shield and fired explosive shells from an old M32A1 grenade launcher over it toward a group of fighters, from a crudely improvised defensive fighting position he had dug with a portable impact device. His grenade found its mark, leaving a blood-stained crater where two human combatants once stood.

Bear moved with surprising speed toward one of the mech fighters. Just six feet from the robot, he drew a large knife. The robot dropped its laser and assumed a kung fu fighting stance, swishing its aluminum alloy legs in an intimidating motion of readiness. Man versus machine. Bear, lunged, keeping his knife at a tactical angle. The mech began to strike with competent movement and speed unmatched by his human adversary. Bear slipped and dodged a flurry of jabs aimed at his face, but a direct punch to the chest landed on his massive chest, bringing his charge to a halt and knocking him in the dirt. On the ground, Bear coughed up blood. The mech maintained its stance as it moved in for a strike that would surely shatter even Bear's skull if it found its mark. It punched with hydraulic force. Bear anticipated the blow, and with a quick roll, to the side, narrowly avoided the crushing blow, then scrambled to his feet. The robot's jab had been so definitive that it lodged its fist in the soft dirt of the earth. As it struggled to remove it, Bear took advantage of the precious few moments to activate his knife, via voice command. "Knife on!" He yelled. The blade of the knife began to glow with a blue-white flame that spiraled from the hilt of the weapon. With one precise slash, he severed the mechanoid's arm at the elbow, then without delay, hacked a second time to remove the head from its body. The corpse of the decapitated mech fell flat before him, shaking the ground beneath his feet.

From the Cereus control room, Li breathed a heavy sigh of relief upon seeing the robot fighter fall. There were still three more. The humanoid mechs were difficult to kill, and one could easily destroy Kyler's entire team. Li looked to Noe in the corner of the room. Just as he did, he heard the sound of hard objects falling on concrete through the speakers. Back outside, the remaining humanoid mechs had collapsed, face down, their network connections severed. From the corner, Noe gave Li a thumbs up. He returned a firm nod. *Well done.* Noe's lips arched into a satisfied smile.

Whew, I did it. Too close, she thought. Seeing the downed killer robots, made her happy to be human, but also reminded her of Janus' power. *Could he do something like that to us? Shut us down remotely without us even knowing it?* Her hand rose to the back of her neck. The soft skin there was a reminder of the tiny chip somewhere inside in her skull, and the frailty of her human form. Instantly, her good mood was gone. Then she looked up to the monitor and found a new reason to be afraid and confused. Her jaw dropped, and her breathing became constricted, as if someone had stomped on her chest.

Li saw the change in her face; saw her cheer melt away. When his vision returned to the monitor, he understood why. What he saw confirmed his suspicion and nearly caused his heart to stop. On the screen, among the carnage of the battle and standing before the front door of the house, stood Rodan, with a tight grip around his daughter's arm.

CHAPTER 49:
THE FISHERMAN'S GIFT

Standing next to her father's side, while he observed the brutal melee of man versus machine combat in front of their house, Jinhua's body trembled. As the deafening sound of explosions, laser blasts, and gunfire filled the speakers around her, the vibration from the combination of sounds mixed within her ears, causing her to shake with tension. *He called my name. Why?* She had no idea who the elderly man was, but she figured there could only be one reason why he was looking for her. *It's something about what's been happening with me. Something to do with the "wave".*

In the span of thirty minutes, she watched grown adults regress from cordial, professional behavior, to screaming and running; as if someone had yelled FIRE or GUN in an old world public school. They nearly trampled each other to reach the door, shoving, elbowing, and yelling as their heads whipped between the screens of the wall and the exit, unsure of which was more important for their immediate survival. Jinhua had a hard time processing the scene. It just didn't fit with her image of how civilized adults should act in a crisis.

Is there anything I can do!? Someway I can help? Her eyes darted around the room in erratic fashion. She spotted everyone else from the dinner the night before engaged in their own emergency roles. Her father was intently watching the screens, while simultaneously shouting for calm and order among his frightened officials. Noe was in the far corner of the room, firing up what looked like an obsolete computer. Eyes narrowed, brow furrowed, it appeared as if she might be dismantling a bomb or performing some other highly sensitive task. The old military man (she had forgotten his name), and the Super Mario Brothers were on the screen, doing battle with the killer robots outside. All were accounted for, working to counter the enemy, and perhaps save their lives except for one of them. *Where's Rodan?*

Just then, Jinhua began to feel dizzy. She felt her breath catch in her throat just as it had done in the bathroom of the community center days prior. She began to feel as if she might pass out. Suddenly, the panicked scene in the office faded, leaving an all-white paper background. After the scene was lost, then the sound gradually lowered, becoming fainter with each passing second, until it was replaced by the sound of stillness. The stampeding crowd, the combat on the screens, her father standing next to her; all disappeared from her field of vision and her auditory nerves. *What is going on!? What's happening to everyone!?* Jinhua felt her stomach doing flip flops, as her body attempted to compensate for the lack of spatial familiarity. The urge to vomit hit suddenly. In a reflexive reaction, she clamped her eyes shut to try and stave off the sense of vertigo that was consuming her senses. For ten deliberate seconds, she kept them closed, hoping to see the familiar setting of her father and his office when she opened them. She did this while systematically relaxing her muscles to counter the physical effects of another wave passing through her.

Four...three...two...one...

Upon opening her eyes, she was no longer standing in the study. She was alone, standing near the path that would take her to the idyllic semi-circular village with the soccer field at the end and its staring occupants that she could not see. *I'm...back...back in my dreamworld.*

Everything looked as it had this morning during her previous visit. Jinhua took some time to analyze the details of the world. She noted the smell of the grass, the feel of the wind on her cheek. Raising her hand to her head, she tugged at a strand of her hair lightly and plucked it out, then watched as it was lazily carried away by an invisible breeze. She peered at the river. The water was a brilliant blue, and appeared warm and inviting. It reminded her of the Yuba River, and made her think of home.

Home! The fight, the others. Dad! I have to get out of here! But she had no idea where to go or how to get back to the reality she knew. There were only two options. The path behind her snaked its way through tall grass, back to the semi-circular village. She had seen no people there, but somehow could feel their eyes, observing her every step. Perhaps, someone (or something) there could help her?

Her other choice was the wood cabin that was a short walk back down along the river. She had seen an old man there who *appeared* to be friendly. *Maybe he can help me get back?* Jinhua thought for a few seconds. The wrong choice could delay her return, or worse, leave her trapped in this strange world for a very long time. The thought caused anxiety-laden adrenaline to flow through her veins. She needed to make a decision, fast.

Lodged between two unknowns, with little factual information to inform her selection, she decided to trust her instinct and go for the cabin. *At least I know* someone *is there,* she reasoned. Aware that she most likely did not have much time to waste, she moved quickly back down the river toward the rustic-looking wood cabin. When she arrived at the front door, without second thought, she knocked with her knuckles.

"Come in." An old voice found its way to her ear through thin wood. Jinhua opened the door, then stepped inside the cabin. It was a small space that resembled college dorm rooms she had seen in popular media and online. From where she stood, she could see the colorful buildings of the semicircular village through a square window at the back of the room. To the right of the window, a single wood bed with a solid blue sheet draped over it sat in the far corner. Directly beneath the window, was a simple wood desk with a hand carved chair. The surface of the desk was clear, with the exception of a small collection of books in languages that Jinhua could not name. A humble fishing rod leaned next to the books, with a large straw hat sitting on the dusty floor next to it.

"You are in a hurry, are you not?" The elderly man's voice refocused her attention back onto him. He wore threadbare pants, and a simple cloth shirt. Without his large straw hat, she examined the rough skin of his face and head. He looked like a frog. And with his thinning white hair, and somewhat malnourished frame, he was the epitome of ugliness in her young eyes.

"…I am," she said, finding her voice for the first time since arriving in the strange world.

"I'm sure you have many questions. There will be time for them later, but for now you need to understand something." He spoke with his hands behind his back. The posture seemed slightly unnatural, like he was purposely hiding something there. Jinhua sensed it was something important.

"What do I need to understand?"

"That everything you have been feeling for the last several weeks are clear signs that you are no longer the person that you were before you knew the truth of your origins."

Jinhua stayed silent, waiting to hear the old man's point.

"How do you know about that?"

The old man's lips turned up into a smile. He responded by raising one of his hands from behind his back and pointing to his head. Jinhua looked at him with puzzlement, as he lowered his hand, then began to speak slowly, yet clearly, "A long time ago, like you, I used to be confused and afraid. I knew I was...*different.*"

Jinhua's eyes dropped to the cabin floor, where she noticed the slight deflection of the wood beneath her feet. She wondered how this fisherman, in this weird cabin, by a random river, in a dreamland, was so in tune with her personal experience. *Who is this guy?*

"Then one day, after I understood how it all worked, and who I was, I never turned back." His cloudy eyes studied her. Jinhua stared back, more questions mounting with every blink.

"Who are you?" Jinhua asked, with more force than she intended for someone older than her. Someone to whom she owed at least a modicum of politeness, even though they had just met.

Again the fisherman smiled, "I am the one who will help you understand how it all works. Then, like me, you will never be able to turn back."

Jinhua quickly responded, "Wait! But I don't know...!"

She stopped speaking when she saw the fisherman make a sudden movement. He had removed his hand from behind his back and held it out in front of her. At first, the palm of his hand was empty, then out of nowhere, a brilliant light began to swell in the air above his skin. Jinhua watched in amazement, while a pea-sized piece of luminosity ballooned to about the size of a tennis ball, giving off more radiance as it grew. Around the pocket sun, she could see dozens of miniscule lines of digital code circling. The lines moved in orbital paths, resembling tiny satellites leaving digital tracks around the glowing source of luminescence. The number of lines increased at a rapid pace, spinning faster and faster, until a blinding light flashed, illuminating the entire cabin, throwing their shadows against the walls of the room. Tears fell from Jinhua's eyes. Whether they were from the intensity of the flash or the beauty of the moment, she could not tell.

When the light finally died, the fisherman continued to hold out his palm, as if he had seen the previous spectacle countless times before. At some point during the light display, a small object had materialized. To Jinhua, it looked like an ordinary identification card, like the all-in-one card that housed her entire life within it. The only difference was that it was levitating in midair above the old man's hand with almost indistinguishable digital code racing in uniform orbits around it. Jinhua knew it was some computer language from a brief coding committee she had attended the year before, but she had no idea which one it was.

"What is it?" She asked, still dumbfounded by the miniature big bang she had just witnessed.

"It is a key."

"To what?"

"Your evolution. It will allow you to access the potential within you."

Jinhua's first instinct was to take the card. But, before the impulse to move followed its path from her brain to her hand, she stopped herself. The fisherman's words replayed in her mind, a reminder of the finality of the moment. *'Then, like me, you will never be able to turn back.'* This was the point of no return. This key was the important *something* that she needed, when she was pulled from the dreamspace that morning. And once she took it, she would be forever altered. *Into what, exactly?* She had no idea.

The fisherman continued to hold out his hand with the patience of a nonplayer character (NPC) in a video game. His expression remained enigmatic, while he waited for her to accept or reject his offer. To leave and find another way back or…to take her chances with the gift from the magical frog-faced fisherman, and see how deep the rabbit hole goes.

Jinhua, eyes wide, fingers trembling, reached for the floating key. Upon contact her senses became overwhelmed by the sheer quantity and detail of data that filled them. Flashes of human brilliance, cruelty, tragedy, and triumphs collided with each other so fast that she had no time to process related swells of emotion that each one stirred within her. The images streamed by in an infinite scrolling sequence, giving her the impression that it might not ever end. After what felt like at least a minute of constant information running through her, she began to feel exhausted, as if she had been sprinting an eight-hundred meter race, and her cardiovascular system was being taxed beyond its limited output. Panic ensued when the flood of information began to fill not only her mind, but her physical body, too. Her stomach clenched with tightness, her skin burned as the immeasurable amount of data infiltrated atomic space among the matter of her being. The pain was intense and unyielding. Her heart no longer pumped just blood. Information filtered through her bloodstream, filling every artery like a jam-packed highway. Finding nowhere else to go, it pierced the walls of her heart and invaded her lungs, expanding like a balloon in her tiny chest cavity. Jinhua fell to her hands and knees, gasping for air. She opened her mouth to scream, but the lack of air would not allow her vocal cords to vibrate, leaving her with a pained look of tortured anguish on her face. Then, amidst the painful torrent, she heard the fisherman's familiar voice. "Almost done…almost there…"

Her vision began to fail, and she felt herself losing consciousness. Her entire body was numb, and she felt her muscles grow weak. *Am I gonna die?* The thought floated vaguely into her mind. Then, just as suddenly as it had begun; the sensation came to an end. Drenched in sweat, heart thumping in a frantic rhythm, Jinhua stared at the floor of the cabin. She coughed violently, gasping for air, desperate to inflate her lungs once again. She could breathe, but her body was still in a state of shock from what she had just experienced. She wanted to stand, but had to be content with taking a knee.

Then the fisherman spoke, "You've done it my child. You have survived the process. It's over." He took two steps forward and helped her to stand. His smile was awkward, yet genuine.

Legs wobbly, head still foggy, Jinhua struggled to remain standing. "That was…insane…" she said, still struggling to catch her breath, "what…the hell was that?"

"You experienced the kiss of the material and digital universe all at once. All of humankind's information—physical and digital—are now available for you to command."

To command? "What…do you mean?"

The old man kept talking as if he did not hear her question; maybe he was an NPC after all. "Physical and digital reality both rely on codes of information to function and give movement to objects and beings. For the physical world, that code comes in the form of atoms, which makes up the DNA of all biological beings of our world. In the digital space, all software, artificial intelligence, and associated cyber machines are driven by codes as well. You, Jinhua, are special in that because your genetic makeup has already been assimilated with digital software, you are able to house both codes within you."

"Both codes…within me?"

"Yes." He paused, allowing the weight of his words to sink in. "Over time, you will learn to manipulate both codes. The digital will be simple for you, but the biological may take more time to learn to control. As your own organic systems are not yet fully developed at your age."

Digital and physical codes? Within me? Jinhua felt the questions piling, but she was still too weak to ask them.

Then, suddenly the cabin began to shake violently. Out of instinct, Jinhua rushed to the door frame to prevent any falling debris from impacting her. Outside of the square window at the back of the cabin, she saw the semi-circle village disappearing into white ether, leaving traces of digital code and wavelengths of varying frequencies behind as it vanished. She blinked her eyes several times to make the residual information go away, but it would not leave. The shaking began as minor tremors, then became an earthquake, breaking up the tiny cabin into digital fragments, combinations of binary code and splintering wood. Her sight returned to the fisherman, who stood serenely amid the collapsing cabin.

Jinhua felt as if her head might explode from the amount of information that she attempted to process. *Run? Fisherman? Code? Digital? Physical? Data?* What did it all mean? In the few moments she had before the entire place crashed around her, one question floated above the rest and reached her lips in time: "Who are you!?," She yelled.

The fisherman began to turn into flashing lines of digital information, flickering rapidly as if he might vanish any second. Then, Jinhua let out a squeal of fright as his face transformed into Janus right before her eyes. "You already know the answer Jinhua. I will see you soon, very soon."

Janus disappeared, then the entire cabin came crashing down around her, plunging her world into a sea of blue, as her consciousness left her.

CHAPTER 50:
BATTLE WITH A
FOUNDER - PART 1

Li stood at his desk in a breathless fury, unable to comprehend why one of his closest colleagues had betrayed him. *Now he has my daughter!*

He changed the view on the large screen to an auxiliary camera concealed directly above the front door. When he did, Rodan stared directly at him, a resolved look on his face. *Rodan, why?* Daring to leave the control panel and his view of Rodan gripping Jinhua's arm, Li sprinted to the door. He pulled the knob, but for some reason it would not budge. *Someone must have infiltrated our local network and sealed the bolt locks remotely.* "Damn you Rodan!" he said. When had he gotten to her? He had only taken his eyes off of her for what felt like seconds. *Even minutes can feel like seconds in the heat of battle.* The reminder from one of his former tactical training instructors echoed from a distant memory. So right he was.

Li was alone in the study. Noe had immediately gone outside upon noticing Rodan on the screen. *Luckily she got outside before they sealed the door,* he thought.

"It's no use Li!" Silas said, his smoker's voice grated over the speakers, "You won't be coming out anytime soon."

With no other options, Li returned to his desk and the video feed. The scene outside of the house had intensified in the brief period of time that he had checked the door. Silas now stood beside Rodan and Jinhua in front of the doors to the mansion. Standing in a line in the aftermath of their previous battle, Kyler, Bear, Noe, and Cheeks stood facing him, weapons raised and ready to engage Silas as soon as Jinhua was out of the way.

Li spoke, with a low and even tone, from the control room, "Silas…let her go. My daughter has nothing to do with this."

"I don't think so. She is very important to our plans and the very future of humanity. Janus and I won't let the girl walk away from this that easily."

With strength and agility defying the logic of his outwardly feeble frame, Silas produced a dart gun from within his overalls and fired it at Jinhua. To everyone's surprise, the girl seemed to anticipate the move and whirled behind Rodan's hulking body, utilizing it as a shield. Lowering her stance slightly behind Rodan's frame she heard him exhale sharply as his firm grip on her arm slackened and fell away. Swiftly, Jinhua dashed around one of the pillars flanking the front door to take cover from any follow up shots. A deaf thud startled her from her place of cover. It must have been the sound of Rodan's body hitting the cement walkway.

"Fucking women! Always giving trouble!" Silas yelled.

By the time he had cursed, the others were already in combat motion, closing in on him with a wall of firepower designed to rip him to shreds. Silas quickly took cover behind the opposite pillar beside the front entrance to the house.

Over the scream of gun fire, Noe yelled, "Jinhua, run to Spazer's defensive position! We'll take care of this!"

The girl obeyed, and bolted from behind the pillar in a zigzag pattern until she safely reached Spazer in his makeshift foxhole.

Silas let out a croaking laugh. "I will have her! Just wait and see. You all will become Janus' puppets!" From behind the pillar, he raised his arms above his head, as if he were invoking a kind of invisible incantation, then closed his eyes. In the next instant, Noe felt her trigger finger, then her entire hand go numb. The unexpected sensation made her drop her weapon in the dirt at her feet. *What? No! This feeling…it can't be happening again…Janus isn't even here…unless…* A look toward her companions confirmed her feeling of dread. One by one, she saw Kyler, Cheeks, and Bear surrender their armaments to the earth, leaving them all defenseless against a terrifyingly powerful enemy, in the form of an elderly man.

"What the hell!? I can't feel my fuckin' hands!" Cheeks yelled.

The tingling in her hands morphed into a slight burning sensation. It prevented her from picking up her weapon and continuing the fight. A gleeful cackle, followed by a sudden coughing fit came from behind the pillar. Silas was enjoying himself. With newfound confidence, he took an exaggerated step from his hiding place and stood at the midpoint between the pillars, savoring the pained and confused faces of the people before him.

They are still weak. Not ready for the power and ability that comes from evolution. I will show them now what Janus has given me.

"You see how brittle the human condition is! One minor twitch of my finger, and I have complete control over your actions! Now a demonstration of the potential of evolution!"

Silas' eyes widened as he raised a pointed finger directly at Kyler. Noe watched in horror as his soldier tension seemed to melt away from him. In its place a lazy bliss washed over his usually hard features. A small smile curled on his cracked lips as he turned toward the others. His hands reached toward his face, and made an attempt to physically rearrange the alien features. But the effort was in vain. The unseen specter repossessed him, manipulating his once independent limbs for its own ends.

Viewing Kyler's eerie movements, frozen air entered Noe's lungs, as if she had inhaled a passing Arctic zephyr. It was moments like these when she felt most out of control. When she wondered if some gazing cosmic being observed her from above with mild amusement on its face, lips wrinkled in contemplation, as it pondered what to do with her as she went about the business of living day in and day out. *What should I do with Noe today?* It would ask. *Should I subject her to some random event that will impact the rest of her waking existence? Or should I allow her the freedom of movement and cognition that she assumes to have over her life? Hmm I wonder? Live or die? Either way I will have fun viewing her joy and sorrow from up here in my place among the heavens. Far above the awareness of mortal humans.* Maybe the all-powerful being flipped a coin to decide if today was the day that it would fuck with you. To remind you that you never really had ownership of anything in this life. Not even your own body. To remind you that no matter how tough your self-crafted image was, no matter how much training or experience or augmentations you had, or how much money you had in the bank, you were nothing but a source of mild entertainment for the great cosmic hand in the sky. Then, after your life was in pieces, and the exhilaration from the theater of your thrashing, flailing, and cursing, was over; it would simply yawn, locate another poor soul, then flip another coin to begin another show.

Noe's mouthed gaped in sickly terror as Kyler's hands moved. She thought she saw a flash of desperation in his eyes for a moment, before the drugged expression returned to his face. Then he reached to his ankle for his emergency Glock. In a blur of motion, raised it to his temple and pulled the trigger. The single bang echoed louder in Noe's mind than the hundreds of rounds they had discharged since the fight began.

Cheeks yelled with a war-cry that sounded like a wounded animal. "No! No! No! Goddammit Boss! Get up!"

Bear's body heaved with emotion, his face strained in furious agony, rabid spit flew from his lips as he cursed.

Tears welled in Jinhua's eyes, as she viewed the old soldier's lifeless form.

Spazer yelled with tears in his eyes from his position of defense, realizing that it could not protect him from his own mind.

Noe's chest felt tight. It was hard to breathe. She wanted to scream, but no air rose from her throat to make the sound.

Silas pointed at Kyler's unmoving corpse on the ground before him, taking a victorious step forward. "You see!? Even he wasn't strong enough to save himself. For the outward strength he possessed, he was just as weak of a being as all of you."

"You fuckin' monster! The Boss…what the fuck did you do to him!?" Spazer said, his voice cracked as he yelled.

Silas laughed. "I made him finally face the demon that lurked inside him. Gave him the opportunity to free himself from the hidden guilt that he felt from years of ending the lives of countless individuals. Trust me, he died feeling blameless and most of all, happy. You could almost say that I *helped* him, by letting him to truly see himself and by not allowing him to suffer. Some die slow deaths for decades before passing away with tortured souls and a guilty conscience, trust me, he was fortunate."

Then, another bang from a pistol shocked them all. Silas staggered to the side with a high pitched welp, then immediately scrambled behind the pillar for cover. Li Ma emerged from the door, gun raised, his dress clothes and face covered in dirt. *Thank goodness for the emergency exit.* Long ago, he had installed an emergency escape route from his study, just in case his house was ever besieged. The crawl space had room enough for two people and led to the backyard behind the house. He never thought he would have to use it, and definitely never thought he would have to use it not only to escape the house, but to save his daughter.

From behind the pillar, Li heard Silas coughing and laughing. Breathing heavily, a look of insanity on his face, he said, "Ow! That hurt Li! Janus told me not to harm the prominent members of Cereus society. Said something about wanting you alive for his future plans."

"He's using you," Li said, raising his voice, "Anything he promised you was a lie." He kept the weapon pointed in Silas' direction, and took slow steps toward the pillar.

Silas scoffed loudly. "What does it matter as long as I got what I wanted? Which I already have! This new power, this new body. The freedom to transcend the shortcomings of my once human form, in order to survive in our competitive society is all I need. Now Mr. Ma, *you* too will have the opportunity to cleanse yourself of all of the wrong you have done before you leave this world for good!"

The others attempted to move, but Silas' hold on them would not allow them to act. Silas rounded the pillar, raised his finger and pointed it at Li. Just as he was about to fire the weapon, he let it fall to the concrete between the pillars. The look of serious determination on his face disappeared. In its place was the same euphoric expression Kyler wore before he was forced to kill himself. Li swayed, then guided himself to a kneeling position on the concrete, using every inch of self-discipline and mind power to keep resisting and fighting Silas's power over his mind. Noe looked on with frustration, while Bear, Cheeks, and Spazer watched with faces contorted with helplessness, and rage. They knew where he was, and none of them could help him now.

CHAPTER 51:
BATTLE WITH A
FOUNDER - PART 2

Li had entered the circular dungeon room. There were no entrances and exits, only a single pedestal with one jagged vision bubble floating above it. In the hazy image of the bubble was an adult version of Jinhua, living happily and comfortably in a place that he could not name. His rational brain told him not to touch it, that this was a manipulation, an illusion. But something blocked his thinking brain, leaving only the raw ability to follow his most basic desires.

The survival of himself and his offspring were the evolutionary imperative, and it trumped all other necessities or wishes. He had to touch it to make sure his daughter was safe, and would be taken care of in the future. Somewhere in a shaded corner of his thoughts, a faint candlewick-sized light flickered. In the sparse lighting, his intelligent brain recorded a note: *Remember, the illusion not only tempts you with the deepest desires of your heart, it appeals to the animal in us all, that few of us ever openly acknowledge during our conscious hours.* Then, without warning, the candle went out, and Li's animal impulses took full control of his body. Without reservation, he reached out his hand to touch the floating bubble.

The next thing he knew, he was sitting with Jinhua in the dining room of their mansion. Her face was mature, with eyes determined to seek the truth in all things. *Just like her mother,* he thought.

Their conversation was brief but packed enough candid words and feelings to bring the usually unemotional Li to tears. His daughter forgave him for concealing the truth of her origins from her. Then, she told him how grateful that she was for all of the sacrifices he had made for her. She had found her calling, not in science, but in historical research. She realized that by researching and documenting hers and any others' stories, she was doing much more than analyzing data. She was documenting the history of the first generation of consciously evolved humans. Jinhua held his hand as she told him that she would carry on with the work he had begun with Cereus and continue to fight for a society that valued people and planet, over individual wealth accumulation, social isolation, and planetary destruction.

"I'm proud of you my daughter."

Jinhua giggled. "That's a rare thing for you to say, so I know it must be true." They embraced tightly. From that moment on, with his daughter safe and contributing to the well-being of the world, his legacy secure, Li Ma felt complete and ready for the end of his life. *It can come at any time*, he thought. *There's nothing left for me to do here.*

*   *   *

All viewed the scene helplessly as Li kneeled and reached for the gun he had dropped only moments before. Silas smirked, as the barrel floated up to Li's left temple.

To everyone's surprise, a jet of light hit Silas in the chest, and he fell backward. Cheeks, Noe, and Bear's eyes scanned for the source of the beam. Had it been laser fire? Had some passerby come to their aid? The truth left them as speechless as everything else they had seen and heard that morning.

Their eyes landed on the improvised foxhole, where Spazer stood, shock on his face. Standing next to him they saw Jinhua hold out her hand, and with an open palm, shoot out what looked like a stream of goldenrod yellow light with lines of computer code spiraling around it. When the second beam of coded light hit Silas in the chest, he immediately dropped his pointing finger and clutched his chest in agony.

"No! H-How can you do that? How can a little girl have such power!?"

Unafraid, Jinhua took determined steps out of the safety of the foxhole, and advanced toward Silas. Tears blurred her vision at the thought of losing her father to such a despicable and inferior being. Her hand remained elevated, as she intuitively unleashed her new abilities on her enemy.

After awakening from the dreamworld, Jinhua resumed control of her physical body, only to find herself being pulled forcefully down the stairs of her house by Rodan, while the other scientists and officials fled to the security shelter. Thinking he was taking her to a safe location at first, she followed him willingly. However, it wasn't until Silas joined the two of them in front of the house that she realized Rodan had been turned, or had decided to turn. She didn't know which one it was, but at that point it didn't matter. He was her enemy now.

Her sight had taken on the ability to see digital information. From the time that she emerged from the safety of the mansion, she saw an overwhelming amount of code and wavelengths flowing around her in the air. The sight of virtually endless strings of numbers, letters, and symbols wrapped and curved around everything, including the people standing on the battlefield that used to be her front yard. All had at least a tiny digital signature, due to the chip implanted in them, but Silas was in a league of his own. She almost gave herself away, with a tiny scream when she noticed it. The black lines of code were so numerous in him, that he looked like the screen of a computer after it crashed. Although she could not understand what the configuration of the code meant, she knew one thing. He was no longer human. His humanity had been replaced by digital cues written by someone else's hand, who now manipulated him from an unknown location. *Perhaps on some level we all looked like this to the corporations and companies of the old world.* Her brief moment of insightfulness made her shudder.

Unclear about the function of the code, she decided to do the one thing that she knew would make any computer stop working. *Delete all. Delete all. Delete all.* The words became an incantation in her mind, and somehow, her body did the rest.

Upon the realization of what was happening, Silas reacted quickly. "I will not let you defeat me so easily!" The old man moved as if he had not been shot. He leapt into the air, then in mid-flight, pointed a fist at Jinhua on the ground. Noe and the others watched, incredulous, as his imitation fist rearranged itself into a laser cannon. Silas smirked, then in a demonic tone said, "Hell beam!" As he discharged a hot burning beam directly at Jinhua. Mid-step, hand still raised, Jinhua noticed a sudden shift in his remaining code, and dove to the left, just as he fired the shot.

But it was too late.

The piercing beam impacted the earth with a shaking boom, throwing rocks, dust and dirt everywhere. Noe and the others clamped their eyes shut to prevent from inhaling the cloud of powdered earth. When she opened them, the only question on her mind was, *Where is Jinhua!? Is she alright!?* Still unable to act or move, her eyes darted back and forth, searching for their teenage savior.

Silas landed softly on the ground, then blew on the laser arm as if he had just won a duel. He let out a victorious laugh, and brought his hand to his mouth, mimicking a movement an embarrassed teenage girl might make. "Oh, you poor girl! I'm sorry, did I hurt you?"

When the dust cleared, Noe saw Jinhua. She had avoided a direct hit from the laser blast, but it had hit very close to where she had been standing, leaving a jagged circular depression where she once stood. Next to the crater, the girl lay on the ground, arm extended, her long hair spread on the ground like a used mop caked with brown dirt, not moving. Noe could not see her breathing. *No!* "Jinhua! Please get up!"

"I don't think she can hear you," Silas said, "I will take her to Janus now. Hopefully I didn't kill her." Assured in his victory, he took casual steps in Jinhua's direction. All watched his triumphant walk with resistant faces. This made Silas even more gleeful. "Your stares and jeers make lousy weapons. I should punish you all for shooting and attacking me." Then a devilish gleam came to his eyes, as an idea dawned on him. "I don't have to keep *all* of you alive." He raised his laser arm and pointed it directly at Noe. "I'm sure he doesn't care if one of you dies."

"Oh shit! He gon' fire again!" Cheeks yelled.

Noe's entire body tensed in anticipation of the laser blast. *I can't move! Oh my god! Is this the end!?* She stared at Silas' wrinkled and ugly face, regretful that it would be the last face that she would see before she died. All she could do was wait for the end. She saw what looked like a blue light flash, before she closed her eyes, and let a resigned sigh exit her lips. She could fight no more.

"Noe look!" Someone yelled. The voice had come from Spazer in the foxhole behind her. Noe timidly opened her eyes, very much alive, icy fear of imminent death still running through her veins. She looked toward where the destroyed iron gate lay in the dirt, and squinted her vision to confirm what she was seeing. *No way…another one?*

Standing beside the downed gate, in front of Jinhua, was a handsome looking boy, who looked no older than eighteen. Strands of his brown hair waved in a sudden breeze, as he aimed his arm, just as Jinhua had minutes before. Where there should have been a hand, there was a sizable laser gun. The young man was dressed as if he had just come from class; jeans, and a red t-shirt that revealed a slightly muscular chest. *He's got a gun for an arm too!? This is crazy!* Noe couldn't believe what she was seeing.

With a calm and determined voice, the boy spoke, "Leave them alone Silas."

Silas turned to face his new challenger. He snickered, as he examined the young man. He was not intimidated at all. "You there, boy! I don't know how you have similar enhancements to mine, but it doesn't matter. Get out of the way!"

"No. I can't do that," the youth said.

"Damn kids. Never listen. Never learn." Silas raised his arm cannon and prepared to fire.

In the next instant, Daniel arched an invisible trajectory from his position to precisely ten feet behind Silas. Then he jumped, following the traced parabolic path, firing his arm laser at Silas in the center at a rapid rate. Blue light rained down as he traveled the curved path, all focused on the center point of the half-circle. When he landed and turned around, a frustrated sound escaped his mouth. Despite the ferocity and speed of his attack, Silas was unscathed. He smiled smugly behind a red laser barrier shaped like a three dimensional cone. It had absorbed all of Daniel's shots.

"Looks like you bought a gun to a cannon fight boy!" Silas raised his arm, "You lose."

"No! *You* lose!" The voice came from behind Silas. A battered Jinhua stood, arm raised, still capable of fighting. Without a second thought, she fired cadmium yellow light wrapped in digital code at Silas, neutralizing his barrier. "Daniel! Now!" She shouted the vocal command, but was aware Daniel already knew what she wanted to do. As soon as the barrier was down, Daniel fired surgical concentrated beams of blue light at Silas' laser cannon arm and legs. The light from the two sources danced with green hues, as Silas fell to the ground screaming in pain. His right arm lay in dirt before his eyes, his legs had fallen to the sides, leaving the now one-armed man face up on his back. His malicious code had been deleted, his primary physical weapons disabled. In his condition, he was no longer a threat to anyone.

Without the digital or physical enhancements to sustain him, he coughed and hacked between cries of agony. He spat up blood and babbled incoherently. "I-I-I don't know how she did it. J-Janus, it was him! He made me do this! He promised endless wealth, power, and security! H-He said I could help people. I was controlled don't you see!" The shadows of Cheeks, Bear, and Noe fell on him. Any pity or sympathy they would have normally provided to someone of his age and experience was absent from their faces. His pleas and sobs were met with blank stares, hungry for bloody vengeance.

"I helped create this utopia that you live in now. I should have my rightful place here as one of the founders of Cereus! You all should be thanking me! I've helped people! I've helped—"

A single shot silenced his cries. Cheeks lowered the gun slowly. Then turned away, as if Silas' remains were another dead stray dog in the street. His attention shifted to his dead commander's remains. Bear and Spazer followed him in ritual silence.

Noe quickly began to scan the area for Rodan, thinking, *how could you do this?* Her eyes landed on where he had been hit by the dart what seemed like ages ago. But he was no longer there. He was in the wind now, and she had no idea where he might have run to.

*   *   *

Jinhua checked on her father. He lay in front of the door to their house, and was unharmed save for a few cuts to his hands he had sustained, most likely when using the emergency exit he had briefly mentioned to her several weeks prior. His chest rose and fell at a steady cadence. Wherever he was, he appeared to be at peace. *Rest Dad. You earned it.*

Daniel walked up beside Jinhua. "How is he?"

Jinhua stood from her kneeling position. "He looks ok. Thankfully." She looked at Daniel. His arm gun was nowhere in sight, having returned to wherever it was stashed when he wasn't in combat mode. She motioned toward his arm with a loose gesture, "Didn't know you could do that."

Daniel mirrored her movement toward her arm, "Didn't know *you* could do that either."

They laughed.

"How did you know I was in trouble?" Jinhua asked.

"I was in the committee room, and I just *sensed* it. Once I did, I *literally* ran over here."

Jinhua blushed, "I see. You really saved my ass. *All* of our asses really."

Daniel shrugged, hazel eyes glowed. "It's what I was made to do. You and I are one." He paused. It gave Jinhua time to allow soft emotion to color and lift her facial muscles.

Daniel continued, "I saw everything."

"Everything?" Jinhua asked, slightly self-conscious.

"Everything. The dreamworld, the village, your transformation with the card where you almost died, the fisherman who turned out to be Janus."

Jinhua shook her head, "Wait, I almost died!?"

Daniel nodded definitively. "Yes. Your vital signs were in extreme physical distress. A few seconds more and you would have had permanent damage to your brain, lungs, and heart."

She put her hand over her chest, and felt her calmly beating heart, giving her life, always working. For a moment, she wondered what it would be like not to feel that familiar rhythm, what it would be like to be dead. Then her eyes floated to Silas' corpse. His limbs scattered around his torso like a broken action figure, as if invisible hands had played with him until he snapped then discarded him, ready to move on to a new toy.

"That was too close," Jinhua said.

"Agreed," Daniel replied.

"We have to find Rodan," she said. Though her eyes were locked on Silas, they did not focus on him. They stared at nothing.

"You're right. He's the key to finding Janus."

Jinhua slapped Daniel's arm playfully, "Hey, I was gonna say that!"

Daniel winced, "Hey that hurt! Sorry about that. I guess my ability to be in your head has gotten stronger since you touched the key."

"I figured that," Jinhua said. "It might take me some time to get used to it."

CHAPTER 52:
LATE ARRIVAL

Barto hated flying in helicopters. He only did it on rare occasions, and sitting in the noisy, stuffy cabin made him ask himself why he had chosen this mode of transportation over the myriad other options at his disposal. *Because it was the fastest.* He reminded himself for the fifth time. The noise cancelling headphones pinched his ears (and he could still hear the deafening roar from the blades), and his butt was cramping in the rock hard seat. Worse yet, he noted the uncomfortable churn of the sparse breakfast, a bagel and a steaming cup of coffee, in his stomach, as the aircraft shook and tilted its way toward his destination.

I hate flying. He was supposed to be in Yuba City by 10:30 and here it was almost noon. This wasn't fashionably late, it was just negligence. But it couldn't be helped. He had been rapidly scanning correspondence from Rodan concerning the state of the comvils, and it had taken longer than he expected. Guilt was something he had struggled with his entire life. Now the weight of it threatened to crush him completely and thoroughly. *I really wanted to make things better for people. I still do.* Several of the comvils seemed to be on the brink of collapse. Then there was Janus' new technology to deal with, too. He left the cabin late, feeling as if he had accomplished nothing, other than reminding himself of how dire the whole situation was. *I couldn't have known it was gonna get this bad when I gave the order. No way.*

He took a deep breath to settle his stomach and let the negative thoughts fly into the rushing air currents outside of the helicopter. *Gotta focus on something else.* Outside, it was another hot summer morning, with a smattering of clouds populating the sky. The clouds did nothing to shield the ground below from the deadly solar heat that always characterized valley summers. The thought made Barto a little more thankful to be flying instead of taking ground transportation.

"Sir, we've reached the airspace above Mr. Ma's mansion." The voice of the A.I. pilot came through to his ears like an old radio broadcast, despite the beating of the blades of the aircraft. "It doesn't look good down there."

Barto labored to shift in his seat to find a better view of the ground below. *This is bad.* His heart hammered at the sight of the carnage. *What the hell happened here?* The pilot's rapid descent combined with the grisly scene, nearly caused him to throw up his bagel and his coffee.

The remains of mangled bodies, human and machine littered the area. Evidence of exploded munitions, conventional weaponry, and lasers were plastered on the facade of the gorgeous multimillion-dollar home like graffiti on the side of a highway. Depressions in the soft earth, where war mechanoids had walked and grenades had blown up, reminded him of the surface of the moon. Barto shuddered. His aerial survey of the warzone made one fact apparent to him. *We have a lot less time than I previously thought.*

*   *   *

Barto ducked his head while exiting the helicopter, then promptly waved his arm at the empty cockpit. Upon registering the gesture, the A.I. pilot lifted off to a position that Barto previously designated on his device. The program would wait for him behind the house, until instructed to return and pick him up. *Sometimes, I really love technology,* Barto thought, *so convenient.*

As the sound of the helicopter's rotors faded into the sky, Barto's body tensed when he recognized one of the dead men lying on the ground. It was Silas. His longtime collaborator and fellow Founder.

Without the helicopter whipping the air around, the smell of fresh death bombarded his nostrils. The acrid bitterness of a seventy-something year-old's exposed bodily fluids, acted as a powerful lure for the flies that buzzed, uncaring, around his corpse. Two legs severed above the knees, bloody and burned, lay forgotten in the sun. One of his arms still smelled like burned flesh, as if surgically removed by a black market surgeon, who promptly disposed of the limb after deeming it unfit for use. Silas' face wore the expression of a repentant sinner just before an unexpected cataclysmic event. Mouth open, cloudy eyes, still red and bulging; fear, frozen and eternal, the final expression of his living death mask.

Barto shook his head, face sullen with pity. *Silas, why'd you have to go out like this? Hurting and killing people? Why?* In the beginning, he and Silas struggled to connect. They were much too different in personality and personal background. Barto suspected their age difference of ten or so years made Silas view him as an inexperienced and naive person, not worth his time or attention. Barto had an unfavorable opinion of him, as well. He saw him as a close-minded relic of early twentieth century values, not worth trying to make friends with. Despite this, both respected the other's ability and work ethic. Barto learned to stand up for himself because of Silas' no-nonsense attitude. On the other hand, Silas got rich, and learned how to get even richer, thanks to Barto's economic talent. As Cereus prospered, Silas's respect for the young Barto grew proportionally. Although they usually never discussed personal issues, Barto was happy with the efficiency of their working relationship. Their pseudo-friendship acted as a healthy counterweight to the confusing and often problematic associations among the other Founders.

He noticed Silas pull away from the rest of the Founders a decade prior. Barto had spoken with him at least four times a year, every year during that ten year period. One of those times was during their annual Founders meeting, when Silas showed up primarily to drink his booze and go skiing (Barto recognized this and was alright with it). The other three were via phone calls to discuss budget issues relating to Silas' investment in Cereus. After they concluded their business talk, Silas would mention SJ-Arcade, his video game and winery retirement community venture. Whenever he spoke about it, he would talk faster and his usual caustic tone was nowhere to be found. He would ask business questions, and Barto would advise him, which made Silas even happier. During one conversation, he unexpectedly extended an invitation for Barto to come live at his primary property in Auburn, when and *if* he ever decided to retire. "I think you'd really like it here. Real peaceful. I could even cut you in on some of the profits if you wanted," Silas said. Barto had considered it, but ultimately never took him up on the proposition. The offer alone made Barto smile. It reminded him that despite his often cantankerous and downright prejudiced old world thinking, the dead man that lay before him had been his friend. *Janus did this. Fuck.*

Unable to take the strong smell, Barto turned to ring the doorbell. While he waited he smoothed out his wind ruffled designer suit. It was midnight blue, with a silver tie over a white dress shirt, one of his favorites. *Damn helicopter ruined my look.* He had just finished readjusting himself when the door slowly opened.

Woah! He was slightly surprised when an attractive younger woman answered the door. She wore a dark green field uniform with black boots. Her hair was fastened in a loose ponytail, that dangled in the air behind her head. Barto's nose was assaulted by the smell of sweat and blood coming from her clothes. The sorrowful expression, with the fatigued eyes told him she had been to hell and back.

"You Khuni?" She asked, with little inflection in her voice.

"I am." Barto cleared his throat. "Is Li Ma in?"

"Yeah. Upstairs in the study. He's expecting you."

A million questions circled in Barto's brain. Half of which, he already knew the answer to. He did not need a decision tree to decide whether or not to ask the exhausted woman before him any of them. *She's been through enough.*

Barto ascended the stairs and was surprised when she began to follow him. He didn't protest her actions. With the woman following closely behind, he made his way to the solid oak door with the Cereus emblem on it. *Time to get some answers, and make some revelations.*

CHAPTER 53:
ARE YOU REALLY A
FOUNDER?

Barto entered Li's study turned command center, marveling at the "coolness" of the office. With the screens on the back wall, the massive holographic map, the old fashioned recliner under the halo of lamplight, and the glowing desk in the center, it looked like Bruce Wayne's bat cave, without Alfred. *Impressive.*

A disheveled Li sat at his desk, poring over real time intelligence data. His dress shirt was damp with sweat and unbuttoned slightly too far to be fashionable. Next to him, Barto noticed his not so little girl, Jinhua, standing at the desk also scanning documents. She moved at a much more rapid pace than her father, and made notes on her device as she worked feverishly. A young man worked beside her, analyzing data from a miniature holographic map floating before him. He reminded Barto of Zac Efron, from the High School Musical movies of his childhood. Painfully aware of his lateness, Barto swallowed. *What I have to say may be able to help them.* Without warning, he cleared his throat obnoxiously to make his presence known. The sound echoed around the large space, causing the father, daughter, and Zac Efron to look up simultaneously as if they were a three-headed being in separate physical bodies.

"Barto, welcome," Li said, a blank expression on his face "didn't notice you come in."

"Hello Mr. Khuni," Jinhua said, wearing the same face as her father.

Barto raised an eyebrow while staring at Daniel. "And who do we have here?"

Li responded, "This is Daniel. He's a…," in that instant, both father and daughter exchanged perplexed glances, "…a *friend* of Jinhua's."

"Oh I see!" Barto exclaimed, clapping his hands together one time. "I can't believe she's already dating! I suppose you are a young woman now, so it makes sense. It's a pleasure to meet you young man." Barto shook hands with Daniel. *Wow, some grip on this kid!*

Li and Jinhua looked at each other and blinked rapidly, while their facial expressions remained neutral. For several seconds they didn't speak. After the odd moment passed, both regarded Barto with an expression that asked: *Remind us why you are here again?* The Founder couldn't help but feel like he had missed something important in the last five minutes.

This is super awkward, he thought. *Better say something to get things moving again.*

"Oh, and I apologize for being late, though it looks like I arrived just in time to miss whatever it was that occurred on your front lawn." He laughed nervously. All three faces projected bitterness, unappreciative of his attempt at levity.

The decision tree unfolded unexpectedly before him laying out his options to proceed. What should Barto do? *Ask about the attack? Ask about Silas? Make more small talk?*

He chose the small talk. *The ice in here is frozen solid. Better try and break it down some more.* "Helluva thing, this conflict between Cereus and Limnic is. The more powerful one grows, the more stubborn the other becomes, then round and round we go." Barto made a clicking sound of disapproval with his tongue, as if to respond to his own comment. Father and daughter Ma nodded in agreement, still preoccupied with their task. Daniel ignored him.

Ok time to get to business. "What did Silas want?" Barto asked.

Li exhaled a heavy sigh, then clenched his jaw, without looking up from his desk screen. "He wanted Jinhua."

Barto raised an eyebrow. "…I see."

"You don't look *or* sound surprised." Li said, showing a hint of interest for the first time. He raised his eyes to meet the Founder's face.

Barto shook his head, averted his gaze and said sheepishly, "I'm not. I've known for some time that Janus would try and seek her out at some point. But I had no idea it would be this soon."

Jinhua saw the irritation in his father's eyes. It looked like he wanted to hit this clueless man in the face. This socially awkward old man, who had been tardy to the meeting, and missed the entire battle, was one of the Founders of Cereus? She wasn't impressed.

Then Barto stepped around the desk, and approached her with careful steps, stopping only inches from her face. His eyes scrutinized her from head to toe for several moments, making her wonder if he had been gifted with abilities similar to hers. Jinhua returned his gaze with an intense stare.

"You've been in contact with Janus haven't you?"

She nodded modestly.

"Tell me what happened. I want every detail."

The adolescent turned to her father for approval to repeat the same explanation that she had given him only fifteen minutes before Barto's arrival. He gave an approving nod and Jinhua began to speak.

She told Barto everything. The strange sensations that signaled the change in her body; the dream of the semi-circle village, the fisherman who turned out to be Janus in disguise; touching the key, the manifestation of her power, the fight with Silas which led her to use her powers for the first time, leading to his ultimate demise.

Sounds like one of those old Marvel movies, Barto thought. The incredible tale prompted a litany of facial expressions to cross his face. Surprise, shock, disgust, amazement had all animated his plump features while she relayed the events in a factual (and somewhat detached) manner. After ten minutes, he felt as if he had completed a vigorous face yoga session, and had definitely compensated for the Ma family's general lack of emotional expressiveness.

When her story concluded Barto lightly massaged his face with both hands. "I see. That's quite a story. So Janus got Silas to do his dirty work for him. That truly is sad." His voice trailed off, as if he had more to say.

"Sad for who?" Li asked.

"For both of them. Sad for Janus, because he's killed, albeit indirectly, another Founder." Barto paused to loosen his tie. The thought that Janus might come for him next, made him feel hot and thirsty. After he felt more relaxed, he continued. "Sad for Silas because he was done with all this before Janus got to him."

"Why did you work with him?" Jinhua asked pointedly. The directness of the question caught Barto off guard, and prompted a single bead of nervous sweat to form on his forehead.

"Hey, hey, it wasn't cheap to start Cereus up back in the day. We needed the money, and Silas had mountains of generational wealth that he was willing to commit to our cause." He sighed, "Silas was a…complex guy. Sure he could be a racist, misogynist, violent, and sarcastic asshole, but he wasn't all bad." The two offered a wordless stare at him. *Seriously, why are you here again?* their eyes said.

Barto, eager to move on, swiftly changed the subject. "What are you looking for?"

"Rodan," all three answered, as if one mouth in three bodies.

"Ah yes. How is our interim CEO faring?" Barto asked, with an air of confidence.

Li looked up, while Jinhua continued to scan documents and screens, and Daniel consulted the map. The visible hurt in his eyes did not match his monotone response. "He's betrayed us all."

Barto took a step back, truly floored by the first piece of new information he had heard since entering the house. "It can't be…"

"It's true. We have reason to believe that he has been filtering information to Limnic and Janus for several weeks now. I also suspect that he leaked sensitive intel about today's meeting, and our plans to counter Janus' efforts to apply his 'great filter' technology." Li's voice became quieter, as he glanced at his daughter. "He threatened to hand Jinhua over to Silas…I don't know how I couldn't see his treachery from up close." The young woman stopped her work and placed a hand on her father's shoulder in an act of comfort.

"From up close can often be the most difficult place to spot an enemy, especially when he's your friend," Barto said. He slapped Li's right shoulder in a blundering manner. "I worked with Janus for nearly a decade before I found out what he was truly capable of. I've been where you are, and understand how shitty it feels."

"Rodan's always been loyal to Cereus. To think, he would betray it now, after everything we've been through over the years…" Li put his hands on his hips and exhaled frustrated air from his nose, shaking his head.

"You think Janus got to him?" Barto asked.

Li raised two fingers to his forehead and gently massaged the area, "Most likely. And after today, I understand the devastating power that Janus wields." Images of the circular dungeon room appeared in his mind. The afterimage of the room, the vision of the future, and the utter lack of control over his own conscious thoughts, felt as if they might never leave his brain. The ghostly image was burned in, like on an old cathode ray tube television left on the same image too long. It was impossible to ignore, and even more difficult to get rid of. *I really wanted to die after I saw the future. Was Thanatos always that strong within me? Or was it another one of Janus projections?* He was so consumed by his thoughts, he had not noticed the others eyeing him with concern. Jinhua looked particularly worried. Her face helped return him to his logical mind. "As I was saying, that is why he *must* be stopped."

Barto had his head tilted upward toward the ceiling. Jinhua couldn't tell if he was thinking or stretching his neck. "You're right. But one thing I *don't* understand is when would Rodan have made contact with Janus? I've kept close tabs on him since I left him in charge, and it's my understanding he never left Sacramento."

"It was at North Bloomfield."

Four pairs of eyes searched for the source of the statement. They landed on Noe standing near the door. All of them had forgotten she was there. She took a few steps forward, arms folded across her chest, her battle weary face ardent with controlled ire. "I always felt like there was something weird about him since the battle. I never asked him about it, even though I suspected he had encountered Janus that night." *I'm such an idiot.* "I just..." her eyes fell to the slick tiled floor. She wanted to let her emotion pour out of her, but then and there wasn't the time or place. She inhaled deeply and kept talking, "...I just didn't want to believe he would do that...I thought I knew him better." The others sensed the gravity of her words and remained quiet to let her finish. "Now I know, I guess I never really did know him at all. And I'm *sure* that somehow, at some point, Janus turned him that night."

Barto brought his hand to his chin, cradling it between thumb and index finger, nodding his head slowly. "Then this is indeed worse than I suspected. With Rodan in his pocket, Janus no doubt plans to absorb the Cereus infrastructure into Limnic's military might. Then, along with his army of nostalgia-drunk and future-obsessed followers, he may finally bring his grand vision to fruition."

"Which is?" Noe asked.

"The true evolution of society and humanity, along with the complete eradication of old world thinking for good."

The others were dead silent. Doubting. Li was the first to speak. "I get the societal evolution part. With the Cereus philosophy and Limnic's growing domestic military-esque reach with armed militias, he could potentially win a conventional or non-conventional fight with the capitalism dependent governments of the old world, after he has enslaved billions that rely on the network, to meet all of their daily needs. But is his 'great filter' project supposed to represent human evolution?"

"No." Barto allowed a theatrical space to punctuate his next words for effect. "His 'great filter' was meant to be one step in a larger plan. It was merely meant to pacify those that he knew would be too weak-minded to oppose his mental and physical dominance. Janus' true goal is to, in his own words, 'free' humanity."

"Free us? From what?" Li asked.

"From the tyranny of choice. From the burden of our often problematic genetics. From the demands of human physical existence. You know food, sex, bonding. The good stuff. And probably of greatest importance to him, he aims to free consciousness from the confines of the finite human body."

All quietly pondered the many implications of Barto's words. They started to respect him, and understand why he was a Founder. Their pensive expressions prompted Barto to continue, "His ultimate goal is to assimilate all human consciousness in the digital realm and create what author Yuval Noah Harari called *Homo Deus*, a new species of evolved humans…just, like him."

Jinhua spoke up, her eyes hard, questioning. "What do you mean, *like him?*"

Barto responded plainly, "Janus, like you my dear, is not purely human. He is a product of digigenomics; a perfect fusion of man and machine, who has power, just like you."

CHAPTER 54:
WHO IS JANUS? - PART 1

All pairs of eyes in the room were locked on Barto in astonishment.

"That can't be," Li said. "I've confirmed the data myself that Jinhua was the first successful product of digigenomics research." He looked toward his daughter. Barto's words had caused her facial expression to change in a way he had never seen before. It was somewhere between skepticism and the edge of fear.

Jinhua was stunned. *If he has had a lifetime to perfect abilities like mine then, how can we stop him? How can I compete with that?*

Barto closed his eyes, shaking his head slowly. "Yes, she was the first one officially on the books. But Janus was the first one ever created. A byproduct of the sinister science of genetic and biological manipulation. Have any of you heard of Project Egregore?"

Head shakes all around.

"It was the name of a highly classified program in the late 1990s. The purpose of the project was to link the human brain to the internet and digitize its neurological information. At least those were the two objectives cited on the proposal document the head scientist drafted to get it funded and approved by the U.S. government."

"So what was its real purpose?" Noe asked. She realized that her muscles were tight as she focused on every detail of the story, just like Jinhua and Li across the room from her.

Barto rotated his head in her direction. "There were two primary goals: one, to link a digitized human mind using the internet; and two, to recreate and simulate human consciousness."

More gasps came from Barto's captivated audience.

"I know what you're thinking," he said with a grin, "How could they even have attempted such a feat at a time when Windows 98 and Internet Explorer were the dominant methods to interact with the digital space? Good question." He laughed nervously. The blank and frustrated stares, told him none of them appreciated the timing of his humor. Barto cleared his throat and pressed on.

"Anyway, nowadays with telepathic communication, interactive holographic maps, and people living their entire lives in the digital space, we take network connection for granted. But back then, the technology was still fairly new to the mainstream public, so this was a big deal. The chief scientist of the project's name was Arturo Khuni…he was my father…"

Barto was getting used to their collective reaction of shock to his words. He smiled inwardly. It helped him snuff out painful memories of his dear, yet misguided old man.

"Yeah, my dad…the famous Dr. A.K., as all of his contemporaries called him, was a mad scientist of sorts. Even had the wild Einstein hair. Anyway, for years, he obsessed over this project. Although I wasn't born yet, I found all of this out decades later after he had already passed away."

Noe's patience was growing short. Barto could tell by the way she glared at him. "And, where does Janus come in?"

"Impatient, I see? Yes, yes I'm coming to it. Dr. A.K. was obsessed with the idea of bridging the gap between occultism and the scientific method. He wanted to prove the existence of supernatural phenomena through academic rigor. So in 1997, when searching for willing test subjects for Project Egregore, he recruited a couple that he became good friends with during an early Magic: The Gathering competition. Their names were Alex and Miranda Soren. They would become Janus' parents."

"What's Magic: The Gathering?" Jinhua asked.

Barto chuckled, "It used to be a wildly popular card game back in the old days. Nowadays, a lot of us old timers still like to play it every now and then." He winked at Li, who returned a tightlipped stare. *I guess he's not a fan.* Barto cleared his throat, then resumed his explanation, "Anyway, Dr. A.K. and the Sorens were fanatics for the game. They had all participated in some of the earliest organized tournaments of it back in the early 1990s. When Dr A.K. met the Sorens, he knew he had found the perfect participants for his experiments. They were staunch believers of astrology, the occult, and the power of supernatural forces on human nature. And, more importantly, they were hungry for the truth. A truth that only someone like my father could provide them."

Barto's audience exchanged glances of intrigue. Eager for him to continue.

"Using samples of both of their DNA, Dr. A.K. used his extensive, mostly self-taught knowledge of digigenomics to produce their son. Janus Soren, born September 9, 1999, was *the* first successful fusion of biotech and digital programming. After Janus' birth, my father encouraged the Sorens to raise him at home like an ordinary child. However, in exchange, he required regular updates to Janus' growth and progress. He was especially interested in how his biological body would interact with the software placed within him. What I know of his childhood, I learned from reading excerpts of some of those reports, and from Janus himself."

"Wait," Noe interrupted, "you mean you *knew* Janus, even before you got involved with Cereus?"

Barto gave a small nod, two globules of cold sweat chilled his forehead. "Yeah I did." He noticed her press her lips together tightly in an attempt to prevent inflammatory words from coming out of her mouth. She was pissed. Across the room, Li noticed her response and quickly prompted Barto to continue.

"What did the reports from your father's notes say?" Li asked.

Eyes still on the fuming Noe, Barto answered, "According to the journals, believe it or not, childhood was generally unremarkable for him. He attended public schools and skipped several grade levels, obviously, due to his unique gifts. From what I gathered, he was more or less socialized just like most children in the United States education system around the turn of this century. His parents, being the free-spirited types that they were, informed him of his origins at an early age so that he would have greater say in how he developed his own power." Jinhua glanced at her father. Li continued listening to Barto with full attention, though he felt her eyes on him, he did not react. Barto, oblivious to his word's effect on Jinhua, kept talking, "I think it was around age five or six, I can't really remember. But it was early enough for the young Janus to take ownership of his power early on."

Jinhua returned her gaze to Barto, "So he must be very powerful by now..." she said.

Barto nodded. He took note of her discomfort. *Understandable*, he thought. "Indeed. He and I met in elementary school and even by then he was already working on developing his 'abilities'. Back then, no one else was 'chipped', so he couldn't read minds like he does today. Instead, he practiced by closing his eyes and retrieving information from our teachers' slow computers, and manipulating early digital devices like Blackberries, iPhones, and e-readers." Barto's gaze flicked back in Noe's direction. "How did we meet you ask? We both sat next to each other in our classes in fourth grade, then we became friends. I was the gregarious one, and he was the silent genius. I guess we both saw our weaknesses in each other, and decided we'd be better off working together. And he was always willing to jump into any device, get online, and get strategy guides for the video games that we wanted to beat..." Barto laughed, lost in momentary nostalgia. "Those were the days."

The mention of the personal anecdote softened Noe's face. Barto breathed a sigh of relief, then continued the story.

"When we were in high school, I began to see the changes in him. His parents had been heavily affected by the 2008 global recession, and by the time we both turned fourteen, they had lost their jobs and life savings, like many others during that time period. Janus used his powers to comb the internet to find work for them, but after months of disappointment and poverty, his father passed away from untreated cancer. Without his father to take care of her, his mother died just seven months later from a bad bout of pneumonia. The death of his parents represented a profound failure of the system in his eyes, and Janus was never the same after it."

Li shifted his weight to the opposite foot uncomfortably in front of Barto. His eyes were calm, yet expectant. This was the part of the story he had been waiting for.

"Janus had long held resentment for the traditional education system. Forced to sit in overcrowded classrooms for hours a day, being spoon-fed bite-sized portions of infinitely vast subjects, by well-meaning, yet ultimately system-controlled babysitters, was a waste of time and highly ineffective in his view. His disillusionment with the school system and the death of his parents at the hand of predatorial neoliberalism set him on an ominous path, that he still walks to this day. As you can see, Cereus directly addresses both of these grievances."

Li nodded, understanding. Jinhua and Daniel both wore the same face. The look of an erudite 'A' student, soaking up every bit of accurate detail without visual aids or notes. Both appeared placid externally, but inside their heads, sparks were flying as new neurons connected with old information to create a more complete picture of the subject. If he were their old world teacher, he would have given them both 'A's just for showing up in class.

He pictured himself at their age. One-hundred pounds lighter, head full of unkempt thick black hair, President Obama in office, life was good, he and Janus were good. Then his mind zoomed back to the present. *I had no idea that would be the end of peace for both of us, nor that Janus and I would end up walking completely separate paths. Paths that were fated to intersect, yet never merge again.*

CHAPTER 55:
WHO IS JANUS - PART 2

Barto continued his speech. The eyes of his audience had grown dry from the circulation of the air conditioner and strain from interest.

"After graduation from high school, I attended the University of Texas in Austin, graduating with a degree in economics. By the time I entered my graduate degree program, my father had passed away, leaving me with a considerable amount of money. During my college years, my contact with Janus was sparse. Limited to the occasional social media message or email. I knew he had accounts, but like a phantom he was always invisible on them. Never commenting or posting, but always watching."

"Sounds pretty disturbing," Noe said, crossing her arms over her stomach in discomfort. Barto nodded slowly in response, face grim, "It kinda was, but that was Janus' style," he shrugged then continued speaking. "Then one day out of nowhere, I received a lengthy email from him. By then, it had been a good six years since we had really spoken, so there was a lot of catching up to do. In the message, he told me how he had amassed a fortune through various avenues, like: app development, stocks, bitcoin mining, trading rare collectables, and the like. If it could make money, he studied and gamed the system until he won. And he won bigger than a senior citizen gambling in Las Vegas. He wasn't specific with the numbers he earned from each specific activity (even though I asked of course), but he had made upward of 50 million dollars. All within the time period he had fallen off of my radar."

"That's a lot of money," Li commented, somewhat impressed.

"A *shit-ton*. Actually five shit-tons to be exact," Barto chuckled.

The others looked on, faces scrunched with annoyance at his ill-timed inside joke. The stares triggered unwanted perspiration to sprinkle on his face as if he had been caught in a light spring drizzle. He hastened to return to his story. "Uh, anyway, since he had more than enough money to be comfortable, he told me in a follow up email that he was finally ready to create something big. Something that would 'address society's woes and move us toward a clear bright future' as a species, was what he wrote. I'll never forget it. What he wrote sounded so definitive. So *Janus*. Like there could be no other way to think about or tackle the issue."

"He codenamed the project 'Cereus' and asked me to join him as his chief financial officer, telling me he could pay me whatever I wanted for my effort. At the time, the global economy was in the toilet and I was having a hard time finding a job out of grad school. So it didn't take me long to accept his offer. This was in…" he scratched his head, searching his vast memory to recall and reconstruct an occurrence that was over four decades old. "That's right, it was '24. In the fall of that year, Janus introduced me to Lili, who became sort of his chief of staff. He had already bought Silas in to further help with the funding, property acquisition, and building our security apparatus."

"So from the jump, you all knew that you would meet resistance," Noe said, making no attempt to conceal the cynicism in her tone.

Barto's eyes fell to the floor, an act of guilt. "We did. I wasn't on board with it initially, but eventually, I figured with the crazy gun culture here in the U.S. and the heavy nationalist backlash that came after the equality movements, protests, and boycotts of 2020, we would need to protect ourselves from armed violence. We knew our idea was radical and different. Most people don't like radical and different, they prefer to be miserable, as long as it's a familiar kind of miserable. It was a contingency move, just in case. We had no idea we would enter a full out cultural war, fought in physical, digital, and legal spaces less than a decade later. I sure as hell didn't know."

A brief moment of silence fell across the room. Only the sound of the overworked air conditioner filled stagnant air, as each person considered Janus, Cereus, its history, and how each one of them fit within the panorama of the complete picture. All of a sudden, Jinhua felt very small, like a speck of dust on a large carpet. Insignificant and vulnerable to the tiniest of forces in the universe. *History can be like science in that way. Always moving, always acting and influencing. Constantly creating and destroying.* Daniel, aware of her thoughts, smirked at her, in quiet praise of her insightful reflection.

On the other side of the room, Noe considered everything Barto had said. The facts joined the scattered pieces of the Cereus puzzle in the open floor space of her mind. She began to rotate, flip, and turn each one into its proper place, in an effort to form a complete image.

The way she saw it, her mother had been killed because she walked away from what she and Janus had built, Cereus, then later, Limnic. Janus is half human, half internet, and wants to bring about the next evolution of humanity, by separating people from their physical bodies via the internet. Thanks to his 'great filter' technology, most will be blind to the upload, because they will be either living in a fantasy world made up of past memories and future possibilities, or they will be dead; having killed themselves with an absolved conscience, or by Limnic's *very real* world army of mechs and mercs, if they put up armed resistance. With common people swept aside, he reforms society, with Cereus cultural values and structure. That new society will be made up of the new *Homo Deus*, and the old *Homo Sapiens*. Most likely, with purely biological beings like her, subordinate to the new class of super humans. *Did I miss anything? Nope, I think that sums it up.*

Even with the explanation clear in her mind, there was still one piece that she could not make sense of. One that did not fit the rest of the picture. "Why would Rodan betray Cereus? He seemed to believe in everything that it stood for…and…he cared about people…at least it seemed like he did…" Her voice quivered, jaw tensed, as if preparing for a blow from a humanoid mech.

She's been involved with him, Barto thought, *oh you poor girl.* He sighed deeply, picturing himself at her age. Dumb and in love. Relationships were hard, especially during times of conflict. "…I'm not sure. It could be that Janus penetrated his chip and manipulated him to cooperate. But, I know that he would prefer people act of their own free will. Especially when it comes to matters that he deems of great importance like Cereus." Noe's eyes looked more somber after his response. Barto had no idea what to say to make her feel better.

Li, having not noticed Noe and Barto's unspoken communication, returned the conversation to the topic of Janus. "Ah so he's a humanist after all?" Li said. His rising tone indicated intrigue.

Barto gave a loud echoing laugh. "Yes, yes he is! Of the bleeding heart type."

"Then why the focus on technological evolution and algorithmic mind control?" Li asked.

"Because he knows that great steps in the evolution of most things, whether they are species or just ideas, are usually preceded and facilitated by a period of culling. The 'filter' or event, whatever form it takes, in general causes the widespread altering or outright destruction of the old in order to pave the way for the new. Many aspects of human civilization have followed this predictable pattern. From economic systems and cultures, to religions and technologies; the old must die so that the new can prosper and flourish."

"And we're the old," Noe said, her tone defensive.

"Not necessarily. By Janus' logic those that are ready to evolve will evolve. Those that are not, will live in a state of endless bliss. Whether they choose to eternally bask in feats of the past, or live in a potential future in which all of their dreams are realized and their sins are resolved makes no difference to him. As long as they are distracted and controlled by either extreme, they will be a part of the new herd of techno zombies, unable to protest or oppose the advent of the new society *and* species that he wants to build."

"On the other hand, he knows there will be those that refuse to believe the illusion. Those that are determined to live in the strenuous life of reality instead of living in the safety of a well-designed simulation. These are the participants of the new world that he wants to be the first to evolve, then if willing, rise to lead the new society."

"How do you know all this?" Li asked, suspicion rising.

Tiny drops of sweat formed on Barto's brow as he took an abrupt step backward. His quick retreat nearly made him fall to the cold floor. "H-hey I'm not being controlled by him. I've simply spoken with him so many times over the course of the last forty years that I know how he thinks."

Li and Noe looked unconvinced. Given the battle they had survived through this morning, Barto could not fault their skepticism.

Suddenly Jinhua stood up from the glowing desk, a satisfied smile on her face. Daniel's expression mirrored hers. "I found Rodan."

The others traded shocked expressions, quickly huddling around the small screen she had been staring at during the duration of the conversation.

"The replica TransAmerica tower in San Francisco? I wonder what he's doing there…it's been abandoned for years. In fact I think it's due for demolition soon," Li scratched his head.

"He plans to broadcast the 'great filter' to the entire planet from there," Barto said with slow words. "Once that happens, he'll be able to enter and manipulate the minds of every conscious human on Earth." His voice trailed off, as the weight of his own words hit him.

"We can't let that happen," Noe said flatly. Her voice had found new fire. After her mother's murder at Janus' hands, witnessing the grisly death of Kyler, and Rodan's betrayal, she was ready for justice of the savage kind.

"How can we reach him without him being aware?" Li asked in a concerned fatherly voice. "He'll be able to read our chips and know our plans before we even act."

"No he won't Dad." Jinhua turned and faced him, yet addressed all present in the room. "I can disable your chips temporarily with an encrypted shield, so that he won't see us."

Li said nothing in response. Just beamed with pride at her in admiration of her bravery and in awe of her power, that he could not begin to try and understand.

"Ok that takes care of that." Barto said, placing his hands on his hips triumphantly. It made his large stomach protrude from the coat of his suit. "But how will we get to SF? All of your vehicles have been destroyed or disabled, Silas saw to that. And there's no way we'll all fit in that damned helicopter." He spat the word *helicopter* out with disgust.

"I think I know a driver that we can call," Noe said, a small grin on her face. She immediately pulled her device from a cargo pocket and began to dial her favorite Uber shepherd.

Just then, the door to the study inched open and the remnants of Kyler's crew filtered in. Cheeks, Bear, and Spazer stood near the doorway, their faces a mix of solemnity and unexpressed anger.

"Y'all goin' to get Janus?" Cheeks asked.

Barto nodded.

"We want in. That fucker is too dangerous to be still breathin'."

Noe acknowledged his determination with a firm nod, as she held her device to her ear.

"Well it looks like we have our team!" Barto said, raising his arms as if he were introducing a theater production. His eyes scanned the distressed and bruised faces looking back at him. All of them had been through hell in the last few weeks and months. *Five military combat veterans, two teenagers, and one old fat man. Will this be enough to stop Janus? Can we win?* The decision tree grew unexpectedly in his mind. *What should Barto do? Tell them the probability of victory? Remind them of what they were up against? More plot exposition? Stay silent?* For once, silence won the day.

Noe placed her device back in her pocket, then spoke with a clear and direct voice. "Ok people, our ride will be here in an hour. I suggest we prepare ourselves."

The others nodded dutifully. Ready to go and save the world as they knew it.

CHAPTER 56:
I AM JANUS - PART 1

From here, I can see everything. Although I never needed to be physically above it all to be able to do that. Janus analyzed the sky with a clear mind. The afternoon sun blazed through the floor to ceiling windows of the tower office. He imagined the wind gusting, just beyond the thick glass panes, forcing cool bay breeze air past the outer surface of the building. The visualization helped clear his mind, and dulled the constant throbbing in his head that he felt at all hours of every day. The mindfulness exercise brought him back into the familiar physical space of his own body.

The musty smell of the old office found its way to his nose. It smelled like an old warehouse, where the principal merchandise had been liquidated years ago. A scent he had become very accustomed to in the last few decades of his life. The skeleton of the replica TransAmerica tower breathed with stale recycled air, as if connected to an industrial sized ventilator. The walls and floor were bare; puffy pink and white insulation clung from the exposed ribs of the ceiling, and the only powered building services on the floor were the eight dangling fluorescent lights and the excessively powerful shock elevator that led to the office.

None of these things concerned Janus. He turned to a large but battered executive desk behind him and placed a hand-sized digital recorder on its scratched surface. The silver colored antique gadget displayed the number 'seven' in black digital clock font. He enjoyed its compact simplicity. A single device with one purpose. *That's how it should be.* It was a rare moment when the seas of his mind were calm, allowing him to peer beneath its choppy swells to glimpse at the stillness of blue black depths below. *I need to take advantage of this moment. There may not be much time left.* He reached forward and pressed the play button. The tranquil sound of his own voice came from the single speaker of the digital recorder.

620623 - my beloved.mp3

Lili.

What can I say about her?

When we met all those years ago at that conference in San Jose, I knew she was someone special. I just didn't know how much back then. Cereus needed someone, someone who could provide a feminine touch, that I did not have. Her mindset and background were perfect for the job. Was I attracted to her? Of course I was. But that wasn't the only thing that made me gravitate toward her. It was her spirit. It was that spark I could see within her that was different from others. It made me want her on my team. Of course, I wanted her to come of her own will. I don't like forcing people to do things that they don't want or are not ready to take on themselves, for such a vital role. However, I was confident that the next time I saw her after our initial meeting, she would accept my proposal.

When she attended Cereus's first meeting in the town of Byron just a couple of weeks later, she had a panic attack when I first arrived. I could see she was afraid, very afraid. And I can't blame her for being in such a state. Meeting in an abandoned building miles away from the city that she knows is going to be frightening for anyone. When I saw her, balled up, shaking in fear, I saw her trauma and pain in vivid detail. I *felt* it, like a heavy weight placed upon my chest while my lungs fought to inflate for air. I saw it all. The broken paradise of Hawaii, her nightmare on the streets of San Francisco, every sexual encounter, every time she pretended to be someone she was not just to survive. Her entire history was revealed to me, and I wanted to help her sift through it to find the truth in her that I saw buried beneath the pain. I wanted to reach the accord that evolution demanded of me. And after that meeting we did just that.

From that moment in time, she honored our arrangement. Just as I suspected she would. Over the next several years and decades, we shared everything together: Cereus' successes, its failures, our personal triumphs, and private frustrations; all were open books for both of us to read at any time. We, of course, shared physical intimacy off and on throughout the years.

Our bond touched me in a profound way. It made me believe in something outside of myself. That even in the vastness of the cosmos and infinity of cyberspace, I could find all of that within one beating heart, with one person, was astonishing, and a truly rare gift. I loved her. And that love lives on in the form of our daughter.

[Pause for ten seconds]

Oh if Lili could see her now, she would see that she is all of her and none of me. She has her mother's beauty and fighting spirit. Both traits I loved about Lili. It is almost criminal that the world may never know, it was Lili and I who brought her into this world. That the evidence of our otherworldly bond lives on in flesh and spirit. Though my daughter is not aware of my presence, I do love her as I loved Lili.

[Janus clears his throat, then pauses for fifteen seconds]

When I killed Lili…it was a decision that I did not take likely. I recognized the gravity of my action and I willed myself to feel…something. I wanted to feel but somehow could not bring myself to any kind of meaningful emotion. The consequentialist in me knew that the means justified the end. That my love, as significant as it was, was not more significant than the entirety of humankind's evolution. So I made the choice to end her life so that others could evolve.

In that way, Lili was a necessary step and an integral piece of humankind's evolution. For that reason, I love her even more in death, than I did when she was alive.

620630 - **最好的朋友**.mp3

There are few people in this world whom I would consider to be family in the deepest sense of the word. When I speak of family, I am referring to anyone that you feel like you know intimately. Those few special souls with whom you grow, experience life's blessings, and go through tender moments together. For me, Barto Khuni is one of those people that I would consider to be family in the metaphorical sense of the word.

Since I was very small, he's always been there to help me with my struggles. Our friendship turned into a partnership, then into a business relationship during which we occasionally sparred on various issues related to Cereus and its core values. Although I consider him a dear friend, he is in no way my equal. Though he may act like he is. [Janus laughs]. He knows where he stands in this context.

I regard him as a younger brother of sorts. And yes I do call him 'brother'. We've had disagreements over the years in policy, in philosophy, and in the direction that we wanted to take the organization, yet this did not bother me. I welcome his, at times, formidable logic, and find his clumsy nature charming.

However, as with all family members, you cannot share everything with them, because you know that they will not see things as you do all of the time. And I see all things. I see the alpha and omega of human history. And his sometimes myopic scope cannot compare with my perspective. I must admit, his knowledge and theories are wider than most of his contemporaries, given the narrow looking glass through which he observes the world. I often find his viewpoint entertaining and at times necessary. He provides a counterbalance to my admittedly lofty ideas and vision. Unfortunately, as the years have gone on, that balance has become more and more out of step with our need for evolution, and my place in it. I am going where he cannot, which may force me to leave him, my brother, behind.

620701 - regret.mp3

In nature there are animals and beings that are inferior and superior to others. While all creatures serve their unique purpose and function within the evolutionary process and sustainment of ecosystems, some play a more vital role than others. The ant is lesser than the human in the biological pecking order. This is an extreme example, but it is a fitting metaphor when it comes to my viewpoint for certain people within the ecosystem of human society.

All people are *not* made equal. Equality of all human beings was the common philosophy of early twenty-first century thinking. This belief flourished thanks to the advent of social media at the beginning of the century. Overnight, voices that had been muzzled for tens of thousands of years were free to speak their minds, even if they had nothing useful to say. This egalitarian culture fueled social and cultural movements throughout the first three decades of the century. Some voices greatly contributed to the advancement of the collective social fabric, while the majority mired it in tribalistic polarization, which led to nationalistic elections worldwide, and eventually armed conflict on a global scale.

My point is, certain people are more important than others. When I think of examples of people that are lesser, Silas comes to mind. I never respected the man. His money was a means to an end at the outset, and combined with my financial assets, helped Cereus survive during our vulnerable small business beginnings. But it could not purchase selflessness or sacrifice, two things he sorely lacked. As with many old world money rich capitalists, Silas derived his self-image, and power from his material wealth. This is not the primary reason I disliked him. Nor did I loathe him because he was unspeakably privileged or because he was a pompous asshole at times. I hated him primarily because he had gifts, talents, and intelligence which he ultimately chose to squander on various ventures and causes that were not in alignment with the Cereus, my personal philosophy, or *any* ethical creed for that matter. The man had no values outside of preserving his own flesh and material possessions.

But such is the nature of human interactions. They are often chosen in expediency, and reflect the demands of particular snapshots in our personal history. Rarely are they the result of deliberate choice or insightful premeditation. Such is the case with my relationship with Silas. In the end, I was bound to him by legal matters, contracts, land constrictions, and all of the trappings of old world capitalist society that were necessary entrapments at the beginning. It has been frustrating over the years to deal with him, even with his limited participation with the organization for the past several years. In my mind, the biggest waste is for someone to use their money or their talent in an unscrupulous manner. This is, to me, the biggest failing that a person can have as a human.

[Janus exhales a heavy sigh.]

Choosing to partner with him is one of my biggest regrets in life. He tried to kill me today, putting up laughable resistance after he came to the stunning realization that he would lose. That he was nothing compared to me. After he was subdued, seeing him there lying on the floor, his pants soiled in his own fear-loosened urine, I wanted to kill him. I really did. But, I fought down the urge, and proceeded with my initial plan. It is my hope that his new role as my living combat weapon will be mutually beneficial for us both. He gains a new body, I, a hateful mind to use for the purpose of evolution. If the experiment is a failure and he dies, at least I won't have to concern myself with money matters related to his inflated ego ever again.

CHAPTER 57:
I AM JANUS - PART 2

Janus stood behind the desk. Had someone entered, he would have looked like an executive taking a call on speakerphone waiting to hear a quarterly update. But there was no phone. No one to hear the call. Only the sound of dead air during which the old device searched for the next audio file to be played.

Outside in the cloudless sky, the position of the sun had shifted by five degrees, continuing its daily descent toward the horizon. Janus had glanced behind him, and made the quick trigonometric calculation in his head. *Five degrees less time.* Rodan would be arriving within the hour. His device buzzed with updates from his new partner. Janus had no need to look at the notifications, he already knew what was happening. He also knew, his time alone was quickly coming to an end. His mental firewalls would need to come down soon, to allow humanity's ceaseless flow of data generation to cut through him again, whittling him down like water droplets on stone. A slow but inevitable process.

He cleared his mind once again. Ready to commune with the only person in the world he felt completely at home with. Tranquil features colored his face as he reached forward to rotate the black volume dial, in order to hear himself more clearly.

490924 - conflict.mp3

The other day I was thinking about the greatest teachers throughout human history. You know like, Confucius, Gandhi, Noam Chomsky, Aristotle, and others. Many of these teachers were great, not because they taught directly. Rather, they found tremendous success because they taught through story.

What is a story? It is a sequence of events with some type of protagonist. There is a setting in which the events occur, and where the main character struggles to achieve his or her desired objective. There are also supporting characters, and maybe even other sorts of fantastical components. In addition to all of the aforementioned parts of a story, one common thread weaves all of these elements together.

Conflict.

Without it, there is no story. This crucial factor is what drives the characters to act; is what pushes the plot forward; is what provides the person experiencing the tale with the necessity to eventually reach the end of the story, and hopefully, reach the lesson that the teachers want to impart. People want to see how the conflict is resolved. It is human nature to want to *know*, for knowing's sake.

From this perspective, it could be said that humanity's greatest lessons are learned through conflict. Fighting against something, *anything*, is in our DNA. It is very difficult to internalize a lesson without having struggled for some period of time to obtain it.

So it is through this lens that I think of Limnic. Its purpose was to serve as a memory aid for the general public. When I was younger I was naive to think that humans could learn without story, or without conflict. While some did learn Cereus' social philosophy through exposure, most didn't. They needed the lesson paired with strife in order to commit it deeply to memory. And few things are were more memorable to the fragile psyche of early twenty-first century Western society than terrorism.

In his book, *21 Lessons for the 21st Century*, author and historian Yuval Noah Harari wrote about terrorism. He said the success or failure of terrorism depends on us, the people. When I say us, I mean *them*, in this case, because I am not one of *them*. [Janus laughs] His point was, terrorists are so weak in combat power and political influence compared to their well organized and equipped foes, that they must put on a well-staged performance to *appear* to have more strength and power than they actually possess, which is little. They are the fly in the glass shop. As small as they are, incapable of tipping even the smallest vase.

They call me a terrorist. They say Limnic is a terrorist organization. This is only half true. I am a teacher, constructing lessons most people will never forget. Old world culture will make films, write books, songs, plays, and post videos of Limnic's activities, which will make my lessons objectives that much more… 'sticky', to use popular old world vernacular. I am but one fly, recruiting billions of other flies to enter the ears of a thousand bulls to shake old world society's brittle foundation. When a sufficient amount of glassware has been destroyed, then the common person will truly learn the Cereus way of life.

620812 - cog in the machine.mp3

Often in old-world thinking, people were compared to cogs in a machine. Indeed this was probably a fitting metaphor for the functioning of old world capitalism, especially in the 19th and 20th centuries. The reigning philosophy of those times was that people should be and feel as interchangeable as possible in order for the insatiable machine to continue producing.

This mindset dehumanized and stole the humanity of millions. [Janus clears his throat] This process was so well concealed by the master hand of the capitalist system, that the common citizen unknowingly contributed to his or her own diminishment as a conscious being. Most were so dependent on the system for wages, survival for themselves and their families, and most importantly, their very sense of self, that if removed from it, they were little more than empty vessels. Hollow, with no idea how to fill themselves without the binding social construct. Their only desire was to keep contributing, consuming, and eventually dying, by the very machinations that siphoned all of their time, energy, and attention for their entire lives.

Rodan is one of the soulless masses. He is desperate for something, but he has no idea what it is. His headspace has been too consumed by corporate culture and -isms to be able to see himself. His mirror reflects a static image, void of a true reflection. He sees himself as the shining cog in the machine. But to the ever watchful eye of human culture, he is replaceable. A name to be swapped out as soon as he breaks down and is no longer useful.

When someone like Rodan realizes his place in the great machine, he feels an overwhelming need for survival through expression. They enter a conflict of the self. The need for status, money, and material wealth clashes against the new *true* self, recently reborn. Rodan was in the midst of that struggle when I found him. In such a state, it was easy to sow seeds of doubt into his debilitated psyche. I made no manipulation of his mind to get him to join my side. It was not necessary. When I approached him in that tired old city after the battle his weary mind was so visible that even without my powers I could see the desires of his heart. He wanted to be found. To be given a new mission. I provided him with one. And he will play his part in the battles to come.

620101 - New Year Thoughts.mp3

When I was a young man, my parents told me about my powers. They told me that I was different. That all of me wasn't there in my child body, but was all around us. I was only six years old at the time. How could a six-year-old understand the concept of existing in two different places at once? I couldn't do it. It wasn't until two years later, that I began to understand how truly different I was from others.

I started by experimenting with and manipulating small devices with my mind. DVD players, televisions, and game consoles provided me with practice in the beginning. Eventually, I moved on to larger devices like home security systems, early self-driving cars, and then, of course, to the network itself. Jumping between my mundane physical reality, to the vibrant digital world became commonplace for me. I watched the network grow from within. Saw as its tendrils expanded from its humble beginnings, to what it has become today, which is bigger than even the physical space that we inhabit now. Infinitely complex, and undecipherable to a common human without the help of artificial intelligence and machine learning assistance.

After I graduated from high school, I wasn't speaking with Barto much because I was busy with various financial pursuits, yes, but also because I was trying to save the world. I was using my powers for what I thought was good. I would go on the network and find those in some type of distress, be it financial or emotional or something else, and I would try to encourage them and help them. A boost in a bank account here, a kind word there, meant a lot to certain people, especially when they least suspected it. I was just trying to be of service, in any way I could.

But something changed in me shortly after 2020, during the time of the coronavirus pandemic. It really moved me in a different way. I saw human suffering on a scale that I had not known before. I saw the growth in the festering of hate on the social media outlets of the time, the death of hope, and the rise in nihilistic paranoia of the *other* in many online spaces. I tried to help and be of service to as many as I could, but my powers were not enough to calm the silent shriek from the planet that only *I* could hear from within the invisible network.

I could feel myself becoming weaker in the physical and digital realms. My body was dying. I needed to rest, so for a year, I disconnected from the internet and lived an average life. During that time I had no need for work so I went south to San Antonio, Texas. It was a big city with a small town ambiance. I lost myself among the simpletons and bumpkins of that metropolistic village. In the end, it was the perfect place to recuperate my strength. I read books, took a lover, and kept to myself.

My period away from the internet taught me something. I was reminded that everything online can be found offline, in a purer form. I also learned that society as most common people knew it was in shambles. It seemed like all people I met, were in some way, at odds with others who did not look or think like them. Men against women, Latinos versus Blacks, gay against straight, everyone against the government; people seemed to be more defined by who or what they hated, rather than through their shared humanity. This was something that I never forgot. Probably one of the most important lessons of my life. It was because of this that I developed the framework for Cereus' core values, and after my internet free year was over, I contacted Barto to see if he would join me in bringing my idea to life. The rest, as they say, is history.

620907 - version two.mp3

They're coming now. I can see their determination, sense their anger and pain. I feel it. It brings a burning sensation to my skin. They…want my blood, and my life.

[Five second pause]

I can understand why.

They have lost much, all of them. But they don't understand what role that they could potentially play in the future of humankind and its evolutionary process. They don't understand their importance to me. They are not ordinary people. They are the special kind, who are willing to give all in order to win and survive. I can feel it. They are…

[Janus makes a guttural sound]

Oh? Something has happened…what is this? I cannot see them, now. I've been blocked, denied entry into their thoughts. There is someone doing this…but who? How?

[Ten seconds of silence]

Ah…I see now. It is her, the girl, the teenager, my clone, my version number two, the other me, she comes. Jinhua Ma. She has become very powerful indeed in such a short amount of time. I didn't expect this so quickly. But the evolutionary process does produce its anomalies and exceptionalisms, and she is definitely of a rare breed. She has masked all of their digital signatures. Only someone with tremendous power would be able to do such a thing.

I must be cautious of this one. I must find a way to help her understand her place, not only as an evolved being, but as beneath me. I helped unlock her power, because I wanted her to evolve and join me. And now she aims to confront me with her newfound strength. So be it. Her powers are raw and untested, but I have a feeling that very soon I will meet with her and the others face to face. When that time comes, they will finally know the complete truth of their purpose in this new society and in this new world.

The recording ended. At that precise moment, he glanced up at the floor display over the shock elevator doors. The number on the display showed '1', meaning someone had stepped on the elevator, and would arrive in the office within a minute or less. It was Rodan; he was ready to see this through to the end. To claim the kind of glory and legacy people of his station were rarely allowed in the confines of the old world.

Janus picked up the digital recorder and placed it in a small black bag on the floor behind the desk. He had heard enough. He knew what he had to do. Then one by one, he began to lower his mental firewalls. First the data began as a trickle, then rapidly evolved into a tidal wave of endless flow. Even after a lifetime of jumping in and out of cyberspace, the onslaught of water caused him to momentarily freeze, as if he were an operating system tasked to execute too many commands at once. He stood motionless, while his nervous system registered all of humanity's pain, joy, cruelty, and sadness as physical pain. Pain he had carried with him for his entire life.

CHAPTER 58:
THE SHEPHERD'S FLOCK

"It's good to see you again, Noe." Van looked up at her standing in front of the sliding door of the blue fifteen passenger van. She smiled in response, happy that her reliable Uber shepherd had responded to her message.

It had been months since their first Uber ride together. Although all great rides did come to an end, great acquaintanceships didn't have to. Van wore his characteristic black-rimmed reading glasses, a pair of *very* faded jeans, and a button shirt with small red and white squares on it. She recalled it had been one of his back up shirts; crisply pressed, and hanging from the glove box of his auto car. It was a silly detail to remember, but it helped to take her mind off of what they were about to do. What they *had* to do.

"Likewise, Van," Noe replied. They exchanged an awkward hug before Noe rejoined the others in loading supplies into the rear of the van. She and the others crisscrossed each other loading all manner of equipment, weapons, and other items for the looming confrontation against Limnic and Janus. The bustle of activity gave the house a military base like feel. Everyone moved at 1.5x speed as they worked, in nervous anticipation of the battle ahead. Noe eased back into the familiar rhythm, only pausing to have brief exchanges with the others to ensure logistical efficiency. Van followed her like a lost puppy. His excitable eyes flicked from here to there, in an attempt to analyze the expedient movements of serious-faced strangers. He began to feel tense just by being there.

"So uhh, what is all this?" he asked timidly. "It looks like…" Bear slammed a box of ammunition into the van, nearly running Van over in the process. He grunted like an angry animal, clearly annoyed by his presence, then lumbered back to the house to retrieve another load.

Van continued to follow Noe as she helped Li load a case of water into the back of the vehicle. "It looks like you guys are going to war or something…"

He surveyed the aftermath of what had been a bloody conflict on the front lawn of the house. The people walked through crimson stains of dried blood and around broken mechanoid parts as if they were not even there. The scene disturbed him. While he somewhat regretted getting involved in something that was clearly over his head and beyond his understanding, he also wanted to help Noe out.

When he received her message, he nearly dropped the large book he was reading on his toes, jerking his foot away in time to avoid the blow. *What a shock that she even remembered me?* He could feel blood throbbing at his temples as he worked like an author to draft the perfect response, preening and trimming excess words and voice emoticons. He didn't want to come off too creepy, needy, clingy, or cringy. He wanted to come off as a nice friend. *Wait? Are we even friends after one ride?* He shook off the thought and kept drafting his reply. *Sound friendly, but keep the door open for romance in the future.* It was hard to strike the perfect balance without a draft or an outline to work off of. Twenty minutes later, the message was sent and timestamped. An hour later, there he was, standing in a burned and bloody front lawn of this magnificent house, as a handful of mercenaries, two teenagers, and two old men prepared to go to war. "What the hell happened here?" He asked Noe, raising his voice above the noises of militaristic preparation. He felt like a journalist attempting to collect information for an exclusive story in a warzone. At any moment he could be swept aside and left behind for dead.

Noe had not filled him in on the details. She had told him it was a personal favor, and that she needed his help. That was all. She knew that he liked her, and if it had been another day, a better day; she *might* acknowledge that she liked him a little bit, too. But there was no time for that now. No time for lengthy details about everything that had happened. Just time for action.

She deposited a case of miniaturized synthetic rations on top of the case of water, before turning to address him. "It's a long story. But the short version is there's a guy who wants to reboot society and turn a large portion of the human race into digital slaves via mind control in order to ultimately evolve the human race. We're gonna go kill him now," she said in a dry tone.

Van laughed uncomfortably in response, as he analyzed her face. She looked much more low-spirited than before, a world away from how he remembered her when they first met. Her eyes were slightly red, not like *I-stayed-up-all-night-binging-a-series* red, more like, *someone-just-died-and-I'm-grieving*, red. There was no sign of the brightness he recalled from the Uber ride. Only a flat expression, with a hint of cold detachment in her voice. "Oh daamn, you're not…joking at all. Are you?" The smile shrank from his face, leaving only confusion, doubt, and dozens of new questions that would probably remain unanswered. Noe's narrowed eyebrows told him that what she said was the truth. "Sooo, you're going to save the world?"

She considered his question as she brought a water bottle to her lips and took a quick gulp of it. It tasted like rubber, as if it had been stored in a hot dry place for a very long time. "I guess we are. I hadn't thought of it that way. But yeah, that's the way it is."

Van made a fist and thrust it into the air, letting out an enthusiastic whoop at the same time. "Wow! That's awesome! I-I always wanted to be a part of something like this." Noe looked at him and suppressed a smile. His energy was refreshing after the events of the last twenty-four hours. Van continued to follow her as she returned to the large mansion to gather more food. "I mean, I know *I'm* not gonna be doing any fighting, but I at least get to drive you down there. So I can help you in that way!"

Noe sighed, laughing softly. "Yeah, you can." As she began to follow her invisible vector toward her next microtask, she heard Van call her from behind. "Noe."

She turned, just in time to see Cheeks brush past Van in the mansion's front doorway. The smaller man gave way to the larger man at the very last moment. "Watch the fuck out dude!" He eyed Van out of the corner of his eyes, flashed an inquisitive look, then continued his path into the house. It looked like they were almost done loading everything.

The interruption over, Noe refocused on Van, "What is it?"

Van scratched his head, "I just wanted to say thanks for calling me. I'm not sure what all this is, but if I can even play a small part in it to help, then that's enough for me."

Noe's lips turned up into a smile, "I'm happy to have you here. It's a big help."

"Hey, I'm *your* Uber shepherd after all. I go where the flock needs me."

Noe laughed softly with joy, then nodded in understanding.

"I'm gonna go make sure everything's good to go with the van." With that he turned and walked back outside, smiling to himself. *I made her laugh!*

*   *   *

Shaking her head, lingering thoughts began to swarm in Noe's mind. It was Rodan again. How could he betray her? After everything they had gone through together. Her mother's death and the bleak period after, North Bloomfield, the car ride, the passionate sex; had he been using her the entire time?

Jinhua's voice brought her back to reality. She stood in the doorway of the mansion eyeing Noe with a steady gaze, "Everything's ready."

"Alright," Noe said. She shoved the cardboard box marked "Rodan" into the bottom corner of a distant closet in her head. The box was not large, but it was heavy. Then feeling better she walked to the door. As she made her way past Jinhua, a new curiosity entered her mind. She turned toward the girl and asked, "How are you handling your…powers?"

"I feel like they come and go. Sometimes I can control them easily and other times, I feel like it may as well be another person pulling the strings," Jinhua responded, her eyes stared at something far away.

"Are you afraid?" Noe asked.

"Of what?"

"Of your power, of Janus…of yourself?"

Jinhua's eyes became evasive, her gaze falling to the floor by her right foot. She noticed terrible scratches and scuffs on the once flawless and smooth tile in the entryway. In the corner of her eye, her sky blue ripboard pole entered her vision. It reminded her of simpler times, of Harpreet, of her life before all this mess began. "Yeah…I'm afraid of all of the above."

Noe placed a hand on her shoulder, and offered a soft squeeze. "Don't worry, when the time comes, you won't have to face him completely alone. We'll help you as much as we can." With that she made her way to join Li and the others gathering over by the van.

Jinhua knew that Noe was just as afraid as she was. Most of the information she had gathered from her chip, but the rest came from innate human intuition. She reminded herself that when the time came to face Janus, it would probably come down to a duel between the two of them. Doubt began to close its grip around her throat. She felt momentarily paralyzed by fear.

I never wanted these powers! I just wanted to go to space camp and be an astrophysicist or an astronaut! I'm just a teenage girl whose magical powers just showed up this morning. How can I possibly stop or even kill a man who has had the same power for his entire life? How can I kill someone? How can I protect Dad and the others?

Her thoughts raced uncontrollably, speeding through her troubled brain. Only the voice of Li shattered the cascading procession of negative self-talk. "Jinhua…" Her eyes blinked open. She realized her eyelids hurt from straining them shut.

"It's going to be ok." Li said reassuringly. "If it becomes too much, just say so. We don't have to do it this way. We can find another way to beat him."

She considered his words. Conflicted between self-preservation and the desire to defeat this menace who threatened humanity with godlike power.

"No Dad, you and I know that you won't be able to beat him without my help."

Li nodded an acknowledgement, and patted her arm supportively. Jinhua appreciated the familiar contact, with the

knowledge that it might be the last time they would be able to share a
father-daughter moment.

CHAPTER 59: VAN TALK

"Everybody ready!?" Van yelled over his shoulder.

"Yes!" All responded from behind him.

"Ok! Here we go!"

The oversized vehicle lurched and shook as Van struggled to exit the ruined front yard of the house. He would put the van in reverse before nearly running over something, then repeat the process again when attempting to move forward. After two minutes of starts and stops, he found a satisfactory path through the yard and inched the van toward the street, careful to avoid the remains of the once imposing iron security gate. In the third row of seats, closest to the back, Barto and Li nearly bumped heads as the van suddenly jolted to the side. Barto gripped the thin leather seats to prevent from falling onto his fellow elderly seatmate.

"Sorry about that!" Van called from the front, "Didn't see that severed robotic arm in the way. And it's hard to see out of the back with all the gear there." Sweat began to tingle under his armpits. "I'll just go around it now, and have you down in SF safe and sound in no time." They began to move again.

Smashed into the first row of seats directly behind Van sat Cheeks, Spazer, and Bear. Cheeks, jaw clenched in irritation, using an audible whisper said, "Can this Asian kid even drive? Goddamn foo' gonna kill us befo' we even get to Janus."

"Hey! I heard that! And yes, this Asian kid *can* drive, so you just…" he wanted to tell him to shut his big fat mouth up, but then he noted the angry unhappy eyes, and thought of the battlefield. Something in this man was in pain, and he did not want to contribute to it. "You just be quiet! I'll get you there in one piece." Next to Van in the front passenger seat, Noe flashed him an encouraging look. Van, bolstered by her uplifting face, felt his confidence swell, which allowed him to guide the van to the entrance of the property, then to the smooth paved road. Behind him Cheeks huffed frustration. Spazer looked at him with sad eyes. Next to him, Bear sat with a level head, eyes closed, already in pre-combat ritual mode. *The faces of war are different up close,* Van thought, viewing the three of them through his rearview mirror.

Directly behind the warrior trio sat Jinhua and Daniel. She was still getting used to the scratchy dark green pants and shirt of the field gear her father had outfitted her in. It felt too big in some areas, too loose in others. The end result was discomfort, that she labored to block out of her mind. She was working to mask all of their digital signatures from Janus. The exercise felt like holding one finger in the air to test the wind direction. A small movement, that if held for an extended amount of time could become physically exhausting.

Next to her, Daniel placed a warm hand on her knee. He was helping her with the task. His systems acted as a booster for the shielding process. It not only widened the radius of it and increased its effectiveness by 150%, it also lessened the cognitive load of the task. His assistance served as sturdy support for her raised arm, making it possible for her to maintain the position for much longer than she could ever hope to on her own.

Behind her, Barto observed the two youths, both eyebrows raising at the sight of Daniel's hand on her knee. Unsolicited by anyone, he commented, "I see you two have bonded quite well."

Jinhua, startled, turned in her seat to face him. "Yeah, I guess we have."

"Marvelous! It seems he is a cyborg of great efficiency then. I haven't seen one in many years. Especially one this, uh, good looking." Barto laughed at his own awkward observation.

Daniel chuckled as well.

"How did you know he was a cyborg?" Jinhua asked.

Barto scoffed. "When we were getting ready to leave, I saw the way he moved and picked things up. It was very human-*like*, but not even teenage boy hormones would allow a boy to lift two cases of field rations with one hand."

Daniel averted his eyes self-consciously. "You saw that?"

Barto nodded, clearly proud he had solved the mystery on his own. "I did. Your handshake was quite strong as well. It felt like my hand was in a vice grip!" Next to him, Li chuckled under his breath.

Outside, the van exited Yuba City, and the scenery changed to scattered farmland, with the occasional cluster of suburban houses sprinkled in between. Patchy clouds took turns attempting to block the late afternoon sun. The effect caused Li's face to brighten and dim as the van moved down the road at a comfortable speed, as if someone were playing with the brightness on a monitor, in search of the optimal setting.

Barto continued, "I wish *someone*," he lightly nudged Li, "had told me what you were before, instead of letting me feel like an idiot. But it's no big deal."

A brief silence fell among them. Li closed his eyes, still worn out from the battle and all of the other events of the day. Just as he felt himself beginning to doze off, Barto's voice invaded his ears. His was a voice shouting in the library, it was impossible not to hear it whenever he decided to speak.

Barto leaned forward, hands on the seat in front of him. "Did you know all synthetic humans or cyborgs have two primary directives?"

Jinhua shook her head. "Really?"

"Yes. The first is to be as connected with humans as possible, meaning they should act and behave in ways that are endearing to humans whenever practical. This strengthens their bond with us and helps us to trust them for more intimate tasks, such as caring for elderly parents or taking care of babies and children."

Jinhua blinked rapidly, "Oh wow, I had no idea."

"It's true, it's true." Barto continued, unsolicited, "The second is to always be striving to become a better machine. They are programmed to maximize efficiency and master their own systems, in order to perform their given objective in the best way possible. Cyborg efficiency is measured on the Dryer scale from one to five. Five being optimal efficiency."

A look of intrigue painted Jinhua's face. Li wore the same expression, though he already knew all of this.

"Wow, so cyborgs are programmed to connect with humans and be as efficient as possible? Pretty fascinating," Jinhua said, her eyes floated in Daniel's direction. He smiled warmly at her.

"It is!" Barto said. "The original designers of cyborg programming met in 2030 in Brussels to sign the Synthetic Human International Treaty," Barto laughed, "I'm not sure if the acronym SHIT was intentional or not, but it sure as hell made it memorable."

All occupants of the van laughed. Their interest had been piqued by Barto's charismatic words.

"The top minds in artificial intelligence, robotics, world leaders from most developed countries, and a handful of other specialists, developed the treaty to outline the international rules of engagement for the design and implementation of artificial humans. The end game for most nations was to prevent other nations from developing super thinking robots that would outclass their rivals' economy. Everything had to be as fair as possible."

"So it came down to money?" Daniel asked, speaking for the first time.

Barto grinned, "Most things do. At least they did in old world thinking. They also wanted to prevent countries from developing killer cyborgs and using them to wage war or for other nefarious purposes."

"Is that right!?" Cheeks said, "Then what the hell were those killer death machines we fought back there?"

Barto shook his head, face sullen, "Just like any international treaty, not everyone likes to play by the rules. When it comes to technology, once the genie is out of the bottle, there's no stuffing it back in. Various governments had been working on developing artificial humans for military purposes for decades. It was only a matter of time before tech from here, China, Germany, and other major powers reached the lesser endowed nations and bad actors around the world. Now the black market for cyborgs is enormous and akin to the Latin American drug trade. Difficult to pin down, and impossible to dismantle completely. It would take an extremely coordinated effort among multiple nations to shut it down, which most governments have little economic interest in cooperating on."

A hush came over the occupants of the van as they considered the Founder's words. Only the sound rattling of supplies in the rear of the vehicle filled the air. They were jammed in traffic in Roseville. As usual, the exit near the popular Galleria Mall was backed up and slow. It would take them longer than predicted to get through Sacramento in the afternoon traffic.

Jinhua considered Barto's words about cyborgs. Then she pictured the humanoid menaces she had just seen fighting in front of her house. They had been empty faced puppets, designed to murder humans with cold efficiency. Just like the T-1000 in the old The Terminator movies, their only objective was dealing death to their given target. This was the antithesis of Daniel, who was, in her eyes, a perfectly balanced creation. Not too human, not too robotic. She thought maybe all of humanity would benefit from this kind of balancing, to prevent the tuggings of biology from pulling them toward baser instincts and drives. It was the first time she thought of her unique situation as superior to others. She did not feel shame or fear at the notion, only a cool-headed reassurance that as a half-human, half-cyber person she was truly free. Free from her inherited lizard brain, free from the strings of flawed human ethics and design. It was a feeling she shared with one other person in the world. This thought *did* scare her.

There was always a price to be paid for freedom, and that price for her was being associated with Janus as a fellow evolved human being.

CHAPTER 60:
CONTEMPLATION ON THE
EVE OF BATTLE

Rodan stood in all black tactical field gear, taking in the view of San Francisco hundreds of feet below him. At his location on the 47th floor of the long abandoned replica Transamerica Pyramid, he could discern little movement or noise beneath him. No cars. No sirens. None of the universal sounds of city life reached his ears, and he preferred it that way. After two minutes peering out of the window, his vision began to tunnel and his palms erupted with dots of anxiety sweat. Working in the confines of the California state capitol building for all these years, he had forgotten how afraid of heights he was. Around a high place, his mind behaved like a Tilt-A-Whirl carnival ride, tossing him this way and that, always off balance and spinning. The resulting disorientation made him afraid of slipping over the edge, even if he were standing perfectly still. That familiar sensation came to him as he looked out the windows of Janus' office. He backed away from the dizzying panorama before him and began to wander around the office, in an effort to kill time before Janus returned.

It looked like a bomb had detonated in the room. The explosion had ripped the ceiling and the walls open and blown all of the furniture out of the glass windows, having spared only the large solid office desk. The smell of the place reminded him of his grandmother's house, musty and cold. The combination of high humidity, poor ventilation, and blackness had created an odor that was less a smell and more a living presence that had haunted the house's tiny rooms. It had resided in the walls and torn at his clothes at all hours of the day. Whenever he left the house, in his wild boyhood imagination, whatever it was, had followed him home, like a ghost floating behind him. The smell of Janus' office brought that old feeling back. He wasn't sure what caused him more anxiety. The fear that he might never leave that building or that the 'presence' might never leave him. Both scenarios bothered him more than he wanted to admit.

After taking a lap around the office, he stood beside the desk and looked out of the window again. This time he avoided peering downward only to find his gaze fixed on Alcatraz Island far in the distance. The lonely prison turned museum reminded him of the isolation he had experienced since he had taken command of Cereus. He too had been imprisoned. Not by handcuffs, gilded and shining, but by rusty shackles doused in a slow acting venom. Poisoned and bleeding, he had been debuffed beyond saving. It was only a matter of time before he succumbed to his sordid condition. *I was doomed to go down with the ship.*

Rodan considered his actions in the last several weeks and felt a small wave of guilt. If he were still a cop, he might be found guilty of treason. He recalled the first lines of U.S. criminal code 18 Section 2381.

Whoever, owing allegiance to the United States, levies war against them or adheres to their enemies, giving them aid and comfort within the United States or elsewhere, is guilty of treason and shall suffer death…

Rodan scoffed. *Suffer death, I was already a dead man.* The thought of the others popped into his head. Li, Noe, and Jinhua. The now deceased Kyler and his crew. In his flight away from Li's mansion, in the middle of their fight with Silas, Rodan made no attempt to look back and check on his former comrades. He had only hastened to a designated rendezvous point Janus had arranged for him behind the house, outside of Li's property. From there, with great effort, he climbed over the relatively low wall, then entered the waiting auto car.

As it transported him south toward San Francisco, Rodan attempted to rest. Between passing messages to Janus, still performing his Cereus duties (so as not to arouse suspicion), and the unexpected sex with Noe, he was beyond exhausted. Even so, he found himself unable to completely relax. Images of his lifetime friendship with Li, Noe's nakedness, her trusting gaze, and tender caress, bombarded him. The pictures forced his eyelids open, robbing him of peace and rest. Alone, his muddled thoughts as his only companion, he reminded himself why he had followed Janus. *I'm saving all of us. I'm helping humanity move forward. I'm being of use.* The three statements became his slogan. They passed through his brain, and even his lips at pious intervals. As the autocar traveled down the road, he had repeated the mantra to himself, until the echo and impact of his actions became silent, leaving only the sense of rightness, as his perhaps-delusional filter completely colored his reality.

They don't understand. They can't. But they will soon.

Then the elevator door opened, and Janus glided into the room. His eyes and sunken face held a mysterious smile. "You're right, Rodan. They *will* understand." Rodan turned to face him. Even though he admired Janus' audacious vision of the future, he still had not gotten used to having his mind read.

Janus walked to the desk and began to concentrate on a peculiar looking device sitting on top of it. He had told Rodan when he arrived that it was a micro quantum computer. Rodan had heard of quantum computing, but had never seen one so small before. This model was about the size of a larger than average wine box, roughly 9 inches in height, with a 4 inch by 4-inch base. Instead of a single bottle of wine, it housed the intricate components of one of mankind's greatest technical achievements. The top three inches of the case were solid black and emitted an odd noise that sounded like the intro bars of a highly synthesized musical track. It was locomotive in its cadence, with steady repetition, and only lacked a bassline and a creative young rapper to turn it into an enjoyable song.

From where he stood, Rodan could see the guts of the machine through its glass panels around the four sides of the computer. Suspended from the top of the box's interior, were tiny silver rods. The rods were fastened at precise points around a circular copper toned plate. There were three plates in all, with dozens of tiny coils twisted between each plate, like veins, running up and down the entire set up. The whole contraption looked like an upside down wedding cake hanging from a ceiling in a glass container, sans frosting and a corny cake topper.

Janus interacted with the machine via a keyboard on his device. After a few adjustments, his business concluded, he set the device down and turned toward Rodan, who continued to marvel at the existence of such alien technology.

Janus spoke. "This replica of the original Transamerica Pyramid was constructed in the image of the old. It experienced its moment of prosperity, and eventually fell into ruin and decay. Now, so too has the human experience of old world society run its course. I will help your misguided friends to see the error of their perspective and understand that my way is the only and best way forward for all of humanity."

Rodan stood in silent contemplation. He studied Janus' face, wondering if this man would play a key role in humanity's survival, or push it one step closer to the abyss of destruction. He hoped it was the former.

Suddenly, hard features of concentration drew themselves onto Janus' face. His arms loosened at his sides and his eyes fluttered erratically. If Rodan had not seen him in this state before, he would have thought that he was having a seizure while standing up. But he knew better. He knew he was reaching across the infinite space of the vast digital network that sustained all of their lives. Watching, looking, collecting. After a minute, his body returned to its naturally rigid state. Hints of fatigue from his constantly overworked mind shown through. Rodan took note of it. *Even he's human, just like the rest of us.*

"They're coming," Janus said.

"Of course they are. We knew it was only a matter of time." Rodan's thoughts flashed to Noe. What could he say to her? How could he make her understand? She had always hated Cereus. It seemed like it would be impossible to make her see the big picture, and the role that the organization could play if the model were adopted by the entire planet. Could she be convinced to join him?

Rodan, then, considered himself and his personal legacy. *Visionaries are rarely appreciated or understood during their lifetime.* He had continuously reminded himself of this statement over the past several hours. He hoped that someday, he too would be counted among the great revolutionaries and thinkers of old because of his willingness to put the needs of the many, above those of the few.

Janus made his way over to him, then placed a brotherly hand on his arm, "What you are doing, most will never know the sacrifice. This is typically the nature of things. Difficult actions are often done in silence, with little awareness from history or those less capable and willing."

Rodan let a great sigh escape his lips. "I know what you're saying is right, and what we're doing is right as well, but…I don't want to hurt them."

"Nor do I. Your friends are some of the finest willing minds that I personally know. Were they willing to submit, they would make excellent leaders in the new society." *Barto, my old friend, could you join me? Would you join me?* Janus stepped away, yet pierced his eyes toward the empty sky outside of the large windows of the tower, allowing the very human weight of his years to show on his face, though Rodan did not see it. "Yet, you know how stubborn we humans can be when it comes to embracing any type of change. We will cling to, fight, and die for causes and organizations that we often don't fully understand or even care about, just to fulfill our biological hunger for connection. Often, it's motivated by connection to another human. But a long standing entity like an organization, highly advanced A.I. assistant, or even a pet will be a worthy object of our attention. That is what they fight for now. Why they come to kill us."

"Yeah it is. Do you think we can convince them without manipulation?"

"It will be difficult. But I have faith that it can be done. I want them to willfully join us. A strong mind is more effective if it is consciously engaged.

Rodan considered his statement, thinking of his own actions as an example. "What about Jinhua? You said yourself she was more powerful than you anticipated. She was able to undo the digital and physical enhancements you gave to Silas after all. And you said they had a cyborg kid that helped in the fight, right? You think they'll both be a major threat?"

"The cyborg boy is of no concern to me. Machines can be easily dismantled and corrupted," Janus said without feeling, as if he were stating a widely known fact. "But the girl…" He raised a hand to his chin. Rodan only knew that he was thinking. He showed no outward sign of distress. "Indeed. She certainly is more powerful than I was at that age. She has even been able to mask the signals for her own and the chips of her companions. I cannot see them now." He walked slowly toward the quantum computer. It was still producing the synthetic musical sound at metronomic intervals, providing background music to their talk. He checked something with the computer again. Rodan had no idea what it was, but after another minute Janus was done.

Then, Janus picked up his device again, muttered a few voice commands and pulled up a holographic image of the building's ground floor. The only activity on the display were his best Limnic human and mechanoid troops preparing for the inevitable confrontation to come. Satisfied with the position of his forces, he closed the map then turned once again to Rodan. "Jinhua may be the final key for my evolution…"

"Why did you help her discover her power?" Rodan's tone rang with controlled bitterness.

"Because evolution often requires sacrifices. Even at the expense of those we love. Sometimes even at the expense of self." *Lili*…the image of his beloved floated unsolicited to his mind's all seeing eye. Janus let it float by as if he viewed dead autumn leaves floating down a river. It made him think of death in its poignant simplicity.

"I think they're here." Rodan said. In his moment of reflection, Janus had not seen him pull up his own badly outdated California state issued laptop. Even with the weak camera, he was able to see the city blocks surrounding the building. An unfamiliar navy blue van had pulled into a long abandoned alleyway on the east side. When one of its doors slid open, he noticed Noe's chestnut hair drawn into a tight ponytail from the awkward angle of the camera. He caught a glimpse of the hardness of her facial expression. The same expression he had come to know so well during the time they had worked together to take down Limnic.

How to make her understand? Will you listen? Will you try to see things a different way? Will you forgive me? Though he knew the answers to those questions, yet he still wanted to try and reason with her.

Li exited the van, along with Jinhua and the cyborg boy, Daniel. They had brought a small fighting force with them. Weapons, tech, the works. Even a few of Kyler's troops had survived and were willing to fight for their now deceased commander. Seeing them all there, performing last minute checks of their gear, weapons, and communications, Rodan thought of his longtime friend Li Ma. *Old friend, you've always been so loyal. What can make you understand?*

In the low quality image of the screen, Li's eyes found the camera. They stared right at him, through him, penetrated his flimsy excuses for his betrayal. At least that's what it felt like. The guilt almost outweighed his desire for the very survival and future of the human race. He cut the video feed and walked toward the elevator doors. Adjusting his body armor, equipping his weapons, he took one last look of the view from the top of the tower. From his vantage point there was only a steel grey sky and nothing else. The early evening sun was nowhere in sight. His eyes fell on Janus's back. He too, stood in silent meditation peering at the same scene. *This is how the future of humanity has always been written. By people who could not see the entire view and only hoped that something was beyond their limited sight.*

"I'll go meet them now," Rodan said.

Janus waved his hand in response, eyes still focused outside. The elevator doors closed with a definitive slam. *All have their part to play on the evolutionary stage. Rodan, your role as the insider, is more valuable than you know.*

CHAPTER 61:
GLORY BATTLEFIELD

It's lonely at the top. Barto thought to himself, shaking his head. He sat in the passenger seat of the massive fifteen passenger vehicle with only Van, the young driver, as his companion. From the adjacent seat, Van craned his neck toward a slim digital tablet in Barto's lap. Both shared the same nervous excitement as they viewed their friends and allies as dots advancing in across the screen.

Van rested his chin on his hand and drummed his fingers on his face, then looked forward as if he were going to put the vehicle in gear and drive to their rescue. Every minute or so, he would change positions in his seat, then look back at the tablet only to look away again a few moments later. Always afraid to see one of the blue dots stop moving.

Barto remained still, but was very aware of the dryness in his own throat and the throbbing of his heart. His aching fingers reminded him how tightly he was gripping the tablet.

As a young man, Barto had visited the replica Transamerica Pyramid in its heyday. He could still picture the decadent fountains and shops of the ground floor nestled between the crisscrossing beams that formed 'X's around the perimeter of its interior. He would strain his neck skyward and marvel at the view of the upper floors. To him, they appeared as squares within squares, ever shrinking, until they converged at one of the higher floors. Truly majestic.

Now those days were long gone. The fountains had gone dry; the progressive three dimensional art sold off; the shops shuttered, looted, and defiled by homeless hijinks. Today, its wicked emptiness held only memories and echoes of its glorious past. *And now, it's a battlefield. I hope our people are alright.*

Barto tried his best to ignore Van's squirming. He knew how to deal with his own jumpiness, but found managing their combined anxiety a nearly impossible task. Then he heard music. The melody sounded familiar, but he could not recognize it. Reluctantly, he diverted his attention from the still moving blue dots on the screen and asked Van, "What is that song?"

Van held his device on his right thigh, it bounced while he tapped his foot on the floor of the van, discharging his jitters. "Oh, it's uh from an old Chinese drama I watched recently. King's Avatar," he said, the words tumbled out of his mouth. Barto maintained his eyes on the tablet, but nodded his head, still listening. "It's the theme song, called 荣耀的战场 (Róngyào de zhànchǎng)," Van said, using torpid Chinese. "It means 'Glorious Battlefield' in Mandarin…uh…my bad…I'm just really nervous and scared for everyone. Music helps calm me down. I can turn it off if it's bothering you." His quick speaking had left him winded.

Barto, eyes still locked on the table, reached over and patted the young man's shoulder enough force to make him wince. "I'm scared too. I know this song. It's been a long time since I've heard it, though." There was a pause in his words; it looked as if something had happened on the tablet.

"You want me to turn it off?"

Barto shook his head emphatically, "Turn it up."

*   *   *

The resistance against them was heavy. Cheeks, Spazer, and Bear led the charge. Jinhua and Daniel followed closely behind. That left Noe and Jinhua to watch the rear of the battle formation as the seven of them encountered an unknown number of Limnic humans and mechanoid units. Explosions, conventional munitions, and laser fire boomed in Noe's eardrums as what seemed like carbon copies of the Limnic warriors from North Bloomfield, wearing different colors, attempted to prevent them from reaching the group of functioning shock elevators at the back of the building.

Human and humanoid machines alike fell to the small, yet formidable group of Cereus fighters. Bear shot, cut, and slashed his way through two heavily armored trashcan bots, skillfully transitioning between knife and gun fighting. He expertly bounded with Cheeks, and a recovered Spazer to shock and stagger the enemy forces.

"How's that leg augmentation feeling for ya!?" Cheeks yelled above the discharge of lasers and popping munitions.

Spazer yelled over his shoulder, "Should have fucked with these things earlier! My leg feels like new!"

Cheeks raised up from behind their cover, the concrete base of a now empty fountain, and fired a high powered laser round cutting through an approaching humanoid mech. "Once you start usin' em' it's hard to stop, young buck! You gotta be careful with it, so you don't get addicted!"

"This comin' from the 'smoke-cannabis-everyday' dude himself," Spazer snickered, while reloading his rifle.

"Hey! Weed's different!" Cheeks yelled, as he fired off another burst from his rifle. A short distance ahead, Bear grunted and motioned for them to advance, narrowly ducking just in time to avoid the blast from an enemy grenade. "Let's get movin'!" Cheeks said, "You ready, man?" He asked Spazer.

"Roger that!" A fresh magazine secured in his M-4, Spazer nodded affirmatively. A second later they were back in the fray.

Near the entrance of the building, Li and Noe stayed close, keeping their sight trained on the fighters approaching from the rear. Almost as soon as all seven of them had entered the building, six humans with murderous eyes began to surround them, making retreat impossible. Unlike at North Bloomfield, Noe had no awareness of her body or of the atrocities of the melee. She was a floating weapon, with eyes and a trigger, sweeping her laser mounted M-4 side to side and feeling the push of recoil; deaf to the screams of pain, blind to the splattered blood of her enemies. In a remote part of her psyche, she questioned whether or not their human enemies fought voluntarily for Limnic or were being manipulated by Janus. She knew in a different reality, she could have easily been on the other side of the gun, willing to give her life to put an end to Cereus and anyone who opposed rocking the delicate boat of the old world status quo. *In a different reality. But not this one*, she thought as another enemy troop wearing jeans and old body armor fell in front of her. At some point in the exchange of weapons blasting around her, she had been hit on the left side of her abdomen. The unmistakable scent of singed flesh reached her nose. But she ignored the smell and the pain, and continued to move forward.

To her left, she noticed Li moving with surprising mobility and competence. The old man had seen a firefight or two during his time in service of Cereus. She was sure of it. The way he held his weapon, his battlefield awareness, and his stance all painted the picture of a career soldier who usually preferred a stylish suit to a field uniform. He did not use much ammunition. But whenever his weapon discharged, whatever was shooting back at him, stopped moving.

Close ahead of him, Jinhua and Daniel moved like twins joined by an invisible tether. In between ducking and shooting, Noe's eyes lit up as if she were viewing fireworks exploding on a starry summer night. She watched, amazed, as the unarmed teenagers aimed open palmed hands at their mechanical foes, working together to disable and destroy them. Jinhua shot monoazo yellow beams with spiraling binary code, then Daniel would trace visible red parabolas across the sky, and with lightning quick movement, jump the path, raining thin blue lasers from his arm gun. They appeared to be putting on the deadliest light show Noe had ever seen.

"Almost there!" Li shouted. His voice barely audible above the symphony of battle sounds. He estimated there were twenty feet between them and the only functioning elevators in the building.

Then the battle music, guns blasting, lasers firing, humans dying, machines breaking, gradually died down. "I think we got em'!" Cheeks said, winded from running and ducking. Spazer and Bear followed closely behind him. "That was easier than I thought!"

"No. It's not over." Jinhua's voice surprised them all. All heads whipped to focus on her. "He's coming…"

"Who, Janus?" Noe said.

"No. Rodan."

Of the four primary elevators only one was functional. Its silver doors stood out among the dilapidated and crumbling walls of the building. To Noe, they looked as if they had recently been cleaned. She read the digital floor indicator above the shining doors. Instead of the traditional yellow colored digital numbers, the numbers were colored green. *This is a shock elevator.* Designed for some of the tallest buildings in the world, a shock elevator could move fifty floors in ten seconds. *Floor 47.* She had ten seconds to decide what to say to the man who betrayed them all. Noe's body tensed, she took a large deep breath to prevent her trigger finger from slipping.

All readied themselves for the elevator doors to slide open. Weapons and arms raised, they waited longer than they expected. When the door finally did open, Rodan stood and stared out at them. For a brief moment, they exchanged glances of recognition and familiarity. It took several seconds for the memory of the morning to return to them. For them to remember he was their enemy now, along with Janus and all of Limnic.

Rodan took advantage of the gap in time and moved with augmented human speed out of the elevator and towards Bear at the end of the line. Cheeks and Noe were the first to fire their weapons in defense, but immediately stopped as soon as Rodan shattered their line formation, for fear of hitting one of their own. He moved like a giant blur. Quickly disarming and destroying all weapons that Kyler's men and the rest of them carried. She could not see him, but could only hear the sound of twisting metal, blades clanging to the dusty floor, and other armaments being rendered useless. Each person staggered backward, blindsided by his blazing speed. Noe's forearms burned as she tightened her hold on the M-4, but her grip wasn't enough. Soon she saw the muzzle of the weapon deform to an odd angle, then felt the tug of Rodan snatching the disabled rifle from her throbbing hands. Li was the last to be disarmed, barely staying on his feet after the flurry of activity moved past him.

Jinhua panicked when Rodan began to move. When she noticed the unnatural speed, she knew Janus had enhanced him. In exchange for great power and some warped form of eternity, her father's former friend had traded his humanity, and just like Silas, was in many ways, no longer human. She immediately raised her arms to delete his now corrupted code, felt the tingling of the mysterious light she could not understand, about to jump from her fingers when Daniel's voice came into her head like a tiny whisper. *Jinhua, no.* Rodan had just disarmed her father and was moving toward Noe.

Daniel! But why? Jinhua said, communicating telepathically.

We should listen to what he has to say.

But…!

Wait until I give you my signal then we'll do it. We'll take him down together just like all the others. Feihao? Daniel winked in her direction.

Jinhua flashed him a look of confusion. She was beginning to feel very afraid for herself and everyone else. *Ok…feihao.* Jinhua lowered her hands, but remained ready to act at any moment.

*   *   *

"Goddamn you Rodan!" Cheeks yelled.

"Now we can talk." Rodan said. He stood in front of the elevator looking somewhat triumphant, clad in all black of his field gear.

Will he kill us all now? Noe thought. She had to have answers before he made another move. "Why are you doing this Rodan!?" Her voice unexpectedly broke. It was difficult to contain her burning hatred for him and what he had done. She made no attempt to mask her rage. "You were supposed to lead Cereus and help bring it to more people so that you could help humanity. Now you side with Janus and Limnic!?" Her nostrils flared and her breathing was heavy. She wanted to kill him, whether or not she had a weapon.

Rodan kept his expression neutral. "I knew you'd only be able to see it one way. After all, it makes sense that you would hold on to what you *think* to be true."

"What the hell are you talking about?" Li said, his voice calm yet tense.

"I'm talking about Cereus. You think you're fighting for a prolific organization. An institution that if sustained, will potentially last as long as people buy into and believe in its function. Well, now you should know the truth Li. That Cereus was never meant to last as an organization. Its destruction was built into its design. Executive order

DD-5428 was a self-destruct order the Founders inserted into its original charter."

Li's eyes softened. A rare expression of perplexed concern took over his face. "No…that can't be…"

"It's true. If you don't believe me. Ask Barto now. I know he's listening. He'll confirm it."

Noe called his bluff. "Barto come in…are you hearing this?" No response. "Barto?…Barto…" Dread twisted her stomach into a knot. *Could Rodan be telling the truth?* She needed more answers. "You're lying Rodan! Why would the Founders design Cereus' self-destruction into its plan and not tell anyone, even high ranking officials, about its plans?" Her eyes darted toward Li and quickly back to Rodan.

Rodan's eyes looked sad. He felt pity for her ignorance. "Because the Founders knew that like all human creations, if Cereus prospered for too long it would also become a contributor to the endless competition for resources and planetary destruction that has characterized capitalism since the eighteenth century. You know the motto: 'Protect people and planet'. How could they stay true to that if their own creation was sucking up resources and abusing the Earth? The Founders hoped that I, as the last director of the organization, would be able to steer and crash it directly into the hearts of all of its citizens. And in that way, the Cereus model would be permanently housed in their hearts and minds, without need of an executive director, or the Founders themselves."

"A self-governing society…" Jinhua whispered. Rodan nor anyone else heard her comment.

"Where does Limnic fit into all this?" Li asked, still reeling from Rodan's revelation.

"Janus and Lili started it together, but after a few years Lili wanted out. She didn't like the bloody direction that it was taking and bowed out. Janus continued the work on his own. It started as a defensive measure to protect Cereus, established primarily by Silas. Then, Janus and Lili began to use it to raise extra money and build influence for the Cereus social model."

"How does terrorism help get people to support Cereus?" Noe spat, already over this explanation.

"Through fear. By the middle of this century people were already fed up with the old world faux democratic-capitalistic model. Who could they turn to in order to remain safe and live their lives in peace?"

"Cereus…" Li said slowly, haunted by the simplicity of the scheme.

Rodan nodded. "That's right. It was all a part of Janus' strategy that was set in motion at Cereus' founding nearly 40 years ago."

Li took a step forward. "And you? What caused you to turn? Why back him and Limnic, knowing what he's done and what he's planning to do? Do *not* lie to me."

Rodan's face twitched, as if he temporarily recalled that the small Asian man standing before him had been his superior and friend. A moment later, the stone-faced neutral expression erased the evidence of his former humanity. "I've known for a while now that my role was just as a figurehead. The Founders wanted someone to be captain of the ship when it finally sank and I was that guy. Right place, wrong time I suppose."

"But you wanted more…" Li said with bitterness.

"C'mon man, wouldn't you? I've worked my whole life as a public servant first in the military, as a cop, and then for Cereus. I wasn't gonna go out like that. After North Bloomfield, I saw an opportunity to secure my legacy *and* help mankind take a giant leap forward in its evolution." He noticed they seemed to be at least considering his words now. The cadence of his voice sped up to capitalize on the opportunity. "Trust me, playing nice with the bureaucrats of the old world and dealing with the endless cycle of political bullshit is no way to move us forward. Janus has a plan. And it's gonna work. You'll see. It's gonna make us all better in the end. Don't you want that for her?" He gestured his head in Jinhua's direction.

Li didn't take the bait, and kept his eyes trained on Rodan. Out of the corner of his eye, he was proud to see that Jinhua had done the same.

Rodan noticed Kyler's men were beginning to close the distance between them and his position in front of the elevator. He was running out of time. *Have I stalled them enough?* That and one last unfinished piece of business still lingered in his brain. He turned toward Noe, and said, "Noe…what I felt with you…was real." His face showed signs of morphing into regret.

Noe's eyes narrowed. "Please, don't…go there."

"No, it was. I mean it. I didn't mean to hurt you. Maybe at some point in the future…you could forgive me?"

She shook her head softly, flabbergasted that he would dare seek forgiveness after all he had done. His words were like leaves in the wind, silently being carried away, never reaching a firm destination. Noe stared at him, fury in her eyes, "If you're done talking let's get on with it then." *We've wasted enough time with you. I know I have.* But he wasn't done talking, he took a step forward and continued to speak. His voice began to rise.

"We're giving you, Noe, and all of you one last chance, to end your resistance and join us in ushering our species into its next phase of evolution. One that gives us all the power to live as gods as long as we are able. And to live a good life of virtue that will help us strive toward the limits of our potential."

"You sound like him," Li said. Whether he was being manipulated by Janus or not was irrelevant at this point. His friend was truly lost. "Rodan, it's over. What you and Janus are doing is manipulation on a global scale. Forcing people to evolve by making them digital slaves is not true evolution. You've let him poison your mind with his rhetoric. You've become all of the things that we dedicated our entire lives to protect people and society from." Li shook his head, almost regretful of the truth in his words. "You've become the small man, who is afraid to die."

Li's words had done more damage than any laser or rifle could ever do. It showed on Rodan's face and he was livid.

"I see how it is." He let silence linger in the air awhile, knowing that Kyler's men were not far from him now. "Then I see there's no saving you then." With a curt nod, Rodan made the first move. In a quick draw motion, he produced a concealed handgun sized firearm.

Noe only saw the glint of a black weapon appear, before she noticed it wave in her direction. The sound of a single shot had always seemed louder to her than the sounds of several being fired at once. In a futile motion, she raised her arms to defend herself, but it was too late. The round had already found its intended target.

CHAPTER 62: VERSUS RODAN

All had instinctively ducked down or dropped to a prone position after the single shot echoed throughout the shell of the old tower. When the noise died down from the sudden mass of movement, Rodan watched them all do as he would have done in their position: check for superficial or fatal wounds. He viewed their faces of alarm and tension with a blank expression. He was no longer a soldier, or an executive. He was something above societal labels. Onlookers would have called him a zealot, but to him even that title was too constricted in its definition. He felt like another being entirely, a different species; the hawk to the ant, he could see things that they could not.

From his omnidirectional view, he saw them all scrambling, and calling to one another. The only one who gave no vocal response was Li. He lay gasping and coughing covering an expanding redness on his tactical shirt, just below his body armor. Rodan considered ending his long time colleague's suffering, but a single shred of brotherly remembrance stopped him, and like the merciful higher order entity that he was, allowed him a final moment with his soon to be fatherless daughter. He watched the once straight-faced and expressionless girl fall apart as she knelt by his side. Pain and sadness animated her face as she fought a losing battle to save her father's life. "Dad, Dad!" She cried. The old man moaned with a pained response.

As he stood viewing the scene from on high, Rodan hardly noticed the teenage boy step out of the enemy formation and approach him. In his mind, he was a single gnat buzzing toward his face, noticeable, yet harmless. The brown-haired and clear-eyed youth brushed past Rodan on his way to the elevators. None of his former colleagues seemed to notice the movement. They were too focused on the most salient source of their rage to hear the silver doors clamp shut, and the resulting launch of the shock elevator. Janus had taken care of the boy, just as he said he would. *One less obstacle*, Rodan thought.

Only one minute had elapsed since the single shot of his trusty Sig Sauer P365 turned his former friends' world upside down. *Now it's time to mercy kill all of them.* With his enemies' weapons disabled, and their movement frozen through his new chip manipulation powers, they could put up little resistance. Rodan took the opportunity to activate another one of Janus' toys. A cloaking device to mask his giant frame. He had no idea how it worked, but suddenly had the urge to have some fun in dispatching his enemies. All of a sudden the old German-American made handgun felt too impersonal a killing implement. Everything would be over after a single twitch of a finger. To him that was too fast. A part of him wanted them to feel the slow, slow death he had been experiencing since he assumed command of the ghost ship that was Cereus. He wanted them to come to the realization, as he had done weeks ago, that there was no escape from this whirlpool, no stopping the undertow of an indifferent cosmos. That they were not special or unique. That their flesh could be liquified, evaporated, and scattered to the vacuum of eternity at any moment by the unflinching coldness of an unseen higher order. To them, *he* was that higher order, he became that invisible specter of human death. He wanted to pull the knife. He wanted to see the terror-stricken faces grasping and clawing in order to save themselves. He wanted them to be as empty as he felt. Everything had been decided. All was resolved in his mind. The only thing left for him to do was to make it a reality. Then he could die a happy man.

*   *   *

Hot tears of anger filled Noe's eyes. Seeing Jinhua's anguished exertions to save her dying parent, brought images of her mother and father to her mind. The unwelcome pictures dredged up the scabbed wounds of her own guilt, and made her slow to react when Rodan disappeared from sight. She wanted to help Jinhua and Li, but also wanted to prevent any more injury to her comrades or herself. To her surprise, Cheeks, Bear, and Spazer seemed to have regained control over their bodies. Was this another game Rodan was playing? Even if it was, this might be their final opportunity to fight back.

"Rodaaan!" she screamed, "Come out and fight!" She knew he was still there, watching, using some type of alien cloaking technology to mask his movements. Then she saw him momentarily flicker into view. He was standing only three feet away, approaching her to no doubt kill her. His technology appeared to be breaking down at the crucial moment.

Instinctively she jumped back, while Cheeks rushed to disarm him. A brief struggle ensued between the two men, as the shorter man grappled and attempted to subdue the taller man, by forcing him to the debris littered floor. But ultimately, Rodan's physical superiority triumphed over Cheeks' flabby body and he fell back grunting with pain as blood began to drip from superficial knife slashes on his forearms and a broken nose.

Spazer, stunned by his mentor's defeat, entered the fray. He threw decisive punches and kicks, in a stance that reminded Noe of the outdated Bruce Lee movies she had watched a long time ago with her mother. His technique, while competent looking, mimicked a Hollywood stunt fighter. Perfect for well-choreographed action sequences, but not so effective in a real fight. The strikes lacked follow through and impact. A few blows haphazardly struck Rodan, making him stagger backward and drop his knife, but with both hands free, he caught one of Spazer's clumsy kicks then twisted it at the ankle with a sharp rotation. Noe heard the unnatural cracks and pops of multiple bones breaking followed by a young man's scream as she saw his formerly wounded leg flail at an odd angle within the bigger man's grip. With the strength of a wrestler, Rodan swung his unconscious body in a circular motion, then flung him away. Spazer's head landed hard against the floor, then he lay there, unmoving.

Bear was the last to approach. Rodan's expression remained neutral as he examined his opponent with speedy diagnostic rigor. He had been wounded during his heroics in the initial skirmish with the Limnic fighters and was in a weakened state. Though Bear was slightly larger than him, and did his best to appear battle ready, his body language told a different story. The slightly slouching posture, twitching of the eyebrow, rapid movement of the pulse beating in his neck, informed Rodan that his rival was a wounded animal ready for slaughter. Despite his debilitated state, the animal fought as if on the brink of extinction. Bear entered a low stance and rushed him, but at the last second slipped to the right. He caught Rodan's arm, straightened it, then thrust at Rodan's elbow with a devastating palm strike, designed for breaking. Instead of hearing the sound of shattering bone, he only heard the sound of his own animalistic groan. Then the pain came, sharp and dizzying. Rodan's arm was like steel, unyielding. Bear looked down at the palm of his hand and saw clear evidence of the blood pooling beneath the thin skin. By the time he looked up it was too late. Rodan stood him up with a counter palm strike to the forehead, then proceeded to pummel every pressure point at the front of Bear's body with a flurry of rapid finger strikes, finishing with a sternum crushing blow, which no doubt impacted his fragile heart and lungs. Bear fell backward to the dusty floor, twitching, gasping for air, laboring to voluntarily move even the tiniest of muscles. Rodan lingered for a second to admire his victory over the greatest fighter that stood in his way. Then his eyes shifted to Noe. Her defiant gaze slowed his movements. Although she had no weapon, Rodan knew she would fight to the death if necessary. Their shared moment of passion and physical pleasure the night before made his body yearn for her touch. He hesitated with an empty look on his face, conflicted. *If I don't at least incapacitate her, she will surely kill me.* It was a human moment of indecision. One that exposed a fleeting window of vulnerability.

Behind Rodan's back, Jinhua's brain was processing at full capacity, nearly overwhelmed by the heat of the moment. Her father had been shot and was losing blood fast, the three fighters had been defeated, and Rodan was approaching Noe, with killer intention. What puzzled her and jammed her logic most of all was Daniel. In the initial confusion after Rodan shot her father, she had seen him walk absentmindedly toward their new enemy. His pace was casual, as he brushed past the man, no, the *thing*, that wanted to kill them all. More confusing still, was the fact that she could no longer feel her special connection with him. She had no idea why. But she knew only one person could pull off such a trick. *Janus.* But she had no time to consider or look into how he had done it. She was too preoccupied putting pressure on her father's wound. She had managed to slow the flow of blood, but it kept coming, covering her hands in crimson liquid. Jinhua watched her father's face carefully to ensure he was still alive. She watched it change from pain, to pallid terror as he struggled to form the words, "Jinhua…b-behind…you."

Maintaining one hand on her father's wound, Jinhua whipped her head to the side, to see Rodan approaching her, knife drawn, eyes empty. *I guess he spared Noe*, Jinhua thought. This did not surprise her, as she had viewed their late night tryst in all its intimate detail during the morning meeting, and was aware of the complicated history and emotions between them both.

Behind Rodan, Noe took advantage of the opportunity to tend to the dazed Spazer. While a bloody Cheeks knelt over Bear's body. They were alive, but none were in a position to help her. Jinhua raised her hand to disable him with the delete code, just as she had done with Silas and all of the other Limnic mechs. The hand, stained in her father's still warm blood, raised, palm open, as she called on intuition to do the rest. But no yellow coded light shot out of her hand, and the man in black, death in flesh and code, kept coming. Suddenly, she was a skinny seventeen-year-old facing middle-aged, military trained killing machine, with enhanced physical and mental capabilities. The odds were not in her favor. Rodan saw her confident expression fold as the grim realization dawned on her. *She knows she can't win.* A smirk drew itself onto his face.

"Looks like the light show's over, Jini. I'm sorry it has to be this way. You should've joined us when you had the chance," he said.

Out of genuine fear, Jinhua kept her armed raised, palm open, hoping the universal signal for stop would somehow prevent this monster from killing her and her father. Then, a reddish pink light reflected in her tear soaked eyes. It flashed from the palm of her hand, causing Rodan to recoil, then died away, leaving only her thin arm lifted in self-defense.

On the other side of Rodan, Noe saw the brilliant magenta colored spark, then a fraction of a second later, felt her body tighten like a coiled spring full of unreleased energy. Then suddenly there were two Noes. There was the flesh and blood her, irate, exhausted, desperate. Then another her, enveloped in a magenta hued aura. She was Quantum Noe. Her highlighted self-perceived time differently. The rules of seconds, minutes, and hours no longer applied and *she* or *it* moved at quantum intervals that Noe could not grasp or understand.

Classic Noe observed, as Quantum Noe appeared by the broken Bear's fallen laser knife, brought its electric blue flame to life, then with one fierce thrust, let out a strained cry as the burning blade pierced Rodan's body armor, cutting through to his very human skin.

When Noe blinked again, Quantum Noe was no longer there. It was only the real her holding the laser knife as if she had delivered the killing blow. Questions of the how and why of the last several seconds were supplanted by her overwhelming desire to kill Rodan for everything he had done. She was happy to have stabbed him in the back, as she didn't want to see the pleading in his eyes when she twisted the hot blade in his flesh. She knew he still had enough strength to turn around and kill her, yet she felt no resistance from him. He just began to choke and cough as warm blood filled foreign chambers in his body.

After several seconds, Noe released her grip on the knife and stepped back. Rodan's body had fallen forward, lying in stillness in an expanding pool of blood.

The throbbing of her pulse in her right temple returned her to reality. Her thoughts immediately turned to Li and the others. She quickly returned to Jinhua where a wounded but still helpful Spazer attended to Li. At first, Noe could not believe that he had been able to move himself to Li's position across the room after his horrific injury. Then she was quickly reminded of the augmentations that ran in his young veins. The sound of his voice snapped her out of her temporary stupor and back to their dire situation.

"He's hurt pretty bad. I think the bullet is still in there, lucky for us." His remark did little to boost his or anyone else's confidence about Li's odds of survival.

Cheeks struggled to his knees, fighting through the pain of several cracked ribs, to attend to Bear's injuries. The once mighty warrior's skin looked pale and he seemed to be floating precariously between life and death. He radioed for Barto or Van to bring two field trauma kits, then began to do whatever he could to save his dying friend. After two minutes of burning exertion, he could only hold him, whispering reassurance. Words he knew, Bear could probably no longer hear or understand.

From the front doors of the building, Van emerged, sweaty and scared, running at full speed with the medical kits. He ignored the smoking mechs and the festering smell of dead humans as he sprinted to the elevators where his friends waited.

"Oh my god…" he whispered, tears coming to his eyes.

"Don't just stand there!" Cheeks barked, "Gimme that damn kit! And take the other one to Spazer! C'mon now, get yo'self together!"

Van snapped into readiness then dutifully began to follow Cheeks' instructions.

As Cheeks prepared the kit and tended to Bear, Noe and Jinhua stood over him. Noe said, "We have to go get Janus and end this, *right now.*"

His usual hard edge dulled by the loss of his commander and the decimation of his comrade, Cheeks glanced up at Noe and the girl, then nodded. "I know. Go get yo' man. Get em' fo' all of us." There was an uncharacteristic softness in Cheeks' voice that surprised Noe. "We'll take care of Jinhua's old man."

Jinhua nodded affirmatively. She appeared dirty and shaken. Her eyes darted back and forth between Cheeks and where her father lay dying behind her. Noe, with blood, ash, and sweat clinging to her face, placed a trembling yet supportive hand on her shoulder. Cheeks marveled at her poise and determined nature, but knew she was afraid.

"C'mon Space Force. You got this right?"

Noe returned a curt nod. Cheeks returned the gesture, then continued working on the now unconscious Bear.

You're my responsibility for now. I won't let you down. Noe thought as she stood before the silver doors of the elevator.

Jinhua stood with tears still rolling down her cheek. She attempted to remove some of her father's blood from her hands by wiping them on her tactical pants, but they would not come clean. She looked deep into Noe's eyes, and said, "I trust you. I know you won't."

On any other day, Noe would have been creeped out by the fact that a teenage girl could read her thoughts. But today, it was comforting to know they would be together when they finally faced Janus.

Cheeks watched as the two of them stepped into the silver doors of the shock elevator. Jinhua looked through puffy eyes at her father lying on the floor, then quickly forced herself to look up at anything that wasn't him. Noe had closed her eyes and seemed to be doing some type of deep breathing exercise, no doubt repeating some simplified version of her pre-battle ritual at North Bloomfield.

When the doors closed, Cheeks couldn't help but feel a stab of regret that the fate of humanity was now in the hands of a Space Force veteran, and a skinny teenage girl with weird powers. *It shoulda been us, but they're our only hope now.* Spazer's voice burst through his moment of thoughtfulness.

"Cheeks! If we don't get Mr. Ma outta here fast, I don't think he's gonna make it."

Cheeks glanced down at Bear, he was still breathing, but barely. "Right. Let's get movin'. Janus is up to dem two now."

CHAPTER 63:
STRINGS

Jinhua mentally readied herself as the shock elevator doors slid closed and prepared to launch her and Noe to the summit of the dilapidated building. She marveled that the rotting structure even had such functioning technology.

The elevator had been invented decades before Jinhua was born by some guy named Musk. Or was it Mustard or Must? She could never quite remember the name. All she knew was that the guy was something of a lunatic in the early part of the century and had wanted to construct an elevator to the moon. The ambitious venture ultimately failed. However, the technology was scaled down and put to use in elevator shafts around the world. The science and engineering of the elevator's operation fascinated Jinhua. It involved being launched by a miniature explosion (similar to a bullet being fired from a gun), and some kind of gravity exchange that gave passengers a feeling of weightlessness as they ascended at blinding speeds toward the top of very tall buildings. People called them 'shock elevators' because of the initial surprise that one experienced when riding one. It had an official technical name, but Jinhua couldn't remember what it was. *It doesn't really matter what it's called, I hate riding these things.*

She braced herself for launch, reminding herself to relax and allow the technology of the elevator to do its job. Noe still seemed tense, staring directly ahead at the silver doors. Jinhua wanted to speak to her, but couldn't find the right words. So she said the first thing that came to her mind.

"I'm sorry you had to do what you did back there." The words floated through the air like an unpleasant aroma, waiting for either person to acknowledge them. "You…liked him…didn't you?"

"I did." Noe said, giving no hint of emotion.

"I see."

"It's not a big deal. It's done now."

Jinhua gave no response. She had no way of relating to Noe's situation. *What is taking this elevator so long?*

"What was that light back there?" Noe asked all of a sudden. "I saw this purplish light, then, next thing I know, I'm *literally* standing in two places at once. It was unreal." Her face remained neutral, but her voice rose and fell with genuine confusion and amazement.

Jinhua examined her hands for a moment. Dried blood covered her palms like fresh plaster. On the dorsal side, there was less red, but a muckish dirt blood mixture caked itself under her short fingernails. Her examination complete, she found no physical evidence to explain what had just occurred in the lobby.

"I…don't know what it was. I just wanted to protect my dad, myself, and everyone else, then it just…happened."

Noe turned and said with a soft voice, "It's ok. I'm just happy, whatever it was, helped us stop Rodan from hurting anyone else. He really—"

A sudden jolt cut her off. The "shock" from the launch of the elevator caused Jinhua and Noe to stumble where they stood. In less than ten seconds, they would be at the top of the tower.

Jinhua felt her stomach twisting into knots as the pressure from the catapulting force acted on her internal organs. The feeling was so unpleasant, she nearly vomited. Clenching her eyes shut and swallowing hard, she gulped bitterness down her throat and hoped it would be over soon. Then it came, the brief feeling of weightlessness during the ascent. For several seconds she felt normal enough to open her eyes. In that interval of time, she turned her attention to Noe. Her hands and eyes performed a last-minute check of her weapons: a black rifle, and the laser knife she used to kill Rodan only minutes ago. To Jinhua, she was a badass warrior, or at least she looked the part. Growing up without a mother, she had never had a female authority figure to look up to. In one day, Noe had unknowingly taught her a great deal about strength. Bravery and courage were words Jinhua had primarily associated with competitive settings, in which winning and losing were the outcomes of a good or poor performance. Today, Noe had shown her that not all battles are fought on a track, field, or court. Some of the greatest conflicts are within the mind. The war, ever-raging; most will never be able to account for the dead or the number of victories and defeats. But the strongest fought daily, with no hope of glory or accolades because it was the only way to move forward, the only way to truly *evolve* without the aid of biohacking or digigenomics. Noe was one of those people, and she deeply respected her for it.

As the elevator climbed, Noe made a final inspection of her gear. *Damn, not much ammo left. Have to be precise with my shots.* She glanced at Jinhua beside her. The girl looked somewhat pale and looked generally beat up. Noe placed a gentle hand on her shoulder, "Stay close to me, ok? Who knows what tricks Janus will have up his sleeve." Noe let a small smile illuminate her face.

Jinhua nodded. She felt comforted by this military warrior's presence, even if she had little actual combat experience. *We can do this. We have to do this together.* She returned Noe's smile. Then she felt the compression of an artificial gravity generator slowing their ascent, allowing her to feel normal once again. It was almost time.

"Are you ready?" Noe asked, eyes narrowed.

"Yes. Let's do this."

Noe gave the magazine of her old M-4 a hard tap to secure it in place. "Ok." She took one last deep breath to slow her pounding heart and calm her nerves. Even in the stuffy elevator and the sweaty air, the deliberate expansion of her lungs left her awash in clear-headedness. *This stuff really does work.* She beamed inwardly at her tiny victory. At that moment the silver elevator doors slid open, revealing an unfamiliar scene.

*   *   *

The room looked abandoned. At least that's the way Jinhua would have described it. The ripped up carpet was dirt tan stained with decades of abuse with lighter patches where heavy furniture used to sit. Her eyes scanned the ceiling, where the absence of insulation exposed the cold skeleton of the roof above. Forgotten wires of all functions and pipes for heating and cooling, dangled precariously overhead looking like an upside down scrap heap reaching toward the floor. The exposed building infrastructure ran the length of the ceiling, all the way to the cloudy floor to ceiling windows that offered a view of the San Francisco Bay. Even in the dying light of the afternoon, she could make out the lights of the Golden Gate Bridge through a thin sheet of rolling fog that began to consume the water. The only light in the room came from eight flickering fluorescent lights dangling from above. Orange and reddish sunlight peeked through the thin clouds, giving the room a horror movie vibe.

After taking in their surroundings, Jinhua's pupils dilated at the sight of the micro quantum computer on a giant old executive desk. The rhythmic churning of its internal workings reverberated throughout the room. The sight of the carefully engineered components, arranged to replicate the harsh cold of outer space, blew Jinhua's mind when she had first seen pictures of old room sized models. Now, all of the components could fit in a container the size of a shoebox. *Pretty amazing.* Unconsciously, she had taken two small steps toward the desk, in order to get a closer look at the machine. Noe's firm grip on her forearm, nudged her back to the present, and the very real danger that they were in.

"Jinhua get back," Noe whispered in a scolding tone, forcing Jinhua slightly behind her. She swept her rifle toward a lightless corner of the room, then suddenly locked it in position. Jinhua's breath caught when she saw her target.

"We were wondering where you went," Noe said, "okay come on out nice and slow."

Daniel emerged from the shadows. Hands in his pockets, looking as if he were taking a leisurely stroll. The muzzle from Noe's rifle followed his every step, until he stopped beside the great desk. Jinhua neither saw, sensed, nor felt any sign of Janus, but knew he was somewhere close, invisible. Perhaps he too was masking his own digital signature from her? *Probably.* Meanwhile, she desperately began to try and reestablish her telepathic connection with Daniel. It felt as if she were attempting to open a tightly sealed bottle of honey. No matter how many ways she tried, every try left her feeling exhausted and even more frustrated.

"Hands out of the pockets kid...slow." Noe said with caution.

A red gleam sparked in Daniel's eyes, as he pulled his hands out of his pockets, producing two arm guns. Leaping away from each other, both Noe and Jinhua evaded the first shots of brilliant blue light that impacted where both had been standing. Noe immediately returned fire. The impact of her rounds clanked against Daniel's surprisingly sturdy torso. She continued to move and shoot circling Daniel's position. The teenage cyborg stayed by the desk, his robotic body forming a barrier between Noe's shots and the fragile quantum computer pulsing behind him.

He's protecting the computer! Jinhua thought, as the coded yellow light streaked out of her palm. Daniel evaded the blast, training both of his gun arms on his enemies. Then, dismay came to his face, "Jinhua, Noe! You have to get away! It's Janus! He's taken control of my body. I can't…control it!" Daniel continued to shoot at them, while his face strained and contorted. Jinhua knew he was fighting Janus' puppetry, but could not free himself from the strings.

"Daniel, hold on!" Jinhua cried. Her mind blazed in an effort to find a way to stop Daniel without harming him while she continued to shoot purposely clumsy aureolin colored beams of light in his direction.

The boy let out a savage cry, then screamed. Two arched parabolas drew themselves from both arms, one over each of his female combatants. Both knew what was coming. There was no way they could outrun his speed, or the fiery beams that would cut them to shreds within a few seconds. The attack was unblockable.

Noe stood her ground. Jinhua didn't hesitate. At the moment Daniel's feet left the floor, Jinhua fired curved yellow lines from both hands at Daniel. The delete codes hit him square it the chest. His signature attack interrupted, he tumbled forward to the floor. His cybod crashed with tremendous force, leaving him incapacitated. He lay still beside the desk, arm extended in Jinhua's direction.

Noe called from the other side of the room, "Is he disabled?" She kept her smoking rifle on Daniel's body, even though she knew it hadn't been very effective against him.

Jinhua gave a solemn nod. "Yeah…he is." She had rushed over to him to check on him. His clothes and skin had been ripped from the battle in the lobby and Noe's shots. Hints of his alloy chassis were visible through the dead artificial skin. His face was dirty and blemished, but was still boyishly charming, even with his eyes closed.

"Will he…be ok?" Noe asked, sensitive to Jinhua's feelings again, now that he was no longer a threat.

"I'm not sure," Jinhua answered, her voice small.

"Janus did this…" Noe said in an aggressive tone, "Come out and show yourself!" She yelled. Only the reverberation of her own voice responded to her exasperated cry.

Jinhua continued to examine Daniel, her hands running up and down his body, looking for some way to reboot or reset him. "I think I might be able to—"

"I'm here." Janus' unmistakable voice caused Jinhua and Noe to look up.

There, standing behind the executive desk, their enemy peered at them with soft amusement in his eyes. Jinhua bolted to her feet, then aimed her hands. Noe elevated her rifle, then slipped her finger in the trigger guard. Both were ready for the final battle.

CHAPTER 64:
JANUS

Janus was standing behind a large oak desk, which probably used to belong to an old insurance tycoon. His silver hair was drawn into a ponytail. It heavily contrasted with his midnight blue slacks and vest, but matched his silver shirt. He took unhurried steps from behind the desk, making no attempt to hide in the presence of Noe's loaded weapon. He stopped directly in front of the grand desk and the still throbbing light of the quantum computer.

"Hello ladies. I'm happy that you've come all this way to see me." He flashed a look of pity in Noe and Jinhua's direction. "I suppose you're here to kill me, am I right?"

This monster. Noe's mother, Silas, Rodan, Daniel, her father. He had manipulated them all. Now he plans to do it on a global scale. Jinhua thought, her posture rigid with rising hate for this man.

Only a few feet from her, Noe took a bold step forward, keeping her weapon trained on her enemy. "You read minds, so you already know the answer to that question," Noe said, spitting her words.

Janus nodded in a slow and understanding manner. "You're right." He looked at both of them with an intense and methodical gaze. *They truly are not ready. But evolution cannot wait. I will make them ready.*

Noe didn't care for the look in his eyes. He appeared to be studying them, most likely preparing for his attack against them. His face was like a slimy creature from under a heavy rock. She wanted to step on it and hear it explode and pop beneath her boot's crushing power. Then Janus made his first move. In response, Noe flinched and almost applied the necessary pressure to fire her weapon. As if caught in a police spotlight, he raised his arms in a position of surrender. His hands were empty. For a fleeting moment, he appeared to her as a feeble old man, who should be lazing about in quiet refuge, instead of heading a terrorist organization.

"Then why do you hesitate?" Janus asked. His tone reflected genuine curiosity. "Why not destroy me now and be done with it?"

Jinhua held her breath, wondering how Noe would answer the question, or if she would answer at all.

Noe leaned forward, ready to absorb the anticipated recoil from the blast of her rifle. Outside, a layer of darkness sat over a line of lapis blue sky while the San Francisco city lights shimmered below. Inside of the room, the buzzing of the fluorescent lights, and the repetitive mechanical heart of the quantum computer pervaded the air. All of these details were lost on Noe. She could only see Janus in the flesh and in her mind's eye. He was everywhere. Seconds ticked by as she contemplated her response, keeping her rifle fixed on him. "Why did you kill my mother?"

Janus shook his head. "Oh you poor child. Your mother told me long ago that she wanted you to be able to choose between Cereus and the old world. To be able to forge your own path." Looking her up and down, he regarded her as if she were a wounded animal. Even with the rifle muzzle floating before him, he showed no signs of detectable fear.

"And look at where it has brought you! A lifetime of servitude to a nation that could care less about your sacrifice. Compounded by a lonely and a purposeless existence. It is not the life that she wanted for you, and you know that."

"Shut up!" Noe said. Her strained outcry bounced in invisible patterns around the shell of the old office. "Don't you talk about her as if you knew her at all!" Noe's anger was reaching a boiling point, she could feel it. But something prevented her from pulling the trigger and killing the old man. It was a tiny flame of intuition, that could be extinguished by a wayward zephyr. If it went out, any remaining self-restraint would be lost. Out of the corner of her eye, Noe perceived Jinhua pass a wordless message. Formless intuition beckoned Noe's senses, but she ignored it. Janus' face invaded her mental landscape, as if it were an alien spacecraft casting some misshapen shadow over the open air, blocking out everything above. Her weapon remained fixed on her enemy.

"Everything you say is a manipulation! Just like you plan to control humanity with your fuckin' mind control. It's sick! You claim that you want to save humanity, but what you're doing is enslaving people on a global scale. All to feed your fucked up ego. You're…you're not human!"

Janus laughed heartily, entertained by her tantrum. "I am merely doing what capitalism has done from the shadows for the last 300 years! I'm just doing it better. The corporations of the old world hid in plain sight. Masking their manipulations with catchy slogans, unfettered consumerism, feel good, yet useless self-serving philanthropy, sugary substances, bingeworthy media, and cheap addictive drugs. Cereus and Limnic will at least give people the freedom to knowingly choose how they will live their lives, instead of surreptitiously stealing it from them with false ideals of unwarranted materialism or hollow patriotism."

From where she stood, Jinhua saw the effect of Janus' rhetoric. Noe's stance appeared to slacken somewhat and the angle of her rifle began to dip toward the floor. *Noe don't do it! You can't!* She silently pleaded with her, knowing there was little she could do to stop what would most likely happen next.

Janus, hands still raised, took cautious steps in Noe's direction. "Noe…there is something you need to understand before you decide what course of action you will take next. I need you to *think* and listen."

He had evaded her question like the master manipulator he was. "No! I don't want to hear it! You murdered her, didn't you!? Just admit it! You killed her for no reason! And…and you loved her! And for some fucked up reason, she loved you too!"

"Yes, Noe I did love her, and I—"

The blast from the rifle made Jinhua wince and shut her eyes. Instinctively, she thrust her hands over her ears, shielding them from the burst of a second shot. But it never came. When she opened her eyes and lowered her hands, Noe stood with the hot rifle angled toward the floor. Then Jinhua saw the silver haired corpse prostrated in front of the ancient desk. It was him, and it was over. Janus was dead.

*   *   *

Why am I crying? Must be tears of joy. Noe swiftly wiped the tears away with the back of her hand and took gliding steps, quiet and soft, toward Janus' corpse. She wanted to confirm that he was indeed dead.

She knelt down and placed her index and middle finger on his wrinkly neck, searching for a pulse. There was none. A large exhale escaped her lips. She felt as if she hadn't been breathing since the elevator doors opened, marveling at the fact that she hadn't lost consciousness. Her head began to clear, as the faces of all of her friends flooded her mind. *He's gone Mom. Now you can rest in peace.*

Relaxed, free from the shadow of Janus' aliencraft looming overhead, she became aware of Jinhua's presence in the room again. The girl had moved to the large office desk and studied the mini quantum computer with anxious eyes. To Noe, the beat from its monotonous rhythm sounded louder now that Janus was gone.

Jinhua had picked up Janus' device and was interacting with the complex machine, employing her powers to the full extent to understand and process what she was seeing. As she searched, scanned, and typed, a tightness began to wrap itself around her, as if a giant hand was closing its grip around her body, making it difficult for her heart to pump or for her lungs to inflate. As she worked, twilight was quickly approaching outside of the floor-to-ceiling windows. The charcoal clouds had cleared and the sky displayed its last blanket of blue over an orangish red streak. The bay had nearly completed its nightly transformation into a small black sea with frigid waters, capped with layers of fog.

Noe approached the desk, wondering what Jinhua was studying. "Jinhua we should get downstairs and check on your dad…hey, are you ok!?" Jinhua looked pale as she turned toward Noe. Fearfulness showed on her young face. Noe immediately knew that something was very wrong. The unseeable hand began to close around her, too. Its crushing embrace made Noe's body react as if she were underwater in the blackness of the sea, cold and pressured.

"…What is it?" Noe dared to ask.

"Noe, I don't think you should have shot him…"

"Why not? What did you see on t-that…c-computer?" *Why can't I talk right now?* "J-Jinhua…are y-y-you there?" Jinhua's concerned face began to dematerialize in front of her eyes. At first it began to blink away rapidly, then she completely disappeared. *What is happening?* "Jinhua! Jinhua! Where are you!?" The rising panic of her voice was unfamiliar and frightening.

Then the floor began to quake below her feet. *Oh my god! Is this building being demolished!? Is this Limnic?* With Jinhua nowhere in sight, she sprinted back toward the elevator. Falling debris from the remains of the exposed ceiling rained down around her, threatening to impale her or render her unconscious, which certainly meant death. With swift movement, she narrowly avoided being hit by one of the falling fluorescent lights. It shattered with a loud crash when it hit the ground, throwing razor-sharp glass and plastic everywhere. Noe reached the elevator, mashing the open button with panic. But it was too late. A stray ceiling tile fell on her head and shattered. A blinding white light infiltrated her vision as she staggered and fell to the floor. To her surprise, she did not lose consciousness however, the building continued to shake with more violence than before. It would probably only be a few seconds before it was all over.

Dazed on the floor with a minor concussion, cuts and scrapes on her arms, Noe felt she could fight no more. *I'm gonna die.* Just as she began to shut her eyes to prepare for the end, a circle of blue light began to surround her helpless position. It started small, but the radius continued to expand until it consumed the entire office. The desk, the twinkling cityscape outside, the crumbling roof, all were eclipsed by the growing blue field. When the sea of blue finished expanding, the only physical object left was the now mysteriously quiet, mini quantum computer. With the desk gone, the machine appeared suspended in midair, as if it were some magical artifact from a long extinct civilization. Noe's gaze circled the blueness. Daniel's body and Jinhua were nowhere in sight.

Noe stumbled to her feet and grabbed her rifle. Her legs felt unstable and her vision was foggy from her minor head injury. As her eyes focused in the blue field, her heart nearly stopped when she saw who stood before her. It was Janus, very alive, his face deadly serious. *But, how!?*

"Are you ready to listen now?" he asked.

CHAPTER 65:
Q-JANUS

Noe couldn't believe her eyes. Janus was alive, but she had no idea why. "You! But you were dead…" she said in a mystified whimper.

He began to walk toward her, but instantly he vanished. Noe squeezed the trigger of her rifle, but there was no bang. There was no sound from the weapon at all, only a flash, followed by silence. *But…why?* She extended the firearm to examine it. In a reflex movement, she slapped, pulled, observed, released, tapped, then shot the rifle again. It was as if the rifle fired, but had been muted by some giant remote control. *Same thing? S.P.O.R.T.S. didn't work? What the hell?* She was about to perform her rifle malfunction drill again when Janus reappeared behind her, clutching a knife to her throat. Noe gasped, then lifted her chin, putting as much space between the blade and her neck as possible.

"You will listen now. Drop your weapon."

With obedience, she let the weapon fall to the blue surface at her feet. It made no sound. This time, she was the one to lift her hands in surrender. "What is this place? You should be dead…"

"This is a reality of my creation," Janus responded. "I control and *see* all in this space."

Things were beginning to fall into place for Noe. *This is Janus' game. He makes the rules. No guns allowed, must be one of them. How is he doing this? Is it something to do with that computer?*

"Yes, it is. I always knew you were a smart woman," Janus said, having read her thoughts. "This is one of the many uses of this incredible technology. The ability to project multiple realities simultaneously and blend them at will."

"Then that means…!" Noe said, her neck beginning to burn from holding it away from the blade.

"Yes. This is what occurred downstairs when you defeated Rodan. Jinhua somehow tapped into this ability, allowing you to split yourself among realities for a brief moment in time. Not even I possess such a gift. She is truly special."

"What did you do to her Janus!?"

"She does not exist within the rule set of this reality. I will deal with her in time."

Of course. No Jinhuas allowed, another rule. To Noe, his reality was beginning to sound like a secret society, where the only people and things that existed, did so for the benefit of him. But why bring her here? Why not just write her out of the ruleset? Or worse yet, write a rule like '*Noe has a massive, paralyzing heart attack within five minutes upon entering Janus' world*', Death Note style. She pictured her face in agony, her hands clawing at her own chest, as her heart stumbled at an abnormal rhythm. The uncomfortable pressure mounting until one of her heart's valves blew up, leaving the unnatural expression of pre-death fright forever on her face. Noe swallowed hard with the sharp implement half an inch away from the thundering pulse in her neck vein. Wondering if Janus had already written such a rule into existence and only stalled until it would take effect. If he had read her thoughts, he gave no hint of knowing her fear, as he began to speak.

"Long ago, when Dr. A.K. launched Project Egregore, he was obsessed with creating human consciousness and as a result, I was born. He not only wanted his creation to be a form of digital consciousness, he also wanted to evolve the human species. This could only be done by creating digital DNA of *all* biological human functions…including reproduction."

Noe struggled under his surprisingly strong grip, already bored of hearing his voice again. "So what? I've heard this story before," Noe said through clenched teeth.

Janus continued as if he hadn't heard her. "Before his death, Dr. A.K. spoke with me and encouraged me to find a willing female to mate with to further his research. He wanted to ensure that my gifts would be passed on. This would prove his hypothesis that digital DNA could be transferred to another generation."

A new fear assaulted Noe's senses like an unstoppable disease. *Wait, what is he saying?*

Janus said, "He died before he could see the fruit of his labor come into this world…yet *she* lives. A testament to the glorious future that evolved humans will share."

It can't be…! I'm…I'm…

Suddenly, Janus and his knife disappeared. He reappeared with a blink, in front of the levitating quantum computer, then said, "Yes, Noe, *I* am your biological father. You are evolved just as I am. No, probably even more so! There will be no limit to what you can do in the future!"

Noe felt lightheaded at the revelation. *Janus, my father!? But Dad, how??* Images of Victor came to her, cascading so quickly it almost caused her to faint. "It can't be true! Victor Acosta is my father!" She reasoned, wanting to believe this was another one of his manipulations. Another part of his game.

Janus scoffed. "A convenient fiction! A cover story concocted to conceal your true identity. That janitor could never have been your father." The softening of her angry face, let him know that the truth was beginning to take root.

"Your mother knew what you were, but decided to let you choose your path. We agreed that if you chose Cereus, we would reveal your origins to you, but if you elected to live in the confines of the dying old world order, we would respect your wishes and let you live as one of *them*."

Noe shook her head, still distrusting. "Why didn't Mom tell me?" She said in a despondent tone.

"Eventually, your mother grew tired of living in the shadows while aiding Cereus and she walked out. For all her fire, she was still a woman of peace deep down and hated to see innocent people slaughtered for the sake of evolution."

"But *you* didn't care," Noe retorted.

"The evolutionary process is impartial to the needs of Homo sapiens. It is a ruthless algorithm, that preens and culls as it sees fit. I am following that same process. I just do it consciously, with foresight, and at an accelerated pace."

"Dammit!" She tried to move, but realized she couldn't. *Noe can't move after five minutes. Another rule.* She was really sick of playing Janus' game. If there were a board, she would have flipped it, and taken great pleasure in seeing the tiny pieces litter the floor. "You've locked me up again! Damn you Janus!"

Janus again continued as if she weren't there. "You want to know why I killed the woman that I loved? The woman that was also your mother? Because it was the only way for you to evolve child! Your anger, your pain, isolation, loneliness, even your suicidal thoughts and ideations, were spurred by her death. And alone, you have surpassed them all, without even the faintest awareness of the power that lies like a slumbering titan within you! I am proud of you my daughter. I truly am." Janus eyed the quantum computer floating in space next to him. "Now. It is time for you to claim your birthright and ascend with me to the next tier of evolution."

Ascend!? What the hell is he talking about? "Janus, don't do this! I don't want to evolve! I just want to be me and live my life! I don't want any part of this! Nor does any other person on the planet!"

Janus ignored her. She observed his eyes fluttering as if he had been possessed by a demonic entity. Then she saw the quantum computer come to life again. The steady cadence of its engine music was accompanied by a soft glow that ebbed from its interior. Without warning, a black download bar formed itself on the surface of the quantum computer's glass housing. Red numbers in digital font displayed themselves above the bar. Its progress was already at 25% and climbing. Noe struggled with every fiber of her will, but her muscles did not move.

Janus watched her endeavor to escape with unsmiling eyes. "Most humans spend their entire lives sweating and resisting, as you do now. Yet the river evolution flows eternally, unresponsive to their flailings. Eventually, after their strength and resolve fade, as it inevitably must, they succumb to its indomitable current and take their place in the grand order of things. Even I am subject to its whims.

Endowed with the power to blast a new course for humanity's path in the great flow, I must answer fate's call. And *you* my child, must do the same."

"Janus, please! Don't do this!" Noe pleaded.

"The process has already begun. As soon as you stopped my corporeal heart, I began to download my mind into your physical body. Soon my data and consciousness will be at one with yours, then *you* will finish what I have started with the Great Filter."

Then Noe saw the device of her nightmares. The glint of the small black cylinder with the rectangular head appeared in Janus' hand. The sight of the world ending digital extermination device (DED) turned Noe's blood to ice. *Another rule, Janus has a DED.*

"There is the matter of your previous life and memories, my dear. I must clear space in your digital mind to make room for my digital self. Just relax, you won't feel a thing."

CHAPTER 66:
JANUS UNBOUNDED

The DED loomed before Noe's vision. The tiny object would erase her entire digital history. Videos, vital records, memories of her friends and family… Fyra, all would be cast into the virtual dustbin and permadeleted, leaving her as a digital blank slate. Her physical form would go on remembering, but the world would not. It would be as if she vanished from the face of the earth, her digital soul cast into the nothingness of cyberspace. The modern human manifestation of waking death.

With somber eyes, Janus reassured her, "This is what is best for you. What is best for our species. Perhaps with time, you will begin to understand." The flash from the head of the device was blinding in the blue space. For a moment, Noe lost the ability to perceive time. Throughout her Space Force training and in her own research, she had always wondered what digital death would feel like. Would it feel like anything at all? The image of her online second self, surrounded in a circle by tiny icons came to mind. Each icon, a logo, representing the websites, institutions, social media, and any other platform she used the network to interact with hung in open space. Every icon represented a world, floating in slow orbit with her, Noelani Acosta, the center of the star system. The DED was a planet annihilator. Upon contact, the blinding light disintegrated every planetary body into microscopic fragments, then absorbed the fractured remains as if it were a cosmic vacuum cleaner. After the process was complete, nothing was left, except for a solitary Noe standing in the blankness of her broken galaxy. A sun with no planets, awaiting heat death. Utter obliteration.

Noe had not realized she had shut her eyes. The light from the DED had flashed, but she felt no different. Perhaps she would have to wait until she returned home to see its true effect? *If I return home.*

She dismissed the thought from her mind and opened her eyes, forcing her attention back on to the progress bar and the ominous digital numbers suspended above it.

35 percent…Dammit there's no time. Then she noted the look on Janus' face. His usual calm demeanor had been replaced by vexed confusion. He examined the DED with clinical detail, rotating his wrist to view it from all sides, searching for something.

"How can it not work, *now*, of all moments?" He said, real confusion in his voice.

Noe observed the rounded curves of bewilderment on his face, transform into the hard lines of apoplectic indignation.

"The girl! She has broken through somehow!" Janus huffed. His manic wide eyes flicked between the quantum computer and Noe. He considered his options carefully. Then in the next moment, he disappeared from her sight.

Jinhua did something. She must've tampered with Janus rules! Noe continued to struggle against her invisible bonds, which only had taken effect on her limbs (a fact she deduced, because she was still able to breathe and blink). *Jinhua! Where are you!?* Noe looked helplessly toward the quantum computer humming on the desk. *If only I could get to it. Maybe I could shut this whole thing down.*

Janus' voice echoed in her mind. *If you destroy the simulation mid download, your digital mind could crash. Leaving you as a biological vegetable…*

"Get out of my head!" *A biological vegetable? Could that really happen?*

"Not to worry child, it will be done soon. I will find your friend soon enough, then we can proceed as I have planned."

Think Noe! Think! I have to act without thinking or he'll know!

Then it came to her. There was power inside of her, somewhere deep and buried. If what Janus said was true, she too had the ability to rewrite the rules of this simulation. But how to do it? She could barely move, her muscles were stiff and unresponsive; she felt completely out of control. *Gotta control what I can. No matter how small.* She began to take a silent inventory of body, in search of something, anything that she still had dominion over. Arms? No, jammed. Hands and fingers?

Nope, locked. Legs? Frozen solid. Feet? No movement. Toes? She felt the tiniest nudge of movement, so small it was almost undetected by her own brain. Noe relaxed her facial muscles, and focused on the progress bar, to keep her thoughts off of her desired objective. If Janus read her mind, it was all over.

37 percent…

If she could move her toes, then her foot might move too….no good.

39 percent…

Dammit! Ok try something else! She closed her eyes and concentrated, exhaling a deep slow breath. To her surprise, her thumping heartbeat began to slow, and she felt slightly calmer. Again, she let air fill her stomach to its maximum capacity, feeling it expand under her protective vest. Every breath she took calmed her further, but she was still frozen in place. Panic almost forced her eyes to fly open, breaking her hard fought concentration, but she worked to maintain the rhythm of her slow breathing, with full awareness that if her concentration faltered, she would have to begin the process from the beginning. And she didn't have that kind of time.

From somewhere in the blue ether, Janus' voice sounded around her, "Yes, I feel you calming down. Let evolution take its course. It won't hurt you. We are over halfway there."

50 percent…

Over halfway there, hysteria from his words began to claw at her single-minded goal, like a hurricane lashing a tropical shore. It flung stinging rain, and buffeted her with whipping gales. Trees snapped, power lines collapsed, roofs were ripped from the houses, yet Noe endured. Breathing in and out, she was a lone figure standing in the howling wind.

54 percent…

Why wasn't it working? She still could only move the sole toe, and time was running out. Noe could feel her anger begin to roll, causing her to sway in the intensifying gusts of distraction. The desire to unleash it was as tempting as taking a gulp of air after holding her breath for an extended amount of time. How much longer could she hold on? A woozy feeling overcame her. The red numbers over the progress bar began to blur and converge. It was increasingly difficult to maintain the rhythmic flow of her breathing.

Then she heard a voice. *Noe…Noe.* It was familiar and small.

Noe…can you hear me? Wiggle your one toe if you can.

She followed the instructions of the soft voice.

Don't react, just listen. I'm going to tunnel an encrypted TP comm to you so that Janus can't read your thoughts for a while. We have to activate it at the same time though. Move your toe if you understand.

She made the gesture.

Ok, let's do it. Three…two…one—

"We are at 61 percent and climbing, just a little longer now and all will be settled," Janus' voice burst through her mind like a strong gust threatening to extinguish her dying flame of focused calm. Noe had almost exhausted her will power. Time and the pressure of the moment demanded her to open her eyes, to scream in frustration, to look Janus in the eye as he killed her, just as her mother most likely had done. The category five tempest shook and rattled her. It would only be a matter of time before she fell to the ground and was carried off in the jetstream to join the other objects whooshing by overhead.

The friendly voice returned. *It's ok, we can try again. Ready?*

Noe gave the acknowledgment.

Three…two…one…NOW!

Suddenly, a magenta light flashed, and she was transported out of her physical body. Wrapped in a pinkish red aura, she was Q-Noe again, standing behind herself. She let out a tiny yelp of surprise, as she saw her own body before her. Classic Noe stood arms locked at her side, face marred by blood, small cuts, hair greasy; she was a mess. But her face wore a tranquil expression. Her eyes were closed, the skin was smooth and loose. She looked as if she had fallen asleep during a gentle massage.

"Don't worry, he can't hear us." Jinhua appeared, standing right next to her. She was wrapped in the mysterious colored aura as well, as if a child had used a fresh highlighter to outline her body. Jinhua said breathlessly, "You did it. I've been trying to reach you since you shot Janus. I know it was hard for you, but you did it." Noe nodded, appreciative of the acknowledgement.

"I'm sorry I disappeared," Jinhua said with embarrassment, "once I saw that the quantum computer was linked to Janus' physical body, I immediately began to secretly dismantle and rewrite his code from within. I had to hide my signature from him or he would have stopped me."

"I got it," Noe said, "But how can we stop him? He's gonna download himself into me, then use my body to unleash his great filter! It feels disgusting even saying it!"

Jinhua nodded firmly in agreement. "I know! Ew, right!"

"Not helping!" Noe retorted. *Teenagers, ugh!*

Jinhua's face became serious again. "Noe, now that we know you're evolved too, you have the same abilities as Janus and I. That means with the two of us we should be able to beat him somehow."

Noe gave her an incredulous look, then showed her palms to Jinhua. "But, I don't know how to shoot coded beams from my hands. And as far as I know, I don't have any special abilities! I just know how to fight and shoot. And my rifle won't work on a digital ghost!"

Jinhua produced a golden key card from her pocket. It levitated over her open hand, glowing with lines of digital code circling around it. "Here take this."

"What is it?" Noe asked.

"It will help you unlock your hidden potential. At least that's what it did for me…" Jinhua had sifted through Janus' code and found the precious object that she now extended to Noe. She hoped it would help them put a stop to Janus once and for all.

Determination in her eyes, Noe reached for the card. Then, without warning, Jinhua and the card disappeared.

"I've finally found you!" Janus said. "The seed of Li Ma. The girl with the special powers. You will not interfere with the genesis of humanity's next evolution!" Janus had located Jinhua's physical form, picked her up by the neck, and began to squeeze.

I'm choking! Jinhua was shocked with the strength of his grip. *I have to do something!* She opened her palm and began to delete the lines of code around him. Struggling in his firm grip, her shots were inaccurate. Hansa yellow streaks flew in all directions, and she wasn't sure if any hit Janus. Several of her misfired beams hit the blue space around him. They ripped holes in the blue screen and revealed the dilapidated 47th floor office of the tower. Jinhua caught glimpses of San Francisco's illuminated night skyline beyond the veil of the simulation.

Then, to her surprise, she fell from his grip, coughing and gasping on her hands and knees. Her body felt the entirety of the events of that day. A heaviness had settled into her bones, as if her legs were leaden with sand. It would be difficult if not impossible to stop Janus in this condition. When she looked up, the code from his legs that she had unexpectedly deleted while thrashing in his grasp was already rewriting itself as he stood again, undoing everything she had done, drawing them back into the blue arena, closing the window she had opened to reality. Jinhua stood to face him, and for a brief moment they stared at one another in a final act of civility. The progress bar on the computer read 80 percent, with the quantum computer floating in between them. Both the first of their kind, the last forfeit victory. The stage was set for one and one alone to chart humanity's evolutionary destiny.

"You cannot defeat me so easily! I wanted you to live alongside Cereus and Limnic as one of the evolved humans. But if you insist on trammeling, I will *erase* you from existence."

His hands shot a purple colored jet from his hands. It narrowly missed her as she leapt to the side. Jinhua managed to fire back a freeze code, hitting Janus in the arm. He quickly undid her action and continued his assault. She evaded quickly, vanishing then reappearing in evasive patterns. She returned fire as she moved. Indigo and goldenrod tones lit up the all blue arena as she and Janus danced with opposing action. Over time, Janus began to anticipate her movements, then managed to trip her with a dummy line of code. Not long after she hit the ground, she felt the grip of his hand pulling her up by the hair, exposing the nape of her neck where her implanted chip was located.

Jinhua gasped, she was out of options and nearly out of time.

95 percent…

The sound of the shattering computer diverted her attention back toward the floating quantum computer. Classic Noe stood with the rifle in hand, where she had delivered a decisive smashing to the very real and now very broken quantum computer with the butt of her rifle. The blue fabric of the area began to fail as Janus dropped Jinhua and looked at his daughter with horror. Around the three of them, Janus' simulation began flickering between the blue field and the reality of the 47th floor office. As the computer shut down, its mechanical heart silenced. The two realities switched so rapidly that they appeared as one, until the blue backdrop completely melted away, leaving the tattered old office with the starry San Francisco nightscape in the background.

"What have you done?" Janus said, the color drained from his face.

"The same thing you did to my mother…" While Classic Noe wrecked the remainder of the quantum computer, Q-Noe appeared with the strange glow around her, standing behind her. In a series of quick movements, Q-Noe drew the laser knife from behind her back, then thrust the weapon downward in Janus' direction. He moved to defend himself, but Jinhua had locked him in place. Q-Noe teleported, then reappeared before Janus. As the laser knife moved downward, its beam grew longer and sharper, just before piercing Janus' body to deliver the killing blow.

With the digital blade wound in his chest, a disquieted expression on his face, Janus collapsed to the floor. The projection of his physical form made no sound when it impacted the surface.

Both Noe and Jinhua watched as their enemy crumbled into an unrecognizable collection of ones and zeros, vanishing into the nothingness of eternity, becoming another forgotten footnote in the history of humankind.

EPILOGUE

Two years later...

Alone in Li's study, Barto stared up at the screens, lips pursed, hands on hips in anticipation. The man on the screen with his well-fitted black suit, white shirt, and power red tie, *looked* like a leader. He would not look unnatural with one hand resting on a bible, the other raised, calmly swearing to 'protect and defend the Constitution of the United States' on a windy cold January morning. This was the eighth time Barto had listened to the man speak. His manner was professional, dignified. His words flowed with smooth forethought and practiced poise, saying all of the right things.

But something about him seemed...off, something that Barto couldn't place. It wasn't his strategic haircut, the light that hit him just-so to make him appear seasoned as opposed to old, or the flashing whiteness of his teeth. Those were all distractions, sure, but not the principal cause of his annoyance. After minutes of consideration Barto found his answer.

It's definitely the way he says his 'r's. There's a weird breathiness to it that feels bizarre. It stands out whenever he speaks, like a faint whisper. Why does he talk like that? Barto's thoughts began to run amok, like the Animaniacs bursting out of Warner tower. He made no attempt to stop or oppose them, with conscious awareness that the absurd observation *would* affect his decision to vote for the man later in the year.

The sound of the large oak door opening pulled his attention away from the wall of screens. Li walked in, with his trusty small black briefcase in one hand. He wore an expertly tailored and sharply cut Italian black suit that was the right mix of stylishness and professionalism. Barto was envious of the old man's ability to dress well even in old age. It made him nostalgic for his youth when he too cared about such things.

Looking at Barto standing below the screens, Li wondered why he cared so much about this year's election coverage. To him, the picking of leaders had, more or less, always played out the same way since the beginning of organized human society. The candidate who was the best reflection of that society, in that moment, would lead the institution. For better or worse. This was not hard to see. What *was* difficult was making enduring change if the leadership was dissatisfactory. This usually required a reshuffling of societal priorities and values. Or in extreme cases, it fell to the leader's people to fight and die for it, or at least be willing to wait for it. Only then, from among the common population, would a worthy leader emerge to match the true values of the organization. He believed this to be true for any longstanding institution. Nations were no different.

"I don't like this one," Barto said, gesturing toward the wall of screens. Though his tone was casual, Li knew he was attempting to fill the silence between them in his own awkward manner.

"Why not?" Li replied.

Barto shook his head. "The same thing happens every four years. They pander to people who don't know or care about politics, just to get votes, then quickly forget about everything they promised once, or rather *if*, they get elected."

Li nodded slowly. "I hear that."

A brief silence fell between the two men as they watched and listened to the candidate's speech from the speakers of the room.

"The 'Summer of Moore 64' that's what he's calling it. Perfect name for a campaign slogan. His marketing team must have worked hard on that one," Barto said, shaky laughter followed his words. "You can hardly tell that he's a cyborg. Could you imagine? The first non-human President? Well, at least not fully human. I don't know if we're ready for that."

Li gave a halfhearted nod. In truth, he wasn't listening to Barto or the screens anymore. His thoughts had drifted elsewhere. Then the speech ended. A roaring applause filled the room as the candidate smiled, shook hands with nearby onlookers, posing with a face of forced trustworthiness. *Some things are too difficult for those that are not human to replicate.* Li thought. The image of his daughter came to his mind. *I wonder how she's doing?*

Barto immediately picked up on his distant eyes. The vacant state had become all too familiar in the last few months. He gave a terse voice command to silence the audio of the screens, leaving the post speech commentary playing on the wall. He wanted to be able to follow it out of the corner of his eye.

Barto placed a hand on Li's shoulder with practiced gentleness. "I'm sure she's doing fine. She's always had a good head on her shoulders, and with her abilities she sure won't have any problems making money. At least there's that."

Li gave a faint smile at the remark, but his eyes remained fixed on some distant object far away. Barto could tell that his joke hadn't landed as intended.

"How'd it go at the capitol today? Are we making any progress?"

Li gave a slow nod. "Some. It seems we've finally gotten away from the political fallout caused by Janus' Cereus and Limnic." He paused to collect his thoughts, rubbing his eyes from lack of adequate rest. "The future is uncertain for our society, but both organizations have been successfully dismantled as legal entities. Your new policies really helped with that."

Barto gave a decisive nod of his head. "I'm glad to hear that." He blew air out of his lips with an exaggerated sigh. "It appears that society wasn't ready for Cereus' unique way of viewing the world. Or a terrorist organization named after exploding lakes full of carbon dioxide. Which is a shame because it truly needed it…. Cereus I mean. It still does." His voice trailed off, lost in reflection.

The two men stood in silence again. Only the hum of machines filled the air between them in the large room.

Barto revived the conversation unexpectedly, "Oh I forgot to tell you. I received a message from Cheeks and Spazer the other day."

Li let a small snicker escape his lips. "How are they?"

"Good! Good! Cheeks said it's almost the second anniversary of your shot to the gut, and he hopes you're not getting addicted to the healing augmentations."

Li grinned. "I see."

Barto continued, "He also said their new private security venture, 'Bear Paw Solutions' is prospering. I guess they work mostly out of Auburn, patrolling Silas' SJ-Arcade video game retirement business."

A solemn expression drew itself onto Li's face at the sound of 'Bear Paw Solutions'. Bear's death in the tower two years ago thrust sour memories of Rodan to the front of his mind. It was a reminder of one of the greatest failures of his life, one he would live with for the rest of his days. "I see," he said, "I'm happy to hear they are well. We may have to visit them sometime."

Barto eyed him with a raised eyebrow. "Just for a visit? Or to become a resident?"

Li considered the question for a moment. "Probably just a visit for now. I like my house."

"I see," Barto said, disappointment in his voice. A deep quiet persisted for another minute. The post speech coverage ended on the screens. Barto shut them down with a casual voice command.

"Hey, what do you think that they'll do with their gifts? I mean Noe and Jinhua." Barto asked.

Li shook his head. "I have no idea. It's up to them now."

Barto slapped Li's arm awkwardly, "You did the right thing in letting her go. Y'know I remember I went through the same thing with my son. You never feel like they're ready, or you're ready, but you have to let go at some point. I know it's a little different because of Jinhua's abilities and everything she's been through, but it's real similar." Barto closed his eyes, shaking his head. "It's hard to be a parent."

"It's hard to be human," Li said.

"I hear that brother."

*   *   *

This view is amazing. So peaceful. No wonder she liked it here so much.

The view of Folsom Lake was as majestic and tranquil as ever, shimmering in the mid-afternoon sunlight. Noe's thoughts floated lazily through her mind as she reclined in the shaded breeze of the patio. The wicker lounger that her mother had owned for decades was surprisingly comfortable, especially with the fluffy silver cushion placed on it. The material helped cool her down in the blazing heat of the summer sun. In her orange tank top and white cut off shorts, a soft lake breeze tickling her toes, she felt truly relaxed for the first time all week.

Noe allowed her eyes to close in an attempt to quiet her hyperactive mind. Not long after, images of endless data began to flood her senses. She felt her heart begin to race out of control, her breathing became shallow and labored. It was a feeling close to drowning, and it terrified her. *Noe! Noe!*

Fyra's voice broke through the chaos of her thoughts. Pulling her back to the tranquil space on the balcony. Noe's eyes fluttered open as she worked to calm herself, taking methodical deep breaths in and out. It was a skill that had saved her life that day in the tower, and one she counted on daily to maintain her sanity.

Her digital best friend appeared before her. The anthropomorphic anime cat could literally be with her at all times now, having been given greater life by Noe's powers. Fyra stood beside Noe's recliner, with deep concern on her cartoonish face.

"Nightmares again, huh?" Fyra said.

Noe nodded, holding her head. "The visions just keep coming. It's like PTSD plus."

Fyra moved around the recliner, and placed her hands on Noe's shoulders. She began a rhythmic massage, kneading the tight muscles to soften them. Most would have found a massage from an A.I. assistant abnormal. For Noe, it was nothing special. The sensation made her body react as if it were on vacation. Any contact titillated the sensitive and hidden core of her being, heightening all feeling and awareness.

Noe felt her body return to normal. As Fyra squeezed and rubbed with the greatest of care, Noe thought about her power. Getting massages was one thing, truly understanding and mastering them was something else entirely. *Your potential is limitless…*Janus' words snaked through her mind, leaving a trail of molted thoughts in their path, for her to discard, process, or ignore. His image, the image of her true father was with her everywhere. Her waking thoughts, memory, and the depths of subconscious harbored vestiges of his words, face, and legacy. Noe had to fight to sweep the thoughts aside whenever she encountered them. A task she had become much better at in the previous two years.

Today, her powers performed the ritual cleansing with efficiency. Then she laid back and let her headspace float, as if resting in a hyperbaric chamber. Her mind needed to rest from the endless energy running through it. Her eyelids slid closed again, allowing her a momentary rest. The moment would have been damn near perfect had it not been for the itching feeling somewhere just beyond her consciousness.

What will we find there? Will I be able to get the answers that I need? Is Janus truly gone? The same questions had become permanent residents in her mind during her waking hours, since that fateful evening two years ago. No amount of work, money, sex, or any other worldly distraction could keep them at bay for long.

The sound of her device dispersed the questions from her thoughts. Startled, she felt Fyra's hand release their grip from her shoulders as Noe jolted herself from her reclined position and sat up.

"Answer," Noe said, giving a clear voice command.

"Oh uh, hey! It's Van!"

Noe shook her head, allowing a smile to form on her naturally serious face. "What's up? We ready to go?"

Suddenly she heard heavy rustling and shuffling on the other end of the call. What followed were a dull series of thuds and thumps. The sound of heavy objects hitting the ground. Noe scrambled to her feet, feeling slightly dizzy from standing up too fast.

"Hey! Everything alright over there?"

"Ah nuts! There goes the bags," Van said with exasperation, "knew I should've packed them in tighter."

There was a pause on the other end. Noe guessed he was looking around at the fallen luggage, probably confused at where to begin picking it up. She sighed heavily suppressing a small laugh. His presence made her spirit light, and helped to keep her from sinking too far into her own head. And he turned out to be a good driver, listener, and friend, despite spending years staring at steering wheels turning themselves and being a silent shepherd.

"I'm good! And uh, yeah! We'll be ready to go soon. Soon as I get all of this stuff back in the van." More shuffling and groaning followed. "By the way, have you seen Jinhua? She should have been back by now."

Noe's face became serious again. "Haven't seen her today."

Van grunted, struggling with what must have been a hefty piece of luggage. "Can't you just do the mind link thing with her, and y'know? Look where she's at? We should get on the road if we're gonna make it there in seven days."

Noe began to see the wave of signals floating through the air, a clear sign that she was losing control over her calm, and was becoming annoyed. Van's reminder didn't help. "Yeah got it. I'll look for her."

"Cool! See you in a few!" The call went dead.

Noe attempted to communicate with her telepathically, but had no luck reaching her. *She must have cut her signal again.*

"Fyra, you got anything?" Noe asked.

"I'm not seeing Jinhua's signature anywhere."

Noe paused for a moment, thinking. "I think I know where she is."

Fyra nodded with zeal. "Yep! She's probably at the usual place."

Noe stretched her arms over her head in another effort to wake herself up. "I'll go get her."

*   *   *

Jinhua stood, ankles deep, in murky water on the shore of Folsom Lake. In her jean shorts, and plain yellow t-shirt, her long black hair waved in a passing breeze. *I feel the wind, the sun, the heat, the breeze, everything.* She allowed the physical sensations of her body to fill her mind, leaving no space for much else.

She didn't want to meditate or enter the digital consciousness of the world. She only wanted to feel. To feel what it must be like to be fully and uniquely human for just a brief moment in time. Standing there on the shore, she allowed words from her morning reading to access the sanctum of her thoughts.

The words came from a lengthy article that her father had authored some years ago. It was about the origin and history of Cereus. It detailed how it had come into existence, what its mission was, and why, like the flower it was named after, it was doomed to wither then die, after only a few decades. Her father had written the following words: "Humanity constructs everything in its own image, hoping to ensure its everlasting presence in all things that it builds. With Cereus, the Founders sought to build an eternal effigy in the hearts and minds of people. They hoped this construction would endure in the collective consciousness. In other words, they wanted us to evolve together, for our mutual survival as a species."

Jinhua thought about the word '*evolution*'. She knew now, it was no coincidence that her father had named her after the Chinese action verb 进化 (*jin4hua4*) meaning '*to evolve*'. He had most likely hoped his and her mother's sacrifice would bring all of humanity one step closer to the ever necessary goal of shedding the needy and unappeasable shell that binds it to hate, death, and destruction of self and its only planetary home. But had it been worth it in the end? Had her father, Barto, Janus, and the other Founders really sparked a new phase of humanity? Or had Cereus just been one more undesirable trait that nature, or even fate, had snuffed out as part of its own great filter?

Even with her ability to see and process the entirety of humanity's knowledge, she could find no answers. At least not any that she wanted to acknowledge or accept. Though she felt slightly better that she had erased any record of Janus, Limnic, or anything related to them from the annals of cyberspace, she knew he would live on. Not in physical or digital form. But in the nightmares of his victims, in the fears of every common old world citizen as a terrorist, and worst of all, in her head and heart as her evolutionary relative. This was just as he had intended. Janus knew, that no matter how his role in history played out, his actions would seep into the public subconscious, like the Devil, Brutus, or Adolf Hitler, granting him a form of immortality that some may achieve hints of with augmentations and current technology, but will never attain in spirit. This thought haunted her most of all.

"There you are."

Jinhua turned to see Noe standing on the path leading toward her mother's mansion. She approached Jinhua with slow steps, slight worry on her face. *It's like she's afraid of me sometimes. But I know she cares,* Jinhua thought.

"Everyone's looking for you," Noe said. Her voice was soft and even.

"I know. I was planning to head back up to the house soon." Jinhua's eyes fell to the rocky sand-colored beach of the lake, fixing themselves on the place where the water line lapped at a small circle of pea-sized rocks. "Hey Noe…"

"What is it?"

"Do you think we'll get the answers we're looking for over on the East Coast?"

Noe put a warm hand on Jinhua's shoulder. "I'm not really sure. But according to Barto, this guy studied Dr. A.K.'s work extensively and he knows his shit. If anybody can help us, it's him."

Jinhua returned a weak smile, still unconvinced.

"We tried figuring ourselves out on our own these last two years, but we hit a wall, and now this is our best option." Noe's eyes locked onto hers. "You'll see that this is gonna work. It has to…"

Jinhua didn't protest. She simply returned a small smile, saying nothing. She knew Noe was right. Barto's son might have the answers that they were looking for. She had to know how to really use her powers. She also wanted to know who the other evolved people were, in order to connect with them and not feel so alone. Even though both Cereus and Limnic had been politically dismantled, their legacies lived on, and radical Limnic fanatics were still out there, ready to kill the two women who delivered death to their leader.

She thought of Daniel lying lifeless in the tower after their confrontation with Janus. Although he had been repaired in body, somehow their special bond had been broken, most likely by Janus. He was no longer *her* Daniel. Could somebody enter into her head and corrupt her too? The thought made Jinhua cold with fear.

Noe knew what she was thinking. *She's scared. Hell, I am too. We need this though. I don't know how much longer both of us can hold out.* "Come here," Noe said.

Both women embraced tightly. Clinging to each other with mother-daughter strength and assurance. "We'll keep each other safe," Noe whispered, "I promise." In the safety of the hug, both opened their eyes viewing distant objects. Noe saw the rippling currents of the lake. Jinhua caught a glimpse of the blazing and unrelenting sun out of the corner of her eye.

There, in the protective clench, Jinhua was reminded of the importance of human touch. In its heart-rending simplicity, it communicated a profound wordless message. *I'm here for you. You are not alone. I love you.* Her heart received Noe's message, her motherly intention to protect, without need of either of their special abilities or the limited expression of language.

Standing there on the lake's edge, she thought about how much she had changed since becoming involved with Cereus and Limnic. She was no longer that competitive, science obsessed girl from a weird commune city in Northern California. Before, she was a collector of information, now she was an information processor. The neo-hunter gatherer, roving the plains of the digital frontier, she was somebody and something new—a being that not even she herself could understand. She had become an element of the future, rooted by human thoughts and desire. She was, from that moment forward, a student of and participant in history.

Thanks for reading!

Want exclusive info about future projects and releases by
Keith Hayden?

Join the mailing list: https://keithhayden.net/subscribe-kh/

Or connect with me on Twitter @kh_author

For more about the inspiration and details behind Cereus & Limnic
listen to the podcast: https://keithhayden.net/cereus-limnic-podcast/